HUNTING EDEN

THE TRIPLE TROUBLE SERIES

VH NICOLSON

For my family

As I whip by in a flash, a quick glance in my rearview mirror reveals Mr. Slowcoach indicating left, disappearing into the crisp evening. "Oops, that's why."

Well, that was a waste of my efforts and petrol.

I sigh into the dark expanse of my empty car as I clutch the steering wheel.

I'm a bit of a girl racer, so I push my foot down on the accelerator a little more and shift up a gear.

Zooming faster through the late-night curves of the Scottish countryside, on the outskirts of Castleview Cove, the fields whoosh by in a blur.

Take it all in, people. This is my level of excitement for the day; this is as good as it gets.

My fun-sized car doesn't even go quick, but it energizes me and gets my adrenaline pumping like crazy.

I need to get a life. I used to have one. However, four years ago it turned into a shit-show and I can't seem to get over it.

I've been aimlessly existing, not truly living these last few years.

Defeated. That's the only way to describe how I feel.

The creeping tension in my shoulders threatens to take hold. A glimpse of the Cove catches my attention as I stretch out my neck.

Way up here on the high road, grants me the perfect view of the ocean. I glance downward at the waning spotlight moon glittering off the inky blanket expanse of the sea. The steep towering cliffs on either side of the cove stand guard. The sea has so much explaining to do to me; I don't think it will ever give me the answers I need. It's deceptive. Never trust it.

"Asshole," I hiss toward the cleverly disguised calm water.

It's not really the sea I'm mad at. Because it's nothing to do with the sea. Not really. Although it started the unfolding of my life, it's really *him* I'm pissed off at.

"I'm sorry, sea. My bad."

I slam my fist on the steering wheel and clench my jaw, grinding my teeth.

"For the love of God, Eden. Stop thinking of him."

I'm normally a pretty chillaxed gal, but I'm frustrated at myself. Frustrated at life.

It's official, I'm one hundred percent, totally and utterly stuck, and completely bored with everything. Nothing gets me excited anymore. Well, apart from driving and dancing.

Every day is Groundhog Day: eat, sleep, dance, read, repeat. Groundhog Day Syndrome is an actual thing. I'm living proof.

Welcome to Saturday Night's Pity Party with star guest, Eden Wallace.

I think I've hit yet another all-time low. Why, you ask?

Because it's late on a Saturday night. I'm driving back home from the supermarket, when I should really be out partying with my sisters and friends. Instead, here I am. Alone. Again.

Before I ran out the door and jumped in my car tonight, I even waved goodbye to Victor, my cheese plant. He's become a close friend. If you head over to sad Scottish loser Eden Wallace dot com, you'll find me there, you know, just hanging out with my cheese plant, Victor. I'm a loner, and I feel like such a loser.

Lost in my thoughts as I swish this way and that, I think about *him*. The man who consumes my reflections.

I should really cut this invisible cord he holds over my life. I want to feel free and happy again, I really do, but somehow I can't bring myself to cut it.

A sudden thought takes hold. But I *am* out. What if he comes back and I've nipped out? Would he come back this late on a Saturday night?

Stop being irrational, Eden. Don't let yourself go there. Nope. Push that down; push those thoughts wayyyyy down. Focus on driving. And... Breathe...

But I speed up a little more, because you just never know.

The highlight of my day has involved a marathon *Friends* binge-watching session. It's not for the fainthearted. Especially season three with the whole Ross and Rachel breakup debacle. You'll cry, then laugh, and then cry some more.

Chocolate, copious cups of tea, and tissues are compulsory support tools. That's the only reason I nipped out in my car tonight; I ran out of tea bags. Not gin. Tea bags. *Christ.*

I've been moping about my house since my last hip hop class I taught at midday and have since then drunk at least seven cups of tea. Intermittently playing some Candy Crush. I'm on level 347, in five days. Don't judge. I'm delicate right now. Remember? Pi-ty par-ty.

My sad Scottish heart did a little dance when it found the bottom of the laundry basket earlier. Actually, I think that was the highlight of my day. I've since washed, dried, and folded it all neatly back in my walk-in wardrobe.

Having a walk-in wardrobe was always one of my dreams. When I converted my parents' old barn, a walk-in wardrobe was way up there on my list of must-haves. I jumped up and down with glee and made carpet angels in the middle of the room the day we completed it. It's just so grand and organized. Exactly how I like things. Also, I have a bit of a clothing buying obsession. The need is real.

But you rarely go out partying, Eden, in fact, never, so why all the clothes?

I tap my finger on my chin. Honestly? I don't know. I just love fashion. Internet shopping is the shiz.

Hashtag: I buy going out clothes to stay in.

Sad.

As.

Hell.

Consumed by my thoughts, I'm suddenly drawn to a high-pitched squeal.

What the hell is that? Is that coming from outside? Must be. That's not Betsy, surely.

Ah, Betsy. My wee, cute mint-green Fiat 500. She even has car eyelashes lined along her headlamps. Actual eyelashes for cars. Who knew? It makes her look even more adorable. Is that possible, you ask? I can assure you it is.

Christ, wait a minute. That noise is getting louder.

"Is that you, Betsy?"

I'm pretty sure if Betsy could talk, she'd be urging me to be wheesht and to stop singing and daydreaming. To be fair, this is a regular pastime of mine.

A large clatter brings me to my senses.

I dart my eyes briefly toward the entertainment console. In the dark, I fumble trying to locate the volume knob.

From the corner of my eye, faster than my brain can comprehend, my bright headlights illuminate a giant, slender, chestnut-colored four-legged beast leaping straight into the path of my compact car.

A deer.

Not just a deer but a big kick-ass daddy stag-sized deer.

"Ho-ly shit." I let out an almighty yelp.

It all happens so quickly.

The startled stag springs its agile body right over my

baby shoe-sized car.

A fusion of clunks, clatters, and bangs follow, as my screams join in the uproar.

In a whirlwind, my tires screech and squeal against the tarmac.

I completely lose control and spin off the road, smashing through the roadside fence straight into a field. There's no stopping me; I'm flying down through a maze of berry fields. Out of control, my car hurtles, scattering pieces of it as it continues to race ahead. My headlights bob up and down, illuminating a flashing path of towering juicy raspberry bushes.

"Oh, fuck. Argh."

Clearly living so close to the sea has turned me into a pirate. Potty mouth and all.

Eruptions of splattered berries thud against my windshield. It appears I've driven on to the set of *The Walking Dead*.

Making homemade jam this evening was *not* on my agenda.

More screaming... Crikey, that screaming is me... Who knew I could hit that note?

Okay, bear with me here just for a moment. I'm going to ask you to press pause at this point as I have a full-on *Deadpool* moment.

You see, what's happened here is... I was too busy channeling my inner old-school Beyoncé in the car. Imagining I'm the fourth member of Destiny's Child they never replaced. At the same time going a little too fast on these country roads, combined with deep longing thoughts of my past love to return home. I've failed to notice with my tunes on, volume full blast and cat choir evening with Eden, there is something clearly wrong with my car. Plus, I'm having a pity party. But I was lost in the haven of my car, singing my heart out. I sing in the car for a reason. I'm safeguarding everyone from ear bleeds as I can*not* sing for toffee. Just ask my best friends Beth and Toni, and my triplet sisters Eva and Ella. In my head, I'm Ariana. In reality, I'm Geri from the Spice Girls, tone-deaf, out of key, and can't carry a tune in a bucket. Shhh… Don't tell her I said that.

Unpause… Let's continue.

Boom.

The sound echoes throughout the countryside. Poor Betsy continues wildly running down the field.

Bang.

From fast and furious to a complete standstill.

Another *bang*.

My airbag thunders, smacking my face in a blast, catapulting my neck backward. Simultaneously, the explosion jolts my hands off the steering wheel.

Searing pain instantly travels into my left hand and face.

Then silence.

Apart from a seriously high-pitched ringing in my ears.

That is quite something.

I shake my head, trying to gain my bearings and organize my thoughts.

As I unclench my closed eyes, I try to refocus.

In front, a cloud of white smoke puffs into the cold pitch-dark night.

Faint hissing and low humming sounds escape from the car.

The ringing in my ears persists.

"Bloody hell. Make it stop."

As I bring my hands to my head, bolts of dull pain rapidly shoot through my hand.

My fuzzy head thinks I've fought twelve rounds with a

world heavyweight champion boxer.

Time passes. I don't know how long I sit in a daze for, but the ringing subsides.

"What the actual hell just happened?" I tilt my head again in bewilderment, retracing my steps. "Car squeals. Loud music. Volume knob. Deer. Spinning. Field. You have got to be kidding me? Think, Eden, think," I coach myself. "Phone, find your phone."

Shakily, I reach for my handbag. It's kindly bounced off the passenger seat during all the commotion and wedged itself into the farthest corner of the passenger side footwell. Just perfect.

I reach to unlock my seat belt but hesitate. My thumb on my left hand is throbbing like a bitch now. "Aargh, that is so painful." I check my thumb. "How did you swell so quickly?"

I sit crying silent tears and sniffle away, feeling sorry for myself. I'm definitely in shock. I'm talking to my thumb.

Steadying my shaky hands, I use my pointer finger to release my seat belt, setting myself free.

"Sweet baby Jesus."

The shooting pain in my hand is getting worse. Delayed reactions are the worst. Like when you use hair removal cream and leave it on too long and burn your lady bits in the process. You know that first pee you go for is going to sting like a nest of vipers, but you have to go. It's okay for the first few seconds, so you think you've gotten away with it, but then *whoosh*, a burning sensation like you've never felt before sets your nether regions on fire. No? Just me then? Anyhoo...

With slow and careful movements, I shuffle over the center console, conscious not to snag my thumb. I twist my small five-foot-two body far enough to reach over and grab my handbag.

My legs are unharmed, so I twist and maneuver farther over. However, even in my minuscule car, I'm still too short to reach.

I try again.

Really craning this time, I grit my teeth and stretch my hand out, grimacing with the pain that's winding up my thumb and wrist, and cry out like I'm bloody Thor striking down his lightning hammer.

"Argh," I shriek, successfully hooking my middle finger into the lip of my bag. "Gotcha." I drag the bag toward me as I hook-a-duck it up onto the passenger seat.

Huffing and puffing, I lean back into my seat. I take a moment before rummaging through my bag with my unharmed hand.

I begin my phone treasure hunt, sniffling into its depths. "Why the bloody hell is my bag like a trash can?"

Mirror—nope. Sunglasses—nope. Dental floss—nope. Cupcake. Yuck. Christ knows how long that's been in there for.

Gum. Spoon. What? Why?

The dull pain in my hand pounds. I suck my breath in through gritted teeth. I keep searching. Hair tie, tampon, phone charger.

"Come on," I grumble.

Realization washes over me. Crap, I've forgotten to pick up my phone.

"Of all the times, Eden, you're an ass."

I'm in the dark, in a field, late at night, no phone.

I lean my head back and search the darkness.

Where the hell am I? Is this McGregor's fruit field? Was I driving past his place? What road was I on? Why the hell did I not take the low road home at this time of night?

It's late. I've no idea what time it is. My car console isn't working, and I know for a fact my Apple Watch is sitting by my bedside on charge. And yup, I'm one of those sad step counters. I'd completed my steps and exercise quota by one o'clock this afternoon and removed it before my shower earlier. *Go me.*

"Shit. Shit. Shit." I smash my good fist onto the dashboard.

I'm a sitting duck. Hot prey for serial killers.

Are there serial killers in our local area? I rub my hand across my forehead. Have we ever had any murders in Castleview Cove?

"Hello."

I jolt, suddenly startled by a muffled foreign voice calling from the blackness.

"Anyone there? Hello?"

Male, but not a Scottish accent.

I hear it again. "Hello, can you hear me?" The voice is closer this time.

Then I hear a few muffled voices. All male voices. *Oh, shit.*

Tremors of cold sweat skim across my body.

My mum's voice pops into my head. *"Always keep your phone on you, girls. Remember to keep it charged, and no taking the high road late at night."*

And now here I am, on the high road, no phone. I have a phone charger, though. "Fucking pointless, Eden." I silently curse myself and pray.

Please, Universe

I am not exactly one to reach out, having lost my faith in you some time ago, for obvious reasons, but can you pleeease not let them be serial killers? Pretty please. I promise to do more steps tomorrow and reduce my cupcake intake this year. Well, that's a bit of a white lie, but could you look after me, please, just for tonight? Thank you.

Be brave.

I suck in a shallow breath and tremble out into the pitch-black, "Help, I'm here."

They won't hear me as I'm in the car. My windows are up and my doors are closed, so how the heck will they hear me? *Stupid Eden.*

Reaching out, I pull the door handle. It unlocks with a soft click. I pull the handle further. *Clunk.* It opens. I nudge the heavy door just a fraction. That's the problem with a little three-door car and a small body frame like mine. The doors are always too heavy for me to open fully without a tremendous amount of effort. I have no more effort left in me tonight.

I try to shove the door wider. Well, if it's a serial killer out there, I've just given him an all-access pass. There's more than one of them too—great, a gang bang of serial killers. Flippin' fantastic.

Hey, Universe, I'm fully trusting you up there. Please have my back.

A mix of chattering voices scramble together. Maybe three of them.

I'm still a little clunky and disorientated, but I pluck up the courage and cry out again, "Hey, I'm here. Can you please help me?"

I tear up again as the full reality of my situation hits me. I haven't even attempted to get out of the car.

"Please, can you help me?" I plead to the abyss.

"Hey, ma'am? Miss? Are you okay? Are you hurt?"

A strong American accent hits my ears as they close the gap. Most definitely a tourist—we get a lot of them in

Castleview Cove. I love the Americans; they are always so polite and kind.

Thank you, Universe.

A loud knock on the passenger side window startles me.

"Holy shit," I burst out and throw my good hand to my pounding heart. I don't think I can take any more surprises tonight.

"I'm on the other side."

I see the tall figure circle around the back of my car toward me, and I hear him informing whoever else is out there that he's on the wrong side.

Yup, we drive on the other side of the road here, you numpty.

Oh, I'm gnarly.

Don't be mean, Eden. Someone is here to help.

As the stranger moves to my side, I imagine my serial killer invite. It's possibly gone viral on the universal serial killer notice board. *"Eden invites a party of serial killers to a field in Castleview Cove. First come, first serve. Mwahahaha."*

"Please take care of me, Universe," I whisper pray.

Although that thought is being overshadowed by the burning pain I'm experiencing. I feel very woozy as adrenaline and soreness mulches into one.

I just want help. From anyone.

My door flies wide open, triggering the indoor light, illuminating the small space. Why didn't I think to try that wee light above?

Movement from a large figure captures my attention as they crouch down inside the nook of my car door.

"Hey, can you move? Are you hurt?" A deep gravelly American drawl floats over me as my eyes lock with the most sensational jet-pooled eyes I've ever seen.

Holy cow.

CHAPTER TWO

Boke or Boak: *verb,* to vomit; *noun,* an instance or episode of vomiting. **Pronounced:** Boke, like poke.

Eden

Where in the land of Mount Olympus, has this Greek god fallen from?

I look up to the slither of sky through the car door. Did he fall out of heaven like a dark angel?

"Tom, our driver, is calling emergency services. We weren't far behind you on the road. You're lucky we saw you. You spun out of control superfast," he says slightly out of breath. "Your car has run deep into the field. We had to run down here to get you. Apart from your nose, where else are you hurt?"

Even the interior light overhead doesn't hit his melted chocolate eyes. I would like to dip myself in those. Mmm, yeah.

Is there such a thing as fuck-me-now eyes? If so, I think

this is what they look like. Not that I would want to, you know, fuck him. Well, maybe just a smidge.

Nope. Stop it, Eden. It's probably closed up down there, anyway. I'm pretty sure that's what happens after years of inaction. It's in the basement of The Scottish Museum, under Vagina Archives.

I don't know what I'm thinking; there is no way someone like *him* would be interested in someone like *me*, anyway.

Hello hotness. Raw sex appeal is in the house.

I read about hot as hell guys like these in my romance books—or porn books, as my friend Beth likes to call them. I never believed men, like this, existed, until now.

Bloody hell, my thoughts are random. It's possibly the hypnotic citrus scent he's oozing, or it's his divine deep tanned coloring that covers his skin that's messing with my senses. He's so alluring, I can't take my eyes off this mysterious guy.

Dumbstruck at trying to make my brain make words, I can't stop this weird, overwhelming sensation that I know him; however, I'm currently one can short of a six-pack right now; I'm not thinking straight and I feel so sick.

Breathe.

I suck air in and out, drinking in this mysterious guy at the same time.

He's all in black. Uh-huh. Could be a serial killer. If he is a serial killer, I'm not sure I could take much more tonight to be honest. I'd happily roll over and beg Mr. Fuck-Me-Now-Eyes to take me.

What a way to go. Death by hot guy.

Could be worse.

I'm mesmerized by his size. He fills the doorway of my little vehicle. He must be super tall; he's crouched way down, but his head still reaches the top of the doorway. How is that possible?. He's massive.

Stationary, I stare at him because I can't help myself, as I cradle my elevated hand. That's what you're supposed to do, isn't it? Keep it elevated? The first-aid certificate I hold for my dance studio seems to have been a complete waste of time; I can't remember a bloody thing.

Bringing me out of my daze, he says, "Hey, you okay?"

"M... my... my hand hurts," I quietly whine.

"You're doing the right thing, keep it up. Your nose? Is it sore? It looks sore." He motions to it with his head, grimacing slightly.

Must look bad. Moving my good hand, I thumb my gold elephant necklace as my lips and chin tremble.

"Hey." He reaches out and lays his hand on my thigh. "You're alright. I've got you. You're going to be okay."

A wave of calm blankets around me from his welcomed touch. Ah... he feels like home.

Where did that come from?

I feel like I know him; I'm sure of it. I know those eyes.

Curiously, I lift my good hand up to pat my face gently, exploring where the throbbing is coming from. It feels wet and warm. I lower my hand; dabs of blood cover the pads of my fingers.

"Argh, I'm bleeding. Aw, Jiminy Cricket, it's all over my Minnie Mouse tee shirt too, it's ruined. I really liked this shirt." I feel super light-headed. "I don't feel so good; I don't like blood."

Everything tilts.

I clench my eyes shut as a cold sweat swarms again.

Fan, I need a fan. Or someone to fan me down.

I could handle this stranger next to me fanning me down; oh yes, palm leaf in hand, wafting cool air over me, wearing nothing but a white towel... Yeah, baby, that sounds nice...

His deep soothing voice hits me. "Hey, stay with me, you're going to be just fine. Look at me." I turn my head toward him and our eyes meet again. "You like Minnie?" the stranger asks me, pointing at my tee. He's clearly trying to distract me and keep me calm. Or check out my tits. Maybe both.

"Yeah, she's one sassy lady; she keeps Mickey on his toes. I've always dreamed of going to Florida and meeting her and Mickey. That would be so cool."

He smiles at that.

I literally have no idea why I'm oversharing.

"What's your name?" he softly prompts.

"I... I'm..." I stutter, unable to knit my words together.

Never taking his eyes off me, he coaxes me. "It's okay, take it slow, what's your name, ma'am?"

"It's Eden. My name is Eden, and please don't call me ma'am; that makes me feel like an old woman."

Smirking, he replies in a cool, steady tone, "Eden, such a beautiful name. A place of paradise. Suits you. My name is Hunter."

Spellbound, I muster a small laugh. "I don't think I look like paradise right now."

Covered in blood, mascara smeared tears running down my face, and God knows what else in the middle of this fruit field, I'm a far cry from paradise.

"Look at Betsy, poor girl. It looks like a strawberry threw up all over her." I wince as I let out my rambled thoughts.

"Actually, you are true to your name; you are beautiful, Eden. I don't think any rotten situation could ever camouflage that."

Eh, sorry, what?

"Who's Betsy?" he asks nonchalantly, cinching his brows as if his previous comment never left his mouth.

He called me beautiful.

Pressing me, he says, "Eden, baby, who's Betsy?"

Baby?

"Eh, my car."

"Phew, thank fuck for that. I thought you had a child or pet in the car with you. One Scottish girl in a field is enough for me for one night, thanks."

"Just little me."

"Do you remember my name, Eden?"

"Yeah. Hunter? That's what you said, didn't you? Yes, Hunter." I answer my question, shaking my head. "I feel like I know you. Do I know you?"

He flashes a dazzling white smile. "You might."

My heart leaps. Roaming my eyes over him as much as I can see in the faint light overhead, he feels like a good guy. He's shockingly attractive and easy on the eye.

Wide and muscly, he looks ripped. Those lips too, like bouncy castles, very kissable. Yup, I've definitely got a concussion. I rub my hand across my forehead.

Hunter chuckles quietly.

"Oh, poop, did I say that out loud?"

He shakes his head.

"If my name means paradise, what does your name mean?" *Why the heck am I asking that?*

"Simple, it means one who hunts or pursues."

"Mmm, how apt. Hunting or pursuing Scottish girls in berry fields," I tease, surprising myself, as I feel the never-ending thrum of pain still running through my hand. Hmm, I still found the effort to joke.

Something lights up inside of me. An odd sensation I've not felt in a very long time. Years, in fact, if ever.

It ignites. It's small. But it's there. A little glow, a spark.

This feels nice. Unexpected. Warm.

I'm loving this frozen moment in time with him.

He makes me feel safe, and I like the way he called me beautiful.

To the local boys, I'm emotionally unavailable. The local boys stopped flirting and trying to date me a very long time ago. To the tourists and the strangers? Well, I don't entertain any of them and give that whole piss-off-don't-even-bother vibe when I go out on a rare occasion. Like Christmas, it's a once-a-year event.

But this guy, well, he doesn't know me or my history. All my barriers are down with this whole messed-up situation I've found myself in too. It's the banging of my nose that's causing me to lower them; I'm certain of it.

I feel something.

It makes me feel uneasy.

What is that? Is it guilt?

Guilt for feeling an attraction to another man? To this guy?

Or is it something else? I'm not sure.

It's been such a long time since I've felt anything other than brokenhearted, so my emotional compass is way off course.

I try to hide what's going on beneath the surface. But my triplet sisters, Ella and Eva, we have this intuitive shared understanding that we can't quite put our finger on.

We can always detect when something is wrong with one another. My, 'the show must go on' veil I've put on to the outside world all this time, is just that, a veil to hide everything bubbling away beneath the surface.

But Ella and Eva, they know different, because they *feel* it. They've told me many times. It's this invisible bond and deep emotional connection that runs between us. We just know. They know.

After all these years, my friends and family keep telling me to move on, but I keep hoping. Hoping he comes back.

He keeps me anchored here in Castleview Cove.

I'll be here when he comes back. *If* he comes back.

Out of nowhere my stomach lurches.

It's not from the thoughts of my past.

"I think I'm going to boke," I mumble.

"Boke? What the hell is boke?" Hunter questions with furrowed brows.

Just as he asks, my body whips forward so fast. I launch my head out the side; my stomach convulses, and I throw up between Hunter's legs. All over his black boots. Bugger, they look expensive.

I gather myself and wipe my mouth. I'm so embarrassed.

I keep my head down. "Oh my God, I'm so sorry," I blurt. "It's Scottish for being sick."

"Fuck. What?"

As I raise my head, his eyes lock on mine.

"Boke. It's Scottish for being sick. Do you know you are sexy as hell, like so, just gorgeous? I don't look the least bit sexy, but you, you have a whole thing going on."

I think I'm drunk.

Motioning at his big powerful frame, forgetting my newly damaged hand, I clumsily rattle it against the steering wheel, then let out a yelp as crippling pain zaps through my hand.

Sudden exhaustion from everything takes over; the pain is too much, and the last things I remember are baseball cap, deep chocolate eyes, American accent, white smile, Hunter... and everything goes wibbly, then black.

CHAPTER THREE

Peely Wally: *adjective,* pale and sickly in appearance. **Pronounced:** Pee-lee-wali.

Whisky: *noun,* Whisky (no e) made in Scotland, also Canadian and Japanese grain spirits. **Pronounced:** Whisk-ay.

Eden

Soaking in the hustle and bustle of the street outside, I gaze out the window of Castle Cones Ice Cream Parlor.

I've been watching the world go by, lost in my own thoughts for the last hour as I enjoy the sweet fragrance of waffle cones in the air.

Thirteenth Century buildings litter my captivating hometown, and of course, there's the castle that keeps a watchful eye over everyone. It's central to everything.

It's breathtaking, romantic, comforting.

Home.

It's been three days since my car crash.

Sprained thumb. Tick.

Nasal trauma. Tick.

Was the airbag the culprit? Tick.

Car totaled? Double tick.

Turns out my alternator needed replacing, hence the noise. That would have been an easy fix; however, a combination of the crash, the damage the deer performed to my roof, and then the bumper car ride down the field, it's now a write-off. *Deep joy.*

Encased in the pastel-colored seating booth, I'm waiting for my lifelong friend, Toni, to take her break.

I watch as Toni elegantly weaves her way through the parlor, casually chatting to customers and laughing with her staff.

She's one helluva dangerous cocktail. Long brunette hair, deep hazelnut Italian eyes, and all year round caramel skin.

In comparison, being a fully-fledged Scot, I have super-pale skin, although I seem to tan really well in the sun.

Not that we see much of it in Scotland. Rain, rain, rain, and, today's forecast, rain. That's why my skin verges on being a lovely shade of whitish-blue in the winter. Peely-wally is what we call it in Scotland. So technically at least I have one thing going for me. My skin and eyes match. Both blue. *Great.*

Toni lives and breathes the family ice cream shop. Her parents handed over the running of the family business last year, and she's been working her butt off ever since, renovating and updating the entire business from surroundings to systems.

It's very rare she takes vacations, but she never complains. She's in her element.

People queue for hours, all year round. The lure of the handmade rich, sugary Italian goodness that Toni and her team serve up pulls people in, even through the wintertime when it's snowing.

I've already had two ice cream cones today myself.

Toni's been experimenting, yet again, with some new flavors to add to the eighty-one strong flavor menu. Scottish marmalade sorbet and rhubarb with ginger and gin. They were both a big thumbs-up from me. Well, one thumb and one finger because, well, you know, my thumb has a boo-boo.

I've tried all eighty-one flavors. Scottish tablet is still my favorite. Mmm, or maybe it's fudge? It's a tough call, to be honest. They are similar; Scottish tablet has that firmer grainy, super sugary texture, but then fudge, well, it's softer, much softer, more melt in your mouth. It's heavenly. A bit of advice. For the love of God, never tell a Scottish person they are the same thing. Fudge and tablet? Very different. Lots of sampling will prove you wrong, and you will be wrong. They are *not* the same thing.

So, Eden, tablet or fudge?

Gosh, that's a hard choice. Please don't ask me to pick. That would be like asking me to pick my favorite nephew. Nope, not doing that. Although... if you really push me, I may sway more toward little Archie. He's a wee smasher. All ice-blond hair and blue eyes. Just dreamy and cute. Really bloody cute.

Castle Cones stays open late; who the hell wants ice cream at eleven p.m.? I raise a hand in the air. Eh, me, that's who. Toni works a lot of the late shifts, so it's my excuse to 'drop in.' *Yeah, right.*

"Hey, short stuff." Toni smiles as she shimmies into the opposite side of the booth.

Short stuff. That nickname landed and stuck throughout school, and it's never gone away. Petite—now I like that word. It's just a much nicer way to say short, isn't it? I dislike short stuff. Toni is only three inches taller than me. Geez.

"Have we tamed the ice cream beast?"

"Mayyybe." I snigger.

"That bruising is really shining through now, huh? Is the pain any better?"

"A little. It's the swelling I can't handle the look of. I look like a pufferfish."

"A beautiful pufferfish." She blows air into her cheeks.

"Stop it, you. Ah, that's painful." I wince. I keep forgetting not to scrunch up my face or make sudden movements. It's painful when I do. "I can't breathe properly. I'm so happy it's not a break though. Thank you." I roll my eyes toward the sky.

"You still look cute. How did you get into town? Did Ella drive you in?" Toni takes a bite of her cheese and ham toastie.

"Yeah, she did." It sucks I can't drive and I'm at the mercy of everyone. My car is a write-off; they confirmed with me this morning. I hope my insurance gets sorted quickly.

"Ella's coming back to get me. She had some things to sort out at the dance studio. And... she mentioned she wanted one of your famous sundaes you're now making with cherry soda ice cream." I smile.

"You three Wallace girls and ice cream, you're worse than my family. Are you sure you're not Italian?"

I cross my fingers. "Promise. Oh, here's Ella now." I watch as Ella swishes her hips toward us, all eyes on her.

Being a triplet is hard.

Everyone expects you to be the same, but we're not. For a start, we're not identical. We're fraternal triplets. The same, but different. We all sound exactly the same. Our tone and quirks in our voices are identical. This throws Dad into a state of confusion all the time. His rule is... One at a time, please. He gets seriously flustered if we don't take our turns to speak.

Compared to me, on the flip side is Ella. She's our full-on party-loving girl and could out-party the world's greatest party animal. Fact.

I'm not sure if or when she'll settle down. Eva and I are 'let's have a night in,' Ella's more a 'let's go for two weeks to Ibiza and not sleep.' Yeah. Very different in that respect.

Eva's our serene, delicate, and thoughtful girl. More homely all around. Her unique boho chic style makes her look supercool. I'd love to pull off her long dress and chunky Doc Martens boot look. She's a hippy at heart. Her immaculate restored VW Camper Van adds that extra layer to her nomadic style too. It's only ever taken out on sunshine days on the beach.

Eva and I do have similar golden-caramel hair, but that's about as similar as we get. Mine is long, very long. Down to my waist long. It's a labor of love.

I watch Ella pull her black off-the-shoulder sweater up over her long thick shiny ice-blond hair and nestles in beside me.

"Beatches. I *am* pooped. What a crazy day."

I roll my eyes. "Having to work for a change, Ella?"

"Down, girl. You're spicier these last few days. I'm taking you home after my sundae, and then we're going to talk about how we juggle our dance school. I'll buy you some cupcakes on the way home. Will that help tame your inner bitch?" She sniggers. "The only thing Eva has asked for is more of the under twelve-year-old classes. She's much better with the kids than I am. I am way 'too sweary' apparently." Ella mimics air quotes with her fingers.

"Eva's not wrong," adds Toni.

Ella narrows her bright-emerald eyes. "Friends, Toni." Motioning the space between them. "We're supposed to be friends; you're supposed to be on my side."

"Whatever. I'm not getting pulled into you girls' ménage à trois." She rises from the table. "What do you want, a cherry soda sundae, Ella?"

"Bingo. Bring it, baby."

"You feeling better, babes?" Ella turns to me as Toni slips out of the booth.

"Yeah. Much. It was a great idea to get me out of my house today. Being here, at the parlor, always feels like home, doesn't it? How many hours have we spent here since we were kids?"

"Hundreds, I reckon. Me, you, Eva, Toni, and Beth, just eating and chatting about school, boys, and music. Not much has changed really." She laughs.

"I love what Toni's done to the place." She looks around. "All the retro ice cream parlor touches are so cool. I love the addition of the jukebox and the new bar stools. I can imagine Sandy making out with Danny from *Grease*, right there." Giggling, she points with her perfectly manicured fingers to the chrome bar stools in pastel lilac and powder blue seat pads.

I take in the remodeled parlor. It's a three-hundred-and-sixty-degree mouthwatering experience. I've tried *all* eighty-one ice cream flavors, so I know. Taste tester, anyone? I jump up and down, saying, "Me, me, me." C'mon, give me a break; you would too if you were this close to the family.

We sit in comfortable silence.

"Here we go. One cherry soda sundae. And for you, my darling Eden. A wee whisky ice cream. It's medicinal," Toni assures me, winking.

"Thank Christ you're not driving then."

A voice pops up from behind Toni.

"Hey, Eva." I welcome her. Seems like we're all meeting here today then.

"Hi."

"Ciao Bella."

"Can I have one of those, please, Toni?" Eva points to Ella's sundae.

"Sure, coming right up."

"So this is what you two do when I'm at work then, huh?" I ask deadpan.

"Eh, no. We live our lives, Eden. So while you teach all day, try to cram more classes into our timetable, create TikToks, and overplan the business. Oh, and read. Eva has the kids, school runs, a house, a hubby, and I have a house and a dog and the horse. We have a life outside our dance studio, Eden." She points her long sundae spoon at me. "So stick that up your peachy tooshie."

Christ, does Ella's feistiness never switch off? "And you said I was spicy today, Ella?" I quirk my brow.

My sisters and I own a dance school here in Castleview Cove—T3SDS. Short for The 3 Sisters Dance School. Us three girls attended the Scottish Contemporary Dance School after we left school. Surrounded by my sisters while away from Castleview Cove felt more like home away from home. We trained for years together, learning everything about dance and where our strengths lay. We then trained to teach. None of it ever felt like work for any of us. Dance is in our bones.

When we set up a dance school, it was the most natural thing for us to do. We wanted to share our gift.

There was no dance school in Castleview Cove. So we made it our goal to open one. Make it fun, make it accessible, be creative, and nurture untapped talent. We do what we love every day in the town where our hearts belong. My heart is rooted here forever.

We extended the gable end of my barn conversion, that's now my dream home, to accommodate our dance school.

Following the incident four years ago, Ella and Eva oversaw the last stages of the conversion. I wasn't in a good place mentally to do so.

When the sad-looking barn sat year after year perched within the grounds of my parents' estate, Castle Sports Therapy Retreat, without a purpose, I asked if I could buy the building. They insisted I could have it. But we did it all officially. The barn is something to ooh and ahh over now. It's even featured in a few Scottish home magazines. Five years on and I'm still in love with it.

I'm ever so grateful because if Mum and Dad hadn't bought the mansion house and its grounds, then I never would have been the proud owner of my barn, which I proudly named, The West Barn. How super imaginative of me.

Eva asks, "What's happening with your car? Do you know yet?"

We each have a Fiat 500. Minus mine now. They're our advertising machines. One in mint green. Well, no longer. But I'm replacing her as soon as I get the go-ahead from the insurance company. I groan at the thought of the ensuing paperwork. Ella has a black one and Eva drives a silver one —it's our dance school brand colors: mint, black, and silver. We emblazoned each one with our dance school logo.

"Yeah, I found out this morning. It's a write-off. I'm not bothered at the moment because I can't drive for a few weeks until my face and thumb heal, but I hope the paperwork doesn't drag and suck a bag of dicks."

Ella splutters. "What the hell, Eden? When was the last time you sucked a dick? Or saw one for that matter?"

"Shut up." I blush.

"They just get you into trouble; look at me with two kids. Word of advice from Aunty Eva, stay away from dicks."

"The closest I've been to one lately is in my book. He was the size of a sword, apparently." I place my hands out in front of me, wide, demonstrating the length.

Eva drops her voice. "Hey, Ms. Wallace, come here; let me impale you with my thirty-inch sword."

We all shake with laughter.

"What are we all laughing at?" Beth's sultry voice drifts our way. I look up and just like always, Beth's phone's in her hand. With her head down, she struts her lean, elegant figure toward us.

"Yay. Beth's here." I raise my arm with glee.

"Eden's books. She was talking about dicks." Ella fills Beth in.

"You and those bloody books." Beth rolls her dark-green eyes, crossing her long slender legs as she teeters sideways on the edge of the seat.

"You need a dick and not read *about* one."

She's wearing her signature black power collarless blazer, teamed with the tightest matching pencil skirt. How does she walk in that? And those shoes look dangerously high. It's not like she needs the height.

Ah, those legs. They are truly enviable. At five foot eleven, she's so graceful. It's kind of embarrassing when I stand next to her. I look like I came along as the freak show circus act. Although Beth reckons it's the other way around. The thing we do share in common is that we both lurveeee to shop. Oh yes, we do. Internet shopping is great and all, but Saturday afternoons are all about shopping. We are bona fide shopaholics.

Out of our little quintet, I'm the shortest. Ding, ding, winner. *Yay, me.* I definitely pulled the short straw. Literally.

"Yeah, yeah, I know. I need to get out more. Eden's a saddo. Whatever."

I love my books. I love the escapism of a good romance novel. Cozied up on the couch. Just me and the story. It reminds me of my life before, a life I don't have anymore. A life that I had a sneaking glance at. Then boom. Like a clap of thunder, it took all those dreams from me. Four years ago now. Feels like so much longer.

You'll find me with my head in a book between dancing. I choose to only read the books that have a happily ever after. Or if you're a book geek, like me, also known as HEA.

My favorite books all have a HEA. Girl meets boy. They encounter hardships along the way. They conquer every emotion under the sun. Travesty tears them apart, but they always, always, get back together and live happily ever after —or HEA to you and me.

I know that actual life is not like that. I'm living proof of that, but I love to dream, and it makes me feel warm and fuzzy inside. Those books give me hope because of the sheer joy and high they always end on.

I don't think I could handle reading anything other than a HEA.

It just hurts too much.

Miracles, hope, and love happen in books.

Hope.

Such a beautiful word.

I cling on to hope.

I drift off, lost in my thoughts, as an ache pulsates in my heart.

Staring around, I take in the tourists and day-trippers filling up the booths and queue of Castle Cones. Most of them are most likely golfers.

Our town attracts them in droves. Visiting from all over the world with the dream of playing golf on Scotland's finest golf courses.

They all want to eat ice cream at the world-famous ice cream parlor, walk the golden beaches, the harbor, the pier, and watch the sun set. It's the Castleview Cove must-dos.

Castleview Cove, *The Heart of Golf*. That's the town's tagline. Apt for Castleview Cove. Surrounded by nine golf courses, including the mother of all courses, The Champion. It's classed as the best, oldest, and most famous in the world; it's monumental in the world of golf and it hosts the world-famous Castleview Championship Cup, or The Cup for short, and takes place every four years.

I watch as Beth taps away on her phone. Probably answering the copious amount of emails she receives every day.

Ah, the cross is hard to bear when you're the CEO of The Scotland Golf Association here in Castleview Cove. The Association oversees everything golf related.

It comes with weighty expectations and demands. Beth is the youngest to become CEO in the history of the Association, a highly sought-after role and historically filled by a man. She's making waves and setting the stage for new fresh talent to join her team.

The five of us played a cracking game of golf, once, when we were eighteen, following a very drunken-lunch-gone-one-drink-too-many afternoon.

We hired clubs, with no idea what the hell we were doing. Well, Beth did. That is her job to know how to play golf after all. But way back then she was too drunk to teach us, and frankly she couldn't give a monkey's.

We ended up on the wrong course. Lost a few balls. Riled up some tourists. Toni fell in the burn that runs along the length of the course, and then we crashed a golf cart into the sand dunes.

I don't recall leaving the course. Apparently, I swung my bra around my head, catapulting golf balls from it as we walked to the pub. God help poor Beth. That story comes up from time to time. We're twenty-seven-year-old responsible adults now. With proper jobs and everything. We don't do that kind of thing anymore. Well, maybe the girls do from time to time. Just don't let them loose on a bottle of tequila. That. Changes. Everything.

Where was I? Golf. Yup. Golf is the soul of our majestic historic town. It was even part of our school curriculum. I sometimes wish Toni and I had paid attention in those classes, then we might know what the fascination with it all is and maybe look more interested when Beth shares her days with us. That glazed look we often have is a look of 'yeah, we do not know what the hell you're talking about' when she explains golfy things to us. Golfy things, that's an actual thing just for the record. Well, it is in our book.

Us townies love the tourists and love the buzz of the town. Beth, Toni, and Ella like it for other reasons—hot golfers apparently.

Can't say I've looked in a while. I don't want to look.

Beth settles her phone down on the table, looks straight at me without flinching, and three simple words spill out her mouth. "So, Hunter King?"

She's a minx.

I feel my cheeks heat for the second time today.

"*The* Hunter King. Pro golfer Hunter King. Found *you* in a field. Holy shit. Have you seen those eyes, girls?" She looks around the table at everyone, then turns to look straight back at me. "I heard all about your little encounter today when Hunter helped us kick off our promo for the Championship Cup. I'm so over this promo stuff, and we still have three months to go. He told me about how he'd found this 'pretty Scottish girl' and how he rescued her in a field. How her voice was like a siren and how she was as cute as a button." She mockingly swoons.

"He didn't bloody say that." I tilt my head to the side. "Did he?"

"Mmm." She taps her chin.

I'm going to kill her.

"No, he didn't. But he might as well have. I overheard him speaking to his swing coach about you. He's been texting Ella. Ain't that right, hon?"

"Well, I wasn't going to tell you *yet*." Beth flinches under the table as Ella takes a swipe at her shins. "But he likes you, and he's concerned about you. He wants to come see you."

She continues. "He's asked about you several times over the last few days. When Mum and Dad showed up at the hospital, Hunter was there. Do you really not remember? He followed behind the ambulance. Mum told you that too. That bump to the head has made you such a space cadet these last few days." She frowns as I shake my head. "Hunter explained how he'd found you. Of course, Dad knew who he was. Dad was expecting him that night to check in at the retreat. He's staying here for three months. And when I say he likes you, I mean, he *really* likes you."

"How is that even possible? Look at me. Five foot two, a

nobody, average plain old Eden. And he doesn't know me. He likes me?"

"Yeah."

"Are you blind?"

"Hush now, girl."

"You what?"

All at once cries call around the table.

Ella turns to me, curling her leg on top of the leather seat. "You, Eden Wallace, are beautiful." She reaches out and tucks a loose caramel strand of hair behind my ear. "You have a bangin' curvaceous hourglass body with flexibility and strength that even Eva and I can't keep up with. You need a man to share that shit with. It's totally going to waste. You're funny and clever and have the kindest heart. You've lost all your dating confidence and belief in yourself. I know you think you don't deserve happiness, but you do. And also not because you're my sister and please believe me when I say this. You are gorgeous." She bites her top lip. "Although as I'm looking at you, all I see is a pufferfish."

I find Toni's eyes. "See, I told you. Pufferfish." I slap my good hand to the table. "I knew it."

"I just gave you my greatest speech, and that's what you take from it."

We fill our little corner of the parlor with soft chuckles.

"In all honesty, girls, I don't feel beautiful. I certainly haven't felt remotely attractive for a long time. My confidence has taken a full on nosedive for sure." I shrink back into my seat and wrap my arms around myself. "I still can't get my head around why he left, and why I then lost my little angel. I didn't deserve this," I say meekly.

I haven't spoken to anyone about my feelings for a long time, or ever. I try to bury them all. Stay in. Work. Dance.

The show must go on, right? Mask on, shoulders back, tits out.

I have quite good tits too. I think it's because my waist is so tiny it makes my boobs look much bigger than they really are. It makes buying bras and jeans a bloody nightmare—tiny waists are awful things. That's why dancewear is my go-to. Lycra is life.

Sinking myself into dance is my grand escape. I was born to dance. I've dreamed about it since I was ten years old. However, back then I imagined myself as tall and slender. Just like the girls in the music videos I was obsessed with watching. Never did I think that at twenty-seven years old I'd be all grown up and still the same bloody height as I was back then. Just with much bigger boobs and a lot of junk in my trunk with all the squatting and dancing I do.

Sensing my sorrow, Eva slides her hand across the table. "You know we love you?" I take her hand in mine. One by one, the rest of the girls place their hands on top.

"We've got you, babes. But you've got to let us help you," Toni says.

"I don't know if I'm ready... I think I want to go home now. Can we go home and organize what we're doing with classes while I'm off?"

The girls groan in defeat.

"I need to pick the kids up from school and nursery, so I'll let you two sort it out. I trust you." Eva winks.

"Just so you know, Eden, Hunter wants to see you. He's a man on a mission," Beth states firmly.

"He can be as determined as he wants, but he's not coming to see me."

Famous last words.

CHAPTER FOUR

Bairn: *Noun,* a baby or child. **Pronounced:** Bearn.

Scunnered: *Adjective,* fed up, annoyed, unhappy, pissed off.
Pronounced: Scun-urt.

Ma heid's mince: *Adjective,* my head's a little bit mixed up.
Pronounced: Ma heed's mince.

That's pants or this is just pants: *Phrase,* That is rubbish or
not very good.

Eden

"So, let's plan. How long do you reckon you'll be off from
teaching then?" Ella asks, stuffing a cupcake into her mouth.
My bloody cupcakes.

"I don't know if I want to do this now. It's been a long day. I can hardly breathe through my nose. My head, nose, eyes and entire face are killing me. My thumb is throbbing and my car's buggered. I can't think straight. I could hardly even pull up my own panties when I went for a pee earlier. And stop eating the cupcakes you bought me; they're mine," I say crankily and wince with the twinging pains that come and go.

That took an awful lot of effort to say.

Now we're back at my house. I'm lying flat out on my luxurious oversized L-shaped gray velvet couch. I swooned over it for weeks before I finally made it mine. I'm enveloped in my cozy blanket. I've barely done anything all day, aside from eating and yet I feel so tired.

I think it's Ella. She's exhausting.

"This is my happy place. Please don't spoil it." I exhale.

My happy place is my incredible barn conversion. It was such a thrill watching the barn being extended and transformed. We turned the old depressed-looking building into an incredibly airy and uplifting space.

I eye the space, taking it all in, leaning further into my couch. I replaced the tall old rotting double doors of the barn with a soaring double-height glass vaulted ceiling entrance. On the opposite side of the barn, I installed sliding walls of glazing.

Nestled off to the west of the retreat, my barn is all exposed brickwork, high ceilings, and roof-to-floor windows. The architect sprinkled oak beams combined with wrought iron finishing throughout. We used lots of raw materials to give it a real industrial feel. It's edgy but warm and welcoming. I love it and often do a little "squee" to myself. It's hard to believe this is mine.

I wonder if he would have shared this patch of heaven with me?

Stop it right now.

My eyes roam the open-plan layout. I do think *he* would have loved it here. I lit the cozy double-sided fireplace in the center of the room because it's a little chilly outside today. It's built into the wall that divides the living room area from the kitchen diner.

I don't know why I need a kitchen because I'm a terrible cook, but the architect insisted I have one. It even features a magnificent duck egg blue three oven AGA. It's more of an ornament—totally wasted on me, but it looks super pretty.

I could burn water. I'm not kidding you either. I remember the time I placed a whole pizza in the oven along with the plastic base from the packaging. Took me months to scrape the welded plastic from the bottom of the oven. And the time I called my mum to ask why my prawn crackers weren't cooking in the pot. To which she informed me to try using cooking oil to fry them, not water to boil them. I'm no Gordon Ramsay, that's for sure.

I love living within the retreat. I have private access with a drive that leads to the dance studio, and a small parking lot to the side of it for our dance students.

Our parents were bored after we all left for dance school. With the three of us gone, Mum wanted something to fill in her time. Buying the mansion worked out perfectly.

The grand mansion house and its grounds are now home of The Castle Sports Therapy Retreat. It's the go-to retreat for golfers to reset, re-energize, get strong, and perfect their swing.

The mansion and land belonged to some Scottish Earl-of-something-or-other and needed love and renovation.

When the Earl died, his family sold the mansion and grounds, and my parents snapped the place up.

Surrounded by beautiful countryside just a few miles out of Castleview Cove, it's nestled within eight hectares of green and luscious gardens and high walls. They've transformed the mansion into a grand stately home with an even grander entrance with a security station. A huge team of groundskeepers, headed up by Campbell, maintain the extensive hedges, lawns, and shrubs.

Within the grounds, to the east of the main house, are six standalone luxury log cabins they rent out to golfers and other athletes, but mainly golfers.

The retreat hires an elite team of sports therapists, nutritionists, and rehabilitation specialists; the dream team, managed by Arran, the retreat manager. Combined, the retreat and the golf courses surrounding Castleview Cove lure golfers from all over the world. They can sniff a freshly mown fairway from eighteen holes away. However, I'm sure the bespoke indoor sports facility with pool, gym, spa, movie theater, bowling alley, and therapy rooms within the retreat grounds doesn't go unnoticed. There's even an outdoor football pitch, a tennis court, a golf practice range, basketball court, and batting cages too.

There's always an undercurrent of activity around, but it's blissful.

I love the calming surroundings I live in, although I feel less than calm with Ella on my case.

Ella slowly blinks, swallows the rest of her cupcake, and licks her lips. "Calm down, hen, I was only asking when you were coming back to teach because I'm assuming the doctor would have told you how long your recovery would be, right? Christ, we so need to smooth your aura down a bit; its way out of whack and super spikey.

"Believe me, I know you are totally pissed off at the situation, and well, the world, and you're mad at the Universe. But Eva and I have dance classes to cover, and as I've already said today, we have lives to lead. We just need to sort out the next few weeks until you're fit to teach again. Plus, Eva has the bairns to sort out too. So we kind of need to know, Eden. I'm not being a bitch here. So just calm the hell down," Ella retorts with a sharp tone.

Good point. "Okay, sorry. I'm just scunnered. I don't mean to be a moan."

Ella just stares at me, raising her perfectly plucked eyebrows, waiting for an answer.

"So, the doctor said it would be about three or four weeks for my nose to heal. Which is way less time than I thought, actually. It looks worse than it is. It's going to continue to look awful for the next few weeks. I feel so foxy and irresistible. And my thumb is only sprained. Although it's still pants. Like *Bridget Jones*-sized whopping panties. Which is ironic because I can't even pull mine up," I end up yelling out. "The struggle is real. I need a cupcake. Pass me one."

"Oh-kay then." Ella cautiously hands me a melt-in-the-mouth candy-covered frosted cake.

Hello sweetness...

"Well, Eva and I will do a wee shifting of classes here and there for the next three weeks, if not longer. I'm going to take on your over twelve-year-old classes, plus all your hip hop ones. Eva said she would cover dance aerobics and all the under twelves. Sound good? Then you need to show me how to do TikTok and Instagram for the biz; I don't think I have the login passwords for those."

Ella, detecting that I hate not being in control, parks her pert bum next to me on the couch.

"Look," she insists, "I know you don't like this, Eden. Eva and I know you love organizing the schedules, paperwork, people, and shit—well doing pretty much anything and everything to distract you—but we can do this, you know. You can let go of the business strings just for a wee while. Trust Eva and me. We've got this. We've got you, and anyway, we need you to rest and come back with some brilliant ideas for the next dance showcase. It's only a few months away, you know?"

"Yikes, I definitely can't think of that just now. Ma heids minced."

She turns to me, head tilted, with a genuine look of concern and affection, arm hooked over the back of the couch. "Eva and I, Mum and Dad, and well, Toni and Beth, basically everyone that cares about you"—she draws a circle with her arms—"We're all concerned. We all want you to get better. Feel better. Heal. And we don't just mean from your recent car crash, Eden. You heard us in the parlor. You need to move on. We want to help. And you need to allow Eva and me to be more involved in the administration side of the business. You've been hiding from the world for way too long, busying yourself with the dance school, not allowing yourself to have fun and not going out so much. You've almost become reclusive. I actually think you've read more books than Amazon dispatches from their warehouse. Am I correct? You're only twenty-seven years old. You cannot live your life like you have been for the last few years, Eden. This has to stop. Try to move on.

"There is more to life than dance, the business, and reading. And yes, I do want us to have an incredible dance showcase this year. And yes, I would love for us to sit and have some time to create that together when you're off. *But* I want you to come out the other side of the next few weeks a new woman. A woman who can see there is more out there for her. Happiness, and maybe even the possibility of love again. You know Jamie would never want this life for you. He definitely wouldn't want you waiting on him. Or hiding yourself away. You are stuck. You haven't had a vacation in forever. I would love for you to think about booking something for next year. Do you think you could do that?"

"Please don't say his name again, Ella. Don't start this..." I stare at her and interject.

Ella raises her finger. "Nope. Stop, Eden, let me finish. You've put your life on hold. He's not coming back. He's gone. You're keeping yourself stuck. You've stopped doing anything or going anywhere. You've always wanted to go to Disney World. Why don't you go with Toni and Beth? Actually... Mmmm... Mamma Mia, she's got it..."

Ella's whole face lights, her eyes sparkling. Oh man, this can't be good. Time feels like it's slowing down as I rub my little gold elephant pendant necklace. Elephants symbolize strength and power; I'd like them to give them to my mind and body now, please.

Give me strength. Work. Work. Nope, it's not working.

"I've got a great idea." She punches the air.

You never know what the hell will come out of Ella's mouth from one minute to the next. She's unpredictable and wild.

"Eden, are you paying attention?"

"Yeah, continue, but for the love of God, don't make me have to punch you if it's a stupid idea, then we could be bruised nose twins and not triplets for a few weeks."

Ella giggles. "So small but so violent. You really have a stick up your arse these days, huh? Let's see what we can do to remove it, shall we?"

Not giving me a chance to respond, she winks at me and continues.

"For the last few years, you've been stuck and I get that. Believe me I do; we all get it. But it's been four years now, Eden. Jamie's accident and then losing the baby was utterly devastating. I watched you withdraw from us all. But I can't allow you to hermit yourself away any longer. Jamie's parents have been adjusting their life. As have all the other families who suffered on that fateful day. I know you will never fully recover from your heartache, but what I am asking you to do is start adjusting too. Make adaptations to overcome this deep-seated loss and heartache you feel. You're lost. And I don't blame you because your compass was thrown off course.

"That stops now. From here on out, I'm making it my mission to find the old Eden. I'm going to guide you back on that bright and positive path you once walked. Think of me as your fairy godmother, Eden. Your clarity compass. That's good, right? Man, am I on fire today or what?"

"Really, Ella? You're pulling this shit on me. I don't think I can take your level of insanity today, please."

"Hang on, let me go get something to turn your frown upside down." She dashes up the stairs and running back down, she returns with my pair of gold sparkly Minnie Mouse ears complete with organza gold bow. They are my fave.

She places them on my head. "Feel better?"

"A little," I sheepishly reply. My Minnie ears do always lay a blanket of calm over me.

"So just let me finish what I was saying. You're always telling us to *leave me alone, I'll be fine, and I just need more time.* Enough is enough. Your time is up. I've held my tongue and sat back and watched for way too long. I'm not letting you sacrifice your chance at happiness or lack of adventure in your life for one minute more."

I feel like a naughty schoolgirl sitting in the head teacher's office.

She pushes on. "Our consistently happy-go-lucky girl. The girl who would do anything for a laugh or dare. The girl who went skinny dipping just for the hell of it when we used to have beach parties. The one that locked Mr. Stephens in the cupboard together with Miss Peebles in fifth year. The girl who fought savagely with our parents for all three of us to go to dance school together. The girl who made ice cubes with mints, unbeknownst to our friends, that turned them into explosive bombs in our fizzy juice. You were something else, Eden. Mum didn't appreciate that one bit. She was cleaning the ceiling in the kitchen for weeks. Where has our carefree girl gone? I want her back. I really miss her." Ella's fire has turned into a more longing request, which is pulling at my heartstrings. She's good; I'll give her that.

"Well, that's quite a speech you've just laid on me there, Ella. I did not know you felt like that," I whisper into my lap, clenching my elephant necklace—nope, still not working.

"We all do, Eden. We miss our girl. Will you be open to what I propose? Will you hear me out? I want to help you get out of this hole you seem to be in. I feel your pain. I feel it every day. But I want that to stop for you, and I want you to feel better. To see there is so much more than dancing, reading, the barn, and Castleview Cove. This nostalgic heartache you are holding on to, it's become some sort of morbid habit.

"It's time to let go. Will you allow me to take the reins on your life a little? To show you what is possible again? I only have your best interests at heart. I would never make a fool of you; you know this, don't you? I want to break down those walls you have barricaded yourself into. I want to show you there is light at the end of the tunnel, but I want you to light it up yourself, Eden. Are you in?"

I can hardly refuse after she's laid her heart out with all those deeply moving and sentimental things now, can I?

"Aw bugger, Ella, you had me at mints."

"Woo-hoo," Ella whoops with glee. "We're getting our old Eden back."

What have I let myself in for?

"So, this is what we're going to do. I'm going to make a goals list."

"What like a bucket list?"

"Yes. Exactly like that. I'm going to create a list of things you *have* to do. These are nonnegotiable. And... you have..."

Ella ponders, tapping her finger to her chin.

"...you have a year to tick everything off the list. This is going to be so much fun, Eden. I can't wait to tell the girls. I'm going to WhatsApp the group now."

Just as she pulls her phone out of her pocket, a loud firm knock at the barn door grabs our attention.

"Who knocks?" Ella looks at me with wonder. "Everyone lets themselves in."

I let Ella answer the door. I hope it's not old Mrs. Mitchell from down the road. I bet she's been looking for any excuse to come visit and get the down-low on my crash. She's always seriously dehydrated and in need of a full glass of gossip to quench her thirst. She'll pour it over the town, adding an extra dash of mixer to make the entire story more tasty. How Mr. Mitchell puts up with her, I'll never know. He's all, "Yes dear, no dear." Although behind closed doors, I bet he likes a good spanking with a *Reader's Digest*. "Yes dear, no dear, harder dear." I've seen the way he stares at our Ella; it's always the quiet ones.

Giggling to myself, I hear a faint deep voice combined with Ella's.

I recognize that voice.

Oh. My. God.

CHAPTER FIVE

Crabbit: *Adjective,* bad tempered. **Pronounced:** Crab-bit.

Eden

"No way," I whisper under my breath. "Don't let him in. Don't let him in," I mutter to myself, hoping that Ella picks up on our triplet spidey sense.

Sounds of casual chatter get closer. Shit, well, that didn't work.

I slouch into my couch, trying to bury my head under my blanket.

"Hey, Eden. Are you hiding?"

Hunter.

Please, sofa, eat me up now.

His incredible American voice is laced with amusement.

That voice. It does things to me.

I shuffle myself up the couch and pull the blanket down. Peering over the blanket, I slowly meet his eyes. And there it is again. That zap of electricity. It creates a shivery sensation all over my body.

I felt it the other night too.

It wasn't the car crash after all.

What is wrong with me?

We stare at each other. A sincere but cheeky smile floods his face.

He's so skyscraper tall compared to me. He must be like six two or three, higher. Really bloody tall. And he's wafted in here, filling the room with his citrusy scent. I remember that. Familiarity. That smells lush. What is that? Lemon, orange, and like a sea salt smell combined with Christ knows what, but that's everything. I'm pretty sure my panties are taking themselves off. Pure Pantie Dropping aftershave, that's definitely the brand name for sure. *Gee whizz.*

He's so dark and dreamy and he's not wearing a baseball cap today. I can see him in all his glory.

Natural thick eyebrows. Full head of sweeping floppy dark-brown hair on top. Shaved up the sides and designer beard and stubble. And don't get me started on his no-nonsense full lips and those eyes that caught me out the first time we collided. He oozes confidence and sex. I can smell it. It's like an Abercrombie & Fitch model had sex with the Greek god, Aphrodite. Wearing all black again. Black skinny jeans, plain washed-out tee, and chunky black designer sneakers. No socks. *Brave in Scotland.* Strong, tanned, toned arms. I remember those arms. *Mmm... I bet he could swing me about.* No tats that I can see. Definitely takes care of himself. I bet he manscapes too. *Watch it.*

He's divine.

"Eden, don't be rude." Ella shakes me out of my fantasy.

"Eh, hi," I squeak.

Smooth. Real smooth.

"Hi," he replies.

Ella bounces her gaze between the two of us.

"Okay, riveting conversation, you guys. I need to text the girls. They'll be so excited about your news," Ella says as she gathers up her stuff. "We have lots to do and I have a full bucket list of shit for you to accomplish, Eden. No backing out now." She declares before turning on her heel.

Oh crap, where is she going? Is she leaving me with Hunter? And how did he know this was my house?

I whip back my blanket and leap off the couch with way more enthusiasm than my battered body allows, being careful not to bang my thumb. You do not know how inconvenient spraining your thumb can be. I've hit it at least three times today already. Every time, I yelped like a Chihuahua.

"I'll see you out."

I catch Hunter ogle my toned bare legs. *Shufflebums*. I changed into my comfiest clothes when I came home. I only have a skimpy pair of gray jersey booty shorts on with my oversized pink hoodie that says *Fries before Guys* and a bright-pink pair of bed socks with a cute burger pattern. I do like matching my patterns. *Burger and fries to go, anyone?*

I've not got on a stitch of makeup either. With this bruised face, there's no point in trying to cover it. It's way too tender to touch, anyway. And crap, my hair. It's piled on top of my head in a messy bun because I haven't washed it for two days.

Fantastic. I'm winning all the glamor awards.

As we get closer to the front door, I grab Ella's arm and spin her around. "Where are you going? Why are you leaving me here with him? How does he know I live here?

"I'm not even properly dressed. Look at me. My ass is hanging out of my shorts. And you're leaving me here with a complete stranger and I'm half naked. Christ, he might jump my bones," I say, now biting my nails.

Ella laughs. "I bloody hope he does. I'm enjoying your mini meltdown. Look, in the last few days he's become a family friend. He wants to see you. He knows Beth. He's all over the bloody media. He's *not* a stranger. I gave him your private security gate code. We swapped numbers at the hospital the night of your crash. He's living at the retreat for the next three months. Three. Whole. Months. He's hired out several cabins for his entire team. He was the Championship Cup winner four years ago. Do you not remember we went to the final four years ago when he won, for a booze up? That was a mega day." She beams, remembering.

"I was very drunk that day. That summer is a blur."

Forgive me for trying to drown my sorrows and grief. Nope, no clue.

"He injured himself not long after that win. Now he's back to maintain his title. Hunter King. Only the most sex on legs golfer to ever don a golf course. He is dreamy," she says, swooning over my shoulder at him.

"He likes you. Accept that. I thought he was going to devour you right there in the living room. He sent those flowers too. The ones I told you about yesterday. I didn't think you were listening to me. Please remember to thank him.

"Now he's here. In your living room. Sexy as sin. By God, that man wears clothes well. They would probably look better lying on your bedroom floor though. But you, my girl, are going to lean into your bucket list. You need to find out what size his putter is. I bet it's magnificent. First on your list. Tap that." She points over my shoulder.

My eyes widen with panic. "You cannot be serious, Ella?"

"Yeah, I am. Remember, no quibbles, no questioning. Your vagina is coming out of retirement, baby. Your year of adventure starts now."

Winking, she sashays toward the door, waving her hand in the air.

"Shit yeah, so much fun. Bye, Hunter," she calls back over her shoulder as she closes the door. *Click.* Gone.

I'm left there, standing openmouthed, staring at the front door, praying it will magically turn into a portal. I would like to step through it and erase the last crazy few hours of my life. I close my eyes, then open them. Nope, I'm still in my house.

Tucking my hands into the arms of my sweatshirt, I slink back to the living room where I find Hunter admiring the retreat view from my tall side window.

Okay, no one's asking you to staple your nipples to the wall, Eden; you can do this. Just a simple conversation.

"It's some view." I genuinely can't think of anything else to say.

Eden, pull yourself together.

"You live in one of the most incredible places in the world. I love it here. I was here a few years ago but never had the time to explore."

With hands in his pockets, he casually turns to face me, his eyes anchored on me.

I feel that fluttering in my belly again, like I felt back in the car.

That does not feel like sickness. Something else.

"Would you like a cup of tea? We love tea here. It solves everything apparently."

Cringe.

"Or are you more of a coffee guy? Or water, or..."

"Tea would be great, actually."

"Okay." I warmly smile. "I have a new locally blended tea I just bought."

"Does that mean it has whisky in it then?"

I scoff, "Not today."

As I shuffle my way around my kitchen. I take the milk out of the fridge, conscious not to knock my thumb.

Hunter startles me from behind when he asks me how I'm feeling. He's crept up on me like a panther across the kitchen table. So stealthy. I feel like it's open season and I'm his prey.

Does he want to eat me like Ella said?

The lack of actual clothes on my legs is making me feel a little vulnerable.

"I'm not going to lie, I've had better weeks. I've been crabbit with my friends and family too. I don't think I'm in their good books." I turn around and say with a half smile. "They reckon three weeks for my nose to get better. It currently looks like a peacock took up residence in my face."

It really is so vivid blue, purple, and golden in places.

"Did you say you have crabs?"

"Oh my God, no. I said crabbit." I widen my eyes. "Holy crap, Hunter." I snort with laughter, then shield my face. I'm so attractive and in pain. "Ouch, my nose. It means bad-tempered."

"Are you alright?"

I wave off the pain and continue with the tea making.

"I'm good. I'm going to buy you a Scottish dialect book. You need one pronto. Crabs?"

I stifle another chuckle. "You know, I watched a documentary. They said that pubic crabs are uncommon these days because of the deforestation of humans, you know, because of all the waxing and tweezing we do? I nearly wet my panties at that. They had a giant model of one—you should see that thing, it's nasty—and they have these wee pinchers so they can grab on to the hairs." I make a pincher motion with my good hand. "They are not pretty, but you can see why they call them cr—"

I turn around fully to finish my sentence, to face an utterly shocked Hunter across the kitchen who is trying to contain a wild laugh.

Gahhhh... shut up, Eden. Crabs? What am I talking about?

Abort mission, abort mission.

I clear my throat. "Eh, you were asking how I was. My, eh, thumb is probably about the same, four weeks. Which is just as well, because I've had to fight to get these puppies under control and clasp my bra daily." I look down and give my boobs a quick squeeze.

The words spill out of my mouth spontaneously.

Hunter grips the back of a kitchen chair, dips his head, and silently bounces with laughter, shaking his head back and forth.

I feel a deep heated blush wave over me. I'm so shit at chatting to guys.

"Yikes, sorry, I should just keep my trap shut. Sometimes I have no filter. Forget I said that."

He must think I'm a dumbass.

"I should really thank you for helping me, Hunter. You were so kind and nice to me that night. The calm I needed in that moment. And thank you for the lovely flowers. Ella said you sent them. Very sweet and thoughtful of you. You really shouldn't have, though. I did puke up all over your shoes after all."

I cringe with embarrassment.

"I am so sorry. I'm totally mortified. Will you let me buy you a new pair?" I tuck my bottom lip into my teeth.

"No way, Eden. I have way too many shoes, anyway."

The way he's now standing tall with folded arms across his broad chest. Legs spread wide, all masculine and athletic-like—it's a very distracting combination and I can't stop myself from sneaking glances over my shoulder. Every time I do, he's staring back at me. He must be checking out my ass. I should have run up the stairs and changed.

"And you're welcome for the flowers. But they weren't for you."

"What? Who were they for then? But Ella said..."

"Your Minnie tee shirt. She was the primary victim in all of this; I think she deserved the flowers more."

A smile shapes my lips as a small chuckle escapes.

I relax a little.

Okay, he's a joker.

I like him.

He's nice.

"Yeah, my tee is royally pee'd off at me; she's ruined. Rest in peace lovely cotton tee," I say, making Hunter laugh.

"Well, you'll just have to buy another one."

"You may have an overflowing shoe collection, I, too, have an overflowing tee shirt obsession. I literally have another twenty or more Minnie tee shirts where that came from. Minnie is life. She's all sass and ass," I say defiantly.

"Just like you then?" He licks his lips.

I giggle. Bloody giggle, like a teenager.

He's flirting with me. Yikes, and I'm reciprocating.

There is no way he finds me attractive. Look at me.

I clear my throat and shake my body out a little, as if to bring me out of this alternative dimension I seem to have woken up in today.

Change the subject.

"Ella's informed me you went to the hospital that night.

I'm a little confused because I don't remember. I honestly think I have some sort of temporary memory loss after we chatted. And you met my parents there too?"

"Ah, Charlie and Edith. You parents are really cool, Eden. You're really lucky to have them in your life. They adore you girls."

"Yup, they are something. They still act like a pair of teenagers. Although their level of PDA gives me the boke."

"You can tell they really love each other. And hey, I know what that means now. Boke. Being sick? You guys speak funny."

"Oh yeah? 'Cause saying the words aluminum and oregano the way you guys do isn't speaking funny? Yeah, right?"

"We say it correctly; it's you guys over here that say it wrong."

"Whatever tomato, tomayto," I say, waving my hand.

A devilish smile curves across Hunter's mouth.

"Ella tells me you're staying here for three months. And you're playing in the Championship Cup?"

"Yeah, staying here to get stronger and improve my swing. One of my fellow golfers told me about this incredible retreat and I just had to go. So here I am. I've taken a long time off to recover from my back injury, but I feel strong and ready, or I will be in a few months."

"Honestly and please don't be offended, but I had no idea who you were. My friend Beth, who you met today, literally just told me this afternoon. I didn't mean to be rude the night of the accident."

"Is Beth your friend?"

I nod confirming she is.

He says, "You don't even have to explain. You had way more things to worry about, and I couldn't give a shit if you don't, or didn't know who I am; it's better that way. And who cares who I am. I actually found it refreshing. You were just you and I was just me. I was more concerned for your safety. However, I hope I won you over with my, how was it you put it, ah, let me get this right, '*very kissable lips, like bouncy castles.*'"

I slap my good hand over my mouth. Did I really say that? That's so embarrassing.

"I'm sorry if I made you feel awkward. I feel awkward about that. Like super cringe. World, eat me up right now, kind of cringe. I had a bash to the face. It made me feel all dizzy and gave me foot in mouth syndrome." That's my excuse and I'm sticking to it.

Divert, divert...

"Soooo... cupcake? With your cuppa?"

Hunter gives me a smirk and a soft yes, please. Sensing my anxiety, he lets me change the subject.

I usher him back to the living room.

Must walk behind him so he doesn't get a full moon view of my ass again.

He sits on the opposite side of the couch from me. I'm not exactly unconfident about my body. Being a dancer, we wear skimpy outfits all the time, but I hardly know Hunter, so I grab my blanket to cover any bare skin I have on show.

I'm pretty sure my clothes will start peeling themselves off anyway if I get any closer to his aftershave. There are not many items to take off... They'd be off in seconds.

We ease into a comfortable and super easy chat over the next half hour. Hunter fills me in on what he's been doing for the last few days. His training schedule and apparently he's met all my family over the last few days, including my nephews. I'm stunned. He's just slotted right in here at the retreat. Like he's part of the furniture. And I feel like I've known him all my life. It's peculiar.

I wonder if Professional Snake Charmer is listed on his resume.

"How's the car? Do you know when it'll be back from the garage?"

"It's totaled. The only positive is that I can't drive for a few weeks anyway, so I don't need it. I need to sort the paperwork and get a new car sorted, pronto. These things always take so long to sort. The insurance people said they were sending all my information via email later today. I'm just so relieved that I'm okay. That deer could have killed me, you know? Those berries made me look like I already was, and Betsy. Poor Betsy."

"Your dad said it was a deer. I think you should rename it Bambi."

"Call what Bambi?"

"Your next car, we should call it Bambi. You're obsessed with Disney. It's fitting."

"I like that. A lot. You're funny, Mr. King."

I feel light. This feels nice. I hold eye contact with him.

A sudden flush of warmth rides over me.

We sit blissfully smiling at one other.

Hunter tilts his head slightly.

What is he thinking?

To stop myself from saying anything stupid, I take a bite of my cupcake. My third today. Well, if people buy them for me, I'm going to eat them.

I moan loudly as the frosting fills my mouth. Oh, that's heaven.

"Are you enjoying that?" Eyes locked on me, a muscle in Hunter's jaw ticks.

I lick my lips as I try to swallow my heartbeat. Time stands still for a few moments.

"Unashamedly so, yeah," I whisper. "My weakness is cupcakes and ice cream. I've had three of each already today."

I hope I'm not off work too long. Being a dancer keeps the cupcakes at bay. However, if I sit here too long, I'll turn into a cupcake.

"Why, does Mr. King not have any weaknesses, or are you all protein shakes and vegetables?"

"I have a weakness." He laughs loudly. "Ice cream. I love ice cream."

"You're a man after my own heart. My friend, Toni, owns the local ice cream parlor. Have you been yet? They have eighty-one to die for flavors. Hey, you're here for a few weeks. You could make that your bucket list. Eighty-one flavors in three months. Tick." I draw an imaginary tick in the air. "Could you do it?"

"Are you challenging me, Eden Wallace? 'Cause I'm game. Tell me. Your sister mentioned something about *your* bucket list. What's that in aid of?"

How do I say this without going too deep?

"Ella has it in her head that I've become somewhat of a bore over the last few years and that I need to find happiness and love and inner peace and yadda yadda. So she's making me her pet project. No, sorry. She said she was going to become my clarity compass or fairy godmother or something stupid like that. Who knows? All I know is that I am now in a world of having to yes to everything she sets me to do for the next year. Can you believe that? It already sounds exhausting." I scrunch my nose—ow, that is painful.

"You know, I think your bucket list sounds fun. If I can do eighty-one flavors of ice cream in three months—and is it individual cones I have to have for each flavor?—then you can do all the things your sister sets you to do. If this is going to be your year of yes, what's the worst that could happen? You find love, happiness, and inner peace. Yeah, that sounds just awful." Hunter rolls his eyes.

I could listen to his voice all day. I love his accent. It sounds a little raspy, but rich and sensuous.

"Are you mocking me, Mr. King? And yes, each flavor needs a separate cone."

"I like when you call me that; it's when you get all commanding, feisty, and shit with me. Your challenge is accepted, Eden Wallace."

"Uh-huh." I squeeze my mug in my hand a little tighter. He's mesmerizing.

I feel my pulse race a little, acutely aware of how he makes me feel. I've thought about him a few times over the last few days. Wondering if he was, in fact, real or a figment of my imagination in the field. I didn't even really know who he was until a few hours ago. But he's handsome. A golfer. A pro, no less. The golfers I see always look so serious on the course when I'm down on the beach walking. The game looks boring as shit. But if they all look like him, I need to start watching golf, Stat.

Hunter is far from boring. Hunter King. Ella's right, I need to Google him. I'm doing that as soon as he leaves. He's here, in my living room, with little Eden Wallace from Castleview Cove. What a surreal week I'm having.

Do you think if I go back to the front door the portal will have opened yet?

Sinking his teeth into his bottom lip, I catch Hunter staring at mine.

What is he thinking? Does he feel what I do too? This pull?

"I think I should head off now. I just wanted to see how you were recovering." He rises abruptly. "You have an impressive home, Eden." He motions around the space and my ego jumps with joy.

"Thank you for letting me visit you today. Or well, thanks to Ella for letting me in to see you. Do you need anything before I go?"

Who the hell is this guy? Where did he come from? Why does he care?

"No, I'm good. My mum is coming over later to help with my dinner."

I go to stand, but he gestures for me to stay put.

"Stay. Rest. I can see myself out."

On his exit, he confidently makes his way over to where I'm sitting. Swiftly leaning down, facing me eye to eye, he places his hands on the back of the couch, encasing me with his arms, carefully brushing either side of my head. I can feel my eyes bug out in shock. I think he's going to kiss me. I feel a nervous tightening in my throat. What's happening here?

I can hear and feel my breathing becoming heavier and faster. My pulse racing. Feeling energized. Feeling a connection as warmth spreads between my thighs.

He softly tucks his head into my neck. His hot breath whispers into my ear, "Just as an FYI. I have a new weakness. Do you want to know what it is, Eden?"

He doesn't give me a chance to reply.

"Scottish girls. One in particular. See you around, Cupcake." His luscious lips airbrush my neck, causing a tingling wave of goosebumps across my body.

In the blink of an eye, he stands, leaving his fresh aroma everywhere.

Did he mean me? Does he like me? Shit, I think he means me.

I watch him swagger toward the door. Casually reaching up, he drums the wooden beams overhead as he passes. His tee shirt rises slightly. I catch a glimpse of a deep red, fiery orange, and black tattoo on his toned lower back.

The last thing I hear is him bantering back over his shoulder.

"You should definitely do all the things that your sister says you've to do on that list. Including me. I want to know what else is on that list. My putter is enormous, by the way. It's definitely time for Miss Minnie to come out of retirement. And yes, I am talking about your vagina.

"And I love your Minnie ears you have on. You are cute as fuck, Eden Wallace."

I reach up to my head. Oh shit, I've still got my ears on.

And he heard what Ella said about me fucking him.

I'm going to kill Ella.

He named my vagina.

Although I quite like my new nickname, Cupcake.

Enormous.

How big is enormous?

I need a ruler.

Holy shit.

CHAPTER SIX

Irn-Bru: Carbonated Scottish soft drink. Tastes like? No one knows, but it's awesome. Looks like? Orange toxic waste. **Pronounced:** Iron Brew.

Boggin: *Adjective,* dirty, disgusting, smelly. **Pronounced:** Bog-in.

Hunter - 4 weeks later

I'm tired. There's no other word for it.

A solid month of intensive training and strengthening has been relentless, and our new daily training routine here in Scotland has really taken its toll on my body.

As a professional golfer, I've always been fit and healthy. I feel strong but blow me; I need a break. I am goddamn tired. My limbs feel like lead weights today.

On the bright side, my back feels better than it has in months. I've had a few twinges now and again, but nothing to write home about. The team isn't worried and I'm surprised my back isn't giving me more grief given the new plan my coach and best buddy, Luke, has been putting me through. He's upped the pace massively on all fronts. No wonder I've been stifling yawns and forgetting things in the last few days.

It's a means to an end. We have a purpose and I'm driven. I'm finally feeling good about my form, control, and swing. I've improved mentally and physically, and everything seems to be falling into alignment. About time.

My body giving out on me under four years ago gutted me, and I felt like I'd let everybody down. My team, the fans, my mom. Watching the fallout of my demise over social media was more painful than my back at one point. They couldn't understand how I had been fine one minute and then down on my knees the next.

It was my fault for not seeking help sooner. Popping painkillers, letting my pain and injury spiral out of control.

Almost, and I really mean almost falling down the rabbit hole of medication dependency. Thankfully, my team never let me get that far.

They dragged me to my senses. They made me seek the help of consultants and surgeons I so desperately needed.

I don't know where my head was at in those moments, but I clearly wasn't thinking straight.

I just wanted to keep going, touring, competing, winning.

As a Major tournament winner, I was approved for a Major Medical Extension, allowing me to keep my tour card.

As soon as I was fit enough, I was getting sponsor invites again left, right, and center, and I've played all the specified events in order for me to hold on to my tour card. Being a major winner sure has its perks. It took another eighteen months to work my way back up the world rankings. It was tough some days, but I did it.

I'm pumped to be competing in golf tournaments again fully. Bring it on. Although I'm not sure I'm prepared for all the traveling, press, sponsorship negotiations, and prepping we do. I find that part of my job less than thrilling and exhausting. Press conferences don't float my boat. They're necessary, but not fun.

The only good part about traveling now is owning a jet —well, I am part owner along with five other golfers, meaning I can travel in peace. No more bothersome air crew pestering me with hopeful eyes to join the mile high club. Yeah, that got boring pretty fast throughout the early part of my career.

I couldn't be in a better place location wise either. Castleview Cove feels like coming home. I was here four years ago, when I won my first Championship Cup. I fell in love with the place and left a little of my heart here. Even better, winning on the world's oldest and most famous golf course, The Champion. It was pretty special.

It all went downhill after that.

I'd been in pain and having spasms for months but said nothing and kept on pushing through the grief in my back. At thirty years old, I never thought for a minute I would have to undergo major back surgery.

When I started limping about three weeks after winning, my back went rapidly downhill. I was at the top of my game too. Known for my power, speed, and distance, I had it all. And then the Universe threw me a curveball. A degenerated lower disc in my back was the epicenter of all my discomfort. When I sat with my team and surgeon on the day of the results, it felt like the only thing I knew how to do was slowly slipping away from me.

The news and the scans and everything around me are a big blur from that day. It felt like I was in a tunnel and everyone around me was whizzing by. *"Never play again." "Long recovery." "Risky surgery."* Those phrases were banded about like they were handing out candies.

I've never been more scared in my life. Since the age of ten, all I ever wanted to do was be a golfer. Growing up in Seminole, Florida, I learned on the beautifully built courses and learn from the best too. It was coaching at its finest.

Thinking of home, I am craving some sunshine. Scotland is stunning, but, man, it's cold and unpredictable. You seem to get sunshine, rain, and wind all at the same time. But then it's warm one minute and freezing the next. And the wind. Jesus Christ, it's fresh.

Coming here to Castleview Cove with my team was the best decision I have made in ages, and believe me, I've made some pretty stupid decisions in the past. Jess. Now she was a king-sized one. Let's not go there.

In fact, fuck it, let's go there.

Jess, my ex-girlfriend. The bitch that wormed her way into my life with claws so sharp I didn't even notice them going in. I was blinded by all the fake blond hair and boobs to match. It only took a few months for it to turn sour, but I stuck with her for way longer than I should have. Our relationship sucked. It threatened tournament games on more than one occasion. She sucker punched me left, right, and center, and she turned me into someone I didn't recognize. She brought out the worst in me. Things went rapidly downhill between us. Turns out she was also fucking around behind my back when I was touring.

Jax, my agent, had great pleasure in informing me.

Asshat. Jax Parks—stupid fucking name—is my agent. He's also a sleazy dick, but he gets me the best sponsorship deals. I'm so relieved he's only flying in for the tournament days because dealing with him daily is enough to make you voluntarily push yourself off a cliff.

When I returned from winning the Championship Cup, I confronted Jess about breaking up and she pulled the *"I'm pregnant"* card, insisting the baby was mine. It was a ruse to keep me. I actually convinced myself that it would be great and having a baby might settle her down.

A few weeks later and once it was announced I was unfit to play, she confessed her lies, showing her true colors. All she wanted was the money and the fame. Once I faded into the shadows, she was there with me too. But she wanted spotlights. The glamor. The attention.

Money and fame changes people. Me, I've never changed; I'm still Hunter King from Seminole who loves to shop at Target and still does his own grocery shopping. I'm just able to buy the nicer things I want from time to time. Like the time I surprised my mum with a new house.

Mom has tirelessly supported me throughout my golfing career. My father unexpectedly passed away when I was twelve. He would have been so proud to witness my first big win. My mom and dad were my biggest cheerleaders. Mom still is. She's joining us for the tournament with my stepdad once they've finished cruising around the Mediterranean.

I never loved Jess. Cared for her, yes, but not love. There was never any closeness. The only time she made me go weak at the knees was when the monthly credit card bill came in every month. Who needs that many shoes?

I loved the idea of coming home to someone. Cozy nights on the couch. Movie night. Meals out. But she wanted to party all the time and rub shoulders with stars and celebs.

So not my thing at all. I really wanted someone to share my love and excitement for my wins. It turns out she was never interested in my profession. She liked the competition money wins, though. Oh, yes, she did.

I was so good to her too. I never cheated on her. In fact, I've never cheated on any of my girlfriends. I appeased her endlessly. Showered her with gifts, but nothing was ever good enough. She wanted more and more. And more partying.

Eventually I kicked Jess out of my house and told her to fuck all the way off and to keep ongoing. Best decision ever.

However, being here in Castleview Cove, this may actually be my greatest decision ever.

Contentment has well and truly settled into my bones. My recovery has been a long and arduous one. Some of those days felt dark and hopeless. I've paced myself. I've gotten strong. I put the work in. I'm back.

My team was fully on board when I suggested a three-month intensive retreat, not just for me but for them too. Who wouldn't jump on the 'let's spend three months in Scotland' boat?

Especially when it's all-expenses-paid and they can bring their loved ones if they want. Not that any of them seem to have anyone of great significance in their lives at the moment. So we're all here flying solo together. We travel a lot, so most of us never have the time for relationships. Traveling complicates everything. I've had a few one-night stands and some casual dating.

Jess was a mistake I won't make again, and the sex was meaningless. It was just sex, and we lived entirely different lives. I don't know what the hell I was thinking. I've never found 'the one'.

Again, the joy of tournament life.

Could Eden be the one? She seems different from anyone I've dated before. You're not dating her, Hunter. Get a grip.

Clear your head for the game...

I've given the team the weekend off. I'm looking forward to the next few days. Pippa, my assistant and little sister, flew in today for the rest of our stay. My team works hard for me. They all want the best and they need this as much as I do. A break. A new plan. Get strong. Win.

My body groans into the soft sofa. Hands behind my head, I relax into it, and take in the surroundings of my cozy cabin.

I've spent little time here aside from sleeping with all the training I've been sticking to. But tonight I am going to sit on my ass and enjoy the peaceful views across the estate. I'm definitely lighting the wood burner 'cause even in June, Scotland is freezing. It's really not summer. I can vouch for that. I crave the warmth of home in Florida.

A solo Netflix and chill for me with the fire blazing. 'Cause why not? I've been having sex with my hand for months now, so no difference there. *What a loser.* I have this glorious life and no one to spend it with. Romantic night in and meal for one, please. Pathetic.

Although my team, and when I say my team, they're my friends—scratch that, they're my family—we're all having a break for a few days, but inevitably we'll always end up spending our days off together, anyway.

I know Pippa mentioned she wanted to go out dancing tomorrow night; she'll drag us all along for that. There will be no complaints from the boys about heading out for a night out. Luke and Evan are my dream team. They're built like brick shithouses and attract women like bees to pollen.

Luke is a phenomenal golf fitness instructor slash coach, and Evan is my personal trainer and physical therapist. Both push me to my limits and beyond, always striving for me to be the best. It hurts when they push me, but damn are they good. Since my back operation, the team's focus has always been on winning the Championship Cup again. So here we are, back in Castleview Cove.

I employ a couple of bodyguards from time to time, Liam and Noah, but only for the tournaments themselves. You've no idea how deranged some fans have become over the years. I must get at least a dozen marriage proposals every week. The women on Instagram are pretty forward. *Oh yeah, I have no idea who you are, but of course I'll marry you, darling.* Yeesh.

I would rather not have bodyguards. It seems ridiculous to me, but they keep me safe from the crazies when I'm playing a golf tournament.

This is our first chill out weekend since we arrived. I want to head to Castle Cones tomorrow because I'm now twenty-seven flavors into my ice cream bucket list challenge Eden assigned me.

Ah, Eden. Before I get to Eden... Who the hell ever thought Irn-Bru ice cream was a good idea? And what the actual fuck is Irn-Bru, anyway? No one, not even the Scottish, knows what the hell it is. It's like a fizzy drink that's totally indescribable. Shocking neon orange. It looks like Oompa Loompa piss. Maybe that's what it is? Hmm, it could be, you know.

And don't get me started on marmalade and haggis ice cream. I'm sure that's gotta be an April Fool's joke. Please tell me it is. Sounds boggin. Boggin, this is another new word I've learned since being here. Means vile.

I love the Scots. Not only are they charming and funny, but they treat everyone like family. Kind and generous, too. Eden's parents, Charlie and Edith, have welcomed me with open arms. They love the team and have been ensuring we are well looked after. Nothing is ever too much bother. Such a great couple.

Contrary to popular belief, Charlie does not wear a skirt, or kilt as it's called here. A kilt is saved for special occasions, not for grocery shopping in. Also, another little stereotype to banish is that they are not all whisky drinkers either. Charlie informs me he and his mates, or pals as they call them here, love a good lager.

My thoughts shift back to Eden. I've been feeling like a giddy schoolboy for the last few weeks, catching glimpses of her around the estate. I can't help but thank fate we found her crashed in the field all those weeks ago. Then discovering she was the daughter of the retreat owners. It felt like it was exactly that—fate.

She was so vulnerable, but sassy that evening. Like a silent volcano. And, man, is she funny. And sexy. Her voluptuous yet slender body is hypnotizing. And her peachy ass. Holy shit, does she have a nice ass. I caught a delightful view of it at her house that day. I've had to adjust myself multiple times over the last few weeks just imagining my fingers digging into her pale backside. Christ, she does things to my cock.

But it's not just that. She makes me feel things I've never felt before. She sets my heart racing, and she has me worrying about her, when I don't even know her at all.

She's an innocent angel with a dash of fire. She's a little thing too, short, but she holds herself like a queen.

I overheard her parents outside the mansion house talking one day. Something about an accident that happened years ago. I didn't hear everything, but her father mentioned how she needed to move on and how the family wanted her to find happiness again. Ella said the same too about her bucket list.

I'm eager to find out what happened.

I want to get to know that little pocket rocket and discover why she's so guarded all the time.

If someone hurt her. Man, I can't even think about it.

She has walls up; that's for sure. I'd like to penetrate those. And her.

She froze in place when I abruptly left her home over a month ago. I had to leave before I jumped her bones, like she said. The way she was biting her lip and roaming my body with her eyes.

I chuckle to myself at the look of utter shock that swept across her face when I encased her with my body. I came so close to kissing her. It took everything within me to stand up and leave.

I've only visited her that one time because I've been respecting her need to grow stronger. But it's been tearing at my inner sanity to visit her every day. I've really had to restrain myself.

And her name. I've played out several fantasies in my head of exactly what paradise would be like with Eden.

However, she needed to heal, and I'd only make her sore, in a good way.

I feel her pulling me in with her sparkling eyes that dance between the colors of ice blue and green. And those plump, luscious lips. I would like them wrapped around my cock, watching her moan. *Fuck me.*

And don't get me started on that Scottish accent of hers, too. She's like a siren. It's sexy and melodic. It's like she's singing to me. It's gotta be the softest, gentle, sexiest voice I have ever heard and I want to hear her screaming my name.

"Aw, man, I need to get laid," I groan to myself.

She felt the connection between us. I know she did too. I could sense it.

There were telling signs. I could read her body. She was rubbing her thighs together under that blanket, trying to ease her urges, and she couldn't take her eyes off my body for a minute, unconsciously biting her teeth into her lips. I don't even think she was aware of her own body language. She was nervous, but I could tell she wanted me.

I reckon she's only about five foot two or so. Will sex be weird with such a big height difference between us, I wonder?

I'm Googling that. I get my phone out and type in 'tall and short couple's sex.'

The answer is... Nope; it makes no difference and suggests a fuck ton of hot as hell positions that work best for short women and tall men.

Seems like reverse cowgirl, spooning, and spread eagle are the winners. A rush of warmth spreads to my cock as the visual of Eden and me plays out in my fantasy. Yeah, that will do nicely.

Man, what it would be like to fling her about the bedroom.

I have *got* to stop this. I rub my hand down my face to wash away my dirty thoughts. I close my phone and slide it onto the table.

Just find something to watch on Netflix, Hunter, you sad dick.

Grabbing the remote, I flick through the menu. I don't think I want to watch a series; I can't commit myself during training. A film it is. Still scrolling through the menu, my thoughts drift back to Eden.

She's taken up residence in my subconscious.

It hasn't helped that she's never too far away. Catching

glimpses of her daily when out and about walking the grounds with her parents' dog, Dave. Dave the dog. God, I love this family. On the occasions she's spotted me from afar, she watches me. She thinks she's being covert. She's so wrong. I feel her eyes on me always.

There's an old magnificent tree within the grounds. Several times I've watched Eden lay sunflowers at the base of the trunk. Curiosity got the better of me last week and I stood at that very tree. The flowers arranged neatly at the foot of the tree next to a little silver plaque engraved with the words, 'Chloe Farmer. Rest Little One.'

Who is she honoring the memory of?

Eden has many layers. She is shy but has some spunk.

She's battling an inner demon.

I want her to share them with me.

I want to ease her inner pain.

I sensed her hesitation. With me. With her sister's bucket list idea.

I didn't want to scare her off early on and come on too strong. So I backed off and gave her space. For now.

I'm here. I'm just waiting.

I know she's single and not dating. Ella told me that. Also, my key clue was Ella's first item, "Tap that," referring to me, her words, not mine.

Find happiness and love.

She's beautiful, so why is she not dating?

I can't wrap my head around it.

Her sisters are both gorgeous too. Not a patch on what I see in Eden, but they are striking.

I've had the pleasure of meeting Eva too. Eva is married with two incredibly cute kids. Ella is a firecracker. On more than a few occasions when she's been visiting her parents, we've chatted, mostly because I've been fishing for information on Eden's progress and to find out how Eden was feeling. Ella has alluded to going on dates and partying. She's a party bus kinda gal.

I actually think Luke has a bit of a crush on her. I spotted him chatting with her out in front of the training facility, and I am pretty sure there was an exchanging of numbers going on.

We'll see how that pans out.

I've never met triplets before. Every man's wet dream. Triplets. In reality, though, so *very* different.

Eden, Eva, and Ella are all unique. They sound the same, but their individual personalities and physical features are incredibly different. I'm glad of that; I'm not sure my cock could take three Edens.

Ella and Eva suit their names too. Just like Eden fitting her name. Ella means goddess—says it all really—Eva means mother of life. Spot on. Ella is more motherly and more grounded, so it suits her really well. I love doing this. Checking the meaning of people's names. You'd be amazed at how fitting some people's names are to someone's personality.

So here I am on a Friday night by myself. I am so rock and roll.

"Okay, how do I light this woodburning stove then?"

I can't see any instruction manual, and I don't have a clue what I am doing.

After trying for ten minutes to light the wood burner, I give up and decide to head over to the mansion. I've still not successfully picked what I'm watching tonight either.

Charlie can help me light the fire before I work on my couch groove for the night.

As I slip out my cabin door, I take in the rain that's now pelting down at an insane rate.

I'm telling ya, man, it was sunny earlier on. Scotland, home of the most unpredictable weather.

Screw this, I need help.

Crouching my head down as I dash across the long gravel drive that widens out to the circular entryway, I run through the expansive double doors at high speed, shaking off the rain. That's quite some shower.

I enter the warm ambient chandelier lit reception area to find it unattended and ring the bell on the marble desk.

As I'm waiting for assistance, an eruption of yelps and gasps flies through the main entrance, causing me to twist on my feet to see what all the commotion is.

"Holy crap. Dad, it's hoofing down outside and I've locked myself out the house."

Eden.

CHAPTER SEVEN

Messages: *verb,* meaning shopping for the groceries. **Pronounced:** Messages.

Drookit: *adjective,* extremely wet, drenched or soaked to the bone. **Pronounced:** Drew-kit.

Hunter

My heart flutters unexpectedly.

With her head still down, sheltering herself, she then looks upward.

She gasps out loud and shivers as the chilly gust of wind blows across her back as the door snicks shut.

For a moment, everything stops.

Eden sweeps her eyes up and down my body, then slowly wraps her arms around herself, pushing her delicious boobs upward underneath her thin tee, setting my cock ablaze.

Shit.

"Hi. We have to stop meeting like this," she pants and flashes a wonderstruck smile.

No we don't. I want to see you all the time.

"Did you say you've locked yourself out of your house?" I ask.

I want to reach out and touch her.

She rolls her eyes. "Eh, yeah. Dad has a spare key. I have a tendency to lock myself out from time to time. I let myself into my house, then stupidly flung my keys on the console table. Just as I was heading back to Ella's car to unload my messages. I heard the wind slam my door closed. I must have forgotten to snap the latch back to keep it unlocked. So here I am. Typical me."

"Messages?" I say, somewhat confused.

"Eh, shopping. Getting the groceries. Messages. Make sense?" she answers with amusement.

"I will say this again. You guys talk funny."

"Again, Mr. King, you guys talk funny, not us. The word coffee is not pronounced kawfee."

This girl.

"Smart-ass."

"Uh-huh, that's me."

She swooshes past me, carving the air with her dainty body in behind the reception area.

"Are you needing anything? Were you waiting on someone?"

She doesn't seem too shy around me this time. Must be the lack of ass spilling out of her shorts and being in neutral territory. Plus, she must feel better; she looks great.

Maybe it's time to make my move.

I wonder if she feels well enough for me to bend her over the reception desk and fuck her into next week.

I'm so distracted by her erect nipples poking through her white off-the-shoulder tee. With the slogan, Teaching is My Jam, inside an illustrated jam jar. It's soaked through from the rain and clinging to her killer curves. She's clearly oblivious to the fact she's the winner of the wet tee shirt competition that's playing out in my head.

I'm trying my best to remember why the hell I came over here.

"Um. Eh. So. Yeah. Well. What did I come over here for again?" I say, scratching my head and clenching my eyes shut.

Don't look. Be a gentleman.

I open my eyes again. My eyes lock on to her puckered nipples. It's like my eyes are on a rocket launching mission. Target located.

Fuck me.

"Hunter?"

I clear my throat. "Eh, sorry. Yeah. I need some help with the log burner. I've never lit one before. I wondered if your dad would help me. But he's not around, it would appear."

"I can help. Let me grab my spare key and I'll come over with you."

She's coming to my cabin, alone with me. My heart beats more rapidly. "That would be great, thanks."

Eden ducks under the desk. I can hear her rummaging about, clattering through the keys, giving me just enough time to pull myself together and readjust myself.

What in the ever-loving hell is wrong with me and this girl?

"Got it." She jumps up like a jack-in-the-box from behind the desk. Her bewitching boobs bounce up and down in response to her sudden quick movement.

Good God, give me strength. I'm never going to survive this.

"Aw, man," I grumble, rubbing my fingers into my temples. I clench my eyes shut again and scrunch my face, mentally picturing her nipples. What color? What size? Are they sensitive?

"You okay, Hunter?"

"Eh, yeah. I have a sore head," I lie.

I turn on my heel. Not looking at her.

"Shall we go?"

I hear her follow behind.

"You're in Cabin One?"

"Yeah," I mumble. "Let's go."

The pair of us run across the gravel as the rain falls down in sheets. Dashing through my cabin front door at high speed, a wall of warmth inside instantly hits us.

"It's drookit tonight." Eden laughs and shakes herself out.

"I have no idea what that means." I lift my eyebrows, confused.

"Eh, it means *it's* wet, or *I'm* wet or soaked."

Fuck.

Me.

Sideways.

Just as she stops talking, our eyes both look down at our interconnected hands. I'm not sure who grabbed whose hand as we were running through the rain.

She lets go of my hand suddenly.

"Sorry," she answers shyly.

That answers that then. She grabbed mine.

My stomach flutters again. She wants me.

She motions to the living area. "Wood burner. Let me show you."

Just keep your eyes off her wet tee.

Must keep eyes off her wet tee. Must not look at hard, puckered nipples.

I groan.

"You okay? Is it your head again?"

"Eh, yeah. My head."

"Do you have painkillers? If not, I can go get you some. I have lots for this I haven't used." She smiles widely as she points to her face.

"Nah, I'm good, thank you. Eh, your face has healed really well. You can hardly tell where that peacock landed now."

"It's great. Still a little tender. But look at my thumb. It bends and everything, although it's still stiff and painful. I am loving on my opposable thumb. I can even put my bra on and everything. Woo, go me. And my new Bambi car is on order too; she'll be here in a week." She gives herself a little cheer with a cute fist pump, then flushes with embarrassment.

She's absurdly beautiful.

"So, wood burner..." She turns toward the living room. "Take me to it before I really make even more of a tit out of myself."

We kneel on the floor and she shows me how to light the wood burner—how to get it going, what kindling to use, when to use the logs, and then how to keep the fire burning.

"I think I got it." Although I'm not sure I was fully listening. I was too distracted by everything about her. She's recovered well from her accident and I'm seeing a more confident side of her.

As I study her face this close, in this light, for this amount of time, I can finally see her properly. All the bruising and swelling has gone. Her delicate, heart-shaped face with high cheekbones and full lips. Her startling blue eyes encased in the longest lashes I've ever seen. I'm transfixed.

"Let me start this for you. Then you should only need to add a wee layer of logs to keep it going tonight."

I turn to face her and notice she has something stuck to the side of her lip. It looks like frosting.

Pointing, I say, "You have something on your lip."

"Oh, do I? I ate a cupcake in the car. Here?" She swipes her tongue out, missing it completely.

I reach out. "Here, I'll get it."

I gently scoop the frosting off her rosy lip with my finger.

She grabs my wrist and opens her mouth. In a rush she unconsciously sucks my finger into her warm, wet mouth.

I pull in a quick breath as I feel a gentle tap of her tongue on the tip of my finger. She is fucking hot. This preview of what she'd do to my cock sends floods of arousal to my groin, making my cock twitch with delight.

I swallow the strangled groan rising from my throat.

Eden slowly blinks.

A tremble waves over her as a buzz of energy flows between us.

Suddenly she catapults away from me, sitting upright on her heels, and my finger leaves her mouth with a pop.

Her eyes blaze with a cocktail of desire and shock.

"I'm sorry. I don't know what came over me," she looks down and says shyly.

I take a long deep breath.

I lean in slightly and tip her chin upward with my just-sucked finger, forcing our gaze.

"Do you feel this between us?" I motion to the space.

Softly she whispers, "What do you mean?"

"Please don't deny it. You know I want you, Eden. And I think you want me too."

Fumbling with the hem of her shirt between her fingers, she says, "I just want to help you with the fire."

"Sure thing, Cupcake. Keep telling yourself that."

"But I haven't seen you properly in weeks. I've seen you around. You've been keeping your distance. You don't want me." She shakes her head.

Uh-huh. So she's been waiting for me to make a move.

"I've given you time. Space. I'm a lot of things, but I'm not an inconsiderate dick. I see how your body reacts to me, Eden. I do know you want me."

"You think you know me, but you don't."

"I want to get to know you. Part of me feels like I already do."

"Is that so? Are you always this confident?"

I lean closer, our faces only inches apart. "I am. I know it will happen. I know what I want. And if you think it's wet outside, Cupcake, I'll show you what it's really like to be wet. You'll be more than soaked. Don't tell me you haven't imagined us together. I see how you look at me."

"How's that?"

"Like you're famished and I'm a three course meal."

She sucks in a breath. "Please stop." Her lips twitch.

"Will you go out for dinner with me at the very least?"

"I don't think that's a good idea."

I reluctantly back away. "Keep denying yourself. But if that's what you want." I hold my hands up. No one has ever turned me down before. This girl is in another league.

"I do," she whispers.

Not now. Maybe soon.

I rise to my feet and move across the room, adjusting my cock because, amen, she just sucked my finger.

Turning around, I now have a painfully perfect view of her curvy ass. She's on all fours, focusing all her attention on lighting the fire for me.

What the fuck just happened? She wants me, I know she does. She's denying herself.

I don't know what surprises me more, her lack of awareness of me staring at her ample toned ass or the fact that there is not even a hint of panty line to be seen through her thin formfitting workout leggings. Is she commando?

I move over to the back wall so I'm standing further back. Shit, that's made it worse. I can see everything now.

As she's leaning over, prodding the fire, her soggy wet tee has gone baggy at the front and is now gaping open at the hemline, dipping toward the floor. It allows me a flawless view straight through her thigh gap, over her lean flat stomach, and a sparkle of jewel glints from her belly button, like a beam of light guiding me to the precipice of her cleavage. She dips her head lower to adjust the open and close controls. Almost stretching, back arched, ass in the air, like a luxurious cat. Her tits dip lower, giving me full access to a see-through white mesh and lace bra. Holy hell balls.

"Give me strength." I stuff my clenched hand into my mouth, biting my knuckles.

"You alright, man?" Luke's voice suddenly startles me.

Where the fuck did he come from?

"Shit, man, don't creep up on me like that."

"Enjoying the view?" he whispers.

"Fuck off. And you stop looking."

Luke chuckles.

"Done." Eden rises swiftly and turns herself around to face us.

She looks straight at me, then Luke.

Clearing her throat, she says, "Hi," then waves at Luke cheerily. "I'm Eden and you must be Luke? I promise I'm not a stalker. It's just Ella's told me all about you. In fact, she never stops talking about you. And who else has 'to die for aquamarine eyes' like yours." Eden rolls her eyes, clearly mocking her sister's words.

"Are those contacts?" She points.

"Nope, all real, babes," he answers proudly, his arms folded across his body as he sways confidently back and forth, his legs spread wide.

"You'd better watch it; those eyes of yours have got our Ella all in a pickle. And your tats, too. Just don't say I said anything."

"Keep layering on the compliments." Luke rubs his hands together.

Asshole.

"I should get going. You'll be snuggly before you know it. Just as well you're not here in wintertime. This is currently summertime in Scotland. You Florida boys are weaklings, I tell ya." Eden smiles, her eyes sparkling.

That smile could light up the Eiffel Tower.

Interesting, she knows I'm from Florida. She's looked me up.

"Well, we aren't all penguins, like you."

"Ha ha, hilarious, Mr. King. Well then, I'll leave you to it. I still need to get my messages out of the car. Remember to add some wood in about fifteen minutes."

"Thanks, Cupcake."

"You're welcome. You rescued me. I rescued you. We're even. Are you into *Bridgerton* then? Is that your kink? It only really gets going in episode five though." She laughs.

"Huh?" I ask in confusion.

She hitches her thumb toward the television where I

seem to have stopped my Netflix menu, landing on *Bridgerton*. It's been all over social media. I might just watch this.

"Good, huh?"

"Hell yeah. Might give you some tips, you know, for the wet weather you were promising." Amusement glinting in her eyes.

Fucking spitfire.

She's full of light and shade. One minute she's reserved, then the next she's teasing me.

"I'm sorry about the whole finger thing... Cheerio," she blushes and whispers softly, passing me with a mischievous twinkle in her eyes.

"I'm never washing my finger again. See you later, Cupcake."

I watch as she tips her head slightly downward and chuckles her fine ass out the door, waving over her shoulder as she exits.

Snick. I want to run after her and beg her to stay.

Silence.

"Uh-huh."

Luke gives me a knowing look.

"Don't say a thing."

I sit down on the couch, pulling my hands through my wet hair.

"She's hot, right? Like, really hot. And she just says the first thing that comes into her head." I motion with my hands in the air.

She's refreshing. And timid and shy. Then she's cheeky and smart. She's guarded, but I think she likes me. Fuck it, I know she likes me. What am I going to do?

I say, "She's definitely not a one-night girl. She doesn't

give off that vibe at all. I can't stop thinking about her. She's all I've thought about since we found her that night. She's driving me insane. God, that feels good to say it all out loud."

I think I'm going crazy over a girl I hardly even know. She feels like my forever. Christ, I sound like a pussy.

Luke softly chuckles. "Man, have you got it bad. Are you getting all sappy and shit in your old age? I don't think I've ever seen you like this before. She's gorgeous. I'll give you that. But you're only here for a few weeks. If she isn't a fly-by-night girl, then you should stay away from her and continue having sex with your hand," Luke jokes.

"Ella seems different. She's a more one-night-stand kind of girl. But Eden? I'm not so sure. Ella mentioned a few times Eden had a traumatic incident. Must have been around the same time as your win here, give or take. She's never said what exactly."

He's right, but I can't help wanting her. I wonder what happened to her.

I've never met anyone like her. She's cute and funny, feisty, sexy, and her body is fucking delectable. Clenching my jaw, I close my eyes. A low growl thunders through me. That Wallace girl has me in a spin.

"Weeeellll... I happen to know she's off to The Vault tomorrow night."

I look up, intrigued.

"How do you know?"

"Ella and I have been chatting on text. Don't you say a word." He points at me.

I flash the palms of my hands in a stop motion as a mocking smile leaves my lips. "It's none of my business."

"They are going out dancing tomorrow. Eden has a bucket list item to tick off, apparently."

"That goddamn list. Do you know what's on the list? Has Ella shown you? Am I on it?"

"So many questions. Calm the hell down. I've had a brief glimpse at it, and yeah, man, it's pretty far out in places. You should ask Eden about it or even better, ask her to show you the complete list."

"Nope, you're going to get me that list. Text Ella now. And text the team," I instruct, clapping my hands. "We're going out tomorrow night. The Vault it is. Can you book a VIP table?"

"Already done, my man."

Game on.

"What the hell are messages, did she say fingering, and should we watch *Bridgerton*?" Luke asks.

I can't help but laugh out loud.

CHAPTER EIGHT

Eden - Four years ago

"Jamie's fishing boat's been found, Eden," my dad whispers into my ear.

My head spins. "Is he alive?"

"We don't know yet. All we've been told is three of them are missing and one's been rescued. The other families are being told now, too. We're waiting for the Coast Guard and police to confirm, but apparently one of them was found clinging to a life buoy. We have to stay positive. C'mon chicken."

He wraps his loving arms around me.

I look around the shoreline at the sorrowed faces of our friends and families.

Standing here waiting. Shivering from the utter shock of it all, not the cold. We've been waiting for news for over six hours. Then this.

"Oh my God, Dad." I sob in his arms. "Please let him be okay."

Everyone is wrapped in their own pain as cries and sobs slowly weave through the crowd as the news spreads.

The next few hours painfully drift by. The confirmation of three men missing at sea is announced. The search will continue in the morning. Without saying a word, we all know what it means.

It feels like a slow-motion movie.

The ship sunk. Only debris from the boat has been salvaged so far.

Heartache. Pain. Loss.

It feels like I've left my body, detached from myself and watching as it all plays out in the scenes below.

Four families torn apart. Never to be the same again.

❉

"Eden... Jamie's alive."

For a moment I lose consciousness and my legs go out from under me.

I come to with my dad's face hovering above with tears running down his face, smiling happy tears.

"He's alive, Eden."

Hope surges within me.

My voice trembles, "What, how, are you sure?"

"He survived. They have taken him to the hospital. We need to go."

❉

Life was never the same after Jamie's boating accident.

The boys were never found and the families of Ross, Thomas, and Nick were forever changed. The wave of pain was felt by all in Castleview Cove.

Apparently we were the lucky ones.

If only they knew.

I got my boy back, but he was not my Jamie.

Tormented. Withdrawn.

Jamie disconnected from us all.

Jamie suffered deep emotional and psychological trauma of epic proportions.

He denied it for a long time. Months, even.

As time went on, we grew apart.

His flashbacks and nightmares consumed him daily.

Living close to the boys' families became a burden and a painful reminder that he was here and they were not.

He didn't want to be the boy who lived; he wished he'd died that day too.

He told me so when he sobbed in my arms.

Somewhere along the line, part of him died.

And so did our seven-year relationship.

Little did I know I was three months pregnant on the day of Jamie's accident.

Exactly three months following the accident, Jamie left Castleview Cove. Leaving one simple line on a text message. **I'm sorry. I can't stay here anymore. Love always, Jamie.**

No kiss. No explanation. No mention of our baby. No return plans. Gone.

Leaving me, his family, and his unborn child.

I cried myself dry. In deep pain, I wallowed in my sorrow.

Not knowing where he was or where he'd gone.

The uncertainty of my future.

Searching for answers.

I was frantic.

Then I lost our little girl.

I lost Jamie.

I lost Chloe.

At the age of only twenty-three, I lost myself too.

CHAPTER NINE

Bonnie Lass: *adjective,* beautiful girl, pretty, stunning, attractive. **Pronounced:** Bawny Lass.

Baltic: *adjective,* cold, freezing. "Put the heating on it's bloody Baltic outside." **Pronounced:** Ball-tick.

Eden

Only a few more days till I return to work. I'm a little afraid to admit it, but it's been lovely having all this time off. I finally sorted out the spare room, decluttered all my drawers, and reorganized my walk-in wardrobe.

Focusing on being gentle with myself and practicing self-care.

Ella's little chat really woke me up. She's right. I was stuck.

In a short few weeks, I've slowly been changing my daily routine. Ella wanted me to focus on my mindset first.

I received two emails from Ella. The first pinged into my inbox a day after our brief chat, the same day Hunter set up camp in my brain and hasn't left.

Ella's first email is not what I expected...

From: Ella Wallace
    To: Eden Wallace
    CC: Eva McDougal
    Subject: Part I – Eden's Life-Changing Bucket List

Hey, Bonnie Lass,

First things first... this is not the official bucket list email. That's coming. Right now I want you to do the following... Attend Dr. Anderson's office on Old Castle Road at one p.m. tomorrow. This is one of six appointments I've made for you. Dr. Anderson is expecting you. She's an incredible therapist, specializing in trauma. You'll love her and I think you'll really hit it off. This is going to be your first step toward many positive changes in your life. I've filled her in briefly, but it's not my story to tell.

Your mind may be reeling, but all I ask you is to just trust us, babes.

Eva and I want the very best for you. We've got you.

Love you, Ella & Eva xx

I was blown away.

I sat in tears at the realization of how much they *really* cared about me.

My girls love me.

To be honest, looking back, I realize I was an utter mess.

I felt like shit mentally.

Something had to change.

I went to that appointment.

Since then, I've attended four of them. I've made significant progress. *Go me.* I feel it too. My therapist has given me lots of homework and exercises to do. All brain work to increase my awareness of my daily emotions. Leaning into my future and letting go of my past. Well, not letting go completely. More like allowing my negative emotions to flow safely. Not allowing them to hold me back like they have. Something I haven't been doing. I thought if I let things out it would make me feel worse. Who knew it would have the opposite effect? I feel better.

Much better.

I've been journaling daily; it's been deeply enlightening. Writing my daily thoughts has allowed me to see things in a new light.

Over time, I know this is really going to help me. I'm not quite over that hill yet, but I will be. I seriously can't believe I've waited all this time to seek help. It's been difficult talking it through. Seeing a therapist, someone impartial that I could talk freely to about Jamie and losing my beautiful baby, was cathartic. It's something I rarely talked about. By keeping it all in, I didn't realize it was rotting my soul and sanity one little piece at a time.

Slowly but surely, I'm banishing the blame and guilt I've been holding on to.

Dr. Anderson informed me I have been holding on for dear life to a perpetual feeling of guilt over something I didn't control.

When she put it like that, I felt like all the air expelled from my lungs all at once.

I didn't have any control over the boat accident. The unforecasted storm was the criminal that night.

I had no control over Jamie or his choice to leave.

Jamie is out there now, living his life. Without me.

His family denies they know his whereabouts. I'm not convinced they're telling the truth.

If they know, that's their family secret to keep. At the very least, I hope they told him about us losing Chloe. I'll never know, although my gut tells me they did. He chose not to come. They would have been mad at him for not coming to our baby's heartfelt church service. Jamie's parents are good people. They protected me from his no-show. Better to pretend he didn't know than to deepen the blow of hurt and abandonment.

I retraced losing Chloe with Dr. Anderson. I had a problem with my cervix. The doctors called it an incompetent cervix. Combined with the trauma of Jamie leaving me, I was unaware of the signs to look for. I thought my pelvic pressure, backache, and pulling sensations in my belly were normal. It turned out not to be so. It all happened quickly, and an ultrasound scan confirmed we were too late.

I cried in that office with Dr. Anderson. I let it all out. I will not let my tragedy consume me anymore. I now realize my past is my past. Time to look forward.

There is no such thing as a magic wand and it will take time to fully recover from these guilty feelings, but it's a start. Dr. Anderson informs me they will try to rear their ugly head, but I'm better equipped to bash them over the head if they do. I'm going to be on top of the Whac-A-Mole leaderboard when I come out the other side of all this.

After a few sessions I'm finally opening up, talking more

and forgiving myself, practicing gratitude, attending my therapy appointments, accepting that I had no control. Accepting the pain and longing I felt for Jamie and my little girl, Chloe, is normal, but carrying guilt with me was preventing me from living my life.

I was just going through the motions of everyday life before.

Waiting for Jamie.

Having talked it out, I'm bloody mad as hell at Jamie for leaving me. For leaving me to grieve by myself. He just walked away from us. Not being able to talk about Chloe to him. For his absence at her funeral. Dr. Anderson explained his torment that trauma can cause. I now have a better understanding of what he went through. It helped and made me see things from his point of view. She also explained it's okay for me to be mad at him too, but not to hold on to it. Forgiving him has been a huge part of the process. I'll never forget, however, learning to be compassionate and understand Jamie's circumstances around his traumatic experiences is allowing me to release any resentment and bitterness toward him.

Dr. Anderson explained how writing a letter to Jamie would help me express my feelings. Simply for my benefit. It gave me a chance to get everything out, explaining my side of my trauma and loss. I said goodbye to him in that letter. Described our little Chloe. Shared our peaceful send-off. Forgiving him. Letting him go.

Carrying around the heaviness of these feelings and weight of unsaid words was giving him power and hold over my life.

Then I burned the letter. I watched the flames dance as I released and let it go.

The tears flowed.

It was a bittersweet moment, but it was my turning point. I physically felt it in my body. A slight crack opened in my heart and started letting the light in. It was raw and messy.

I'm not broken. I'm opening it to allow love and joy in again. It's been a whirlwind of sensations these last couple of weeks.

Emerging from my four-year hibernation has been liberating.

I'm feeling good. I am stronger; I am still here, standing, still breathing.

I'm using my past to shape my future.

I have my sisters, my lovely friends, my forever supportive parents, my grand home, and of course our dance school. My challenge now is to thread in more fun with huge dollops of laughter into the gifted life I have. It's been in front of me all along. But I'm only just realizing how lucky I truly am. With awareness comes oneness, I've discovered.

I'm sleeping more soundly. I'm breathing easier. I'm lighter.

Connecting myself to the outside world. Connecting with me. I've started watching the news again. Tuning in to the world and the people around me.

Started dreaming and planning for what *I* want in life. Where do I want to be in five years' time? Doing what?

It's exciting. New desires have lit a fire in my belly to do more, be more, feel more. Forget Stella, Eden's getting her groove back.

My bucket list whooshed into my inbox two weeks after my first therapy session. My stomach did a flip. You never quite know what you're going to get with Ella. Apparently, Eva was having the final say on a final version, so part of me felt safe-ish. I held my breath in anticipation before I tapped it open.

With nerves I opened this...

From: Ella Wallace
To: Eden Wallace
CC: Eva McDougal
Subject: Part 2 - Eden's Life-Changing Bucket List

Dearest Eden,
Before we dig into your bucket list, which will be life-changing by the way, because, well, I made the list and I'm awesome. I just wanted to thank you for allowing me to do this for you. I have had WAY too much fun coming up with ideas. I can already hear your mind working overtime from my desk but don't stress; Eva had the final say, so don't get your knickers in a knot. We've got you girl and we are going to watch you blossom and shine, baby. Are you ready? Here goes... Remember, we love you... but first there are rules.
1. You can't delete anything from the list
2. You have to do everything on it
3. You have a year to do it all
4. Never give up
5. Note the date you complete each item. Let us know when you've done them too—we need details about everything. 'Cause we're nosey bitches. Toni and Beth want to know too. Especially all the details on item number one ;)
6. Enjoy it all and have fun
7. Light that tunnel up like I told you to and shine, baby, shine

Are you ready?

Eden's Awesome Bucket List

1. Hunter King—read into that what you will, Eden; we don't care how, just do him :) There's a time limit on this one, he's only here for a few months
2. Buy a new vibrator to loosen yourself up and prep yourself for list item one... How long has it been?
3. Attend six therapy sessions—you're already doing these, and we are so proud of you
4. Go out either every Friday or Saturday night—or both
5. Keep journaling and talking to us daily; we love what you've achieved so far, it's working, keep going
6. Limit your book reading to three a month
7. Attend Pole-Dancing Fitness classes to gain your qualification. These are purely for selfish reasons. Eva and I want to offer more dance classes to mums. My idea. I think this will be epic
8. Go on at least two dates a month
9. Attend a ball
10. Try horse riding
11. Be kissed under the stars
12. Book a vacation to Disney World
13. Ride in a limo
14. Feed a penguin
15. Get a tattoo—I know you've always wanted one
16. Swim with dolphins
17. Attend an outdoor concert
18. Go skinny-dipping
19. Build a sandcastle
20. Visit a museum
21. Have a water balloon fight—childish we know, but we

fancy this and the kids will love it; when was the last time we did this?

22. Watch the closing fireworks at Magic Kingdom

23. Buy new lingerie. Because we want you to...

24. Have a one-night stand—maybe two. It's time to explore and discover

25. Have sex in the sea—we give you full permission to combine this one with number 18

26. Learn a dance routine with Eva and me. The filthier the better and we'll perform it at The Vault. It's all arranged with Roman; we just need to tell him what week

27. Finish decorating the spare room

28. Learn to master your own cupcakes, so you don't have to keep buying them. :) Although you're an awful cook, you may be a better baker?

29. Practice gratefulness daily

30. Keep on booking appointments with your therapist if you feel six isn't enough

31. Fall in love... You don't have to do this in a year, gahhh that is pressure but open your heart to possibility

32. More than anything Eden, we want you to find yourself, celebrate your lovely life, and be happy

We love you, baby girl, you've got this and we've got you.

Ella and Eva - and Beth and Toni too. xxxx

    Some of these freaked me out. Horses. Yup, they scare me. Don't ask why, but they just do. Ella can keep her horses. Fall in love? In twelve months? That seems impossible. Sex in the sea? In Scotland? It's bloody Baltic. I may die of hypothermia. Two dates a month. Gee, I'm not sure I want to do those.

    I have achieved some of the smaller things so far. I'm

continuing to journal daily and attend my therapy sessions. I booked a couple more because they are helping. I practice gratefulness daily, which I am loving. Oh, and this week, because I'm feeling stronger and my thumb has healed, Eva, Ella and I spent laughter-filled afternoons together this week creating a routine for item number twenty eight...

'Learn a dance routine with Eva and me. The filthier the better and we'll perform it at The Vault. It's all arranged with Roman; we just need to tell him what week.'

We're performing there tonight. Roman is Beth's brother. He manages The Vault bar and nightclub. The things I do for my sisters. I hope none of the dance mums are there; they may never bring their kids back to classes.

I really don't think Ella thought this one through.

Doing this one ticks another thing off the list. I'm actually really enjoying it.

Note to self: speak to Toni and Beth about Disney World, so they can book their vacation time.

I can't remember the last time I went out dancing and drinking for fun. I'm so excited, I do a little jiggle in my seat.

I'm currently sitting at my desk reading through my bucket list again.

Hunter King. Way up there, right at the top.

He's got me in a spin. I feel like I've popped a red sock in with my white wash. Mixing everything up, creating something new and unexpected. He's woken the desire and excitement within me that's been buried for so long.

I don't know how I kept my cool around him when I helped him with his fire.

Okay, so I sucked his finger. I don't know what I was thinking.

It all happened so quickly I totally lost myself. It was an

impulse move. Like I left my body for a moment and Miss Minnie took over. Hunter's awakened a desire for intimacy and touch. His touch. I lean back in my desk chair, remembering.

Dragging my hands down my face, I recall the finger incident.

I sucked his finger.

I'm blaming his deep chocolate eyes and his scent; that's what made me do it. Or maybe it's his muscles and lips. Admit it. It's everything about him. He sends tingles down my spine just thinking about him.

Item number one...

Hunter King—read into that what you will Eden; we don't care how, just do him :)

This scares the shit out of me. And there's a time limit.

No pressure, girls, thanks.

I haven't been with anyone sexually, besides Jamie, like, ever.

Jamie was my high school sweetheart. How do you please a man that looks like Hunter? I'm totally out of my depth. I need internet porn Stat.

It's been years since anything or anyone has been near Miss Minnie. I haven't touched myself in forever. I think she has closed up and given up. But she's come alive recently. She tingles and pulses when I'm around Hunter and when I fantasize about him. This has surprised me—I think it's surprised Miss Minnie too. Bloody hell. I can't call her that. Hunter calls her that.

I've daydreamed about him. I wondered what his cock looks like. He's huge all over. He said it's enormous; I bet it's as beautiful as the rest of him. I don't think Miss Minnie can take it. I feel warmth spread between my legs just thinking about him. She's keen.

I open a new tab on Google and type 'Hunter King.'

I Googled him as soon as he left my house the last time. I may have stalked his Instagram too. Daily. I'm an excellent student; I'm being thorough with my research. I didn't follow him though. *Hi, my name is Eden, I love reading romance books, and sunset walks on the beach, cupcakes, and stalking hot guys on Instagram.*

My search throws back rows and rows of images of him on the course, at events, and shopping. News stories, achievements, facts. I know them all. One image captures my attention. I didn't see that last time. I click on it to open. Hunter stands tall with arms around the shoulders of an elegant blond, big-boobed woman. She's wearing the skimpiest of red bandage dresses and black stilettos with those red soles I've been drooling over for years.

Is this his girlfriend? I click on the image to read the article and take a sip of my tea.

"Look out, ladies. Rumor has it, pro-golfer Hunter King is back on the market. An insider informed us Jess Samuels and King have gone their separate ways following a twelve-month relationship. Jess was spotted removing her belongings from Hunter's home in Florida and packing them into her Audi TT. Hunter has yet to confirm but quickly putting two and two together, we suspect the rumors are true. Watch this space to find out who'll be stroking his shaft next, apparently it's rather impressive."

I spit my tea out all over my laptop screen.

"Aw, bumheads."

Quickly, I whip off my shirt and use it to mop up the tea. Luckily, no damage caused.

I keep scrolling through all the news articles.

I find lots more I missed the last time. Hunter pictured

with so many striking women. How in the heck am I ever going to compete with the likes of them?

Impressive shaft. Eeekkkk.

What have Ella and Eva got me into?

Tap that? Fuck that, girls. I don't think I can.

He must be playing me because there is no way in hell he's into me. Look at them. They're all gorgeous, elegant gazelles.

I pull up his Instagram account on my laptop. This way I can pull up bigger images of him.

There's no denying it. He's handsome.

I really like him. *A lot.*

I haven't thought about anyone other than Jamie, ever.

He's been my one and only since high school.

This is all new to me.

Thoughts of another.

My therapist told me it's time to move on.

This is my new beginning, or maybe I just need to buy that vibrator off my bucket list to ease these sexual and unfamiliar feelings I'm having recently.

Better do what Ella says. I pull open another new tab and position Hunter's Instagram window parallel to a new window so I can shop and stalk at the same time. I type in 'Ann Summers' into the search bar. New vibrator, here I come.

After finding the sex toy section, I start browsing. Trying to figure out what I want. Why is buying a vibrator so technical?

I take my time scrolling through. Some of these are huge. Will that fit? *Wow*. What color? With or without ears? How many speeds? Too many choices. I finally select one and add it to my basket, quickly checking out, feeling chuffed with myself. One thing off the list, only another thirty-one to go.

A text dings through on my phone.

Unknown number: Are you shopping for a vibrator while swooning over my Instagram page, Cupcake? Am I your vibrator purchase inspiration?

I slam my laptop lid shut with a swift almighty bang.

I look up and dart my eyes around, trying to figure out where he is.

This is where I should have spent the money, opaque glass in the living room. What a fool. A poor fool at the time.

I text back.

Me: Are you stalking me?
Unknown number: You're one to talk.

I save his number to my contacts.

Hunter: Let me get this straight... you're half naked, shopping for a new vibrator, with my photos splashed across your screen. Are you getting off to my face? Anddd... where is your shirt? Is this your normal Saturday afternoon attire and activity?

"Shit." I blush in an empty room. I leap up from my desk that's nestled into the corner of my living room, positioned next to my floor-to-ceiling windows. Bugger. I am in fact giving everyone an eyeful. Half naked in only my Brazilian lace thong sleep panties and a lace bralette. He's clearly let himself through the security gate that divides my house from the retreat. The groundsmen have Saturdays off. I was not expecting this. Sprinting across my living room, I take the stairs two at a time up my sweeping wood and black metalwork staircase and run into my bedroom on the upper floor.

Not that it will make a difference; there's floor-to-ceiling windows everywhere. As a side note... Always, always, remember to wear your panties and bra, or clothes, just wear something to make sure the groundsmen don't catch you in your birthday suit. Yup, I've been caught out myself a few times. Like now, for instance. I'm positive Campbell, the head groundsman, spends way too much time trimming the trees around my house, hoping to catch me out. At the ripe old age of sixty-five, it would be the thrill of his year. In the words of Ella, "all this glass shows a lot of ass."

I have that clever opaque smart glass in my bedroom, though. You know the one at the switch of a button it turns from transparent to opaque?

Super fancy me. It was too expensive to install anywhere else in the house. Hashtag: pennies were running low. I grab my smart glass controller and switch it on. Then quickly draw my curtains across the windows of my Juliet balcony. Oh yeah, I have one of those too. I really went all out in my bedroom. You can enjoy Castleview Cove in its entirety. Perched perfectly above the treetops. Add a cup of tea. There's no better way to start the day. It's how I start mine. Every. Single. Day. Ah... bliss. It's my sanctuary. In here, I'm now safe.

Hunter: Aw, you're no fun. I was enjoying that.
Me: Where the bloody hell are you, Mr. King?

Hunter: Everywhere.

Hunter: So when does it arrive? Should I add an eggplant emoji to our chat?

Me: It's not called an eggplant, it's an aubergine. Bloody yanks.

Hunter: Bloody weird Scots.

Hunter: Which one did you buy? Did you buy a rabbit?

Me: You're so bad, Mr. King. I'm not telling you.

Hunter: Is this for bucket list item number two to prep yourself for item number one?

Me: How in the bloody hell have you seen that?

Hunter: Did Ella not tell you? We're best friends now. #friendsforlife

Me: I'm guessing this is how you got my number too? Ella is off my Christmas list. We are so done. Forever.

Hunter: She's my best friend now anyway; she won't miss you. So... what did you buy?

Me: I'm not telling you.

Hunter: Come on...

Me: Nope...

Hunter: Okay... maybe you can show me when it comes... or when you come...

Me: You are WAY TOO MUCH, MR. KING.

Hunter: So shouty.

Hunter: And that's right, Eden, I am TOO MUCH. Do you think Miss Minnie can take it?

Me: I'm not having this conversation with you; you're so naughty. I'm off for a shower, good day, Mr. King.

Hunter: Is that to cool down? I know I'm hot from the flash of your lace thong. Did I make you hot and bothered?

Hunter: You've not seen my naughty side yet ;)

Hunter: Two things... 1. You were buying a vibrator while drooling over my face. 2. Who sucked who's finger?

Hunter: Annnddddd... I'm the naughty one? #fingersuckingfantasies

Me: I was NOT drooling.

Hunter: Whatever, were you wet in other places then?

Me: I can't deal with you right now.

Hunter: Maybe deal with me later then?

Hunter: Or I'll deal with you later. Naughty girl.

I fling myself back on the bed and laugh out loud.

Holy shit.

A few minutes pass.

Viewing my phone, arms stretched above my face, I watch as a bubble appears, indicating he's typing.

Hunter: Where did you go? Are you in the shower thinking about me?

Hunter: Are you ignoring me now?

Hunter: Buckle up, Cupcake, you can only ignore me for so long. I'm only getting started.

Hunter: You look beautiful today ;) xo

I stare at my phone as the last texts come in.

He's the devil. A handsome devil.

Boy, am I in trouble.

CHAPTER TEN

Fanny: *adjective,* In Scotland fanny means loads of things… Vagina. But mainly means idiot or stupid. Used in conjunction with wee, as in "you're a wee fanny." Aren't we a delight? **Pronounced:** Fan-nay.

Eden

"You are glowing tonight, Eden." Toni smiles over my shoulder at me in the mirror.

"It's the light bronzer I applied earlier."

Anything to cover up that Scottish blue skin tinge sneaking through.

"Okay, I'm done." I say, smacking my lips together as I finish applying my lipstick.

I've straightened my stream of hair within an inch of its life tonight. Hello, shiny locks.

My caramel waist-length locks are anything but straight. It can be, but boy, does it go frizzy in the misty weather that comes off the sea in Castleview Cove. It makes it go mental…

like totally crazy big. Think Monica from *Friends* in Barbados. Not a good look. I reckon if I invented a frizz free serum for my hair specifically to deal with the Scottish weather, I would be a millionaire, because nothing works. Believe me, I've tried them all. It takes so much effort to smooth it out. Straighteners are life.

"It's nothing to do with the bronzer, Eden. You are gleaming from head to foot, girlfriend."

"Thanks, girls."

I swing my legs around to the side of my gray velvet dressing table chair, drape my arm gently on the back, and rest my chin. I relish the photogenic sight of my four besties —Ella, Eva, Toni, and Beth. All perched on the edge of my bed, dressed up to the nines, smelling like the seven wonders of the world as their perfumes clash, sipping sparkling prosecco with expressions of excited happiness.

"It feels like forever since I felt this alive. I still have work to do, ladies, but I feel so good." I raise my hands in the air and sing.

Eva covers her ears. "You still sound like shit, no change there."

"Well, you look incredible and fucking hot. This is your coming out night. That sounded wrong. Not coming out. Not from the closet. I meant, this is your rebirth. Yeah, that's better," Toni rambles.

"Like a phoenix from the flames." Ella splays her fingers and arms out, drawing a giant arch in the air.

I smile at her exclamation of delight.

"Are we ready? Are we *really* doing this dance tonight?" I question Ella and Eva.

"Hell to the yeah, baby. We've been practicing all week. Let's go. I'll order an Uber." Ella springs up from the bed and teeters out of the bedroom in her black spaghetti-strap heels, black super skinny jeans, black vest, and shiny gold belt.

"Did we really think this through, Eva? What if there's some dance mums there tonight and we're all dancing like some sex-starved women? I know we used to do this all the time, but we have a dance school now." I exhale my concern as we all wobble down my stairs, clattering our heels against the wood. "You didn't think that shorts jumpsuit you're wearing through either, Eva. You are so going to give everyone an eyeful tonight."

"Stop stressing," exclaims Beth, running her hands down her bobbed, chin-length fire-engine-red hair.

"Get a grip, girl; you can do this." Toni nods in agreement.

Eva says, "Yup, we are doing this, Eden. All bets are on. I put money on us filling up our adult dance classes off the back of this. Husbands will line up on Monday, signing up their wives so they can learn how to sway their hips like we do. Just think, when we offer pole-dancing aerobic classes, they'll sign up for those too—it's the seamless upsell. Think of it as the perfect promotion."

"Since when did you get a business head on you, Eva?"

"Since you allowed Ella and me to take the reins a little. It's been the best, and I have so many more ideas on how to grow the business. I'll fill you in on it all next week when you're back at work, but for now we are going dancing sexy lady, let's go." She bellows out toward the end with excitement.

"I can't wait to dance and perform together with you girls. When did we last do this in front of people? All we ever seem to do is teach now. We should do this more often." Ella says with glee, pushing her arms through her black blazer.

"Black on black on black this evening, Ella?"

"I'm a mother-fluffing ninja tonight."

We all burst out laughing. "You're a fanny, not a ninja," Eva says.

Beth chimes in, breaking our laughter. "I can't wait to perv over the performance. I haven't watched you three dance together in forever. You girls make me rethink my sexual persuasion when you start grinding and swaying your hips. And the faces you make... Lord, are you girls a triple shot of sexiness. Wooooo. I can't handle it. C'mon, let's go, taxi's here." Gathering her handbag, she sashays out the door.

Toni rolls her eyes, following everyone. "You girls can deal with her tonight. I'm not sure I can if she starts dry humping the stage while you put on your slut show."

"It's not a bloody slut show, Toni. It's art," I retort.

Yeah right, not tonight it's not.

A burst of laughter from us all again, combined with the clicking of our heels, echoes around the courtyard. I lock up and we all bounce into the taxi.

The Vault is already jumping when we arrive. It's R&B night. My favorite kind of music.

Roman gave us an excellent space in the VIP area, which means we don't have to put up with all the workers currently living in the town.

The Championship Cup starts soon and they've made a start building all the spectator stands and marquees to prepare for the tournament. This is the best time to visit the town. Before, during, and after the entire town buzzes with activity.

I watch the crowd filling the dance floor from the glass balcony of the VIP area, music pumping to the sounds of Usher, Beyoncé, and Ariana.

Nerves keep creeping in and out of my thoughts at the thought of having to dance soon. I've limited my drinks just in case I make a tit of myself and fall over in my heels. Dancing, like proper dancing, in high heels isn't something I've done for ages. The last thing I want is to fall flat on my face in front of this rowdy crowd. I'll wait till we do our routine and then sink a few more cheeky rhubarb gins.

"Okay, I have a game for us all." Toni grabs our attention over the music.

We're all crowded around the black and gold semi-circle seating booth.

Ella's blending in with the surroundings tonight, I note.

We all groan. We do this from time to time. And tonight's game is...

"What's your vagina's name?" Toni cries loudly.

"Keep your voice down, Toni," I hiss.

"No one cares, Eden. Just play the game. Beth, you first. First letter of your first name and first letter of your last name. I have the list. Texting it to our group chat... now."

Ding, ding, ding, ding.

We all dig our phones out and find the photo.

"Go, Beth," Toni instructs.

"Holy crap. Sparkle Flaps," she exclaims as we all burst out laughing.

"Me next," Toni says, raising her hand. "Mine issss... Moist Waffle." She looks up from her phone in shock as we all set about giggling again.

Eva jests. "How is Moist Waffle today? Not blue?"

"That turned out to be a crock of crap meme hoax in the

end," Ella informs the table. "Although Eden has a blue vagina. How long has it been?"

"Far too goddamn long," I say unexcitedly.

If I'm going all in with the honesty malarkey, my therapist so helpfully reminds me on the regular, then I'm going all in.

I clear my throat. I've said nothing negative about Jamie or really spoken about him in a long time. Here goes...

"Although it was never good. I feel bad saying this. But it never rocked my world. It was very vanilla. Like no world-shaking stuff that's in the books I read or in the movies. Jamie never got me off, not even once. I always looked after myself. Eden one; Jamie zero."

The girls stop as if on pause. Three, two, one... then a rapid explosion from the girls all at once bursts out.

"*What?*"

"You're kidding."

"What the hell."

"He must have been shit in bed."

Ella's in shock. "That's not normal. You need someone to take care of you." She sips her drink, shaking her head in disbelief.

"I think I'm finally realizing now he was a crap lover. But anyway, getting back to your question. It may have closed up; it's been that long. I've never craved sex though because I've never experienced this fireworks shit that you all talk about. Is it really like that? The sex? Like amazing?"

Eva pipes up. "Hell to the yes, it is. It should be. It should be so good you cannot wait to whip your clothes off. Having kids sucks now. Ewan and I have to sneak around. That makes it more fun sometimes. But man, the things he does to me. Oshhh."

"I'm so missing out," I whisper out in thought.

Toni peers up over her glass. "How does Hunter make you feel? You know after the finger sucking thing?"

"Sorry, what? Finger sucking what?" Eva exclaims in horror.

I brush it off. "That's a story for another day and it was a mistake. It was... gahhhhhh... Hunter makes me gaga. And I get tingles. I really do. He's just incredible. There is no other word for him. He gives me fanny flutters." I gaze off, thinking about him.

"Whoa. This is all new for you, Eden. Lean into it. You need to get some, baby." Beth thrusts her hips, making me chuckle. "List item number one. You've got to do that. Like, really. I reckon he'd give you the explosive ending you've been missing out on." Beth smiles saucily.

"I think I would like that. Ah..." I raise my finger in the air. "I ordered my vibrator today, as instructed by you all, so that may help ease this newly found ache in my foof I have for Hunter."

"Don't call it a foof." Beth gags into her drink. "You make it sound like it's a farting device; we aren't six anymore."

Our table erupts with laughter.

"Let's get back to the game... What's your vagina's name, Eden? Oh..." Toni points at us in thought. "You, Eva, and Ella share the same initials. Eden, you do first and first letters. Ella, you do second and second letters, and Eva, you're off the hook since you're married now."

I go next. "Oh, holy shiz. My vagina is called Pink Puddle."

That sets us all roaring again. Everyone from the surrounding tables looks over. We are drawing way too much attention to ourselves.

"I think I'm going to wet myself," I cry out.

"Christ, then it really will be a puddle."

We shriek with laughter so much we fail to notice Hunter approaching our table.

"Evening, ladies." He demands the attention of the table as it completely silences.

His eyes find mine.

Everything around me stops.

I try swallowing the sandpaper lump in my throat.

Holy cow. Just look at him. Those eyes. And his designer stubble beard. He's sexual eye candy. I wanna lick him.

Yikes. I hope he didn't overhear my sexual inadequacies.

That would be awful.

"Having fun?" He's asking the table but looking at me.

The girls pull themselves together and swoon with small waves and shy hellos.

"Eden." He tips his head to me in acknowledgement.

I blink.

Shyly I mouth a small hi.

"See, you managed to clothe yourself, eventually."

All eyes snap to me.

He *is* the devil.

Eyebrows raise along the line of the table.

"Eden, do you have something to share with us... again?" Eva asks, her voice laced with curiosity.

"No, I do *not*." I shake my head furiously.

Eva pops an eyebrow in amusement.

"Honestly, I have no idea what he's talking about." I raise my hands with exasperation, slapping them back to rest on my jean-covered thighs.

Deny. Deny. Deny.

I look up and meet Hunter's amused stare. "You're a menace," I say as I grab my glass and down a large gulp of my rhubarb gin.

"I really am." He roguishly winks and asks, "You girls getting up to dance?"

"We sure are. Just you wait," replies Ella.

"Maybe save a dance for me, Eden?"

He's so direct.

I scrunch my nose, then roll my eyes to the side away from him as I ponder. "Maybe."

Make him sweat. Act cool, Eden. Act cool.

He stalks around the table.

"That so? We'll see."

He glides around to the back of the booth directly behind me. He dips down and nuzzles into my neck. "Would you like me to show you what a pink puddle really looks like, Cupcake?" he purrs.

Then he inhales a deep breath. Is he sniffing my hair?

My skin crawls with sparks of electricity.

He suddenly stands back and raises his glass in a cheers motion to the table. "Girls." He turns on his heel and walks away.

I circle my neck and follow his handsome figure as he glides away in his simple white tee, black ripped designer jeans. Paired with dark-gray suede lace boots. Everything about him looks expensive. He saunters to the far end of the VIP area and sits down. He's with a crowd of people, I'm assuming that's his team. I only recognize Luke. There's a beautiful brunette girl sitting with them too that I don't recognize. She's all long bronzed legs and boobs. She looks like a goddess.

How did I not see them all when we arrived?

"I think I just got pregnant from watching that." Toni fans herself with her hand.

I focus my eyes on the table; the girls are all sitting and staring at me.

I put my head in my hands.

"He's a rogue. A great big gorgeous rogue. I think I need more alcohol," I grumble dreamily.

"It's a bloody orgasm you need, more like," drawls Beth.

And the girls all break out into a fit of giggles.

No help at all. Thanks, girls.

✳

Hunter

She's here.

I'm excited.

She's beautiful. There's no other word for her.

I laugh to myself. Fucking Pink Puddle.

Those girls.

I've sat and watched her for the last half hour. That makes me sound like a fucking stalker. Scrap that... Sat and gazed at her with longing eyes... That sounds worse and makes me sound like a creep.

Okay, so maybe I'm being a bit stalkery. I can't take my eyes off her. Now and then she looks up and catches my eyes. You can feel the tension between us; it's becoming unbearable.

I watch as the girls all rise from the table.

Are they hitting the dance floor?

I watch as they disappear down the metal stairs.

I turn to Luke. "Are we getting a front row view of list item number twenty-six? The sexy dance? Do you think they're doing it tonight?"

He smirks. "Come see."

He stands and beckons me to come closer to the balcony.

I watch as Eden, her sisters, and friends weave through

the crowd toward the stage. It's a great nightclub. An old bank is what Luke said. The old teller's desks have been converted into a bar along one wall. Gold and black velvet and metal interiors throughout. Gold lighting floods the floor in the VIP area and features a glitter wall of dotted lights on a black wall. Reminds me a little of The Bank at the Bellagio. Very cool.

I rest my arms on the handrail of the glass balcony, following Eden's every move as she climbs onto the stage with her sisters.

She's wearing light-blue extreme ripped jeans, exposing her lean thighs to her knees and gold ankle tie stiletto heels. I'd like them wrapped around my head.

The faint outline of her erect nipples is evident through her fitted white, sleeveless crop top, accentuating the curves of her ample boobs, tiny waist, and flat stomach. She's wearing multiple layers of fine gold chains, all different lengths and designs. As she stands there nervously, the stage light bounces off a tiny light-blue crystal dangling from her belly bar piercing.

Imagining myself skimming my tongue across her skin and belly button drives my cock wild. I palm my crotch over my clothes to reposition myself.

She's a goddamn wet dream.

The music dies down a little. The DJ bellows over the mic, "Hey, party people. We have something a little bit special tonight. For those of you who aren't from the town, these ladies are the Wallace Triplets. Aren't they gorgeous?"

The crowd cheers in agreement.

Damn straight *she* is.

"Ella's getting it. She's a fox," Luke exclaims.

"Fuck Ella, check Eden. She's mine."

We both laugh at each other. We're like a pair of teenage boys with high school crushes.

We've got it bad.

"Eden... put your hand up, baby girl," the DJ instructs.

"Baby girl. He's a douchebag," I expel in disgust.

"Eden is under strict orders from her sisters to complete everything on a bucket list they set for her. Tonight she is ticking one off the list. The girls are trained dancers and own a dance school here in Castleview Cove. Tonight, fellas... we are getting an all exclusive private dance, just for The Vault."

The men in the crowd give a low whoop.

Bastards.

Throwing his head back, the DJ screams into the mic, "Okay, less talking, more dancing. Let's get this shit going."

The crowd cheers and claps.

A brief hush falls over the club. Eden and her sisters get themselves into their positions before the music kicks in.

The intro of "Dirrty" by Christina Aguilera slowly ticks and clicks through the speakers, then the beat drops. Before my very eyes, the girls start dancing for their lives in a routine they've clearly been practicing. I can't take my eyes off Eden. All nerves have gone, and she's a fucking vixen on the stage.

Her hips sway, pump, and thrust. Hands roam up and down her body.

Holy mother of God. I want to be those hands. I'm a bad boy. A very bad, bad boy.

How is she dancing in those heels?

Persistent, hard-hitting, high-energy movements take over her body. She's lost in the moment. She's someone else when she dances. Like she's possessed.

Hip and body rolls, booty dips... She's the gift that keeps on giving.

Crawling across the floor, arching her back now, she gyrates, like she's humping the floor, circling and rolling her body in time to the music like a cat in heat. Then jumping up to her feet. Bouncing, jerking, flexing.

More hip sways and I take note of her dance face. She's drowning in the moves and music. Smoldering dark sexy eyes. Her splayed hands slide up her voluptuous body, up over her delicate neck, then into her waist-length hair, I'd like to wrap my hands around, giving her that just-fucked look. She throws her head back, shaking it from side to side, hair flying, mouth open wide as she lets it all go.

Oh.

My.

God.

I think I might be having a heart attack.

My heart is beating out of my chest so fast.

I want her.

"Look at them go," Luke booms over the music.

I only see Eden. She's a star. A star that my body now craves.

I want her to light me up.

She's everything.

I'm so entranced, suddenly I realize the song is over and the crowd is going wild.

Eden and her sisters are cuddling each other and bouncing up and down with excitement on the stage before heading back toward the dance floor to meet their two friends, who I haven't officially met yet. I watch her for a few minutes; covered in a light sheen of moisture, she's shining. She must feel me watching her. She glances up and stares directly at me with a wide, dazzling smile, a look of relief on her face.

She spots Pippa wrapped around me to my side and her smile drops.

Mmmm, that's right, Cupcake. You're jealous. You do like me.

Eden hasn't met my sister yet.

To tease Eden a little, I give Pippa a brief kiss on the top of her head.

Pippa looks up at me and smiles.

"Having a nice night, bro?"

As I turn my eyes back to the dance floor, I find Eden watching us.

She does not look happy.

"I am," I simply reply.

"She's beautiful, Hunter. I can tell you like her."

"Do you think she likes me?"

"Have you seen you? Even as your sister, I can categorically tell you, you are a fine specimen of a man. Who wouldn't want you, Hunter? You have an incredible heart. You're like the whole package. You deserve multiple levels of happiness. Jess would have never made you happy. She was a class A bitch. I'm so glad that never worked out. You deserve better, way better."

I pull her into a hug.

"That means a lot to me, Pippa. Thank you."

"Are you going to get the girl?"

"Yes." I beam, pulling away. "I am."

CHAPTER ELEVEN

Yer bum's oot the windae: *saying or phrase,* you're literally talking rubbish. **Pronounced:** Your bottom is out of the window.

Eden

Hands in the air, eyes closed, I'm lost in the music, swaying my hips to the hypnotic beats.

A pair of clammy hands startle me as they snake around my midriff.

I spin around at lightning speed to discover it's some random sleazeball drunk. Leaning backward in surprise, he holds me firm.

"Get your fucking hands off her," a loud growl bellows.

I quickly look around. Hunter. He stands tall, chest puffed out.

"Sorry, man, I didn't know she was taken," the stranger says with his hands still on me. He takes his time, slowly removing his sticky hands along my ribs. *Yuck.*

"I said get your fucking hands off her, now." Hunter launches forward.

There's no messin' with Hunter. His size overshadows everyone here.

Sensing Hunter's intention, Mr. Sleazebag instantly steps back. "I don't want any trouble." As he holds his arms up in submission. He quickly turns on his heel and disappears into the crowd.

My shoulders relax with relief. I dislike confrontation.

Urgh… what a creep. I shiver.

Hunter stalks toward me, eyes fixed on mine, breathing heavy. Suddenly he holds his hand out, beckoning me to take it. I tentatively palm my hand into his and feel an instant zing from out touch. He undeniably oozes the X factor, or sex factor in his case. I can't even describe it. So powerful.

Gently, he tugs my hand and pulls me into his rock-hard chest and envelops me with his hot body.

Sparks race between us as he bows his head and rests it on top of mine.

There are no words needed. It's like we've both been waiting for this moment to be this close to one another.

To feel. To touch. To explore.

We sway together in our own little world for a few moments. Our hearts leap fast together. I can feel and hear his beating against my ear. His fingers gently stroke back and forth across my exposed lower back. That feels so nice. A let out a low moan. "Mmmmmm."

Holy cow, what am I doing? I pull away suddenly, startling Hunter.

"Eh, should you not be getting back to your girlfriend?"

I point to the VIP balcony overhead.

A mocking smile fills his face. "Jealous?"

"No." I reply childishly.

"She's my sister, Eden." He smirks. He knows he got me. I'm telling you, he's the devil.

"She arrived two days ago. Now come back to me, I've been waiting weeks to be close to you and I was enjoying that."

Well, I feel like an idiot now. He's not even mine. Yet here I am pissing all around him, somehow, trying to brand him like he is. Hesitantly, I hold his gaze as I slowly pad toward him again and watch his eyes grow hungry. He reaches out and wraps his strong as a bison arms around me again as I nestle back into him.

"Much better." We dance slowly together.

"I'm not dating anyone, Cupcake. I'm single," he coos.

Relief washes over me, and I relax into him, enjoying every single minute. We've never been this close. He's warm and feels so good.

I've thought about his arms. Thought about me being encased in his arms. I never thought I would ever say this, but he has sexy forearms. All toned and tanned.

"Into You" by Ariana Grande thumps through the club. The floor vibrates with electric beats. I love this song and how the words are so fitting, I am *so* completely into *him*. I've been denying myself, but he's consumed every thought since I met him.

In a room full of people, it feels like it's only Hunter and me. Everyone, the music, the crowd, the noise, it all fades away.

He bows his head lower, then gently sweeps my mermaid-length hair over my back and rests his head in between my shoulder and neck.

"You smell divine," he murmurs into my ear, sending shivers down my spine.

We stay like this for a few moments.

He rubs his nose along my neck and jawline. It's then I feel a soft tap of his curvaceous lips against my skin, the tickle of his stubble sending goosebumps all over my body.

I stretch my neck, allowing him more access to my nape. Moving in closer, his mouth drifts nearer to the divine spot behind my ear, driving my senses wild. His hot breath trickles over my skin and I shiver again as he kisses and licks my neck with more valor. We moan out loud together.

I throb and tingle between my legs as I feel his hard cock press against my stomach. Now fully aware of how tall Hunter is—or actually, more like how short I am—there is quite a noticeable height difference between us. It's almost laughable. But I'm not laughing; I'm so in the moment with Hunter driving my body insane.

Hunter's hands slowly drift down my back, tentatively dipping his fingertips into the waistband of my jeans. All the while delicately ravishing my neck and leaving feather-like kisses across my jaw. Instinctively I arch my back, pressing myself harder into him as a sea of emotions and feelings sweep over me. He must feel how hard my nipples are through the thin fabric of his shirt.

He slides the pads of his fingers a little further down into my jeans to meet the top curve of my behind. Being cautious as he ventures south, desperately trying to control himself.

He lets out an audible gasp, panting into my ear, so I can hear him over the pounding music. "Are you not wearing any panties?"

I lean back, gaze up, and wet my lips. "No." I shake my head innocently.

"Are you trying to kill me, woman?"

"I don't like wearing panties when I dance. I find them too restrictive. I don't wear them when I work out either."

He groans loudly, dipping his knees slightly and rolling his eyes with reverence and longing.

"You are. You are definitely trying to kill me."

Removing his hands from my waistline, he skims the path up my body with his enormous hands, tracing my curves as he explores them for the first time. Finally he cups my face, gently tilting my head upward to meet his lust-filled jet-pooled eyes. A skeptical frown pulls at his mouth.

A moment of doubt.

Hunter's eyes bounce between mine, looking left and right. He's making sure he's reading the signals correctly as he sinks his teeth into his full bottom lip.

I sense his vulnerability. He's second-guessing his next move.

Make me yours, please, I silently beg.

His gaze moves to my lips. "Can I kiss you?" he whispers.

My face relaxes into a reassuring smile, and I lick my lips in anticipation.

Hunter pulls me flush and firmly into his chest and our lips instantly crash together. His hand grabs the back of my head and we breathe against each other heavily, our lips pressing together in a painfully perfect kiss. Threading his fingers through my hair, his other hand pulls my hips into his thick cock, which is getting harder by the minute. Oh wow.

Our mouths open simultaneously.

Taking this as permission, he slides his wet tongue into my mouth, colliding with mine. Fireworks explode. I moan into his delectable mouth as our tongues tango together in perfect timing.

Warmth spreads to my sex. I thrust my hips into his body, with the urge to ease the pulse between my legs. Holy shit. I'm going to come right here on the dance floor and all from a kiss.

It's a scorching kiss. I have *never* been kissed like this before.

Hunter deepens our kiss as if wanting to climb inside my body, our hearts racing together like a runaway train. I slide my hands down from his chest toward the hem of his shirt. I pull it up a little and skate my hands along his side and up his sculpted back, feeling his every muscle contract at my delicate touch.

Hunter swallows a deep growl as I run my nails down his back.

His tongue licks and kisses my lips with blistering heat, biting my lower lip and sucking it into his mouth, then he slides his hand from the back of my head to my side, thumbing the contour of my boob, making my nipples pebble with desire.

Losing himself, he digs his fingertips deeper into my needy, thrusting hips.

I think I may pass out from all the sensations streaming through my body.

He's opened Pandora's box and I never want him to close it.

"You're gonna give me a cardiac arrest," he whispers against my lips.

Kissing me again, more softly this time, he wraps his fingers around my throat possessively. Man, does he know how to kiss. I throw my head back, gasping for air.

This is so erotic.

He dusts a path of light kisses over my cheeks, down my jaw, and buries his lips in my hair. Removing my hands from inside the back of his shirt, I run them slowly to his front and palm my hands softly up over his thick chest again. He removes his head from the curtain of my hair. He touches a lingering kiss to my temple, then rests his forehead against mine with his eyes closed. In an instant, I wrap my arms around him, tracing my fingers back and forth across his neck.

"I've wanted to kiss you since the moment I first laid eyes on you," he says, catching his breath. "You drive me crazy, Eden. I want you."

"I want you too. I've never orgasmed from a kiss before. That was close." I chuckle. "I've never had an orgasm before, well actually, I'll correct that. A *man* has never made me come before. So there's a first for everything." My words are out before I can catch them.

Shit, why did I say that?

Hunter's eyes pop open to meet mine with a questioning, confused gaze.

The next few seconds that pass feel like an hour.

"Sorry, what now? Say that again." Hunter gasps in shock.

"Forget I said anything. Where were we?" I say, leaning back into him to cover my blushes.

"Uh-uh. No way. Look at me."

I look back at him as my cheeks grow pink.

"Are you a virgin?"

"Hunter, no," I yell out and swipe his shoulder playfully.

"Thank fuck. That felt like too much pressure for a moment there. You certainly don't kiss like a virgin, or dance like one either. I kind of figured, but I was checking. Your bucket list said it's been a long time. I didn't know if that meant never, ever or a few months. No one's ever made you come? Holy shit."

"Oh, my... eh, ah, you like the dancing, huh?"

"Are you trying to ignore the question?"

My heart beats double time.

"Okay, baby. I *love* the dancing. But just *your* dancing. You had me hard just watching you."

I slide my hand from his neck to touch his cheek, taking my time to reply. "Hunter King, you are so gorgeous. What the hell do you see in me? Little Eden Wallace making you hard. I don't get it." I shake my head in bafflement.

"Do you really want to know what I see in you, Little Eden Wallace from Castleview Cove?" he teases as he cups my ass with his shovel-sized hands, pulling me close. Yup, he's still hard.

A sheepish whisper of uncertainty washes over me. I'm not sure I want to know. But I'm a sucker for punishment.

"Yes, I do."

He stalls until he finally says, "A new beginning."

I was *not* expecting that.

Then he groans. "Christ, that sounds sad as fuck. Am I scaring you? Please tell me I'm not. I can't explain it, but I feel like I was meant to find you in that field. That I was meant to book in at your parents' retreat. I just feel... like we are meant to be." He raises his eyes to the ceiling as if to hide his confession.

My eyes glaze with emotion.

Is he for real?

"I think yer bum's oot the windae, but you're not scaring me," I say when his eyes return to mine.

His grin turns into a full-blown victory smile.

"What did that first bit mean? Bum's what?"

"It means you're talking rubbish or complete nonsense."

"Silly Scots. I love your accent. It's like catnip for my cock."

I can't help but giggle.

"You are something else, Hunter King. There's so much pressure on me now."

"Mmmmm, talking of pressure. Would you like me to fix *yours*? I want to hear you scream my name, baby. I'll fuck you so good you won't remember yours. I've thought about nothing else since I met you," he whispers in my ear, scattering tingles everywhere.

Holy hell balls.

No one's ever spoken like this to me before. He's so direct. He knows what he wants. Me.

"You can tick that off your bucket list... Come home with me. I promise you though, it won't be a one-night stand, and it'll be an all-night affair over multiple nights."

"I'm not that kind of girl, Mr. King."

A pleased look dazzles his irresistible face. "Yet... I'll show you what it's like to come so hard we'll break the fucking pressure gauge."

Oh, yes, that please.

"And what douchebag has never made you come? I promise that will never happen on my watch. What an unthoughtful, self-centered asshole," he fumes.

My eyes drop at the very thought of Hunter's words. He's not wrong. What a selfish man Jamie was. I'm slowly waking up to his past behavior and how he treated me. I actually thought it was me. Sorry. I'll say that again. Jamie told me it *was* me. There was something wrong with me, *mechanically* is how he put it. Our sex life was always very one-sided, and it was all in his favor. I got used to it and it became normal. He said there was something wrong with me so many times, I believed it. Being high school sweethearts, we were each other's firsts. Jamie was, is, my first and only. How pathetic. Here I am at twenty-seven with hardly any sexual experience. Crikey, a kiss almost got me off. Right here on the dance floor.

"Hey, where did you go? You alright?" Hunter asks with concern.

I glance up, his question lingering in his eyes.

I look him straight in the eyes. "Yeah. I'm great."

He smiles, leans in, and kisses me with a newfound closeness we've just formed.

"Is that a yes to going home with me?"

Am I really doing this? "Yeah. I need to grab my bag and jacket though."

His face lights up. "I'll look after you, baby. Real good. I may not have one of those ladders like they do in *Bridgerton* though, but we can do lots of other dirty things together."

I'm utterly speechless.

Hunter laces our hands together as we drift out of our little bubble. We weave through the crowded flashing dance floor as a loud sound of whooping and cheering startles us from above. It's then we notice our friends lined along the balcony watching us, cheering us on. Ella is wolf whistling and Beth has her hands in the air, cheering.

"Jeez, how embarrassing." I snuggle myself into Hunter's chest, shying away from all the attention.

"Idiots." He chuckles.

Once up the stairs with our friends, Hunter introduces me to his team and his sister Pippa, who's adorable in every way.

"Oh, this night just got better," Toni says, fanning her fingers in a wave as she's introduced to Evan, Hunter's fitness trainer. He's exactly Toni's type. Big, buff, blond, and blue eyes—he's all the Bs.

I watch as our cocktail of friends gel together with seamless ease. A dreamy smile curves my lips as I observe

Ella and Luke who are sitting, playing text message ping pong together. They are kidding no one.

Hunter and I reluctantly agree to stay longer, even though Hunter can't keep his hands off me. He keeps growling into my neck, sharing his thoughts of how sexy he thinks I am and how he can't wait to go back to his cabin.

I'm not used to being this close to someone, certainly not in a sexual way. Jamie barely touched me when we were out with our friends. Hunter's the complete opposite. Very tender and loving toward me, and he doesn't seem to care about his public displays of affection. Sexual confidence bounces off him.

I actually can't wait to go home. I'm getting wetter by the minute just imagining him and me together. If it's anything like how he touched me on the dance floor, then I'm in for a helluva night, I reckon. Miss Minnie has woken up, that's for sure. But not just for any man, nope, just Hunter. He's like the spark and I'm the flame, sparking something more than just attraction. He's right about the connection we have; my whole body burns at the memory of his touch. We connect, we fit together, there's no explanation for it.

As I watch the dance floor below from the balcony, Hunter returns from the bar, appearing behind me. He pulls my back to his front, gathers my hair into a fake ponytail, wraps his hands around it and arches my neck, trailing openmouthed kisses to the side of my jaw and behind my ear. "Let's go home," he whispers, sending a wave of tingles through me.

Holy shit, he is wild.

I want to go home *now,* but I'm also *really* nervous. It's been a *very* long time since I've been with a man. Will I remember what to do? How will I please Hunter? He's been with all those exotic-looking women.

I shake my head, ridding myself of my thoughts.

He said you're his future, Eden. Focus on that.

Okay, sex-starved vagina. Let's get you out of hibernation. It's now or never.

"Hunter and I are going," I turn around and state confidently to everyone.

It's just like riding a bike, isn't it? You never forget.

"You guys heading home too?"

Everyone looks at us with great amusement. They know why we want to go.

A resounding yes is expressed across our little circle as we gather up our belongings and start heading out to grab a taxi.

"Where's Beth gone?" I ask.

"She's with Billy." Toni points down to the dance floor where we watch them for a moment. I've got to admit it. They look good together. Beth has a friends with benefits arrangement with Billy the Gardner. He's hot, yeah, but really? I don't want to know where the hell his hands have been all day. Although Beth and Billy has a nice ring to it. Hmmm...

"I'm too old and tired for late nights. God, Archie and Hamish will be up at the crack of dawn tomorrow." Eva groans. "I want to sleep in tomorrow. Not have a hangover. Have lazy sex with Ewan. A hot bath in peace. Aw, man, I so want that."

The group goes silent.

Eva looks around.

"Aw, shit, did I say that out loud?"

We all descend the stairs with laughter.

"You and your sisters really are very alike," Hunter says laughing, taking his hand in mine.

"I'm just going to head to the restroom before we leave."

I turn as we get to the bottom of the VIP stairs. "I'll be there in two minutes," I hold two fingers up to Hunter and mouth two minutes, smiling.

He pulls me in, grabs my backside, and thrusts his hips into mine. "Hurry up, Eden, you're torturing me. Be a good girl and make it one."

"Okay." I place a chaste kiss to his lips, then turn to walk down the corridor to the restrooms.

"I'll come with you." Ella grins at me, then follows at my heels.

CHAPTER TWELVE

Greetin': *noun,* weep, cry, lament; complain; grumble.
Pronounced: Greet-ing.

Haverin': *verb,* to talk nonsense or foolishly, babble,.
Pronounced: Hay-verr-ing.

Eden

"Holy shit, you and Hunter." Ella rolls her eyes, fanning herself. "You guys are ice-hot together. That kiss was off the charts."

I can't help but swoon as we stumble down the corridor.

"Argh, he's so dreamy. And hot. He's so sexy," I say in a daze.

Ella burst out with abandonment, "Pink Puddle will be getting it tonight." We cackle like a pair of witches. I daren't share my concerns with Ella about my lack of sexual experience. I love Ella but she can be quite flippant, and I have what feels like a thousand butterflies fluttering in my tummy. I throw open the bathroom door, deep in thought, and we quickly find a stall each.

As I'm sitting doing my business, I play back Hunter's confessions to me tonight; it's sensory overload for my soul and it triggers a face-aching grin to my face.

I hear a couple of voices enter the bathroom. "Christ, did you see her? She has no shame."

"She's clearly not waiting for Jamie to come home anymore; that's as clear as day. It's about time. She's been brooding over Jamie for way too long."

I still. I think Ella's heard them too because I can't hear her shuffling about either now.

"Was that Hunter King she was with? How did she get him? He's fucking hot. According to Jamie, Eden was a wet fish or a sack of potatoes, as he put it, in the bedroom. She'll never satisfy a man like Hunter King."

All good feelings gone. *Poof.*

Confirming all my self-doubts and deepest feelings. Hunter will definitely never want to be with me if I'm crap in the bedroom department.

I cover my mouth to silence my shock of what I'm hearing. Anger bubbles in my gut and I start to feel sick.

"Yeah, well, it's just as well you satisfied Jamie, Fiona."

They both burst out laughing.

Am I hearing this correctly? Fiona *fucking* Evans? And Jamie? My Jamie? When we were together? Cheating bastard.

Tears threaten my eyes and quickly become unfocused.

"Yeah, we had many happy years of shagging behind Eden's back. I never understood why he never just left her if he was *that* bored."

"But he left Fiona. He left you too, remember."

"Shut up, Kim, you stupid bitch."

"Sorry, I didn't mean it like that."

Screw this. I make my presence known. Ella senses what I'm doing and we both flush, unlock the latch, and come out from the stalls.

Fiona's face pales as she locks eyes with us both in the mirror's reflection. She whips around; my angry gaze slices her face.

I brave out a sneer. "Fiona *fucking* Evans."

"Shit, I'm so sorry, Eden; you were never meant to know. I, eh, oh, God, I'm..." She stammers.

"Really? Are you really sorry? Because from what I just heard, you were relishing and laughing at the fact you were cheating with Jamie behind my back. For years apparently," I explode. "How long? Tell me now."

"Eh, four years."

"Four years." My voice bellows across the bathroom.

"I lost my baby girl when he left." I stab my chest with my finger. "Was that not punishment enough?" I stalk toward her. "And now, I find out about you. You're a bitch."

Fiona's chest rises and falls with rapid breaths as I march closer.

Inches from her face, I drop my hands to my sides and clench my fists. She scrunches her face up, eyes closed, leaning away from me over the basin unit.

"Please don't hit me." She holds up her hands.

I scoff, breathing deeply. "I wouldn't waste my time. You're not worth it. You and Jamie deserve each other... Please don't look my way ever again. Christ, Fiona, we went to school together. We grew up together. Four years? Behind my back?" I snap as streams of tears run down my face.

"And just so you know I'm not crying because I'm upset about Jamie. I don't love him anymore. I haven't loved him for a very long time. I'm upset because my little girl had a cheating liar for a father who didn't even come back for her funeral. His own daughter."

I wipe the palms of my hands across my cheeks and pull myself together.

I turn to Ella, who's been silent this whole time. She let me have my moment. "Can we go?"

Having my back, she turns to Fiona with a steady voice. "Don't look mine or Eva's way either. I'll remove you from dance aerobics and refund your money, Fiona."

Fiona's shoulders sag as she closes her eyes and lowers her head.

Ella wraps her arm around my shoulders, motioning me carefully out the door, like I'm a fragile package.

"You know what they say, the bigger the hoop, the bigger the ho, Fiona. It looks like you're wearing the biggest hoop earrings in here tonight." Ella seethes.

The door closes behind us. As we enter the empty corridor, I bend down and wail, echoes drown the corridor. My universe moves in slow motion. Ella pulls me into a comforting hug. God, that hurts to hear. 'A wet fish'? *Fucking Ouch.* How humiliating.

The light that's recently shone in my heart slowly dims again.

Pulling away from Ella, I lean against the wall and slide down into a slump, covering my face with my hands.

"What did I ever do to deserve this?"

Ella kneels down in front of me.

"Nothing, Eden. You're an incredible woman with a heart of gold. You thought you were in love and you trusted with every piece of your soul. Jamie's actions were nothing to do with you and everything to do with him.

"You need to open your eyes. Jamie was an asshole. But

you were so wrapped up in him to see it. We all saw it. He treated you like crap. He stayed out with his mates all the time, never took you anywhere. He spoke to you like you were his servant, everything on his terms. When he left, we all sighed with relief because we thought you'd make a fresh new start with you and the baby. And then, well, all that changed. And the funeral? I think his lack of care about you and the baby says it all. You deserve better." She lets out a soft exhale. I think she's wanted to say that for a while. "Now stop greetin', he's not worth it."

"Take me home, Ella. I don't want to see anyone."

Grabbing my hand, she pulls me up to my feet.

"We'll go out the fire escape and down the alleyway at the back. I just need to text everyone to let them know where we are. Give me just one minute, babes. Are you sure you don't want to go back with Hunter? There's more to tonight than just a one-night thing with him, Eden. He really, *really* likes you. Stuff Jamie for still interfering with your life."

"Mmmmmm, I think that ship's sailed. Those two are right. I could never satisfy a man like him. I think it's better to just be alone."

"Stop that now. You're havering. Those two are a pair of bitches." She looks at me. "C'mon, Eden."

Ella drops her phone into her jeans pocket and starts shuffling me down the corridor. We head out the fire door with a loud clank into the fresh nighttime Scottish air. I take a deep breath in.

"Can we go in the back entrance of the retreat, please?" I plead. "I don't want to bump into anyone."

"Now if it was any other time, I would make a joke about your back entrance, but I won't." She arches an eyebrow at me, trying to make me laugh.

It makes me scoff a little.

"I'm sorry. I'm no fun, am I? Shit, what a night. Did you hook up with Luke? I'm so fucking selfish. Sorry, Ella. Here you are with me, and you probably had a sure thing going on tonight."

"It's cool. You're my boo. I have the horses to muck out early, anyway. Plus, I need to clean my house tomorrow. Between working your extra shifts and helping at the riding school, Treacle has barely had two walks these last few weeks. It's just as well he can come with me to the stables. Silly dog scares all the horses though, so Janice might not let me take him anymore. He's a cheeky wee monkey." I listen as Ella talks fondly of her love for her little black French bulldog. He's cute. All big bat ears and droopy mouth. She loves him like a baby and likes to dress him up. He looks ecstatic when she does. Poor bugger.

I keep my horrible train of thoughts away from my recent revelation.

Shall we go back to pushing those feelings down again, Eden?

"What was your vagina's name Ella? We never got to yours."

"Taxi's on its way; c'mon, we'll meet it at the bottom of the road." She loops her arm through mine and we saunter down the lane. I wipe the back of my hand across my nose, then use my fingertips to wipe away my tears. I'm a mess.

"It was Hungry Beaver. Eva's was Pink Fuzz Box."

"Figures," I say with a lifeless laugh.

We stroll down the long lane in silence, huddling together.

Ella's held her thoughts in for such a long time. Turns out she never liked Jamie and neither did my family. This is all news to me. I know they thought he was pond scum, having not shown for Chloe's funeral, but this is a new revelation.

Reading my thoughts, she whispers, "He put you down all the time. He made you believe he's all you deserved and you were worthless. You are *not* worthless. You are funny, kind, caring, gorgeous. You have this weird magnetic aura about you that people become so attracted to. You walk into a room and people know you're there. You are small, but you have this tremendous presence. I don't know what I'm saying, I can't explain it."

She continues. "And you have, like, no idea; you are oblivious to it all. You've had your blinkers on for way too long. Your smile lights us all up. People love you. The dance students adore you. Jamie kept you small because he knew all the other boys at school wanted you. He knew you were different. You deserve everything your heart desires. You deserve a happily ever after. We all do. You cannot let Jamie hold you back any longer. This has to stop. If you don't stop this pining and yearning for what could have been, I may have to punch you in the boobs."

I agree about the happily ever after, but I'm not so sure about the other stuff Ella's just dropped on me. I feel like someone has punched me in the gut at the things Jamie was saying behind my back. I'm so ashamed. Totally betrayed.

People will believe Fiona, so I may as well embrace it. No one will want me now. I still can't believe she, well, Jamie said those things about me. Jamie and Fiona. God, I feel like a complete fool.

Hunter was wrong; I'm no one's future. I'm certainly no one's happy ever after. What was I thinking? Me, worthy of finding love and having a little family I always dreamed of. I couldn't even carry my baby girl. Incompetent cervix? Nah, it's me who's incompetent. In the bedroom, finding love. I've done a pretty good job holding on to my friends, although on some of my darkest days, I thought they'd given up on me too. I wouldn't have blamed them either.

I'm not sure how I will bounce back from this. Here's me thinking I was making significant progress too.

Nope, a happily ever after is not meant for me. I'm destined to be by myself.

A text dings on my phone. I check my on-screen notification.

Hunter: What happened, Cupcake? Are you okay? xo

Then another.

Hunter: Where are you, baby? Let me come get you. oxo

I don't open it and don't reply.

CHAPTER THIRTEEN

Haar: *noun,* a cold wet sea fog. **Pronounced:** Haar - roll the r at the end.

Belter: *noun,* excellent, very good, awesome, we also use this for more sarcastic wit... *"Christ, did ye see her dress? Aye, that was a belter."* Meaning it's bloody awful. **Pronounced:** Bell-turr.

Hunter

Bamboozled by last night's events, I couldn't sleep. Finally, I admitted defeat and jumped out of bed after tossing and turning all night. Walking the four miles from the retreat down to Castleview Pier has cleared my head slightly. The fresh air here is so clean and crisp, I can feel the fog of my sleepless night lifting.

It's just turned five in the morning, but the place is a hive of activity.

Leaning back against the bench I'm sitting on at the end of the long pier, I observe the fishermen in their boats preparing to head out for a day at sea. Water slaps against the boats, gently rocking them from side to side, sometimes bumping the harbor walls.

Quaint colorful houses line the road, set back slightly from the harbor wall.

Crying seagulls fill the sky as the fresh sea salt air fills my lungs. Taking in a deep breath, I feel a sense of peace and tranquility here. I look back to the multicolored homes; I'm a little envious they wake up to this idyllic view every day.

The last time I was here, I didn't take the time to do any exploring. I'm regretting it now. Castleview Cove is so charming; it's like a balm for my soul.

Sweeping beaches stretch for miles on both sides of the harbor, sprinkled with putting greens, play parks, flamboyant wooden food huts, and an outdoor trampoline park.

Mist floods the shoreline to the horizon.

I close my eyes and let the sound of the crashing waves wash over me.

My thoughts drift back to Eden. I don't know what happened last night. She was with me one minute, then gone the next. It all changed at the flick of a switch.

Eva received a text from Ella as we waited for our cab. She never told me what happened, but she looked concerned and instructed us all to get in the taxi. All she told us was Eden and Ella were finding their own way back.

Not wanting to press or push Eva, all I asked of Eva was that she tell me if Eden was safe. She reassured me. I said nothing more after that. Like a magnet, the urge to go to her house last night was pulling me in. A sudden desire to smell and taste her takes over my mind and body. That's why I've left her alone, because I want to reach out and comfort her. I want to wrap my arms around her. But she needs space. What for, I'm not sure, but I want to find out.

I need to check in for my own sanity. I hope someone didn't hurt her last night or say something to her to upset the night, Christ, I don't know; maybe it's not my place to visit her again.

A deep frown creases my brow. I was finally getting Eden to trust me last night. I confessed things I've never confessed with anyone.

A new beginning? What was I thinking coming on strong like that? Did I scare her off? Is that why she disappeared last night? There was no evidence of that before she went to the bathroom. She wanted me. I felt it; she felt it. The intensity between us was, *is*, so strong, like we are in sync with one other. None of it makes sense.

Pushing the tip of my black cap back, I palm my hands into my stinging eyes and let out a yawn, shuffling my cap forward again to cover my eyes. My body craves sleep, but I want to speak to Eden first.

Startled by a burst of laughter floating over from one of the boats, I spot a girl off in the distance passing an enormous bunch of elegant long-stemmed yellow sunflowers to the fisherman. She's laughing and joking with them all. She looks a little out of place in her neon-pink leggings, bright-white sneakers, and white hoodie.

Indicating the boat is about to leave, a sudden growl from the engine bounces around the harbor. I watch the girl wave goodbye to the anglers as they unhook themselves from the dock.

As the boat glides over the water, she walks, mirroring their path along the pier, toward where I'm sitting. Making its way toward the mouth of the harbor, she laughs and jokes with them. As the boat picks up a little more pace, she starts a slow jog.

Getting closer, I realize suddenly it's Eden.

What's she doing here?

She looks tired, but she's wearing a beaming smile as she waves to the crew on the boat. "Bye, guys, come home safe," she calls out to them with her head turned toward the boat, not noticing I'm here.

She takes a couple of minutes to reach the end of the cobbled harbor pier.

Silently she tucks her hands into the pockets of her hoodie as she watches the boat bob across the waves out of sight.

"Hey," I call out from the rocky recess I'm sitting in.

"Jesus Christ." With a loud gasp, she whips around and presses a hand to her chest quickly.

"Oh my God, don't do that, I could have fallen off the pier," she gasps. "Bloody hell, Hunter. What the hell are you doing here? It's like five o'clock in the morning."

"Crap, I'm sorry." I palm my hand in the air in a stop motion. "I didn't mean to startle you. I wasn't thinking. You alright?"

"I will be after my heart stops bouncing; just give me a minute."

Gathering herself, she frowns. "What are you doing down here?"

I watch as she pulls her hood up over her head and slides her hands back into the snug pocket of her hoodie. Slowly she pulls out a small tube of cream.

"I couldn't sleep."

"Me either."

I pat the wooden bench. "Will you sit with me?"

She knits her brows together.

"Please?" I beg. *Pathetic.*

Tentatively she scuffs her heels toward me and sits at the end of the bench, looking out across the shore.

God, I must have done something terrible last night. She couldn't get any further away from me if she tried. I definitely came on too strong. Man, I feel like a dick.

I take my black baseball cap off, place it on the seat, and sweep my hair back off my forehead.

We sit for a few moments listening to the gentle ting of chains as they rattle against the mast of the boats in the wind.

I watch her as she smooths what looks like lip balm over her lush lips.

"Am I reading that right? Does that tube say nipple cream?" I ask, confused.

"Eh, yeah, I use this as it works better than lip salve and your nipple is the same skin as your lips. Did you know your top lip is the same color as your nipple? Well, it is for me. It's one of those top beauty tips, much like the one where they say to use hair conditioner on your pubic hair because it softens it. I suppose it makes sense, not that I have any down there, but if I did, then I think I would use it too. That documentary was right; remember I told you about the deforestation thi..."

"Stop talking, Eden," I interrupt. Around the outskirts of her hood I watch her pale cheeks flush a strawberry pink.

This girl.

Leaning my head back and rolling my eyes to the sky as warmth spreads to my groin. "You can't say shit like that. I have no control over my body when I'm around you. You make me feel things no woman has ever done before. Just stop."

Yip, I'm a sexual deviant 'cause all I can think of is the color of Eden's nipples as I zone in on her top lip and try to envision her bare pussy.

Shoot. Me. Now.

A long silence follows. Okkkaaaaaayyyy then...

"It's really foggy today," I say, trying a different tactic.

"We call it Haar. It's what we call a cold sea fog. It happens when warm air passes over the cold sea. Drives my hair daft and makes it so frizzy."

Eden's shoulders hunch over as she holds her gaze out to sea. I watch as a gentle breeze picks up her hair, stirring the strands around the frame of her hoodie as they stick to her now shiny lips. She's no idea how captivating she is. I capture a mental picture of this moment. She's exquisite.

Gently I ask, "What happened last night, Eden?"

Silence.

"Please talk to me."

"You should forget about me, Hunter."

"That's going to be really difficult after last night. You're all I can think about."

Whipping her head around, she looks at me with glazed eyes. "Believe me, you do not want this." Pulling her hands out of her pockets, she motions to her tiny body. "I'm a mess." Then she rubs the back of her hand across her cheek as a small tear trickles down her rosy cheek.

"What's going on, Eden? Did I do something wrong?"

"This is going to sound so cliché. It's not you, it's me."

Yup, I've blown it.

"Tell me why it's you. Tell me what happened or what's wrong. I want to help you."

The sound of the wind quietly swirling between us is the only thing I hear. Eden has built her wall so high, it's impenetrable.

I hold my hands up. "Okay, I'll go. If *I* did *do* something, I'm really sorry, Eden."

Shuffling myself to the end of the seat, I smooth my hands down my jeans and slowly stand up. Just as I take my first step...

"It was four years ago," she faintly mumbles. "My boyfriend Jamie was a fisherman; he owned his own boat. One night he and his three-man crew came face-to-face with a storm so violent it sunk his ship. Ross, Thomas, and Nick never came home. Lost at sea."

Carefully, I gently perch myself back on the bench, trying not to disturb her story she's now ready to share with me.

Her eyes distant with memories, she says, "It was awful. I'll never forget the faces of the families that night. But Jamie. He lived. They found him floating on a buoy. What are the chances of that? I was so ecstatic. But I felt so guilty for being happy. I had my Jamie back, but those poor families lost their boys. The boat crews scatter sunflowers for them out at sea. Sunflowers are a sign of hope. Hope they may eventually come home. It's too long now. The service we held for them all. We had no bodies to grieve with. It was truly harrowing. This bench you're sitting on." She rubs the seat with her small hand. "This is their memorial bench."

I turn to read the plaque Eden's now pointing to with the names of the three men engraved into it.

"Our lives changed that night. Jamie gave up on everything. He had post-traumatic stress disorder, but he never admitted it and he refused to get help. The word lucky was banded about like confetti. *'Jamie is so lucky to be alive; you are so lucky to have Jamie back Eden.'* But we weren't lucky; we were bloody doomed after that night. I think we were doomed long before that, knowing what I know now."

This is the most she's ever said to me. Not wanting her to stop, I let her continue.

"Jamie boxed himself up. He stopped talking to everyone. He wouldn't listen to me or his family. He hated being surrounded by the families of Ross, Thomas, and Nick. He said he couldn't stand the look when they saw his face. The longing to have their own sons back and looks of unintentional loathing because they wished it was their son back home and not him."

Silent tears one after another slide down Eden's face.

"I'm so sorry, Eden," I whisper.

She continues. "About twelve weeks later, I'd just finished a dance lesson when I received a text from Jamie. Just a one-line text telling me he'd left town. I knew he couldn't stand being here in Castleview Cove anymore. And just like that, he left. No forwarding address. Just gone.

"The worst part is..." She takes a deep breath. "I was six months pregnant when he left. I discovered I was three months pregnant a few days after the accident. Jamie wasn't interested. He was too traumatized by the loss of his friends. Just like that he left me, left us. Then two days after he left I lost our baby too. He didn't even come back for her funeral. He just washed us down the drain like we meant nothing."

"Is that who Chloe is, Eden? The plaque at the tree inside the retreat?"

She bobs her head slightly, confirming it is.

"Heartache from both losses was life-changing. I lost myself at twenty-three. Like someone just blew out the light. Losing Chloe was painful. It was medical. I didn't lose her because of him leaving or stress or anything, although I'm not sure that helped. I now know that I have a medical reason that will affect me if I ever chose to have a baby again. I'm not sure I want to take any risks, to be honest.

"Grief for someone who dies is worlds apart from losing someone who decides to leave or you don't know where they've gone. Chloe was, is, gone, and I didn't control that. But Jamie, well, he was still around, somewhere. Worry tormented me about his well-being, thinking about what he was doing, who he was with, and did he get help? I let *it*, let *him*, consume me. He didn't care about me, but I never stopped caring about him. I don't even know why now."

She graciously pulls back her hood and slides herself sideways; facing me, she curls her leg on top of the seat.

Swiveling slowly, I turn too.

Eventually she lifts her head and my heart cracks open as her icy red-rimmed and bloodshot eyes meet mine. She's so broken. *My poor girl.* Never one to be stuck for something to say, my words suddenly dry up like dust.

"I think you'll know Jamie's brother, Fraser Farmer?" I don't know where this is going, but I raise my eyebrows in agreement. I do know him; he's a pro golfer, like me.

"He left Castleview Cove a long time ago to pursue his career. I haven't seen him since the funeral. Even he came. Jamie's parents have never said if they know where Jamie is. I'm assuming they do. I stopped asking. I'm glad I did because I feel like such a mug after last night."

"Small world. Yeah, I know Fraser. He's a top guy. I didn't know he was from here."

Eden shudders suddenly as she sobs. "He's the nice brother. I got the shithead one." I reach out, straddle the bench, pull her in close, and let her weep into my shoulder.

I place a soft kiss on the top of her head. "You're so strong, you know that, Eden, but you don't have to keep this all to yourself." I soothe her, rocking her back and forth, holding her tightly. "Hey, hey, let it all out, I've got you, baby. You're okay," I coo.

As her sobs subside, she backs up and wipes her face, rubbing the fabric of her hoodie down her puffy, swollen cheeks.

"I don't feel okay. I feel bloody awful. I hate Jamie for making me feel like this." She bites out a snarl laced with venom.

"Last night, well, you made me feel so special. For the first time in a very long time I felt happy, actually happy. I think I'd forgotten what that felt like, but then... flipping heck, I feel so stupid."

My heart does a little jump. I made her feel happy. I need to know what changed. "What happened last night? Crap, was Jamie there last night?" I gasp at that thought suddenly.

"Hell no, he'll never come back. It may be just as well as I might punch him in the dick. I'm such a fool. I've been wasting all these years of my life waiting for him to come back. It's taken me all this time to realize what a self-centered prick he really is.

"No, last night... I don't think I can even bring myself to say it. It makes me feel sick." Turning around, she tucks her head between her knees. I slowly rub her back as I hear her breathing in and out.

"I found out he was cheating on me," she mumbles between her legs.

"What a dick."

"You think? He's the biggest asshole ever," she says, pinging upward suddenly, as if it's just dawned on her.

"I've frittered away all these years, pathetically waiting." She flings her arms around in the air. "Then last night Fiona Evans informs me in the restroom that she was fucking

Jamie behind my back. Not just once, but for years." Her voice echoes around the bowl of the harbor. "It was an accident how I found out; she would never tell me.

"And the things Jamie said about me, are so hurtful. He was talking about *me* to *her*. I got a front-row seat about the shit they spoke about me behind my back while they were playing tonsil tennis together. It hurts so bad." She clutches her chest. "On top of that, Ella informed me last night that my family didn't like him either, like not at all." She draws a firm straight line in the air with her hand.

"So no, Hunter, you did nothing wrong. Last night was my wake-up call." She circles to face me again. "You talked to me about fate and meeting me. I'm not so sure about us. But it was fate last night, me being in the bathroom. I've been miserable over him for years when I should have been living my life. I'm actually relieved... And I can't believe I'm going to say this... But I'm relieved my baby girl didn't end up with a lying, cheating scumbag of a man for a father. I would never have wanted that for her or for me."

"Don't ever feel guilty for saying how you feel. I'm not trying to take anything away from you here, but Jess, my ex-girlfriend, she cheated on me. I know what that feels like. At first I was devastated and my self-confidence took a hit. I rolled through the emotional roller coaster from fear, betrayal, and disbelief to confusion, anger, then relief. It's the ultimate betrayal. But use this to empower yourself. His behavior is not a reflection of anything you did or said. What he did was despicable, and you deserve better. The cheating part aside, to me, it feels like you've been bottling all your emotions up for so long, it's consuming you."

"My bucket list? Did you see it mentioned attending therapy sessions on it?"

I angle my chin up.

"Well, I've been going. I'm not crazy, I just find it hard to talk things through. I was feeling great. I've opened up more. I've learned that my past *is* shaping and *has* shaped me. Last night was the first night I've been out in months, almost a year. And then that bombshell. Well, that was a belter," she spits.

I don't stop her to ask what a *belter* means.

"I'm damaged, Hunter. My grief is ugly." She looks me dead in the eyes, her graceful face now blotched from crying. She's my everything; I know she is. I feel it everywhere, deep down in my soul. I want to scoop her up and hold her until she doesn't feel this hurt anymore. I want to take it all away.

"You may think you want me, but you don't want all the heavy baggage that comes with me."

I really do, I want every part of you. I want to unpack it all.

She continues. "I was thinking about you as I lay in bed in the early hours of the morning."

Oh, my heart skips with hope.

"You're a wonderful man. You're kind, funny, affectionate, and passionate about your profession, and I like everything about you. I am attracted to you, so much. Please believe me when I say this because it's very rare I open up to anyone like I have to you today. I've never felt attraction to anyone, like I do to you. Not even..." She trails off.

She was going to say Jamie. She straightens herself as if preparing for her next words.

"Look at you. You are gorgeous and smart, and you wanting me the way you do, I am deeply flattered. Last night you made me feel wonderful. Your touch and your tenderness were everything I didn't know I needed. Your touch meant something to me. Without doubt, I know you would take care of me in ways I can only imagine, but I need more."

My heart flutters subside. Shit.

"As soon as The Cup is over, you'll leave, and I can't risk getting hurt any more than I already am."

"Please don't say that, Eden." I told her things last night that I have never said to anyone else. Like, ever. I barely know her, but it feels like my soul knows hers deeply. I feel this profound bond with her. There's no explaining how much I already care for her, and I *do* want to take care of her in every way. "Fuck." I drag my hands through my hair and clasp the back of my neck, expecting the next line to cut me like a knife.

"I don't think we should take things any further."

And there it is.

"I can see myself falling for you, Hunter but I don't think I will survive when you leave. I think you would break my heart. I can't let that happen. I read so many romance novels filled with happy endings. Believe me, in real life, my life, it doesn't have a happy ending. I thought Jamie loved me, but he left me, so he never really did. I lost my baby. That broke my heart. Now I meet you and you live thousands of miles away. You have this fabulous life traveling all over the world. But I live here. Let's be real here, Hunter. We're better off being friends, and I know you're on my bucket list, but I can't. I'm really sorry."

"Fuck the list, Eden. I couldn't give a shit about that. Me wanting you has never been about your bucket list. You seriously believe you don't deserve to have a happily ever after? My father died when I was twelve. My mum and dad were besotted with one another, a bit like your parents are. My mum found love again, and she's so head over heels in love with my stepdad."

She shakes her head. "I think for my sanity, I need to focus on myself for a bit and figure out what I want. I waited so long for Jamie; I've lost focus of who I am."

"So you don't believe in a second chance at love?"

She's protecting her heart. Everything she's said, she's right.

"The ironic part of this whole thing is I don't even think I was in love with Jamie. I've been pining over someone I grew up with and cared about but was not *in* love with. He was my high school boyfriend. We were a habit just going through the motions. We were bloody boring together. Hindsight's a wonderful thing, huh? I don't actually think he cared about me. Well, finding out about Fiona last night confirms that. He never took care of me or proudly went out with me to dinner or took me on days out. It was always about him—friends, football, vacations with his mates. Last night when Ella informed me that none of my family liked him either, I realized now I was too blind to see it and I've decided I'm not getting wrapped up in someone else again. I need to be selfish."

Tucking her hands back into her hoodie, she lifts her little body off the bench. "I should go. I'm tired. I'm so sorry, Hunter. Maybe in another life?" She shrugs her delicate shoulders full of sadness and defeat and blows out a sigh. "See you around."

Frozen to the bench, I watch as my forever girl slips out of my life.

She dissipates like the morning haar at the rising of the sun.

And I just let her go.

CHAPTER FOURTEEN

Fricht: *noun,* a fright; *Verb,* to frighten; to scare. **Pronounced:** Fri-kh-t (the kh is more of a throaty, back of throat sound. Imagine having a fish bone stuck in your throat, say it fast, yup, nailed it.)

Scotch Broth: *noun,* traditional thick soup made from lamb bones, vegetables, dried pulses, and barley. **Pronounced:** Braw-th.

Hunter

Before getting out of the black Range Rover we've rented for our time here in Scotland, I pull the cable out of my iPhone, disconnecting it from the car. My phone auto opens. Thank you, Apple, for face recognition; it saves me so much time. I tap open the Notes app and list yet another flavor I tried tonight at Castle Cones. Get Fudged, essentially fudge ice cream with cubes of fudge pieces. My favorite so far.

I'm on flavor thirty-five and it's week five of being here. I still have so many to tick off the list. Toni laughed at me tonight when I started moaning. She's added another two new flavors to the menu, for heaven's sake. I now have forty-seven flavors left to try. She's changed the goal posts for me now. I was not happy.

Yeah, whatever, who am I kidding? I don't care. I'm getting to eat ice cream every day. I'm a man on a mission; competing and winning is in my blood. I will do this.

I think I should set up an ice cream tasting blog after this. First blog would be about the worst flavor I've tried—grapefruit and peppercorn. Bleurgh. You can keep that one. I didn't even eat the whole thing; I hope that still counts. Fuck, it does. Who's checking? Not Eden, anyway. She made her feelings very clear to me last week on the pier.

I've been going over and over our night in the club. It's been driving me crazy thinking about her curves, her smile, the way she giggles, the way she makes me feel—she's breathtaking.

When I was in Castle Cones, I had to bite my tongue not to ask Toni where Eden is. She hasn't been around the retreat, teaching dance classes or in her house for the last week. *Stalker.* I wonder if she's taken some time off to get away and clear her head.

We have spoken not a word between us since she poured her heart out to me on the pier.

I'm craving to see her. To find out how she is. She's so fragile—one slip and she may shatter. Every part of me wants to wrap her in a protective blanket and keep her safe from anyone hurting her ever again.

Listening to the pain she's been through sliced me to my core. It's no wonder she's been so guarded toward the world.

Much like her sunflowers she lays, she was vibrant and bright one minute and wilting the next.

Jamie's a dick. She is right about that. She was right about everything. Me not living here, long distance and leaving Scotland soon, and tournaments. It's all part of my job, which I love, but could I really move here? It doesn't matter where I am in the world because I travel so much anyway. All I need is a base.

That's a lie. I want more than a base; I want a home, with a family and someone to spend the rest of my life with who wants the same. A home filled with love, safety, and happiness. Now I sound like something out of a Disney movie. Luke was right; I am getting sappy in my old age.

I have to admit it; I feel something for Eden I never thought I would ever feel. That instant connection only happens in movies, doesn't it? Eden says the same about happily ever afters too. Just movies. But I feel it. I believe it does.

With every word she spoke on the pier, it cut deeper and deeper. The honesty from her, the trust she had in me to share her story and her emotions she displayed, were raw and real.

I've replayed her words over and over the past few days. She wants me to back off and leave her alone. Friends, she said. I've never been friend zoned. That's a first.

The temptation to pick up my phone and drop a simple, 'Hey, how you doing?' text, without sounding like Joey from *Friends* or that I didn't respect her wishes to be exactly that, friends, was ridiculous. I wrote a text, deleted it, and then did this repeatedly at least ten times. I almost, *almost*, sent one of those texts last night. I'm flipping out, not knowing where she is.

Not wanting to come across like a lovestruck fool, I've

held off asking her sisters and Luke; they'll just poke fun at me if I do. So I've kept my mouth firmly shut.

Jumping out of the Range Rover, I step onto the gravel drive, leaving the door open to get a good look inside the interior. I actually love this car. I walk around, admiring it. It's way too big for these narrow roads here in Castleview Cove. I've had to be so careful on the country and beachside roads, not to damage the alloy wheels or drive into the ditch.

Several times I've needed to remind myself that I am on the other side of the road driving here in Scotland too; it messes with my head. I'm more accustomed to big open freeways and wide-ass roads with lots of space and on the correct side of the road.

As I brush my hand along the contours of the car, I think one of these would work so well back home. First thing I'm going to do is visit the car dealership when I get back home.

Low thumping bassy beats bring me out of my thoughts suddenly as they start up from the direction of the dance studio. I slam the sturdy door closed with a *thunk* and before I know what I'm doing, I'm across the drive, around the other side of the mansion house, and keying the gate code on the security pad that leads to Eden's house and studio.

Closing the gate behind me, I carefully prowl through the trees along the edge of the wall and slink in behind a tree, giving me a perfect view inside the studio. A wall of glass runs the entire length of the studio. Combined with the interior studio lighting and the dusk settling over the retreat, the studio glows like a giant light box through the trees.

She's here. My pulse races.

With her back to me, I watch as Eden fumbles about with the sound system.

The door of the studio is slightly ajar; she must have left

it open as it's warmer tonight. Well, we're in Scotland; it's warmer than normal by only a few degrees. Still Baltic, as the Scots like to say. See, get me picking up the lingo. Give me a high five.

Her beautiful curves, I'm now obsessed with, are encased in figure-hugging high-waisted nude cycle shorts and a long-sleeved matching crop top with chunky white trainers giving her a little extra height. She's giving Kim Kardashian a run for her money. Hashtag: curves for days. She's perfect. Looking naked in that color though, it does nothing to tame my cock. *Down, boy.*

Craving to see her this week, just wanting to be near her, I may have gone a little overboard watching all the studio's TikTok and Instagram videos, trying to catch even so much as a glimpse of Eden's angelic face. But there was nothing from Eden this week, just Ella and Eva.

Sneaking through the trees, I lean against one in wonder, just watching. I'm perving like some sort of voyeur. All I need now is a pair of binoculars and a taser. Wait, no, that's kidnapping. Nope, just a stalker over here.

Tinkling beats of a piano fire through the sound system. I'd recognize that song anywhere, "Dance Monkey" by Tones and I.

With purpose, Eden moves away from the sound system and starts moving in time to the thrumming beats. I'm enthralled by how she can instantly be in the moment with just her and the music.

Elegant and hypnotic, Eden checks her moves in the vast expanse of wall-to-wall mirror, sometimes softly closing her eyes as she slides, kicks, and hops across the room.

Coming to a standstill halfway through the song, she places her hands on her hips, lowering her head to her chest to steady her breathing. Dropping herself to the floor, she flattens herself against the black ocean of floor, her chest bouncing up and down.

Music still pumping, I've no idea how I got here, but I'm suddenly through the studio door, quietly moving toward Eden. Like a moth to a flame, I know I'm going to get burned, but I can't stay away.

Between the loud beats of the music and her heavy puffing and panting, she hasn't heard me softly lie down next to her.

I tentatively reach out and faintly draw a light touch along the outside of her hand with my pointer finger. I'm seriously overstepping the line here. All my common sense gets thrown out the window when I'm around her.

All at once she lets out a shriek, snaps her hand up to clasp it with the other, twisting her head as her eyes fly open, and she lets out another shriek, wide-eyed at the unexpected sight of me lying beside her.

"What the hell, Hunter," she yells. "I thought it was a spider. Holy shit. That's two times you've given me a fricht in the last week. What is wrong with you? I need to change the security code on my gate." She lightly smacks me on my arm.

"Ha, your face. You're just too easy to spook. Your music is so loud, I heard it way over from my cabin. No wonder you didn't hear me," I say over the music.

"Oh crap, my mum will go crazy. Alexa, switch off studio."

Silence. We both lie still, staring at the ceiling.

"I'm guessing fricht means to frighten?"

"Uh-huh."

"I watched you dancing."

"Uh-huh."

"I could watch you dance all day."

"Uh-huh."

"Are you not talking to me?"

She's thinking.

"Eh, no, I am. I'm just, eh, well, you make me nervous, and when I'm nervous, I say stupid shit. Well, you'll know this from all the garbled crap that flies out of my mouth when I'm around you. So, yeah, you, um, make me nervous. And I shared a lot of personal stuff with you the last time I saw you." She puffs out her lips and cheeks, expelling a long noisy breath through her lips.

I'm not sure if this is a good or a bad thing.

I turn my head sideways. "You don't need to be nervous around me."

Slowly, she turns her face to mine.

I roll my eyes. "We're *friends* now, remember?"

Eden lets out a stream of giggles. I haven't seen her in a few days. I miss this perfect face.

"It was the bravest and most honest words I've ever heard leave anyone's lips."

I want to kiss those soft pink lips now.

"Where have you been this week?"

With a mischievous smile, she replies, "Ah, you noticed I wasn't here? Were you worried about me, you know, with us being *friends* and all now?"

Her eyes hold mine. She looks sublime with her super long caramel hair fanned out across the floor, her eyes dancing between blue and green.

Gently she rolls over to her side, slides her arm straight out on the floor, palm down, and rests her head on top of her little bicep, then tucks her other clenched fist under her chin into her neck. My eyes roam the length of her perfect hourglass body. Ample breasts, toned stomach, well-defined tiny waist, and shapely hips. She's so sexy, she should be fucking illegal.

I mirror her position; inches apart, we lie face-to-face.

"Late on Sunday, I received a call from the pole-dancing course coordinator. Someone canceled at the last minute. So I took their place. I've been in Edinburgh for the past few days. I'm now a fully-fledged pole-dancing aerobics instructor. It was nice to get away. Like Scotch Broth for the soul."

"Did you have fun? I would love to go to Edinborough."

"It's not pronounced like that." She titters. "Your American accent is butchering our epic Scottish dialect again. Repeat after me, say Edin. Like Eden but with an *i*."

"Edin."

"Bra. Say if fast and soft."

"Edinbra."

"Excellent. You learn fast, Mr. King."

She's so cute; there's no other word for her.

"To answer your question, yeah, I had fun. I think it's what I needed. Away from Castleview Cove. Learning a new skill. I met some lovely girls who own their own dance studios and fitness businesses. Turns out none of us are as fit as we thought we were. Pole dancing is not for the faint of heart. I'm sore today." She groans. "We're getting poles fitted over where the lockers are next week because no one uses them, anyway. Although I'm not sure how my body will cope with too many pole-dancing classes. The instructors this week were insanely fit. I may need to limit classes to two a week. Pole dancing is brutal on your body. I'm sore today."

Imagining Eden dancing around a pole, I'm a heartbeat away from exploding. Think of something else...

"I'm guessing since you've been gone, you didn't see us in the local paper then?"

Her chiseled cheekbones flush with color. "Of course I did. The girls sent a picture of the article to our WhatsApp group. Bitches. We were in one of the gossip mags too; I bet *you* never saw that. They sent that to me too. We were in a few of the nationals. Brilliant," she says, evading my eyes.

"Are you kidding? I saw them all. We look fuck-hot together in those pictures. God knows who took them in the nightclub. Rats are everywhere. My personal favorite is the one when you're smiling up at me. Did you like it? Or did you prefer the one of us kissing? Or I am guessing you preferred the one with you dancing and your face looks like you're having an orgasm, with the headline 'Hunter's new girl looks O so fine'?" I tease.

"Just stop now," she yells and pokes me in the chest. "You really are a scallywag."

"I know, you love it."

Dropping her hand to mine, she rubs her soft thumb across my knuckles. It's the first time she's touched me unprompted. I stay still and let her strum my skin, as the thrill thrums through my veins at her soft touch.

"Does that kind of thing bother you? I have never been in the paper before. It kind of freaked me out."

I contemplate for a minute. "It used to bother me. But it pushes my brand out. Some articles are accurate and some are so far off the truth, I don't know where they get their ideas from. The sports pages are great for me, the gossip ones, not so much. Are you okay with the paper stuff? That was never supposed to happen. I'm actually quite a private guy. I would never want you to feel unsafe or feel like your privacy was breached. I know you're not my girl, like the headline said, but if I fight it, they will just come back with more stupid shit. I'm so sorry if they overstepped the mark with their assumptions and your privacy."

"I'm fine. I know I'm not *your* girl. We're *friends* though, so I'm cool."

I so *want* you to be my girl.

"It was a shock at first. I read some of the blog comments. They all want my toned abs," she says, her eyes glinting.

"We looked great together in the images, don't you think?"

"The height difference is a little comical."

"Don't lie, we look incredible together," I tell her off. "You look hot in that photo of you dancing."

I want to bottle this moment and I don't want to move from here even though I've got pins and needles in my hand.

"Tell me what you love about dancing."

"Everything. I love dance, but combine it with music, I find it hard to explain... I love moving my body to the lyrics. Movement with emotion. There is nothing better in this world. Every song is so different. I listen to the change of tone, a key change, the emotion behind the words, the meaning behind each word, and it literally fills me with a deep urge to move my body. Moving in harmony with each beat of the music. It consumes me. Dance is my everything, my passion, my love, my life. I've always loved it. I've wanted to be a dancer since I was tiny."

"Tinier than now?"

"Ha ha. Whatever Mr King. But I think that's what makes me and the girls epic dance teachers because we teach our students how to feel and tune into emotion. It's more than movement. Dream, feel, and lose yourself in the words and the dance."

Her whole face lights up and she becomes so animated when she talks about dance, and her passion oozes from every pore of her being.

"Wow."

"I wish I could sing too. Dancing and singing go hand in hand. You know, like fries and ice cream?"

"What?" I exclaim.

"I'm not kidding you. Try it. It's like a brilliant explosion of sweet and salty in your mouth all at once."

All I can think about is sweet and salty in her mouth and it's not ice cream I'm imagining in her mouth.

"I will take you for chips and ice cream one day. You'll see. It's all about the contrast of the taste, the same with dancing, music, and singing. Light and dark, slow and high tempo, leaning in to the peaks and troughs of love and loss and every emotion in between. It's so romantic, so sexy. It's everything. Can I demonstrate?"

"Eh, yeah." I watch as her fair face disappears, and she shuffles to her feet.

"C'mon, get up." She reaches her hand out and helps to pull me upward.

"Last weekend my sisters and I danced to 'Dirrty' by Christina Aguilera, yeah?"

I listen as she becomes really intense and passionate.

"Sit on the table over beside the music system." She points as she readies herself and I hop on the table.

"That song is fast, pulsating, pow pow." She slams a closed fist into the palm of her other hand. "Pow pow, pow pow. Double beats pace through the whole song. The words are sexual, gritty; instinctively your body wants to grind, stomp, and thrust."

I'm speechless. I can only bob my head as I swallow hard.

"But if I do the same dance routine to a different song. It has a whole new feeling and vibe. Let me demonstrate. You ready?"

Nope.

"Alexa, play 'Good Days' by SZA. Just watch."

I will be. I can't take my eyes off her and she hasn't even started.

As the soft gentle tune of electric harp like strings play through the sound system, Eden moves as the smooth beat drops in.

Paying close attention to the words of the mellow song and the way she swishes her hips in slow, steady movements, it's bewitching. I'm dumbstruck.

"See, same dance routine. You'd never know, right?"

I can tell this song means something to her. This song is Eden's song. She certainly has a shield of armor wrapped around her worries, but she does it all with a smile on her face.

Carving the air with her body, she travels across the floor. In a smooth and fluid motion, she circles her arm around her body, then pops her hand out and summons me to come forward.

There's nothing to conceal the raging hard-on I have if I stand up.

"I can't."

"Yes, you can, get up," she coaxes.

I lean forward, let out a growl, jump to my feet and palm my cock, adjusting my jeans as I move toward her, legs bowed as I palm and walk.

"Oh my God, Hunter." Eden zones in on my enormous bulge.

"I can't help it; you're too fucking sexy. Just stop jiggling about and I'll be fine."

No, I won't.

"You can't say that to a *friend,* and dance *is* sexy. It's supposed to be. Okay, think of your gran and grandad having sex and step closer to me."

"What? Eden. Stop it."

"That will work though, I promise. It'll go away." A hearty laugh leaves her.

I seriously doubt that if I get any closer to her, I may come in my boxers like a fucking frat boy.

"Okay, let's calm down. Now, close your eyes; listen to the melodic beat. You should be good at this with all the hip action you do in swinging a golf club. I'll guide you. Just listen. Swish... swish, pah. Swish... swish, pah. Swish... swish, pah. Roll your hips, dipping your legs slightly, left, right, swoop up, left, right, swoop up. Smoother. That's it. You have good hip action, Mr. King," she jests.

"I sure do."

I feel her hands rest on my hips; automatically mine rest on the curve of her taut waist. "And if I follow your lead, imagine we're making an infinity loop with our hips together. Just gentle movements, soft, and soak in the words of the song." She straddles my right leg, her pussy now rubbing against my thigh.

Oh, fuck me.

The attraction I feel toward this girl is undeniable.

Hip to hip, we loop in motion together. I open my eyes. I need to see her. Legs anchored to mine. I watch as she lifts her hands in the air, lost in the music. Her beautifully formed breasts now on full display. I slide my hand up her back and pull her chest closer to mine. "See, do you feel that?" she asks.

Can I fucking ever. My aching cock is doing a dance of his very own.

"It's like you zone out but home in at the same time.

Allowing your mind to wander but feel the emotions of the music. Isn't it magical?"

"You are magical." I exhale slowly.

Eden's eyes flash upward, meeting mine, then she drops them away quickly. She slows down her movements, almost to a complete standstill, before backing away from me. Standing straight, she walks toward the table over by the wall.

"Alexa, switch off studio."

Shit.

"So, you see what I mean about the music," she says as she pulls herself up to sit on the table, resting her hands under her thighs and tipping her chin to her chest.

"You okay?"

She bobs her head up and down.

My girl is hot and cold. Her talk about the contrast in music, Eden reflects the same emotions, light and dark, pain and pleasure, happy and sad.

Sensing her unease, I carefully move toward her. I take my fingers and cradle her soft face upward. "Hey, I know you're not okay. What's up, baby?"

"I don't want to talk about it." Her troubled blue eyes rivet to mine.

Gentle, Hunter. I carefully position myself at the edge of her knees.

Delicately, I feather my fingertips down one side of her neck, slowly moving them back and forth. Eden relaxes at my touch.

Softly I ask, "That song you were just playing, the words? I know that better days are coming for *you* too. You don't have to hide anymore or doubt yourself or your life choices."

I continue brushing my fingers back and forth across the

soft skin of her neck, behind her ear, and dip them into her hairline.

Eden arcs her neck, ear to shoulder, and lets out a soft moan as she closes her eyes at my touch.

"Your life is yours for the taking now. You're free to be, do, and have anything you want. What do you want, Eden?" I ask in a whisper.

Almost inaudible, she breathes, "I'm scared."

"Of?"

"You." Without thinking she wraps a soft grip around my hand with her petite hand and presses a soft kiss to the inside of my wrist. Her simple touch sparks my excitement; I can't take my eyes off her delectable lips.

She scares me too. She drives me wild, and all I can think about is her and her lips, her divine body, and her screaming my name.

"You make me feel things, Hunter. I've had a lot of time to think this week and I still want you. None of it makes sense, because of who you are and where you live, but all of it scares me."

"I would never intentionally hurt you, Eden. Like ever. I really mean this when I say it; I feel this overwhelming need to move heaven and earth to be with you. I listened to everything you said last weekend. Every word you spoke, about us, it's all true. You living here, me living in Florida and traveling all the time. All true. But I can't stay away from you. You're locked and loaded in my head and I can't shake you out. I'm scared shitless too. I never came looking for you, but I found you," I say, carefully moving closer into the space between her thighs.

"You don't know what you're saying." She curves her neck further as I massage the back of her head.

"I know exactly what I'm saying and I know exactly what

I want. I want you. All of you, the good, the bad, even your sister Ella—she kinda comes as a package deal." Eyes open now. This makes her smirk. I love my girl's smile.

Weaving a path with my fingertips from her head down her neck, across the side curve of her breast, down her waist, I sweep across her curvy ass and graze my fingers along her outer thighs. "I know you feel it too. Now, in this lifetime. Me and you. We are meant to be."

I let my words sink in.

Eden shudders at my touch as I dip my head and lean in.

"Please kiss me," I whisper.

Little by little, she closes the gap and takes me with her soft mouth. In one careful fluid motion I pull her lean thighs up and wrap them around my waist.

My entire world spins with the sudden thrill of touching her again.

Losing herself, without hesitation and unrelenting passion, she clasps her ankles together and wiggles her hips into mine, digging her feet into my ass.

Our mouths devour each other with fast and furious intention.

Cupping her bountiful breast, I firmly pinch her nipple through her barely there top. Arching her back, Eden moans wildly into my mouth. Our tongues play together, like they've been lifelong friends and they've not seen each other for months.

Rubbing my cock against her center to relieve the pressure, Eden balls my tee shirt into her fist and pulls at me as if the world's ending. This isn't anything like our last kiss, this is desperate, dangerous, and fueled by pure desire.

"I want to take you to my bed so bad," I brush out the words against her lips.

Immediately, Eden unhooks her legs, pushes me away,

and leaps off the table, holding her mouth and gasping for air.

Me and my fucking mouth.

"Shit, I'm so sorry, Eden." I need to fix this. "I know how you feel about us; I had no intention of doing that, but I can't stay away. I'm sorry. I am trying to respect your wishes. I'm finding this so difficult. I want to be with you. I keep messing up." I pull my hair with my hands.

"You don't keep messing up. I just... I can't do this. You won't want me. Not if you knew."

"If I knew what?" What am I missing here?

She paces back and forth.

"The things that Jamie said about me. Those things."

Fucking Jamie.

"What did he say? Are these the things Fiona said?"

I watch her thumb her little gold elephant charm on her necklace. I've watched her do this a few times now. She did it the other day on the pier.

"He said... That I was a... just horrible cruel things about me not being able to satisfy him. Nasty words. I can't bring myself to repeat them. I feel embarrassed. If I couldn't satisfy him, then how can I ever satisfy a man like you? I've seen those pictures of you online with all those women. I am not like those other women you've been with. I have, like, no experience at all. I'm practically a virgin. My sex life with Jamie was shit. I know this now, and he never, ever looked after me, ever. And I clearly never looked after him after what Fiona told me last weekend. She could, but *not* me. We had a *very* one-sided relationship in every way. I never had an orgasm with him. Or anyone. He was my one and only. Jamie told me there was something wrong with me sexually so many times I believed him. I can't believe I'm talking to you about this." She rubs her hands deep and roughly into her temples. "Just go, Hunter. Please, just go."

I've had enough of this fucking Jamie guy. What an utter asshole. Imagine saying these things about her. *My Eden*.

"Are you sure you want me to go? Really?"

She shakes her head.

"If that's what you want, then I'll go, but before I go, I want you to listen to me and listen to me good—real good. Please, will you look at me, baby?" She turns to look at me with a combination of embarrassment and anxiety written all over her face.

I pad toward her slowly.

"Never, not once, have I ever given you any reason for you to think those things Jamie's said about you. You turn me on like no one ever has. He is wrong about you."

With a steady, soft voice I continue. "These girls you see online with me, the pictures are all taken at social events and parties. I've only ever had two girlfriends and Jess, my last girlfriend, well, she was a big mistake. I've had several one-night stands; I can't deny that, but they were nothing more than that. You doubting whether you can satisfy me? I'm scared I can't satisfy you. You deserve to be loved; you deserve to be made love to in every way— hard and fast, soft and slow—and you deserve to feel wanted and cared for, because your body speaks to mine, and you are one of the sexiest women I have ever laid my eyes on."

I continue my soft pace across the studio toward her, getting closer now.

"You've got this all mixed up because I don't want to mess this up between us. I'm scared I will fuck it all up. I already feel like I am. I want to look after you, physically and emotionally. I know you're scared; we can be scared together. I want you. You've said you want me too. For me, it's more than just sex, Eden. Way more."

Man, that was hard for me to get out and I feel a little out of breath. I can't blame her for wanting to protect her heart. My broken angel.

I ask, "Do you want me to go?"

"I think so," she whispers.

"Okay. I'll go. I don't want to make you feel uncomfortable, but before I do, I just want to say a couple of things."

I reach out, lovingly clasp her face, and gaze into her wondrous eyes.

"I'm not that shallow to believe anything Jamie has to say. I don't know him, but I know enough about *you* to make up my own mind. You are a remarkable woman, inside and out. Never let anyone, ever, let you feel things or believe things that are simply not true or have been twisted to make you feel less than you are. None of it is true. You need to believe this when I say this. I know you already. My heart knows yours. I want to take all this pain you feel away. If I could, I would."

Eden's eyes glaze and her lips tremble. I strum my thumb across her delicate jaw.

"The stuff Jamie said about you. I know from personal experience, people who talk about others says more about them than it does about you. It screams underconfidence, fear, and complete disrespect. I would never be disrespectful toward you. I would never be unkind to you, and I would never cheat on you, ever. I don't want anyone else. I want you, Eden."

I place a soft kiss on her forehead. "I'm all yours. I'm standing here, right now. Take me."

"I don't think I can, Hunter."

Reluctantly, I step back.

As if in slow motion, I tilt my head and softly release my hand from her jaw for the last time.

I know this is it.

My heavy heart stutters as I turn away from her quiet, delicate face.

Bowing my head with disappointment, I stick my hands in my pockets of my jeans and slouch out the studio door.

What a mindfuck. Jamie, shattering her confidence. Eden's grief and broken beliefs. Me living in Florida. Eden living here.

I'm finally falling for someone who doesn't want me.

We live miles apart.

Our professions dictate distance.

My heart hurts.

I've got to give it to you, Universe, you pulled, as Eden would say, a belter.

CHAPTER FIFTEEN

Foutered: *noun,* one who muddles aimlessly or mucks around. **Pronounced:** Foo-tird.

Eden

I raise my hand to tap the door.

I have no idea what I'm doing here.

It's been hours since Hunter left the studio. I stood in the shower and washed away my self-pity, shame, and confusion, watching it all swirl away down the drain.

I replay Hunter's words repeatedly. He said he wants to be with me in this lifetime. We're meant to be, *now.* Does that mean forever or just a few weeks?

My thoughts have been ping-ponging back and forth since I left the studio. I'm not sure what it all means, when he goes, when The Cup is over, what happens then, I don't know.

He'll be on the next golf competition and halfway around the world. I'll be here waiting around like a fool again. Is it just fun for his short time here, or can we do long distance? Would he want to do that with me?

Good grief, I am driving myself insane.

And then there's the whole sex orgasm bit. Like how can that not be true if it's never happened before with a man, well Jamie? Can I really have an orgasm with a man? With Hunter? Having only ever slept with one man, could I have sex with Hunter and not catch feelings? Sex even? It's been such a long time for me. I was ready to go in all guns blazing that night in the club, but then my confidence really did take a hit. But he said he cared for me, didn't he? Did I understand him correctly?

Christ, I don't know anymore. I'm confusing myself.

What I do know is the look of utter disappointment on his face when he left the studio earlier. Like someone blew out the flame from his burning heart. His beautiful heart.

What did I do?

His delicate touches and the way he holds me with such care, I'm stunned by the intensity I feel at his graceful touch. A gentle giant of a man who instantly lights me up and makes me feel safe. The kindness in his eyes makes my heart bounce with delight every time I'm around him. I'm a little in awe of this perfect man.

Sharing so many of my secrets with him didn't even scare him off. He sought me out again today.

These thoughts tapped in and out of my head as I foutered about the house.

Blowing out my mane of hair and straightening it, it then took me forever to dress in a pair of simple black high-waisted leggings and a plain white crop top.

I pace up and down the length of my house before pulling on my black and gold chunky trainers and deciding to go out. It helps me rack up at least another four thousand steps, though. Nailing my step count. Yay. Only thing I seem to be winning at today.

Which brings me to here.

I think I must have floated, because I can't remember how I got here or who I passed or if I locked my house. I must have locked the house because my clenched fist is wrapped painfully around the ridges of my house key with my phone in the other.

I pull my hand back from the door and squeeze it tighter.

Nope, can't do it.

Eh, should I do it now?

Or should I turn back around?

Hmm.

Maybe just a little tap.

Now?

Deep breath.

Okay.

I give the door a soft tap and then another two. Would anyone hear that? Give it a minute, nope just seconds, no one is in anyway, I reckon. Annndddd...

That's my cue to go.

I dart away from the door just as I hear someone. "I told you, Luke, I'm not in the mood, I'm not coming out for a be..."

The door swings open.

"...Eden?"

I whip around.

Standing as tall as The Mountain from *Game of Thrones*, his hand touching the top corner of the door, in nothing but skin-tight black boxer shorts is Hunter.

Holy guacamole.

My jaw must fall to the ground, because Hunter's mouth

twitches slightly at the corner. Little droplets of water scatter across his impressive shoulders from his wet hair, evidence of being fresh out of the shower.

I have never seen an athletic body like his in the flesh before, well, certainly I've seen the athletes around here, but, you know, they all wear actual clothes. And Hunter has, like, literally, no clothes on.

Son of a monkey.

My throat's suddenly parched; I can't even swallow. Someone please pass me some water.

Bravo to Hunter's parents for creating this fine specimen of a man, though.

Tanned and toned muscles galore, watch out, modeling contract, here comes Hunter. I wonder if he's the love child of the Greek god, Apollo.

I feel very hot everywhere, suddenly. "Mmm, hey, I, eh, I wanted to come and see you and apologize for earlier. I'm not really myself and I was, eh, well, you know, I'm sorry." I bite the inside of my mouth that now feels drier than a fossil.

I try very hard to concentrate, but my eyes seem to have a mind of their own as they follow a downward path. Zooming in on his sculpted abs creating that panty-dropping *V* shape. I always thought those were a myth, like the Loch Ness Monster. There are pictures, but no one's ever really seen it in the flesh. Covered by a small sprinkling of dark hair, his deep *V* disappears into his boxers. I clench my eyes shut to prevent me from staring at his massive concealed package.

"Erm, I should go." I hitch my thumb toward the sports facility. "Eh, sorry, no, that way, ha." Opening my eyes, I swipe my other thumb in the direction of my house. I put it in my mouth and start biting the crap out of my nail.

"So, I'll be off then." But I can't move; I'm anchored to the gravel.

Hunter narrows his eyes, motionless, just staring.

Hunter lifts his hand off the top of the door and just as I think he's about to close it, he opens it wide, stands to the side, and leans against the edge of the door. With one leg crossed at his ankle, he closes his eyes, arches his neck to face the ceiling, bites into his bottom lip pulling it inward, and lets out a deep audible breath. Shadows flicker across his muscles, highlighting all the divots of his delectable abs. He is sex on a stick; I really want to lick him like a lollipop.

"Hallelujah." Miss Minnie begs for attention. *Shut up, not now.*

I've said it all along, but I really am in trouble. He is yum-mee.

Authoritatively, he booms, "You've got until five to come in... One... Two... Three..."

Just go in, Eden.

"Four..."

Go.

I hurry toward the open door and leap over the threshold into the cabin.

"Five. Good choice."

Slamming the door, Hunter uncharacteristically grabs me by the waist and pushes me up against the back of the door. He pries my phone and key out of my hand and flings them onto the gray tartan sofa without looking.

Pressing both hands flat against the door, I'm now encased by his brawny arms on either side of my head. Hunter's citrusy scents swirl in the space between us, making my head swim with intoxication. I think I might pass out.

"What are you *really* here for, Eden?" he asks, bringing

his face down, his eyes searching mine. Oh, where did my lovely tender Hunter go? Bring him back, just for a moment, please.

"To say sorry, to apologize for being stupid and emotional and fifty levels of crazy and—" I stutter.

"Wrong answer. Try again."

"Um, it really was to say sorry," I whimper.

Hunter runs his nose along my jaw. "Bad girls don't get to play nice, so try again, Cupcake. Be a good girl and tell the truth. *Why* are you here?"

Tell him. Tell him you want him. Tell him *now.*

"I want you," I blurt out.

Smooth, Eden, really smooth.

He purrs into my neck, "Ding, ding. The girl's got it. Do you know what happens now?"

I shake my head. I do know; please tell me though.

"You, my beautiful girl, get everything your body's been craving since we met. Do you know what that is?"

All I can do is shake my head as my sex starts to pulse between my legs.

"Me inside of you, making you come so hard you won't know if it's New Year or New York. It's time to wake up Miss Minnie and unleash your inner goddess. Come out, come out, wherever you are," he sings, sending chills down my spine. "It's time to play. I'm going to show you what a real orgasm feels like and what it's like to be fucked right. Are you game?"

Holy shit. This is a new side of Hunter I haven't seen.

I blink. Yes to everything, please. Do it all. "Mm-hmm."

Hunters flashes his trademark I'm-so-sexy smile, his lips now millimeters from mine. "You're going to have to speak, but before you do, for the record, once we start, there's no backing out. I'm not playing games anymore. No hot and cold, just scorching fucking heat. You and me. You've to leave the scared version of *you* at this door. I want the confident, sexy dancer version of *you*. You in? I need you to tell me."

I can't wait any longer, I'm pulsating everywhere. "Yes, I need you inside me, now," I pant. I've no idea who I am.

I don't think this was my plan coming over here.

Yeah, right, it so was.

"Easy, Cupcake." With his big sandpaper hands, reminding me of what he does for a living, he cups my cheek with so much tenderness. This is more like my Hunter. *Mine.*

"I have a confession to make."

My stomach plunges.

"As dinky as you are, I can't carry you up the stairs because of my back. So the plan is I'm going to kiss you here and then lead you up the stairs to my bedroom and learn every curve of your sinful body. How does that sound?"

"I really like the sound of that," I whisper in relief.

Feeling brave, I lean in, making the first move. I want him to know I want him. From desperate need, I grab his stubble-covered face. A sense of ease washes over me, like I've finally made my decision and all I want is Hunter.

This witty, passionate, incredible man who said I'm all *his*. He's mine. At least for now.

Firmly, I press my lips to his; I'm done waiting. I want all of him. We groan into each other's mouths, savoring each other, our breaths quickly become ragged and shallow in a rocket-fueled electric kiss. Our hot possessive mouths fuse as our deep, loud breaths fill the air.

Grabbing my hips, he thrusts me into his hard cock. With barely any fabric between his boxers and my snug thin leggings, I feel every part of his impressive length.

Tentatively, I use my delicate fingers to draw a featherlight path down his ripped chest. His stomach contracts beneath my touch, and I relish in the fact that *I* am making him react this way.

"Touch me," Hunter mutters.

Steadily, I reach down and palm his cock over his boxers. Holy shit, how is Miss Minnie going to take that all in? Is my vagina long enough to take him? Is there such a thing as a long vagina? He's long, thick, and rock hard.

"Fuck," Hunter hisses against my lips. Delicately, he bites my bottom lip, then pulls it into his mouth with soft suction.

Hunter then nuzzles into my neck, nipping his teeth into the delicate skin and digging his fingers painfully into my ass.

"Can we go upstairs now?" I ask breathlessly.

"I'm ready if you are." He thrusts his thick cock harder into my hand. "Mmm, are you sure you want to do this?" he murmurs, making me gasp as pinpricks trickle down my neck from the warmth of his hot breath.

I don't want to wait anymore.

"Yes, I really do, Hunter."

Without uttering another word, Hunter slowly straightens to his full height and I have to crane my neck to take in this mesmerizing man in front of me.

Holding my hand in his, I try hard not to stare as his wet erection pops out the top of his boxers. With a shameless grin, Hunter slowly turns toward the wooden stairs.

It's only now I get a full view of his muscular, tanned back, covered edge to edge in a stunning Phoenix tattoo in vivid reds and oranges with jet-black detailing. As he walks me up the stairs, it moves across his muscular skin as if alive, flying as he takes each step, one by one.

As we reach the top of the stairs and enter his bedroom, he gives me no time to think. His skillful hands are instantly on me, lowering his body slightly to accommodate my height. He curls his athletic arms around my tiny waist, leaving no space between us now. Crashing our lips together, boldly nipping and tugging, he's done waiting. So am I. Our teeth clash together, tongues fighting to take power, breaths gasping, demanding full surrender.

Hunter skims his hands over my waist and dips his fingers into the hem of my white crop top, lightly slipping it up over my head.

Yeah, so this is going faster than expected. I'm actually doing this. If someone could round up a cheerleading squad to cheer me on, that would be brilliant, thanks. I need all the support I can get with so many doubts flying round my head. Give me an E...

"I've been imagining what your nipples look like since that night in the mansion reception and you had a whole wet tee shirt competition thing going on," he rasps against my lips. "Then you told me what color they were on the pier, but I need confirmation." He continues to assault me with his lips as he unhooks my intricate white lace bra, then glides the delicate straps down my arms.

Hunter steps back slightly, seeking the answers he needs. "Beautiful. You have no idea how sexy you are. You have the best tits I have ever seen in my life. Big for a small girl." He bites his tongue between his teeth with a smile, making his nose scrunch, and gives me a wicked wink.

Gosh. He thinks I'm sexy. I know he's told me this so many times, but I feel so exposed with him, here now. A deep flush flashes over my chest.

Hunter tips my chin. "Hey, it's time to start believing that you are one showstopper of a woman. Smart, funny, and so fucking hot. It's time to take your control back. Own this shit, baby." He motions to my body. "You barely have to touch me to turn me on. You're already doing everything right."

I can't speak as emotion builds within my chest. He's just everything. Handsome, caring, and he has a massive cock. Yikes. That scares me more than the actual sex part itself. Actually, that's a lie—all of it scares me. My heart is beating faster than a mariachi band. How in the hell is it going to fit? It's been so long for me, and he's, like, *so* long.

Gah, and what if my parents saw me coming here? Crikey.

"You're overthinking. I can see it. Free your mind. I've got you, baby."

His words make my insides squirm in delight. This feels like way more than just sex. It's not though, right? He lives thousands of miles away and he leaves soon. But...

Hunter slowly thumbs my nipple, and it instantly hardens beneath his touch.

"You'll be pleased to know I jerked off in the shower thinking about you. Knowing you were mine all along. You just needed to work that out for yourself. So you'll have me for much longer tonight than you bargained for; otherwise, I don't think I would last two minutes inside of you."

Urgent and wet, now all I can think about *is* him inside me. "Leggings off," Hunter instructs, stepping backward again as if reading my mind.

Okay, I can do this. Channel Eden, the dancer. Be sexy. Wiggling my hips from side to side, I slink my leggings slowly down my short, lean legs, elegantly peeling them from my ankles before removing my trainers.

"Fucking knew it. No panties and bare. But you weren't coming here to dance tonight, Eden, which means you were planning on coming here to work out, weren't you? Apologize my ass. You're a little minx," Hunter pants.

He stalks toward me, urgently enveloping me with his broad body. Skin to skin, our naked bodies touch each other for the first time. In one swift move, he lifts me. "I may not be able to carry you all the way upstairs, but I can lift this beautiful dinky body of yours onto the bed."

Hunter is hot and hard, everywhere. He's breathtaking. My legs lock around his waist greedily, our lips tackling one another. Hunter bites my lip hard. I feel his clothed cock rub against my center, making me wet, and I whimper, the heat between us intensifying as a whirlwind of sensations race through my body.

Hunter roams my body with his hands as he lays me on the soft gray comforter, bodies flush together, kissing me deeply and grinding his hard hot cock against my pussy. I arch my neck, leaving his mouth. "Oh God."

Moving south, Hunter scatters kisses over my neck, sliding slowly down to my nipples, then he tongues one with his wet mouth. Flicking and biting in fast quick licks, he pinches the other between his nimble fingers, shooting jolts of electricity through my body.

Hunter's unbearably hard length rubs against my inner thigh. I want to see him. I slide my hand inside his boxer's waistband. Hunter grabs my wrist with a firm grip. "Nuh, uh, uh... Not yet." He scuffs his designer stubble against the skin of my stomach, licking across toward my belly bar. "So sexy," he says, nibbling and licking my toned stomach, his voice dripping with pleasure.

Repositioning himself, he props himself up slightly and shuffles slowly down the bed.

Placing his head between my thighs, he looks up, giving me a full-on I've-got-you grin. "Such a pretty pussy."

Is this how people talk to each other during sex now?

Oh boy.

"Focus on all the sensations, baby. You've to tell me if anything doesn't feel good. You're the boss of this bedroom tonight, Eden. This is all for you."

I look down. "I'll tell you."

"Good girl. I'm about to take your first orgasm."

Will I be able to, with a man, with *him*? I'm going to be so pissed off if there really is something wrong with me, because I feel like I'm going to explode, and apparently we haven't even gotten to the good stuff yet.

Just relax, feel, let go, enjoy... I slow my breathing, close my eyes, and lean in to this new experience. I want this.

Tickling my thighs with his splayed fingers, Hunter taps gentle kisses from thigh to thigh, moving closer to where I want him to really touch me.

"Touch me, Hunter. Please touch me."

I can't wait anymore.

I feel a soft brush of his finger on my folds. My legs voluntarily open wider as he slides it along my sex. "Wet," Hunter mumbles.

Leisurely he slides his finger back and forth. I gasp at his foreign touch and I breathe out in a rush of anticipation.

The tension's been building between us for weeks and I want him, *now*.

I watch as he spreads my lower lips with his long skillful fingers before leaning in and taking me with his incredible mouth. Holy shit.

Softly at first, then adding more pressure, he sucks my soft bud with tenderness, causing my center to pulsate and tingle with pleasure. How did he find that so fast?

Holy crap, I think I'm going to come within two touches. Flicking and lapping his hot tongue against my clit, I feel him insert his long finger into my wet, swollen flesh with merciful care. "Oh God," I cry out.

This is new, delicious, and freeing. Never have I felt so turned on.

I lock eyes with Hunter as I look down. He smiles against my pussy and winks. Holy shit, could he look any hotter? Closing his eyes in delight, he attacks my clit, sucking and swirling gently, with the trace of a bite. He's enjoying this. He said this is for me, but this is for him too.

The intensity of him massaging my clit combined with his finger pumping in and out of my dripping sex creates the sensation of joyous pleasure building within me. This is beyond extraordinary. I feel him insert another finger as he picks up the pace, simultaneously pressing against a spot so deep inside, it makes me lose my breath.

"Ah, do that again," I beg.

Faster now, I feel this new sensation rise as I writhe against Hunter's mouth. "Oh, yeah. Just like that." The sounds of my breath and wet sex swirls in the air. He's so good at this. Holy shit.

Hunter's warm mouth leaves my pussy suddenly and everything stops. What? I wait a couple of seconds. Then I lift up on my elbows to see what the hell he's doing. "I think we should stop, don't you? I don't think this is working." He looks up at me with a yard-wide smile and warm, dark eyes.

He *is* the devil.

"You need to be quiet now, look pretty, and don't stop what you started," I blow out in a huff, flinging my head back onto the pillow. I don't want tender anymore; I'm teetering on the edge of insanity.

"You have three choices here," he says calmly as he slides his fingers painfully slowly inside of me again, forward and backward.

"Oooooh, so good." Grinding my hips, I urge him to go faster and deeper.

"Slow and steady." He kisses my clit. "Fast and furious." Clit kiss. "Or we can stop and watch some Netflix. Lady's choice. What will it be?" He flattens his rough tongue to my tender bud, hard.

"Ah." I lift my head and command, "Fast and furious."

I've turned into a crazed woman.

Hunter chuckles against my skin as he turns his head and plants a gentle kiss on my inner thigh before dragging his tongue back to my clit.

This guy.

Fire grows hot deep in my core as Hunter laps at my bundle of nerves again.

Pleasure builds, swooping all over my body.

I arch my back off the bed and clasp his head with my thighs. Taking my cue, he licks faster, kissing and flicking my bud with his expert tongue, over and over. He really should have some sort of accreditation for how good he is at this.

Oh dear God.

I sneak a glance at Hunter. He's grinding his hips into the bed to ease his own pressure that's building. Eyes closed, devouring me with his mouth, he's in the moment too, enjoying it all.

Hot, searing bolts of pleasure strike through me.

Untamed, Hunter picks up the pace, pistoning his fingers in and out again and again, arching his fingers inside me in a beckoning position, hitting a newfound spot I didn't know existed. "I think I'm gonna come," I rasp out.

I reach down, entwining his dark hair between my fingers and push his face harder into my clit. Suddenly, an explosion of convulsions scatter outward throughout my body as I cry out Hunter's name.

"Holy shit." Clasping the bed cover with my other hand as if to stop me floating off the bed, Hunter lets out a loud, long, breathy hot groan against my swollen bud. He's so turned on, it's fucking hot.

Warmth and tingles flood all over my body as my heart hammers fast in my chest.

Flushed and tingling, Hunter mercifully kisses my clit again as I release his hair from my tight grip.

"Ooooh, too much, that's so sensitive."

I suck in several breaths, trying to calm myself as my shudders subside.

My emotions take over and a small tear of joy and relief slides down the side of my temple. What is wrong with me?

Placing a small kiss just above my clit, Hunter removes his fingers from my soaking wet center, and I whimper at their removal. Leisurely crawling up my body, his gorgeous face comes into view above me. "Hi," he whispers. "There's my girl."

He takes his fingers and sucks them into his mouth.

"You taste fucking delicious."

Hot damn is he dirty.

"Hey, baby, what's the matter?" His face drops suddenly, full of concern.

'That was—"

"Incredible, Hunter, you're the best. Amazing. Hunter, you made me come so hard."

I giggle as he lightens the moment. He always knows exactly how to handle my emotions. "You're so silly. Stop spoiling the moment. But, yes, all those things. I feel a little overwhelmed. I actually orgasmed with you. It felt wonderful." I can't quite believe it. It felt so liberating.

I taste myself on him as he leans in for a kiss, which doesn't seem to bother me. All of this feels so unexpected.

"Thank you," I say with a shy smile.

"You don't have to thank me." He wipes the small tear away with the pad of his thumb. "Your body is meant for pleasure; let yourself surrender. Your name even means place of pleasure; it's a rite of passage. Let me look after you, baby. I really want to and I want you to enjoy it all."

He whispers into my neck, "Eden, there is nothing wrong with your body, baby. You just needed someone who cares about you and who knows what they're doing."

He cares about me. He's said this before. So this isn't just about sex? He said it earlier in the studio too. I heard that correctly then. Oh God, somebody catch me.

A nervous laugh escapes me again. "Do you really know what you're doing?"

"Damn straight I do, you have firsthand experience now."

I clasp his gorgeous face in my hands and gaze into his eyes. "I feel wonderful, Hunter."

"Seriously, are you okay?"

"Yeah." I smile.

Swooping in, he kisses me with urgency. "I need to be inside you now; it's about to get even better," he says, grinding against me.

"I want to see you." I expel a slow, steady hiss.

Hunter takes his time to lean back on his knees. With my hand in his, he pulls me up.

Don't be scared, Eden, you can do this.

Dipping my fingers into the thick waistband of his tight trunks, I gently slide them down and off, exposing his beautiful enormous cock, glistening with pre-come. He's ready.

I've no idea if there is such a thing as a pretty penis. But he has one.

"Does it ever go down? It's huge."

Hunter loves my words as he proudly places his hands on his hips. "You're about to find out, my beautiful girl."

My beautiful girl.

Hunter leans over to open the drawer of his bedside table. I watch confused as he shuffles about a little. Finally finding what he was looking for, he pulls out a box of condoms.

Worry hits me. Aw crap. "Ah, I, eh, shit, I'm allergic to condoms. Well, latex, those. I never thought. I'm such an idiot." I smack my hand to forehead. "I'm really shit at all this bedroom stuff. Way to spoil the moment."

"You are not. No more of that trash talk. Are you messing with me? About the condoms?" He shakes the box.

"Nope. I get flu-like symptoms and break out in hives. Super attractive."

Disappointment rushes across Hunter's gorgeous face. Mine, too.

I clear my throat. "I have an implant, like the contraceptive pill implant." I point to the top of my arm. "I suffer from bad period cramps too, so it works for me. I'm totally clean. Like Virgin Mary clean. Well, you know this. Are you clean?"

He groans and rolls his neck back as if he's imagining himself inside of me skin to skin. "I'm clean. I haven't been with anyone in a long time." His eyes beam now, looking at me. "I get tested all the time, not that I've needed to in the last few years, unless you count my hand. I think he's clean." He raises his hand and wiggles his fingers.

He's so funny and refreshingly honest.

Gosh, I really do like him.

He leans in. "Are you sure? I've *never* had sex without a condom before."

"I'm positive." I chuckle. "Sorry, that's not the right word to use; I mean yes."

Hunter sucks in a breath. "Jesus, Eden, you're my dream girl."

My heart leaps.

Hunter palms his large hand across my chest, motioning me to lie back. Slowly he drifts over me again.

Face-to-face, he stills, his eyes glinting. I notice something change in them. He's thinking. What is he thinking?

"You're so uniquely beautiful," he says.

Before I get the chance to tell him I think he's beautiful too, he assaults my mouth with his tongue and swallows my words.

Settling between my legs, Hunter nudges my legs wider and slides his knees down. His now dripping wet length rests against my inner thigh.

Flicking my nipples with his thumb and forefingers, I tilt my pelvis to his. I want to feel him inside me. "I need you."

With languid movements, Hunter slides his hard cock through my bare flesh, teasing all my senses. Taking his face in my hands, cupping the stubble of his cheeks, I lock my eyes with his. "Please be gentle."

"Always."

Reaching down, Hunter slowly glides a finger over my clit before sliding it into my wet heat.

In and out he moves, getting me ready, before guiding the tip of his magnificent cock into my entrance.

Dear Lord, this is good.

"Oooooh," I whimper.

"Just relax, baby. You're so wet and ready for me; I know you can take me."

"I like your confidence, Mr. King, but I'm not so sure." I take in the pain and pleasure cocktail.

"Kiss me." He closes the small gap and devours my lips. Passionate predatory kisses bite at my mouth as pleasure sparks in waves between us.

"Suck my finger."

He presses his finger against my tongue and I suck. Hard.

Ravishing my mouth with his, with his finger still in my mouth, we pant quickly, tongues tangling, licking, and me sucking. He growls wildly.

Hunter takes his finger, lowers it between our bodies, then coats my clit with gentle taps. Instantly, I feel a rush of wetness.

I was right back in the field at my car all those weeks ago. I really am going to die... Death by hot guy... Death by orgasm from the hot guy.

Since when did sex become so hot? I've been missing out all this time.

Wanting to take him in more, I lift my hips and drive him a little deeper.

Kissing me to distract me from his size, he tantalizes my senses, pushing his cock further into my body.

Inch by torturous inch, he tentatively slides and glides back and forth. He hisses in pleasure as his strokes become slightly longer and deeper, coating his cock with my desire.

Fudge nuggets, that stings a bit. I clench my eyes.

"Are you okay?"

"You are so big. Mmmm..."

"Do you want me to stop?"

I open my eyes and stare up at this majestic man. "No way, keep going."

"Thank fuck." He smiles and I do too.

Lips locked firmly together, our wet and warm tongues collide in fury.

My body opens up for him as he gently pats my clit, sending molten heat everywhere. I spread my legs wider in invitation.

Hunter removes his hand between us, allowing him to nudge forward as I feel him enter me fully.

"There you are, baby. Fuck, you feel so good. You are so fucking tight." He moans, whispering against my lips in his American twang I've grown so much to love.

This is a little painful, but holy shit it feels great.

We kiss as Hunter stills inside of me, allowing me to adjust to his incredible size.

"We fit together perfectly in every way," Hunter growls into my mouth.

Slowly he starts to move in and out of me. I feel a little burn at first but oh wow, this feels great and close, we are so close.

Then we really move together. Rocking in and out, Hunter buries himself deeper.

He whispers dirty things in my ear, none of which I recall, but they turn me on like an electrical surge.

He's so goddamn good at this.

"Hunter, that feels so good," I breathe. "Give me more."

Breathing hard against each other's lips, we gaze at each other as if we can't believe after all these weeks we are actually doing this.

He lifts himself up slightly, arms on either side of my head, and thrusts his hips in and out with intensity, sending my senses into overdrive.

Bowing his head, he dusts kisses onto my neck and across my chest as I dig my nails into his lower back.

"You're so sexy, Eden. Fuck, I'm not gonna last. Are you okay?"

I simper, "Yes, please don't stop."

Slowly I palm my hands down to his rock-hard glutes and squeeze hard, urging him to move faster.

"Harder, Hunter, Harder," I demand.

But he slows down.

"Greedy girl." He chuckles. "Tilt your hips slightly, baby."

I do.

"That's it."

With a rough thrust, a thrum of sensations fire through me.

Holy shit. What in the hell was that?

"Do you feel that Eden?"

"Hell, yeah."

"G-spot jackpot, baby. You better saddle up for one of the most epic fucking orgasms of your life. I hope you're ready for this."

Hunter circles his hips, thrusting back and forth.

"Ooh, that's amazing, keep doing that," I whimper.

With wild abandon, Hunter leans back and wraps his expansive hands around my tiny waist, two hands almost encircling it, holding me firm. He tips my hips so they're slightly off the bed. "Can you do that again? Pivot your pelvis a bit."

Of course, I'm bloody doing that again. That felt incredible.

He picks up the pace again, his strokes becoming faster and unhinged.

The twilight filters through the curtains shining across

his striking athletic body. Bolts of energy fire through me at lightning speed. Our breathing becomes heavy and loud.

Teasing my newfound magic spot back and forth, I feel him so deep inside me, I can't hold off any longer. Tiny sparks turn into a blaze.

"Are you close?" he asks, breathing heavy now.

"Yes!"

I think I stop breathing before I arch my back; instinctively I cup my breast and pinch my nipple, hard.

"Fuck yeah," Hunter growls. "Come for me, baby. I can't stop it. I'm gonna come."

Hunter pounds into me hard with everything he's got. My orgasm builds so fast, my body shatters into a thousand splinters of ecstasy as wave after wave gives me the most incredible pleasure imaginable.

I come fast and hard around him as I'm overwhelmed by all the tingling sensations buzzing through me.

I gasp for air as white spots sparkle behind my eyes and I feel Hunter spill himself inside of me as he comes hard and fast, pulsing into my sex, roaring loudly as he comes, muttering words of desire.

"Fuck," he groans.

Fluttering my eyes open, I watch Hunter arch his neck back in sheer euphoria. Butterflies dance in my tummy at the sight of this magnificent man before me.

My creamy pale skin stands out like a full moon on a clear night against his deeply tanned long, lean body. We are complete contrasts of each other.

As we ease out of our orgasm haze, Hunter carefully bows down and holds me close, kissing me with featherlike kisses as our breathing calms. My stomach clenches as newfound feelings wash over my body. I feel at peace and at ease in his caring arms.

"You're mine now." Hunter pants into my neck.

What does he mean?

This is only supposed to be a for a few weeks. I'm not his.

All of this feels alien to me. To be this close to someone, so soon. It feels unnerving and intimate.

My heart raps against my chest with each breath.

Hunter pulls back slightly, gazes at me, then beams a dazzling smile from ear to ear.

"I'm a fucking vagician," he says proudly and strokes the pad of his thumb gently against my temple.

I can't help but giggle. "Oh my God, Hunter. Is this how it's going to be?"

"What do you mean?"

"You, spoiling all our special moments?"

"Nope, just this one time. I promise. Making you come twice does things to my ego. Which is currently bigger than the Empire State Building." Then he kisses me again. "I want to stay like this forever. You feel so good," he whispers against my skin.

We kiss for a long time, and eventually he slowly slides out of me.

Rolling over to my side, we lie face-to-face. He smooths his hand across my bottom, pulls me in to him, and kisses me wistfully.

I don't ever want him to stop.

It's crazy to think I've only known this man for a few weeks. It feels like we've known each other forever.

Hunter certainly knows his way around my body. Like a map, he followed the directions perfectly, ensuring my safe arrival at my final destination, twice.

Relishing this heart-touching moment, he holds my gaze with his dark eyes that make me feel luminous.

"You're a beautiful man, inside and out, Hunter King. Where did you come from?"

With a wide white beam lighting his entire face, he says, "Well, that's easy. Seminole, Florida."

A little worry sprinkles over my heart at his words. He lives so far away. I really like him. A few weeks of fun with Hunter sounds fantastic, but I think I want more.

"You give me all the feels, Hunter King."

"You give me all the feels too, little Eden Wallace. Come here."

Tucking my head under his chin, I snuggle in against his brawny hot chest.

"You were incredible, baby. How do you feel? God, I hope I wasn't too rough. I kind of got a little bit excited," he says, rubbing my back.

"Normal. Well, not normal, because that felt otherworldly. I've been missing out all these years. I feel alive. Thank you. I think you're trying to kill me though. My heart's never beat so fast and I think I stopped breathing too," I say, laughing. This is all so new for me; I feel like I want to tell anyone who'll listen what I just felt. It was magical.

Hunter chuckles. "Death by orgasm. There are worse things to die of and please stop thanking me. I am the vagician after all."

"I can't believe you said that. You are so strange." I get a fit of the giggles. I think I'm seriously delirious.

"Stop laughing." Hunter tickles my sides. "It's an actual thing; look it up in the urban dictionary. It means you will never go home unsatisfied. You're not going home tonight, Cupcake. You're staying here with me. First, we're going to have a shower, then I'm gonna show you what your body can really do and how much better it can feel each and every time."

My giggling subsides.

Smoothing his thumb down my cheek. "You and me. We were meant to be. Your orgasms were meant for me, and me only. Miss Minnie feels fucking awesome and is back on the payroll."

I love how he continually flips from being sultry and sexy to deep down and dirty in swift succession.

But he must mean my orgasms are his just for a few weeks. Doesn't he?

"I had no idea how your enormous putter was going to fit," I tease.

He frowns. "You know all that shit you've been told. It's all lies. You look smokin' hot when you come undone. You are so hot, baby. You turn on me on like a dream; your body works beautifully."

"I know that now. Jam..."

He places a finger over my mouth, shushing me. "Ah, ah, ah, first bedroom rule, no ex talk, just sex talk."

I smile against his finger and suck it into my mouth and bite down.

"Fuck, don't do that. You'll make me hard again."

I suck and then softly push it out of my mouth with my tongue, planting a kiss on the end. Hunter's eyes spike with desire.

"Goodie, I want more," I tease.

"What is it with you and finger sucking? It's fucking hot." Dragging his hand down his face, he says, "I knew this would happen. I've unleashed a sex kitten."

"Hmmm, I'm not sure yet. I think I need a few more demonstrations to convince me if I should become one." I shyly look up.

I hope we're having more sex again tonight. Taking my shot, I make my intentions known.

I bounce off the bed and slap his backside. "C'mon, in the shower, I'm ready for round two."

I spin around and dance off toward the shower as Hunter leaps from the bed.

"Who's trying to kill who now? You asked for this; you'd better buckle up."

CHAPTER SIXTEEN

Braw: *adjective,* good, fine. **Pronounced:** B-raw.

Hunter

She's still here.

Sleeping peacefully.

In my bed.

Like a small boy on Christmas Day waiting patiently for everyone to get up, I've never been so excited.

Wake up, wake up, wake up.

I unwrapped the best gift of my life last night.

If someone had told me yesterday morning that I would wake up lying next to this perfect girl in the next twenty-four hours, I would never have believed them. But here I am.

Watching her peacefully sleep, eyes fluttering from time to time, I can't help but think it is wrong of me to find this tiny girl cute and sensual all at the same time. It's kind of like her fries and ice cream combo, a weird combination that just works. I need to try that.

I got a superb taste of her last night and already I'm addicted.

Scanning her face, she looks a lot younger than she is with her natural fresh, fair face framed by her caramel hair, draped against the charcoal sheets.

I love her hair. I've never known anyone to have a waterfall of hair as long as Eden's. I fucking wrapped my hands around that last night from behind as she arched her back and reversed onto my cock. It worried me I was a little too rough with her, but she begged for more, reassuring me that she was enjoying it.

I roam my eyes down her tiny figure wrapped around the bedsheets. My Cupcake.

Having been on a weeklong instructors' course, and not getting to sleep until after three in the morning, she must be exhausted.

We were at it for hours. Last night was incredible. She was incredible.

She showered me with kisses of appreciation after every orgasm, which melted my heart and rendered me speechless.

I uncovered a brave and sensual woman. She's been hiding herself away for too long. Her body blossomed last night, like a creamy-white Queen of the Night flower, she's been waiting for the right time to bloom.

She was a little shy when we tried a few different positions, but once she got into it, she really let go, showing me a cheeky but erotic new side of her.

Surprising me, she's a little spicy, and she likes sex, and when I say she likes sex, she really enjoyed it all last night, becoming a little braver every time. She was instructing me what to do as the hours rolled by. She trusted me to explore new and exciting things last night.

She sleepily thanked me for looking after her and for helping her discover her newfound ecstasy before drifting off. I watched her as her breathing settled to an even contentment before drifting off myself. I could watch her for hours.

There were also moments of raw passion and desire which demonstrated Eden's physical stamina. I'm sure it has something to do with her being a dancer or some shit. She fucking bounced up and down on my cock like a pogo stick at one point, as she discovered it was the ultimate position to take her to the moon and back. Most women give up after a few squats. But not Eden; I may have met my match.

I chuckle to myself at the memory of her seriousness last night. *"Okay, what position are we doing next? I'm super flexible. Try me."* She really did properly get into it. She was soft and hard, fast and slow, tender but teasing all night. She was, *is* perfect.

It makes my heart ache a little at the unwelcome thought of having to leave her here in Castleview Cove. Long distance I've done before, but being away from her *all* the time, I'm not sure I can. Now I've found her, I don't want to ever be away from her.

I drag my hand down my face at my thoughts. I don't want to spoil this little euphoric bubble I've woken up in today.

Carefully, I roll over and grab my phone from my bedside table and prop myself against the pillow. Opening our group chat, I drop a message to my team.

Me: Do we have much on the training plan today or could we take an extra day off?

Luke: Why? Are you not feeling up to it today?

Me: Just tired and feel like I could do with a day to myself.

Luke: He's tired, Evan. Is the old man not managing to keep up the pace?

Evan: Hmm... I don't think it's that. I wonder what it could be... taps finger to chin emoji.

Me: I'm just tired, you pair of idiots. I never ask for days off.

Luke: Maybe it's got something to do with...

Evan: Yeah, it probably has. You're right, Luke.

Me: What is he right about?

Why the fuck are these two talking in code this morning?

Luke: Well...

Luke: Rumor has it "you're the best," Hunter.

Aw, shit.

Evan: But you need to give it "harder"

Luke: Was there an actual banshee in your cabin last night, Hunter?

How did they hear? Were we that loud?

Noah: I believe there was, although there was a full moon last night; maybe it was a she-wolf.

Me: Assholes.

Luke: Next time, close your goddamn windows.

Pippa: What have I woken up to?

Evan: Hunter had a run-in with a starving Scottish she-wolf last night. Did you not hear it?

Luke: It was ravenous.

Me: Stop talking about her like that. That's enough.

Pippa: Oh God, I can only imagine what this means, but it's about time. Would you like to hear about my sex life, Hunter?

Me: Fuck no.

Pippa: You pair stop talking about Hunter's then. I'm leaving this conversation now. Day off, yeah?

Luke: Yeah.

Evan: Yup.

Pippa: Good. We have to organize your trip back to Florida as you have a photoshoot with your new sponsor. A signature is required on some paperwork with them too, plus a couple of interviews. We'll stay here. It just needs you. A pain I know, but they couldn't organize it for here in Scotland. You only need to be away for a few days and then back here again to train before The Cup. I will organize the jet. I'll speak to you later this week about specifics. Peace out.

Evan: I can reshuffle a few parts of your training around and slot it in across the week.

Luke: Same here. I can do that. I wouldn't mind spending the day with Ella, anyway.

Evan: I'd like to meet up with Toni today too.

Are my boys complete horndogs?

Me: Okay. Thanks.
Luke: You're welcome, tiger.
Me: She never fucking called me tiger.
Evan: Nope, but you roared like one.
Me: You're on your final warning!
Evan: Yeah, yeah, whatever.
Luke: Have a fun day off, pony boy.

Christ, we must have been loud if Evan could hear us two cabins down.

I slide my phone back in the side and turn back around to face Eden.

An idiotic smile crosses my lips as I drift my thumb over her pale cheek, staring at her like some lovestruck teenager. She's so peaceful, with not a worry in the world. She often has these little brow furrows, as if deep in thought all the time, but I can't detect a single line as she lies here beside me. Smooth and supple, like all her worries have disappeared.

I don't want her to worry or second-guess herself anymore. I want her to live a life full of wonder, happiness, and excitement. She so desperately wants it.

She's been through so much. I cannot imagine what losing a child must be like, and all by herself. She deserves happiness.

My phone buzzes on the side table, bringing me out of my rom-com movie moment I'm currently having.

Glancing at my phone, I see a text from Ella.

Shit.

Opening it, my heart beats in a different rhythm. Ella is a ball-crushing bombshell; I psych myself up before I open it.

Ella: I hope you gave her the full show last night ;) But please don't hurt our baby girl.
Me: How the hell do you know?
Ella: I have eyes and ears everywhere, and I believe you were both loud last night ;)

Luke. I'm definitely having words with him and Evan later this week about my privacy. No doubt they'll just laugh in my face, but it's worth a shot. Who am I kidding? It's pointless. This happens when you employ your friends. It turns into a frat boy party.

Me: I have no intention of hurting her, ever. That's not my style.
Ella: Famous last words. Just know, I am watching you. Bug eyes emoji.
Me: Message received and understood. To be honest, I don't think I could handle what you would do to me if I did.
Ella: Protect those balls at all costs.
Ella: I'm not talking about your golf balls either.

Christ, I think my testicles just jumped up into my body.

Eden's protectors are fiercely loyal to the core. I don't blame them for looking out for her; she's been through more than enough trauma for one lifetime.

The deep urge to protect her with everything I am, and bring her into my world to keep her safe, runs deep in my veins.

I lie for a few minutes as all these jumbled thoughts run through my head.

Leaving Eden to sleep—I don't think she's waking up anytime soon anyway—I carefully leave the bed and make my way to the shower.

Then I plan on making her breakfast. I'm hoping she can spend the day with me. If not, I'll just follow her around today like a lovesick puppy. Love. Wait. Not love. No, lust sick puppy. Yeah, lust.

Eden

Fluttering my eyes open, it suddenly dawns on me where I am. Hunter's bed. I hear the shower tinkling away in the adjoining bathroom. I've been in this room hundreds of times before, but never like this. It's only ever been to help Mum with the decor or check people in.

I cup my hands, covering my face, not quite believing I came here last night and then the things we did in this bed together. A carnival of giggles escapes my lungs.

Yowza, it was good. When I say *it*, I'm talking about the sex; it felt like more than sex. Maybe it wasn't, but it was intense and mind-blowing and all the things I read in my books. It's all true. Better than true because it happened to *me*.

Hunter wound me tighter and tighter with every orgasm, showing me how good it would feel each and every time. He woke up every molecule in my body. It's the closest thing to heaven I've ever felt.

He was patient and kind, but gave it to me hard and rough when I asked. A flush of embarrassment whisks over me as I think about how forward I was asking him what position he wanted next, I think I was showing off a fraction, wanting to show him the level of my flexibility.

Gosh, who was I last night?

Lazily, I sit up, pull the covers around my still naked body, and cross my legs in a lotus position. My jaw opens as I let out a wide yawn in sheer satisfaction.

Glancing around the room, I wonder what time it is. Looking to the bedside table, I lean over and grab my phone that Hunter must have put there for me. He's even put it on charge for me. My heart melts at his small gesture.

Seven in the morning.

I hover over my WhatsApp icon. This is big news for our little friendship circle. I really want to tell the girls. I may live to regret this. I tap the icon to open and text our group chat.

Me: So, I did a thing.
Beth: A thing, or someone?
Ella: Someone - she did someone.
Beth: Aubergine emoji.
Ella: Water emoji.
Eva: Yup, I know she did someone.
Me: How do you know?
Ella: Luke heard you - you were LOUD
Eva: And Ella told me.

Me: Please tell me that's not true?

Me: Is nothing sacred anymore?

Toni: Why, lovely people in my phone, are we texting so early?

Beth: Eden did someone.

Toni: About time. Please tell us it was Mr. Swoony McSwoonerson.

Me: That's a shit nickname.

Eva: Gotta do better than that Toni, what about Mr. Ankle Spanker?

Beth: Or Mr. Womb Raider.

Toni: What about King of Cocks?

Beth: Love it.

Ella: Did he score a hole in one?

Beth: Good one... more golf puns please.

Toni: We don't know any, shoot, Beth.

Beth: Did he lay you out spread eagle?

Eva: Pahahahahaha.

Beth: Was his shaft stiff and hard?

Eva: Dear Lord.

Beth: Did he play 18 holes and you can barely walk today?

Toni: Can you walk, cowgirl?

Beth: Is he a king in the bedroom?

Ella: Gotta be, have you seen the size of his hands?

Beth: Did he tell you to get into position, lift your head, and spread your legs?

Me: Why do I even bother with you lot?

Ella: We're sorry.

Eva: Sorry, we'll be serious now... go for it... Tell us, what was it like?

Me: It was...

Toni: Incredible?

Ella: Good?

Eva: Great?

Beth: Fantastic?

Me: Earth-shatteringly mind-blowing incredible and I think I saw stars. Like actual stars. And he was tender and rough and then caring and then we had rocket-fueled fun. I have no other words.

Toni: Mamma Mia.

Ella: I'm speechless.

Beth: Holy cow.

Eva: Oh my.

Ella: So were there orgasms? Plural?

Beth: Go on, make us well jell.

Me: Yes, seven times!

Toni: Seven?

Ella: In Len Goodman *Strictly Come Dancing/Dancing With the Stars* style... Sev-en!

Eva: Christ, is he magic?

Beth: He's a fucking King alright.

Me: He actually told me he was a vagician.

Eva: If those words came from anyone else it would be dickhead like, but he's so nice, I think he really is a vagician!

Ella: I just spat my cup of tea out all over Tartan's jacket.

Ella and that bloody horse. She's turning into Mrs. Dolittle with all these animals she's been gathering lately. She's just bought another dog to keep Treacle company. If my suspicions are accurate, then it's filling a hole in her heart that's been empty for a very long time. Like me, she puts on a good show.

Toni: Does he have a brother?

Beth: Piss off, Beth, he's mine if he does.

Toni: I called dibs first.

Me: You lot are on fire today!

Eva: How do you feel? Are you okay?

Me: I feel incredible! Like I've bloody woken up. I had fun. It was fun. I feel excited. About everything. Ella was right. I needed to get a life and get some :)

Beth: Aw, our little girl is growing up.

Ella: Sorry, say that again? Ella was...?

Me: Right! You were right!

Ella: Why, I thank you, my work here is done... I'm currently bowing to Tartan and Treacle.

Beth: So, is this a long-term thing, you think? Or just a few weeks of fun?

Toni: Or a one-night stand?

Eva: Please don't do the one-night stand thing; that's more Beth's style.

Beth: Get stuffed, Eva. I'm not that bad.

Toni: Yes, you are!

Beth: Enough now, I'm going off you lot.

Me: Honestly, I have no idea. I really, really like him. He's not like anyone I have ever met before.

Ella: You haven't met/dated anyone other than Jamie before Eden, but he is different.

Toni: I think it's his height; he's huge.

Eva: Or his dazzling smile?

Beth: Or the length of his enormous cock, perhaps? Is it as enormous as they say in the papers?

Me: I'm not answering this shit anymore. Now bugger off to your jobs.

Me: See you girls tomorrow when we open again for classes, the joiners are expected to be done in a day.

Ella: I bet you get *done* today... again.

Beth: Don't forget to get it rough. That's a golf term, girls.

Ella: And he never misses a hole, so you'll be well looked after.

Eva: You girls are so immature... I love it!

Toni: What does all that mean in golfy terms? Golf sounds more sexual than it is when I'm watching it down at the beach. I think I'm missing out somewhere; I need to get you to explain this all the next time I see you, Beth.

Beth: You're a fanny!

Aaannnnd... that's my cue to leave that conversation. I slap my phone down on the bed and chuckle to myself.

Without warning, the bathroom door opens into the bedroom with a clunk. As if by magic, in a cloud of steam, Hunter appears in the doorway wrapped in a fluffy white towel from the waist down.

A mild storm of butterflies instantly flutter in my tummy. Who knew men looked like this in real life? I fist the sheets with my hands and pull it up, covering my mouth.

"Good morning, gorgeous." Hunter tilts his head.

All I can do is grin like a goofy girl under the sheet. "Hi," I say, my voice muffled.

Strutting toward the bed, Hunter bends from the waist down and plants a delicate kiss to my forehead, then my temple.

Arms straight, towering his hands on either side of me on the mattress, he places another on my eyelid. Everything Hunter does is performed with intentional care and he makes me feel extra special, always.

Using his pointer finger, he drags the sheet down that's covering my mouth.

"I haven't brushed my teeth,"

What a stupid thing to say.

"Mmm, and here's me thinking you were feeling a little shy and regretting what we did last night."

"A little shy, yes. Regret, no," I confirm.

"No regrets, that's a relief." He relaxes. "My tongue was buried deep in your pussy last night and you're feeling a little shy?"

I blush deeper than a cherry and fling myself flat against the mattress. "I don't think I'll ever get used to your filthy mouth."

Straddling over me now, he says, "You had no complaints last night." Then he leans down for a kiss as he laces his hands in mine and stretches our arms above my head.

I scoff.

"You smell of sex and me, dirty girl."

This is all so new and exciting. We simply smile at each other.

"You look so peaceful when you sleep; are you tired today?"

"Nope, I feel good."

"Just good?" he teases.

Smiling, I scrunch my nose and squeeze his hands in mine. "Yeah, just good. Why, what would you prefer me to say?"

"That you feel like a new woman and that you had the best sex of your life last night. It was for me. Please tell me it was for you too?"

"Is this to feed that ego of yours again, Mr. King?" I say, teasing.

"One hundred percent it is." His face drops. "I'm being serious now, promise. How do you feel today? Are you okay, baby?"

I've noticed he calls me baby when we have these close tender moments and then Cupcake when he's being more playful. He's a complete dream; I'm not actually sure if he's real. Maybe if I blow on him, he'll disappear into thin air, like a dandelion seed on the wind.

"I can't deny it, Hunter. I feel extraordinary today."

"Extraordinary." He beams.

"You were. I feel fabulous. A little sore though."

He frowns. "We can leave Miss Minnie alone today. I would never hurt you intentionally. I'm sorry."

"You didn't hurt me. It's just, well, it's been a long time for me and we got a little wild last night."

We both laugh.

"I'll be fine for more soon," I say suggestively.

"Oh, really? You want more, huh? I've never had so much fun. It was fun, right? And beautiful. You're entwined around my heart, forever."

Swallowing hard to fight back my emotion, I tell him, "You always know the right thing to say." I rub my thumb across his hand.

I've never known a guy to open up the way Hunter does. He wears his heart on his sleeve and I really like that about him.

Eyes locked, he asks, "What are you doing today? I wondered if you would like to spend the day together. I've been waiting weeks to spend time with you. Could we do that today?"

"No training today?"

"Nah, I have the day off and I would like to spend it with you. Do you have to teach classes though?"

"The dance studio is closed today as the joiners are coming in to remove the old lockers and install poles, which I'm looking forward to. Once I sort them out, I'm as free as a bird. I need to let them in, actually."

"Can you not stay for breakfast?"

"I'm afraid not. I really need to go to the studio, but we can get brunch when we go out for the day. There's a great little food shack down by the beach where they do the best cheese toasties ever."

"That sounds perfect."

"Crap, I just remembered my new car is being dropped off this morning. If they do that early, yes, I'm all yours today."

More seriously now, he tilts his head in thought, then his tongue dips out slightly and licks his bottom lip. "All mine for today? Or for more?"

I've been asking the same question myself.

"Today and more. You're here for a few weeks, so the more is for those," I try saying as casually as I can.

"Okay," Hunter says with a look I don't recognize, then he clears his throat. "Well then, you better get up for our day of adventure together. I would love for you to take me on all the sightseeing stuff today, visit the castle, and I want to eat ice cream and walk on the beach."

"Sounds like a braw day. I like the sound of that."

"You're wearing a bra today? What?"

"Braw means fine, good. It sounds like a good day is what it means. I never got around to buying you that Scot's tongue guide book I promised you. I need to go to the shops today and buy a book of our wee sayings. Remind me to do that."

"I really need one and I can't wait to see your new car."

"Yay, I'm getting my wheels back, baby!"

"You're so silly. It's time to get up, Miss Lazy Bones. It's going to be Eden and Hunter's Day of Fun." He cheers as he shuffles off the bed, before placing a chaste kiss to my lips and pulling me up out of the sheets.

"Ooppsie, you're naked. Well, this is turning out to be my best morning so far in Scotland." Startling me, he dips his head and takes my nipple into his mouth, sucking hard. He then moves across to the other, giving it the same attention.

Oh, that happened fast, but it feels so good. I grab on to his shoulders as joy leaps around my body and my sex throbs again.

"Oooooh."

"I want you so bad, now that I've tasted you. I'm not sure I can stop, but you need to go for a shower and we need to give Miss Minnie a rest. Also, you'll hate me if I hurt you more and you have to wait another few days longer. Plus, we have a day of adventure planned. My cock hates me right now for saying all these things," he mumbles, still kissing my skin as he travels north to my mouth.

"I know how your cock feels," I say, laughing against his mouth. "But I also agree with you. Later maybe?"

"You sure?"

I bite my bottom lip with my teeth and nod on a smile.

"I really like you, Eden."

My heart stops.

"I really like you too, Hunter."

Goofily, we smile at each other.

"I'm looking forward to today," I whisper. "But first I need clothes. And I need to let these joiners into the studio. They said they'd be here at eight."

"Okay, you go home and get ready. Text me about the time your car is being delivered, and then I'll run across. Sound good?"

"Perfect." I steal a quick kiss and then scurry about the bedroom, trying to find my clothes and trainers.

"Oh, two things, Eden," Hunter says as I'm pulling on my leggings.

"Mm-hmm?"

"First thing." He holds up his fingers. "How many fingers am I holding up?"

I count. "Seven."

He keeps them held up, pulsing his fingers in the air as if they're a flashing neon sign.

"Seven times, baby; that's how many times you came last night. Can we beat that, do you think?" he asks proudly.

This guy. "You are really competitive, aren't you?" I laugh as I put my bra on, then flip my top on over my head.

"Have to be, it's in my blood. And the second thing is… so no panties again, huh? Is this a regular thing? Do you ever wear them?"

"Eh, yeah, from time to time, but just the really stringy micro thong ones."

"Fuck's sake, Eden. Where have you been all my life?" He stalks toward me, rubbing his towel over his cock. "You need to go now, or we will never get out of this bedroom today. I'll walk you to the door. Turn around, you little tease."

Grabbing my shoes and phone, a small scream escapes my lips as he chases me down the stairs. Pulling on my trainers quickly, I hop toward the door.

"I'll see you in a couple of hours then, yeah?" I say, swiping my key off the sofa as I pass it, then fling open the front door.

Just as I leave, Hunter catches me, spins me back around, and lifts me in quick succession. I wrap my legs around him like a koala. I don't want to go. I want to stay with him forever. Our kiss is slow and deep. It lights up my soul and I feel my heart drum hard and fast in my chest. Dragging my hands through his wet hair, I want to ask him to take me back up the stairs. Lost in each other, we kiss and kiss, our tongues caressing. I don't even give a hoot that I haven't brushed my teeth yet. My dirty all-nighter level is through the roof. He pushes me against the doorjamb, rubbing his yet again hard length over my leggings. Our breathing quickly becomes heavy and heated as we lose ourselves in each other.

"Eden?"

Oh shit.

Faster than an Amazon Prime delivery, we stop kissing, pull apart, and turn our heads toward the voice.

"Morning, Mum."

"Son of a bitch," Hunter whispers. "Eh, morning, Mrs. Wallace." Hunter clears his throat as he gently lowers my feet to the ground, then places me in front of him, facing outward in the doorway to cover his massive erection.

So this is awkward, me in last night's clothes. Hunter standing here in front of my mum in just a towel where Hunter's cock has pitched a tent inside and is currently rammed against my back. World, swallow me now.

My mum raises her eyebrows high with a surprised smirk, then brings her hand to her mouth and draws a zip across it. She turns on her heel and shifts her slight figure fast across the gravel path toward the sports facility, her shoulders shuddering up and down in concealed laughter.

Bug-eyed, I draw in a large breath through my nose, then suck in my lips and hold it.

"Ho-ly-shit," Hunter exhales.

We can't hold it in anymore, and we both burst out laughing.

"My mum's seen your hard-on. What the hell just happened?"

"I'm going to get arrested for indecent exposure. How will I ever be able to look your mother in the eye now?"

"She almost saw your other eye."

With hands on his hips, he says, "Stop it. I'm a professional man." He stoops his head. "There is no coming back from this. Should I go across and apologize later?"

He's such a caring man. Bless him.

"No way. She'll be fine. You probably gave her the thrill of her year." My phone buzzes. "My God, I really have to go; that's the joiner. He's early. I need to let these guys in."

I jump out the door, leaving Hunter still in shock at our morning shenanigans. "Get dressed, you filthy bugger. Stop flashing the residents." I run down the path in delight. "See you in a wee bit."

"You are trouble. Miss Minnie is going to get it later."

Still standing in the doorway, Hunter watches me running toward the studio with my hands in the air cheering.

Eden's back in business... Well, Miss Minnie is... seven times... bloody hell.

What a night.

CHAPTER SEVENTEEN

Wheech: *verb,* snatch or remove something quickly. **Pronounced:** Whee-kh (again the kh is more of a throaty, back of throat sound. Remember that fish bone I asked you to imagine having stuck in your throat, that sound again.)

***

Eden

Shower, check. Teeth brushed, check. Hair blow-dried and straightened, check. Cute outfit, check. Keeping it simple, I went for dark indigo wash, high-waisted skinny jeans and a white tee with a large red sequined star. Dark-navy wedge trainers, check. Definitely need them to boost my height today when out with Hunter. Feeling horny still, check. Boy, it's going to be a long day if I feel like this already. Fluttery excitable tummy at the prospect of spending all day with Hunter, double check.

I can do this. I have my big girl panties on—well, my string thong on, but you know what I mean.

Still swooning over last night's incredible bedroom

antics with Hunter, I still can't quite believe how sensual he was. He's a big man with a gentle touch. He's funny, smart, and so fucking hot. Christ, will I be able to keep my hands off him today?

I've been holding back these last few weeks from him, but now it feels like I've opened my social media and can't stop scrolling, he's that addictive. We couldn't keep our hands off one another earlier. If it hadn't been for my mum interrupting, I think we would have had sex right there in the doorway. Note to self, must visit Mum tomorrow to apologize.

A text comes in on my phone with a ding. My on-screen notification shows it's from the car broker... **Ralph will deliver your car tomorrow between 9:00 and 10:00. Please let us know if you need to rearrange by calling us on this number.**

I got my days mixed up, most unlike me. I'm Mrs. Planner usually but so much has been going recently; even though I've been off, I've been busy. Well, I'm as free as a bird now to go out. I've already let the guys in at the studio. I texted Ella asking if she could come down, check the job, and lock up when they leave, so yeah, I'm good to go.

Grabbing my little navy leather Ted Baker rucksack with the gold metal bow logo I love so much, I stuff my phone, wallet, and clear lip gloss into it. I think I'm set. Oh, nope, I need a hoodie. Running back up the stairs, I grab my red hoodie with pink embroidery flowers that run down the arms. I fold it up and slip it inside my bag once I'm back down the stairs. It's a glorious day today so I won't need it now, but I probably will later when the sun goes down.

Dashing out the door, I pick up my keys and sunglasses from my oak console table and quickly check myself in my oversized oak floor mirror.

I've never been on a day out with anyone other than the girls, and I've never really been out on a date before, well, since Jamie. I'm not sure getting drunk with friends around a beach fire classifies as a date. We always spent our time with friends. Looking back, our relationship was stuck in a bad high school movie. I shake my head. No more silly thoughts. This is a fresh new start.

"Bye, Victor." Yes, I know, even though I have more of a life these days, I still chat to Victor, my cheese plant. That's still sad. But it would be a shame to stop. We're great friends; he's been there for me through everything.

Flinging my front door open reveals a waiting and eager Hunter, standing mid-knock on the other side of the door, looking sexy as sin from head to toe.

Fabric skims across his muscly arms and broad chest. He's casually dressed in a dark-forest-green collared button-up polo tee shirt, dark-navy jeans, and designer trainers to match, wearing a smile larger than a coconut crab.

My heart blooms. "Ah, I was just about to walk around to come get you." I smile.

He gently pulls me in close to his hard chest. "You forgot to text me. Who's Victor?" He leans in and kisses me, making me feel all swoony.

"My cheese plant there." I point to the spot on the floor beside my console. "Sorry, I just received a text to say my car is coming tomorrow. I got my days muddled up. Can we take your car today? And you now have really shiny lips." I reach up and wipe it off. "Suits you."

"You'd be as well taking it all off because I'm only gonna lick it off, anyway. I won't be able to keep my lips off you today, so it's pointless, Miss Wallace. What is that taste? Is that your lip gloss?" He licks his lips and rubs them with his long fingers, trying to remove it. I now know the things he can do with his tongue and those hands. My eyes zone in on his actions for a few seconds before I realize what I'm doing.

Get it together, Eden.

Pulling my front door closed and locking it shut, Hunter then takes my hand in his and interlaces our fingers as we walk toward his car.

"It's peach flavor."

"You always taste and smell divine," he replies, his eyes twinkling.

I wave to the workers in the studio as we pass by, although I have to skip a little to keep up with Hunter's long strides.

Some of them are Jamie's old mates and the guys I went to school with. They follow us with their eyes as we pass. One of them, recognizing Hunter, says, "Awright, Hunter, is The King back?"

Hunter laughs, answering back in his relaxed American drawl I so love, "Yeah, man, I sure am. You coming to watch the Championship Cup?"

"Yeah, we all are, eh, boys?" A rowdy, low murmur of yeses is mumbled from the construction team.

He waves goodbye. "See ya there, guys."

Everything seems to come so naturally to him.

Oh boy, it's going to be a long day, and he's holding my hand without a care who sees.

A girl could get used to this.

It's almost dinnertime now and we've had an incredible day together. It's been fun-filled and jam-packed.

We parked Hunter's Range Rover at the beach earlier and

grabbed some brunch from the food shack first, where we sat on the wooden benches lined along the path and made the most of the rare sunshine, just watching the world go by.

Hunter and I have eaten and chatted all day. We haven't been able to stop. It's easy and comfortable. We get on so well, everything feels so natural, like we've known each other forever.

He's shared his love of golf with me, telling me all about how he started as a young boy. He opened his heart to me about his dad passing away when he was just a young boy, but how his mum fell in love and married his incredible step dad. He also mentioned that he can't wait for me to meet his parents who are coming over for The Cup. That freaked me out a little. It's not like we're together, together, you know? He's also suggested we go out for a meal with his sister, Pippa, too, so we can get to know each other. He's such a surprise to me, a loyal family man with a really tight-knit team around him.

I've learned he's very passionate about his family, friends, and his profession, and it turns out he's funding a new golf coaching school in his hometown for underprivileged kids. What a guy.

We walked for miles, touring around Castleview Cove, visiting the castle and the many other little ancient ruins around the town. We even trampolined, and I nearly wet myself with laughter at the silly moves Hunter pulled in the air. His face was a picture, and he didn't care what anyone thought about him fooling around. He enjoys having fun all the time. We also whipped into one of the Scottish tourist shops and I bought Hunter a Scots dialect book. Fingers crossed it helps him to understand me now.

Next we visited The Championship course as he wanted

to show me where he won The Cup the last time. Pointing out the exact spot he shot his winning putt from.

Hunter was instantly recognized. Several golfers stopped asking for selfies and autographs. This was another world to me. I've never been around a celebrity like this before. In the golfing world, Hunter seems to be big and people love him. He took his time with his fans today, chatting with ease, asking what their handicaps were, if they were here on vacation or visiting for the day with plans on coming back to watch the Championship Cup.

Hunter even introduced me to them all, placing his athletic arms around my shoulders as if to protect me. All the fans wished him well and were rooting for his comeback. He's so well presented and knew exactly what to say. You would never know he's only three years older than me. He acts older than his age when he slides into professional golfer mode. I do not know what a golfer makes in terms of money, but he acts like the guy next door, so grounded and very appreciative of his life and his dedicated fans. It was quite special to watch him in action today.

We stopped by for ice cream at Castle Cones. Toni wasn't working today, but Hunter hinted at the possibility of that being due to her spending the day with Noah. Goodness, Toni must like him if she's taken a day off.

When we stood in the huge queue, waiting to be served, Hunter informed me he's now on flavor thirty-five. He's made real progress on his ice cream bucket list, which I had totally forgotten all about. I think I need to check out my bucket list again and get cracking on that bad boy.

Grateful I put my wedge trainers on today, Hunter loved the fact he didn't have to bow so low today when we kissed, because, well, we have kissed an insane amount of times today, and Hunter doesn't seem to care who's watching. He literally hasn't stopped touching and caressing me; it's filled me with energy all day. I think I might be glowing with happiness. Or maybe that's the redness glowing from the stubble rash on my chin.

Just before we headed back to the car, we nipped into Cupcakes & Castles to buy a selection tray of my favorite cupcakes, letting Hunter pick which ones he wanted too.

I'm currently standing and watching Hunter fumble about in the back of his Range Rover and watch as he pulls out a tartan blanket which I recognize from the cabins. He begins to take off his shoes.

"Whatcha doin'?" I ask.

"We are going to sit on the beach, watch the sunset, and eat cupcakes, and maybe we can get some dinner later. I just want to go grab some bottled water from the food shack before we head down to the sand. That okay?"

"Sounds amazing." How romantic.

He struts off to grab what we need as I shuck my trainers off my feet. Once we have everything we need, we plod barefoot a couple of feet down the sand, find a spot, lay the blanket out, and park our bums on it.

My feet throb from a long day of walking.

Covering my hand over the top of the tray of cupcakes, I say, "Before we begin, there are rules, Hunter."

Tanned arms straight out behind him, with his long legs stretched out in front, sunglasses now atop his head, he looks at me, confused. "Rules for what?"

"For the cupcakes. There are cupcake rules."

"Okay."

I start. "First rule." I hold my finger up. "You can't change your choice. What you chose back there in the shop"—I point back in the direction of the town center—"that is yours. You can't change your mind."

He laughs at my absurdity.

"Second rule, no laughing—cupcakes are serious business."

"You just made that up; it's not a rule."

"It is now, Hunter. It is now." I narrow my eyes with seriousness.

"Third and final rule, no asking for a bite of the other person's cupcake."

"What? Not even a nibble?"

"Nope, not even a nibble. That's breaking the rules. Now which one did you pick again?"

"The Yolo one."

"Like hell it was," I say a bit too loudly, turning heads. "That one is mine; that is my all-time favorite. You are so not having that. And if you take it, I will wheech it off you."

"You're a peculiar little thing, Eden Wallace."

"In a good way though, huh?" I cheekily raise my eyebrows as I open the box.

He shakes his head. "Yeah, in a good way. Mine is the bright-blue-and-pink one. I think it was bubble gum or something."

"How very masculine."

"You learned exactly how masculine I was last night, so don't even go there or I will have to give you another lesson right here on this blanket, missy."

I snort as I retrieve my cupcake from the box. "I'm not sure if the mums and dads would like that," I say as I take my first bite and moan out loud.

"Are you teasing me?"

I cheekily grin with my teeth full of chocolate sponge and frosting. "Yup."

"You're an animal."

"I am when it comes to cupcakes."

"And sex, you were a fucking animal last night for sure. Where did my quiet girl disappear to? I unleashed a sex-crazed goddess last night."

My quiet girl.

I blush. Or dear Lord, here we go. "I think someone invaded my body last night."

"Too fucking right they did; it was me," Hunter firmly states.

I burst out laughing, spraying sponge and crumbs everywhere. Hunter screws his eyes closed, crinkling his nose and puffing out his cheeks before he brushes the crumbs off his face, top, and jeans.

I'm so ladylike; I would definitely never have made good wifey material if I lived in *Bridgerton* times.

"Do cupcakes make you gaga or something?"

I hold in a muffled laugh with my mouth full of cake and nod my head furiously. "Oh my God, I'm so sorry. They really do," I mumble, covering my mouth.

"Come here. I need protection. Sit in between my legs before you spray me again."

Crawling over, I rest my back to his front, sitting between Hunter's legs, and let out a sigh of contentment as he wraps his free arm around me.

"That's better. My eyes are safe now from your cupcake spitfire rounds." He chuckles.

We sit in silence, watching the sun kiss the ocean as it goes down for the day, listening to the seagulls shrill and circle above, ever hopeful of a stolen snack. I hold on tight to my cupcake, knowing the bravery of these cheeky gulls, and enjoy the sweetness of my cupcake.

I take my time with mine, nibbling along the bottom first, saving the top part for last—that's the best bit.

Quicker than I can react, Hunter leans over my shoulder,

lunges at my hand that's holding my cupcake in the air, opens his enormous mouth, takes a massive bite, and wolfs it down.

"What in the ever-loving hell is wrong with you? You broke the rules," I cry out. "And you took the top bit with all the caramel. I was saving that." I raise my hands to the sky.

Circling my head toward him, he opens his mouth, showing me the cake inside. "You're a savage. Utterly disgusting."

Hunter puffs out his cheeks full of cake, laughing. He's so funny and so not what I expected him to be like. He's cheeky and playful all the time.

I hold up what's left of my cupcake. "You even ate the caramel chocolate Yolo. That's like the most bestest bit. You know the whole, loving someone enough to give them your last chocolate slogan; I love myself enough for me to eat it, I really do. You have, like, no heart right now."

Hunter stills suddenly. Oh, what did I say?

Leaning into my ear, he whispers, "Do you think you could ever love me enough to give me your last chocolate or cupcake, Eden?"

I actually have no idea what to say to that. Well, that's a lie. I think I could really fall in love with him. I think I've already started to fall for this dazzlingly perfect man who's entered my life like a whirlwind.

But I'm not so sure about sharing how I feel.

Should I share and show myself a little more? He hasn't run so far and I've shared lots with him, even more than I have with some of my closest friends. He's seen all my ugly parts and thoughts.

He clears his throat. "Relax. It's okay. You don't have to answer."

Slowly, I place what's left of my cupcake into the box,

lick my lips, and turn myself to the side to face him. "You know I'm not good at this opening up stuff; however, around you, I think you keep lacing my food and drinks, or the air or something with truth serum, because I want to be honest with you." Not for a second does he take his eyes off me, patiently waiting in anticipation.

"I *really* like you, Hunter. I do believe fate brought us together. We get on so well; it's like instant magic between us. The sex is spectacular." I splay my fingers out in the air. "I feel so relaxed around you. You make me feel safe and radiant. You give me the confidence to just be me, and you're everything I could ever want, but I'm not sure how this works, this whole long-distance thing. I like you so much I'm not even sure that I could bear to be apart from you for long periods of time. I don't know what your golf tournament schedule is like. I'm guessing it's busy. And could you keep up with a relationship, ping-ponging back and forth between Florida, focusing on your career and then me here in Scotland?"

I draw a breath.

"My life has been on pause waiting for another man. And believe me, you are absolutely *nothing* like Jamie— that's not what I'm saying—but it would be kinda the same thing, me waiting again. Continents separate us. My dance studio keeps me here in Castleview Cove. I have a business here. A really glorious business at that. We've just started getting sponsorship opportunities through Instagram and our TikTok account is flying. Eva had some brilliant ideas when I was off. My life is here."

His shoulders sag.

I swallow as I continue my brutal honesty. "If I worked in an office or something and I could work anywhere, then it would be different. Maybe, in fact, I know I would leave with you in a heartbeat. I know this for sure, having spent just a few days with you. I watched you with your fans, the way you treat your team and talk about your family. We share the same values. I value all those things, the same as you.

"But..." And there's that word again. "My family is here. My sisters are here. And I've started to find myself, enjoy my life and my family again. They've supported me through everything. I've had so much fun these last few days with you. Like laugh till it hurts fun. Exploring the town today with you, reminded me of the wonderful place I live."

Hunter squeezes me tight in his chiseled arms and wraps his legs around me in comfort. I feel so tiny, cocooned within him, like a fragile egg in a sturdy robin's nest.

"You are an incredible man, Hunter," I say into his chest. "I want to spend the time you have in Castleview Cove with you, certainly as much as your training plan will allow, and then you have The Cup soon, but we can have some fun together. Honestly, I'm really not sure how I will cope when you go; I already feel so close to you. But I would like to spend more time with you, if you want to," I finally say on a whisper.

My heart constricts.

"This is shit," is all he says in response.

We huddle together in silence as the sound of people shrieking, the odd shrill of a seagull, and the crashing of the waves against the golden sand fizzes around us.

Eventually, he whispers, "Do you think we could we make it work? The long-distance thing? Shit, but you said you didn't want to wait around. I'll shut up."

It's odd how this impressive man really wants to try with me. He has no problems telling me how he feels, and I really like that he trusts me enough to open up to me.

I move out from his athletic chest. "Hey, I would like

nothing better than to make it work. And no, I don't want to hang about waiting; I really don't. I've been there and I've got the heartbreak to prove it, but we've only spent a few days together. Why don't we see how the next few weeks go, and then we can see how we feel, huh?" I say, trying to lighten the mood.

Genuinely, I do not know how this will work. I try to tell myself, even if we get a few weeks together, then that will be okay, won't it?

"I meant what I said to you back in The Vault. I see my future with you too, but I don't know how this works either. Why is everything so complicated?" He skirts around my question.

Hunter's strong arms scoop me up and I straddle my legs around his waist. Pulling me in closer than close, Hunter spirals his long arms around me and wraps me in a giant bear hug, resting his head on my shoulder. As if not wanting to let me go, he holds me tighter and lets out a deep breath.

Into the screen of my hair, he asks, "Tell me your dreams, Eden."

"What do you mean?"

"Tell me what you want to do with your life and the business; where do you see yourself in five or ten years?"

I try to lean back to look at him, but he pulls me into his warmth and I bask in his citrus aftershave that stirs my senses. "Just stay like this. Dream big, baby. Tell me."

I think about this for a moment.

Here goes.

"If you'd asked me six weeks ago, I don't think I would have been able to answer you, but I guess, lately, I think I would like to see the business growing. Moving to a bigger studio perhaps, merchandising, taking on more teachers. Maybe becoming more of an academic school for dance, and I've always dreamed of being married in the small church on the grounds of the retreat. You should see it; it's so pretty." I lose myself in my dreams. "And I would love a family, although I'm not sure I can carry a baby full term, and that's scary, but the love I felt for Chloe was overwhelming. I can only imagine what that must feel like to give birth, you know, properly. And the little flutters in my belly I felt, even when she was so tiny, were indescribable. I want the happily ever after, the two point four children, a house filled with love and laughter." I smile as I say that, imagining this life I've just described.

I'm not sure where all that came from. Sharing all this with him feels raw and really personal.

"That sounds a little too perfect. I'm not sure if I will get that; the Universe keeps throwing me curveballs, like us, now."

Hunter unwraps his arms and runs his hands up my back. I don't know what he's thinking as he stays quiet.

A kiss to my neck relieves some of the tension between us and the words I've just spoken. A soft flutter of tingles waves down my spine and neck at his touch.

Slowly, he moves to my mouth. Hunter encompasses my face with his enormous hands as we share an almost there kiss. Like the delicate wings of a fluttering dragonfly, it's a ghost of a kiss, but I feel it everywhere. I have to choke back a breath as an odd sensation buffers in my throat. This feels sentimental... loving.

We hold motionless, connected by our soft lips touching, neither of us wanting to be anywhere else but here in this moment.

"I want to spend the next few weeks with you. As much as we can squeeze in. I'd really like that," Hunter wisps finally answering my question.

"Me too."

"Are you ready to go home?"

"Yeah. Will you stay the night with me?"

"I would love to, baby." A small smile forms on his lips.

"Okay."

"I don't want to move from here." His forehead touches mine as we gaze into each other's eyes.

The weather has turned. "I know, me either, but it's getting cold; I'm a wee bit chilly."

"Ah, and here's me thinking your nipples were as hard as rocks because I turned you on," he says, giving my ass a little squeeze.

I laugh softly. "Nope."

"Oh, that hurts, you devil woman. C'mon then, Cupcake, let's go. I don't want you catching a chill."

As we shuffle to our feet, we notice the impending dark clouds above us signifying rain. "We'd better hurry; rain always comes on fast here," I say as I pick up our things.

"Tell me about it. I've been caught out a few times already here."

"Hunter?" A voice breaks our chat.

A quick look up reveals its Fraser, Jamie's brother.

Bugger.

CHAPTER EIGHTEEN

Clarty: *adjective,* dirty, filthy. **Pronounced:** Clar-tay.

Eden

"Holy shit, man; how are you, Fraser?" Hunter moves toward him, holding his arm out for a handshake.

This may be a little awkward. I keep my head slightly bowed. I haven't seen Fraser in forever.

"I'm great, fantastic, in fact. What about you? I saw you were staying here on your Instagram; have you've been here for over a month now? Are you staying at the retreat? It's a phenomenal facility. I know the family well. How's your back? Christ, I have so many questions; we really need to catch up."

Fraser seems to have caught a bit of a transatlantic accent while living in the States, I note. I think my mum told me he married an American girl. You can hardly detect his Scottish accent anymore. It dives in now and again, but not much.

Hunter laughs. "We really do. Eh, I think you know Eden?"

Oh heck.

I stop busying myself and lift my head fully, coming eye to eye with Fraser's crystal-blue eyes.

"Eden? How the hell are you?" Fraser rushes in to give me a hug.

I wasn't expecting that. Not knowing where to put my hands, it ends up being an awkward hug from me. "Yeah, I'm good, thanks. You? I haven't seen you in years," I stutter.

Even Fraser had the decency to come to Chloe's funeral, and we both know that was the last time we saw one another.

"Yeah, I'm okay." He half smiles.

I'm not convinced by his reply.

"Is this your son?" I motion toward the boy playing around Fraser's ankles in the sand.

"Yeah, this is Ethan." He points to a very dark-brown-haired little boy who looks about seven or eight years old.

"It's great being back. I have missed Castleview so much."

Silence runs between us.

"So are you two together then?" Fraser asks, pointing to us both.

Both at the same time, we reply.

"Yes."

"No."

Hunter turns his head to me.

Crap, I should have said yes.

"Well, it's new," Hunter says, grinning, but I detect a minor annoyance.

"Ah." Fraser smiles with a downturned mouth.

"How are you, Eden?"

I plant a smile on my face. "I'm good actually, yeah." I don't want to say anything else for fear of giving too much away about how crap the last few years have been or to stop me asking where Jamie is, not that I care, but a small part of me is curious if he still keeps in touch with his numbskull of a brother.

As Fraser stands before me, I can't help but see how dissimilar they are now. Fraser's got his shit together; he's a family man and career-driven. Jamie is like the polar opposite of that; well, he was with me. I wonder what he's like now after all this time.

"My mum was saying your dance school has really taken off and is super busy. How's Eva and, eh, Ella? It's been so long."

"The school is really busy, yeah, and the girls are great. Ella, well, is Ella, as you know. She has a wee dog, Treacle. She bought a house, around from your mum and dad's. The new ones in the Old Courtyard. Have you spoken to her since..." Fraser and Ella were boyfriend and girlfriend back in high school. He's a little older by a couple of years. Eva always said she felt left out because we had a brother each.

Ella was so in love with Fraser, it broke her heart when he was awarded a full golf scholarship over in the States. When he left, it devastated her. They vowed they would keep in touch, they lasted five years doing the long-distance relationship thing, but Fraser got really busy with his training and tournaments. On our twenty-first birthday, he called and ended it with Ella. I don't think she's ever really gotten over him; in fact, I know she hasn't.

I reckon that's why she's never had a boyfriend since, and the reason she's turning her life into a zoo. She's trying to fill a gap, and I don't think she even realizes she's doing it. Us Wallace girls are as bad as each other.

Fraser shakes his head. "No, we haven't, not even at the funeral, Eden. I wish she would talk to me. There's so much I needed to explain, but she couldn't even look at me. I lost my best friend too. The whole Ella and me thing was a mess. Maybe you can put in a friendly word for me, tell her I would like to have a chat perhaps? I'm here now until The Cup," he says with a tentative smile.

Oh, yikes. I'll need to tread carefully with this. Better to speak to her than text. He has a family now too; I'm not sure how that will go down.

Ella cried for weeks when he left, and then months when he ended it between them. Ella never did understand what happened. She still doesn't. Ella and Fraser spent every waking hour together. Ella even attended his golf lessons with him too. She adored him, and he mellowed her out. I always thought they'd get married; I was so positive.

"I'll try," I reply to Fraser's appeal. I don't think she'll listen to me on this one, but it's worth a shot. Fraser's a lovely guy too. He was perfect for our Ella. It was such a shame it never worked out.

"You and Ella, huh?" Hunter jokes.

Fraser bobs his head back and forth. "Yeah, man, she was my world at one point, until she wasn't," he says, his voice now laden with emotion.

Out of the blue, it strikes me. It's like a carbon copy of Hunter and me. Long distance doesn't work. That's a fact. The evidence is standing in front of me.

A gentle tug of pain shoots through my chest.

"And Eva?" Fraser asks, pulling me out of my thoughts.

"Eva married Ewan and they have two wee ones now."

"And you, Eden? You're good, yeah?"

I give him a more relaxed and confident nod this time.

You know what? I am feeling good; I'm great, in fact.

"Yeah, Fraser," I reply. "I'm happier than I've ever been, actually." My mouth curves a massive smile as I look directly at Hunter. He does, he makes me happy. Why am I not showing this?

Oh yeah, I know why. Because my time with Hunter is like a ticking time bomb waiting to go off. We have an expiration date; that's why. Like the sands of time slipping through our relationship hourglass.

And it's only a little fun for a few weeks, right?

Screw it, in the spur of the moment, I walk across the sand toward Hunter and circle my arms around his waist. If we're only together a few weeks, then I'm claiming him as mine *for now*.

The yo-yo of emotions bouncing about in my heart and head are quite confusing to me today.

If Hunter could bang his chest in a Tarzan style, I think he would as his beautiful face is beaming stronger than a lighthouse. He kisses the top of my head and bundles me into him, taking sheer pleasure from my actions in front of Fraser.

"You guys look great together. You look great, Eden, seriously. Man, I'm so glad I bumped into you guys. We should catch up soon. Before the competition. Can we try to do that? Can I DM you?" Fraser shakes his head in revelation.

"Yeah, you're on, man." Hunter squeezes my waist.

"Okay, well, look, I had better go before the rain starts, and we still have bath time to tackle. I'm sure there's sand in places I don't want to even think about. Ethan is clarty."

Ethan cutely giggles.

I wonder if Jamie knows how adorable his nephew is, or if he's ever seen him.

"Well, you two take care, see you soon, and that's a promise. Can you remember to speak to Ella for me?"

"Yeah, I'll will Fraser."

Hunter shakes Fraser's hand as we say our goodbyes and we watch as Fraser dips his hand into his pocket, takes his phone out, and starts tapping on it madly as his son runs behind him... Maybe he's DMing Hunter already?

Hunter whispers, "You okay? That didn't freak you out or anything? He didn't mention his brother, you know; I was hoping he wouldn't. I don't want you to be upset."

"I'm perfectly fine," I whisper back.

As soon as Fraser's out of earshot, Hunter turns me in his embrace with a playful scowl on his face.

"Good, cuz now I can give you an ass whooping. No? You said *no* to us being together?" he says seriously but starts tickling my ribs.

"Stop tickling me. I need a wee." He stops. "I'm so sorry; we haven't talked about what we are. What am I? Are we dating for the next few weeks, or do I say I'm your girlfriend or should I refer to myself as your fuckbunny?"

"My what?" he exclaims. "You are not my fuckbunny. You're the one ordering bloody rabbit vibrators; you're the one with the fuckbunny." He stands back with his hands on his hips.

I love how he flips between being funny and serious in seconds. You just never quite know what's going to happen next with Hunter.

"From now on, you tell people we are dating for the next few weeks. Okay? Me and you." He points to us both. "We are dating. We are exclusive. We've talked about it. That's it settled. Got it?"

For the next few weeks.

He's so serious that I can't help but laugh. "Okay." I then

can't stop laughing. I think I'm hysterical; he said we are dating and we're exclusive. Holy crap.

"You had better stop laughing at me, little girl, or I'll take you as my fuckbunny tonight."

I bend over with shocked, hysterical laughter.

I bruised his ego but now he's claimed me as his and his word is final. That's it and I have absolutely no problems with any of it. Not at all.

As my laughter subsides and Hunter finishes gathering up our stuff, I'm not prepared when he scoops me up like a caveman over his shoulder unexpectedly.

"Argh, put me down," I squeal. "You'll hurt your back. Although I don't mind this view—you have a fine ass, Mr. King. King of the Fine Ass, that's what your nickname should be."

"It's only ten steps to the car. Be quiet, you naughty girl. If you don't, I'm gonna have to spank you."

"Oh good, anything else you have in mind?" I tease.

"You'll see when we get home."

"Does it involve handcuffs?"

"What? Do you want it to involve handcuffs? Where the hell am I getting them at this time of night? I'm so unprepared for you, Eden Wallace."

The pair of us giggle as Hunter stomps up the sand back to the car.

"Take me home, Hunter," I purr as he slides me to the ground.

"I'm doing just that. I have plans for you tonight. Now get in the car," he says through gritted teeth, smiling and bulging his eyes.

❋

Driving in silence into the retreat, with the crunch of the gravel beneath the tires, Hunter pulls into my private drive and swings his large black Range Rover around directly outside my front door.

In a low, joking voice, Hunter turns and says, "You had better run; you are in so much trouble after today. No? You said *no*?" He shakes his head in disbelief.

Laughing again, I say, "Hunter, please don't hurt me. I know I've been a bad girl. I promise I won't do it again." He's right. Where did quiet Eden go?

"Get out of the car."

We jump out the car. I literally have to, it's so bloody high.

Carrying on this playful charade, I say, "What are you going to do to punish me, Hunter?" I unlock my front door.

"I'm going to fuck all the nos out of you."

Yes, please. Do it now.

I start running through the door and up the stairs through my darkened house.

I hear a clatter behind me. "Aw, shit, that's gonna bruise. I don't even know where your bedroom is." I hear him groan.

"Alexa lights on," I command. Instantly he spots me on the stairs. As the lights illuminate the barn, he runs toward me with his trademark grin again.

Holy shit, this is exciting and I squeal. Never has sex or being with a man been so adventurous and fun. The difference is, I want to be. If I'm doing this with Hunter, then I am really doing this over the next few weeks. I'm kicking the backside out of these wonderful feelings he's sparked.

My doors are wide open, so to speak. I want to experience all this newness with him.

As I try to close my bedroom door, a firm hand pushes

it back open. In an instant Hunter grabs me and tackles me to my king-sized bed, roughly smacking his lips to mine.

"Gotcha," he growls.

We start furiously tearing each other's clothes off. Both our shirts are removed in an instant. Then yanking my jeans down, he whips them off my legs.

"How much do you like these panties?" he mumbles against my inner thigh. "Not that there's any point wearing them, fuck me, it's like two pieces of string and a postage stamp."

"Not that much." I laugh. As the words leave my mouth, I feel the fabric pull against my skin and hear a ripping noise as Hunter tears them from my body. Balling them into his fist, he bunches them into his pocket. "These are mine now." Hot damn.

Hunter buries his face in between my legs and dips his tongue straight onto my now pulsating clit. Inserting a finger, he slides it in and out with a little speed.

"Fucking soaking."

Compared to last night, this is more carnal. Like we're done taking things slow and just want to fuck each other's brains out. Crikey, listen to me.

Standing back, he unbuttons his jeans. I pull up to my knees and kneel on the edge of the bed, helping him with his buttons. "No boxers," I say, spotting the top of his dripping wet cock on the waistline of his jeans.

"Two can play at that game, baby."

His beautiful cock springs free from his jeans. I may not be very experienced sex-wise, but I'm amazing at giving head. If you've been paying attention, then you'll remember Jamie was a one-sided lover. Hence the reason I'm great at this. It was all he really wanted.

Softly wrapping my hand around his thick length, I lean in and kiss his glistening crown.

"Holy shit," Hunter gasps.

Gripping his hard shaft a little more firmly, I wet my tongue, open my mouth, and flatten it to the underside of his cock. Licking up and down with care, I curve my tongue upward to a point. I do this repeatedly, up and down.

Slowly I wrap my wet mouth around the head of his cock, taking him in lick by lick, swirling my tongue around, at the same time moving my hand up and down his shaft.

I gaze up from his thick cock to his eyes, taking in this glorious man. "You feel so good in my mouth," I say around his length.

Digging my nails into his ass, I take more of him into my mouth. I continue to suck, lick, swirl, and begin to moan myself, as I really start to enjoy it. He's big, really big, but I'm getting so turned on at the reaction on his face and the sounds he's making. I'm lost in the moment, and a rush of wetness floods between my legs.

"Aw, fuck. Where did you learn to do that? Fuck it, don't answer." He flings his head back and grabs the back of my head.

"Internet porn." I mumble against his cock.

"Good answer." He moans loudly.

Feathering my hands around, I lightly massage his balls. Hunter grips my hair, urging me to go deeper.

I hum against his cock and pull back a little as I flick the tip of my tongue around his more sensitive areas and sheath my mouth over him again and suck hard.

"Baby, you're gonna have to stop cuz I'll come if you don't."

Doing the same again, he moans. "Oh, oh, oh. You do have to stop," he says, pulling back with a whimpered laugh.

His cock leaves my mouth with a pop and I look upward to meet his eyes, now blazing with desire. "You're so good at that, baby."

"I know," I purr.

Whisking off his jeans, Hunter settles back on the bed, pulling me on top of him.

"Get on my cock, baby."

He doesn't have to ask me twice.

Jumping on top, I straddle him and slide the head of his cock back and forth along my wet folds, teasing his head at my entrance a few times before sliding down his throbbing shaft. Ooooh, that feels phenomenal. I'm still a little sore from last night, but I want this so badly.

I swing my hips back and forth, snaking and circling, taking his cock deep into my core. Hunter pulls me down for an angsty kiss and he continues to piston his hips, thrusting hard.

"Now tell me again, what's the word you're not to use anymore?"

"No?" I gasp.

"Are you questioning the no now?"

"No," I pant, clenching and tightening my pussy as his cock teases my G-spot.

"You're a bad girl; you're not allowed to use that word anymore." He slaps my ass.

Oh, that was unexpected, but I quite liked it as a shiver of goosebumps tidal wave across my body and sparks of tingles spread warmth to my sex.

"Ah, do that again, Hunter."

His hand connects with my ample ass with a loud slap, and I cry out in pleasure.

"Get up on your feet and squat, now," Hunter commands.

Placing my feet flat against the mattress, I move into position and start squatting up and down on his thick hot cock. Ah, I won't last long like this; I'm already teetering on the edge of an orgasm.

Hunter grabs handfuls of my ass as he moves me up and down, ramming in and out of me with hungry intensity. "Now what's the word you should have used?"

"Yes," I shout out.

"Again."

"Yes," I whimper as I feel my impending orgasm. "Yes, yes, yes, yes. Don't stop." I pant out in time with every fast thrust up and down his hard cock.

"Come, Eden, come," Hunter begs, unable to hold back his own impending orgasm. Grabbing my hips, he thrusts himself deeper.

I come fast as an orgasm the magnitude higher than the Richter scale explodes across my body from the tip of my toes to the top of my head. My sex pulses wildly, not stopping as wave upon multiple wave of explosions hit me one after the other, ramping up from one to the next, coming in quick succession.

It won't stop; I can't stop it.

Hunter groans loudly, coming furiously inside of me as my pulsating pussy clenches all around him over and over. My heart sprints like it's reached the finish line and my breathing is off the charts.

Each time I have an orgasm, it gets stronger and lasts longer. I actually feel like I'm going to pass out and I'm having an out-of-body experience.

My inhibitions have well and truly gone out the window, allowing myself to experience pleasure with no doubts or fears.

"What the fuck was that?" Hunter pants as perspiration shines across his body.

"I think I may have just had one of the longest orgasms of my life. It wouldn't stop," I say, finally trying to catch my breath. Sliding my feet and legs back, I rest my head on Hunter's rippled chest.

"Holy fuck. That felt epic. You clenched around my cock so tight I thought you were gonna strangle him. Never in my life have I ever felt anything like it." He laughs, flinging his head on the bed.

"I think I'm dead," I say with my eyes closed. I'm so tired suddenly.

Rolling me a little awkwardly onto my back, still connected, Hunter brushes my hair off my face. "You keep surprising me."

"I keep surprising myself," I coo.

I feel so relaxed and at ease.

"I think I've woken up all your brain cells; they're now firing on all cylinders and your body knows exactly what to do. Maybe it was me chasing you; that was fucking hot and exciting."

"It was." I chuckle softly. "Although I quite liked it when you spanked me; that was different."

"Oh, reeealllllly." He shakes his head in wonder. "What was the word you're not allowed to say again?"

"Eh, I'm clueless. I think it's fallen out of my head. You fucked those words all out of me. It worked."

We both laugh.

"You're an incredible woman."

"An incredible woman that needs to go clean up. Wanna join me in the shower? Just for a shower though, I'm shattered," I say.

"You can just stand and I'll wash, no funny business, I

promise, although I find it really hard keeping my hands off your sexy ass and these boobs." He grabs my boobs and sucks my nipples into his mouth one after the other. "I'm a lucky man," he says between teasing flicks and licks with his skillful tongue.

Feeling so turned on by his sensual touch and the friction of him still inside me, I begin to rock against him.

"Oooooooh, that's nice. Keep doing that."

"I thought you were tired?" he says, nipping my pebbled skin.

"I am."

I moan as he pinches my nipple hard, then rubs them back and forth quickly with his fingertips.

He increases his speed, brushing, then pinching even harder each time.

Taking his tongue, he lashes at my nipple with urgency, and flattens it roughly, moving from one nipple to next, heightening all my senses.

Flicks of his stiff tongue pulsate back and forth.

"Ah, Hunter." I push my hands into his hair and feel his rock hard cock inside me.

How is that possible? I think he's superhuman.

Twisting my nipple hard, I feel him moving in and out of me in quick relentless pumps.

"We are filthy," Hunter mumbles.

"I don't care, keep doing that. Fuck me," I breathe.

Sex with Hunter is so *fucking* hot; I want him all of the time.

Hunter gives my nipple a long pull, stretching it out between his teeth, teasing the other with his fingers.

Rolling his hot tongue over my hard nipples, he slams in and out of me, pistoning faster and faster, driving me insane. Over and over again.

I grip my hands in his hair, burying him into my tits before filling the air with ecstasy. "That feels incredible."

Passion and fire rockets across my body as I release an almighty howl as I come again, and my skin screams in pleasure.

"Oh, baby, you're so fucking beautiful."

With intention now, Hunter flings his head up from my chest, slides his forearms quickly up under my back, and hinges his fingers to the top of my shoulders.

Palms to my back and shoulder, giving him the leverage he needs, he bows his head into my neck, impaling me with rapid-fire strokes.

"Come inside me, Hunter. Fuck me like you mean it," I pant.

"I'm gonna," he bellows.

Snaking my legs around his waist, I lock my ankles, digging my heels into his rock-hard ass, holding him firm.

Continuing his onslaught, he buries himself deeper and deeper inside my body; I tense and clench my pussy muscles, urging him on.

Hunter mumbles filthy words into my shoulder. Uttering words of how my pussy feels, how it feels to be inside me, and how he loves how hard I make him come.

He drives himself wild.

Within moments he explodes inside me again, roaring my name into my neck. I feel his cock pulse and twitch as he gasps against my shoulder, then collapses his full weight on top of me.

"Holy shit," he mumbles into my neck.

"I wasn't expecting that."

"That was amazing. Eden, you drive me fucking crazy."

As our breathing levels out, I'm now aware of Hunter's weight on top of me.

"You're gonna have to get up though. Jesus, I can't breathe."

"Sorry, baby," he says clumsily, lifting himself off and pulling himself out of me before rolling onto the mattress, then nuzzling into me.

It's always so explosive with us. We are dynamite together.

"Let's quickly clean up, cuz we are a pair of dirty buggers, order pizza, then we'll have a shower," I say, getting up from the bed.

Having cleaned up quickly, back on the bed, I'm draped over Hunter's body, exhausted from our intense sex session.

"What happened just there, Eden?" Hunter drifts his fingers back and forth across my skin.

"What do you mean?" I ask, confused.

I lift my head to find Hunter's eyes staring back at me.

"Well, your entire body comes alive with me. I only have to touch you and you light up, and ditto for me. There's this level of attraction, intimacy, and trust I can't explain between us. I've felt it from the moment I met you. But it's not just the sex; we click. Like we're soul mates or something. It's like we already know each other. Our bodies talk to one another. We get on so well and I'm not sure I can fight this thing we have or only do this for a few weeks. It fucking hurts already thinking about when I have to leave. Leave *you*." He pushes the fingers of his free hand into his eyes and then drags his hand down his face roughly.

Oh God, he's really upset. Dread slithers through my body.

"I don't know what to say."

"And I don't know what to do," he says, sounding almost defeated.

Reaching out, he places a hand on my cheek and gently smooths his thumb across my face with his gentle touch.

Rolling his head away, his eyes gaze at the ceiling, deep in thought, as he draws in a frustrated breath.

It's not often Hunter is serious, but when he is, he's intense, passionate, and intentional with his words and actions.

I place a kiss on his bronzed shoulder.

"You okay?"

"Yeah, ignore me." He sighs.

I whisper softly, "I feel the same too."

Hunter rolls on to his side to face me and strokes my flushed cheeks.

"Hey, I don't want to upset you. Not after what we just did. That was indescribable."

We gaze at each other.

"You're right though, Hunter. We keep going round in circles about how we feel and only having a few weeks together. We can talk about it all we want, but there's no simple solution; in fact, there isn't one. I think we have to face the facts. If one of us catches deeper feelings, then one of us will get hurt, and that sucks big-time, but what else can we do?"

I gulp as he continues to gaze at me.

"I already have, Eden."

All I can do is blink and breathe as my heart beats uncontrollably in my chest. I feel things for him, just like I said last night and confessed today, but I think Hunter means more than that. Is he talking about love?

I'm not sure if he's waiting for me to say something back.

Hunter clears his throat. "Okay, I'm hungry," he changes the subject as if the last few minutes never happened. "Let's order that pizza."

"Yeah, let's do that." I respect his wishes, not wanting to talk about it anymore.

"I'll order," he says, busying himself, trying to find his phone on the floor. "You go ahead. I'll be there in a minute. Pepperoni?"

"Please with extra cheese."

"Great."

Bugger, this feels awkward.

Something changed in those last confession-filled moments, and I'm not sure if it's good or bad.

Jumping in the shower, I mull over Hunter's words and I let the hot water run over me. Cranking the heat up, my muscles relax and I loosen up.

I close my eyes and let the multiheaded shower rain down on me.

I wait for Hunter, but he doesn't appear. Realizing he's not coming in, I wash quickly, grab my towel to dry myself, and head back into my bedroom to find Hunter sitting fully dressed on the edge of my bed, head in his hands bowed over, resting on his knees.

Oh, this can't be good. "Eh, are you not having a shower?" I swipe my thumb over my shoulder.

He sighs, long and deep, then sits straight, running his hands down the thighs of his jeans.

Looking at his watch, he says, "I'll get one back at my place. I think I should go."

Okaaaay.

"Are you not staying then?"

He takes a deep breath.

"You're gonna think I'm a dick, but I can't do this." His voice cracks.

The realization of what he's saying stabs a pain through my racing, uneasy heart.

"I can't be with you for *just* a few weeks without getting hurt, more than this hurts right now. I don't want to do that to you. Or me. It's not fair to either of us. The feelings I already have for you are beyond what I have felt for anyone. It's shocked me how quick it's all happened with you. Spending more time with you is only going to make it worse. I can't do it, Eden."

My heart's now battering against my ribs. At a loss of what to say, I stand motionless.

"Sharing your dreams with me on the beach earlier, I realize now, I don't think I can give you any of it. You deserve someone who can. But I'm not that man. You are a true romantic at heart. You talk about all those romance books all the time. You really deserve a happily ever after, Eden, but with someone here in Castleview Cove. Get married in the church you so love and have your little family too. But with someone who has a less complicated career and who lives close by. Putting two and two together, I'm guessing Ella and Fraser split because of his golfing career. It's so fucking obvious now. I don't want that for us."

He stands from the bed and walks toward me, then cups my face with his tender hands.

Please stop doing that. I suck in a deep breath.

"Truly believe magical things are going to happen to you, because they will if you believe, Eden. Imagine your happy ending is as if it's already happening. I want to give that to you, but I can't," he says through his pained words.

I swear to God this man has been sent directly from the heavens above. Where has he been all this time? But he doesn't want to be with me, and he's leaving me already. I think secretly I imagined my happily ever after with him, but that's never going to happen now.

"Everything is meant for a reason; everything is all about

divine timing. *Our* time is not now, Eden. I should have listened to you on the pier and stopped this earlier. This is all my fault. It was wrong of me earlier to say we were exclusive.

"I want you to be ready for what's coming, because when you find that special someone that's made for you, I want you to be ready and I want you to be happy."

At a loss for words, all I can do is stand there. I think he's made for me already; I don't want anyone else.

"Please know that this is so fucking hard for me to do. But I can't figure out how we can be together. It keeps creeping back in, all the time in my head; it's a niggle I can't ignore. I have to do this to protect my heart, especially *yours,* which is angelic, sweet, and kind. Please know that I'm not liking any of this either, not one bit. I'm so sorry, Eden," he whispers.

Seeing all the disappointment and hurt I feel reflected in Hunter's eyes, I say, "I understand."

Removing his hands from my face, I step backward, wrapping my arms around my toweled chest. My universe pivots.

"I think you should go now. Thank you for a lovely couple of days. You really are a special guy. I hope you find what you're looking for too," I say, attempting to smile.

Oh, my heart aches so badly as I say those words. I don't want him to find someone else. I want it to be me.

With a final look, he turns his anguished face away from me as he slouches out the door quietly. "Your pizza's on its way," he mumbles flatly.

"I've completely lost my appetite now," I say inaudibly.

Turning my head away, I can't bring myself to look at him as he takes his final steps out the bedroom door.

With a sinking heart, I hear my front door close, and I

can't quite believe how I woke up this morning feeling like a luminous supernova to have my day end on a damp squib.

Still encased in my towel, I pull back the covers of my bed in a daze, wrap myself around them, and roll into a tight ball.

I drift off, entombed in my sweet happiness turned sour. I ignore the loud knock at the door. I don't want stupid pizza. I want *him*.

I hope that as the night enters a new day, it will take today with it and bring a better one for me tomorrow.

CHAPTER NINETEEN

Aw fur coat and nae knickers: *Saying,* superficially cultured, dignified, classy and elegant but you're actually common.

Hunter

Three days. Three *long* days since I've seen Eden. I feel like shit and look like shit.

"Concentrate, Hunter. Your form is way off this week. I need you to focus," I hear Luke call out from behind me.

"Your lower body is overactive at the start of every downswing. You're needing to close your stance dramatically to make that shot."

"Argh." My sudden outburst booms around the practice range in front. Simultaneously, I launch my golf club at high speed, and it sails through the air, landing hundreds of yards away from me as it falls to the grass with a *thunk*.

"Yup, that's gonna fix your problem." Luke laughs behind me. "Break?" He chuckles.

"My swing is screwed. Over, under, too short, off-balance. What the fuck is going on?"

"Your head's not in the game, Hunter. I think if we go looking, we'll find it in somewhere called The Garden of Eden. You're fucking lost."

Facing outward still, I rest my hands on my hips and exhale loudly with a growl.

"You always said you would never, not after Jess, let another woman jeopardize your game. But that's what's happening. Look at you. Just go and see her, make it right. There's no way you can let her go. Not after how you've told me you feel about her. Just go see her."

"No. I can't. I was a dickhead to her the other night, and she probably hates me. And I need a plan to be with her and I can't figure any of it out; none of it makes sense." Turning around I make a beeline for the door and storm past Luke. "I'm taking the day off."

"You can't afford to have any more days off after this one. This is your last one. Go see if you can get a massage with one of the team. Loosen up," he instructs.

I don't need a fucking massage. I need *her*.

"Yeah, yeah. Whatever."

As I stomp back to my cabin, I spot a limo pulling into reception. Someone must be checking in.

Getting closer, I catch a glance of a brassy blond with bright-red lipstick encased in a garish fur coat exiting the car. My stomach lurches. I would recognize that fucking gold digger anywhere. Well, doesn't this week keep getting better and better? What the fuck is she doing here?

Thank you, fucking universe.

I continue stomping toward the limo.

"What are *you* doing here, Jess?" Completely out of

character, my voice booms across the retreat. Clearly, I've lost all sense of myself this week.

Startled, Jess flounders on her sky-high red stiletto heels on the gravel.

As the words leave my mouth, Jax hangs his head out the limo door. Jax Parks. What the fuck? "Is she with you now?" I ask, my voice laced with confusion and anger.

"That's no way to speak to the best agent you've ever had now, Hunter. C'mon, man."

"I'll fucking speak to you however I like; I pay you good money. What the fuck is she doing here?" I say, looking at Jax but pointing at Jess.

"Hunter, don't be like that," Jess purrs at me. "It's really good to see you."

"I wish I could say the same," I scoff. "Is someone gonna tell me what the fuck is going on and why *you* are here, Jax?" I bellow.

Jax's mouth twists in a smirk as he pulls a cigar from the inside of his oversized trench coat. The two of them look like something out of a bad '50s detective movie. What the fuck did I ever see in her? Bile bubbles in my stomach at the very thought.

"C'mon, buddy, calm down. I was going to call you, but I thought it would be best speaking to you face-to-face. Yes, Jess and I are dating now. I didn't want you to find out like this. I thought you'd be training, and I was going to come and see you later. We have a sponsorship deal to do with the Scotland Golf Association. I thought I would personally come and oversee it rather than by video call. You've been here for weeks now and I miss my best client," he sneers.

I'm sure he fucking does. I make Jax more money than he ever needs to last him a lifetime, and I'm not his only client. Although he'll need it all now if he's with Jess.

"You really didn't think to call? And you should have left *her* back in the States," I say, turning to face Jess now. "Has he given you a credit card yet, sweetheart?"

"Hunter, please stop, you're ruining our lovely Scotland trip," she whines and pouts.

My eyes bug out as I glare back at Jax. "How long?"

"How long what?" Jax replies, acting stupid.

"How long are you here for?"

"Just four days. We leave on Sunday."

"Fine. I'll meet you for the deal on Friday." I turn to Jess and shoot her a venomous look. "You, stay away from me, and don't fucking speak to me if you see me. After all that shit you said about me in that magazine interview, you're lucky I'm letting you stay."

"Hunter, I'm so—"

"Save it. I'm not fucking interested." Turning on my heel, I pound loudly back across the gravel. "Have a fucking lovely time in Scotland," I say sarcastically, waving my hands in the air.

Feeling her presence, I spot Eden from the corner of my eye, firmly rooted to the spot. She's clearly watched the whole 'Hunter Having a Melt Down' show. Just brilliant.

Our eyes lock and my fucking chest cracks open. Like Venus in Nike, Eden stands, bare-faced, in her pale-pink dance gear, honey hair up in a messy bun, and white trainers.

She's the complete opposite of the bloodsucking parasite behind me. I'm pretty sure that's why Jess wears red lipstick all the time. Her lips aren't coated in lipstick; it's the blood of men with gold credit cards.

Filled with sorrow, I want to run over to Eden, bundle her up, kiss the shit out of her, and tell her everything's going to be alright and I was wrong. Wrong about everything, that I want to spend the rest of my time with her here, that we can make it work and that we can be together, forever. Fuck, it hurts.

Eden is irreplaceable, and she's consumed my every thought since I've been here. I feel her everywhere, all the time. I don't want anyone else but her. My head hurts trying to figure out what to do.

All I've done is sleep and train since Monday night. I haven't even been out with the guys or spent any time with Pippa either. All I want to do is hibernate and sleep, because when I'm asleep, I don't feel any pain.

Eden probably thinks I'm a class A cock after speaking to Jess and conducting myself the way I just did. Way to go, Hunter.

Thinking about it, it suddenly dawns on me Jax was probably cheating with Jess all along. It's so obvious now. What a pair of assholes. They deserve each other. I need to find a new agent. Stat. I'm doing that straight after The Cup is over.

Eden bows her head, breaking our gaze, and starts scurrying toward the reception entrance. She didn't even wave. This sucks.

It hurts to breathe being so close to her. I really don't want either of us to get hurt. *But it already does hurt, Hunter, so what are you doing?*

That old saying, if you love someone, set them free—I'm doing just that. Wait, am I in love with her then? Not just lusting over her?

Fuck if I know. All I know is that Eden is hurting and so am I.

What a true shocker of a day.

However, I got to see Eden today. *My girl.*

No. Not your girl anymore, Hunter.

Not anymore.

I'm going back to bed. Fuck this day.

Eden

Arms folded against Mum's wooden kitchen table, I rest my head on them, feeling defeated.

"Oh, Eden. What's the matter, hen?"

"Nothing, I'm just tired, Mum."

"She's not tired; she's lovesick," Ella replies.

"Ha, you're one to talk," I mutter.

"What do you mean?" Ella snips back, leaning against the black range cooker with a cup of tea in hand.

"Weelllll." I lazily pull myself back up, squeaking my palms against the tabletop. "I bumped into Fraser down on the beach on Monday." I watch as Ella clenches her jaw. "And I finally figured out why you've never had a boyfriend since Fraser." I stare. "He's the one, isn't he? You can't move on from Fraser?" I question.

"Ella?" Mums says, confused. "Are you still in love with Fraser after all these years?" Mum loves our girly drama and bathes in it regularly.

"No." Ella snorts as I confirm, "Yes."

"You're lying, Ella. He said you were his world when you were together. His world, Ella. I know now that you've been pining for him from afar for all these years. Trying to fill the gap of heartache and pain with dogs and bloody horses." I point to Treacle, who's curled up sleeping next to the warm range. He must be roasting as Ella has him dressed in a gray dog hoodie today. "Knowing what I know now, you should have left with him. It's been years and you've never had a boyfriend. Never. Are you still in love with him?"

"What are you talking about? Left with him?" she exclaims, now playing with her necklace. She's nervous, I know, because I do the same. "How could I have done that? We were all signed up for dance school." She flushes.

"You could have trained to be a dancer anywhere; you could have finished school and then moved to be with him," I state, unblinking.

Silence.

Eventually, she says, "Maybe I should have. Why did we not talk about this back then?" She shuffles in and sits opposite me at the table in the bay window of Mum and Dad's kitchen.

"I think we were too young then to even consider it. Being a triplet is weird. I think we always thought we had to do everything together."

"He asked me to go with him, you know?"

"Ella, why didn't you tell us?" Mum gasps. "You know your dad and I would have worked it all out for you. We would have let you go. We would have made it work if that's what you had wanted."

"I didn't think I could leave Eden and Eva, or that it was even possible. We had never been apart before. Christ, we can't talk about this *now*; I'm going to end up regretting more than a decade of my life if we talk about this and I have always believed that everything happens for a reason. Don't turn around and tell me I messed this up and didn't make the right decision back then."

Resting her elbows on the table, she runs her fingers through her hair in exasperation.

"He asked me to ask you if you would consider speaking to him. He wants to make amends. Will you talk to him?" I ask.

She shakes her icy-blond locks. "He's got a wife and

family and everything now. I don't think it's right that I speak to him. And I'm not still in love with him. I just haven't found anyone that lives up to him. I can't believe he's back in Castleview."

She's lying. And she does know all about his family and new life. She's been keeping tabs.

"Well, what about Luke? He's a great guy. There was Gordon, too. What happened to him?" I question.

"Luke and I are just having some fun while he's here. To be honest, it's all a bit of flirty banter; nothing's happened."

"Yet," I say.

"Mmm, and Gordon, well..."

"He wasn't Fraser," I confirm. "Oh, Ella," I put my hand out for her to take it. "If you change your mind, Fraser told Hunter he would DM him on Instagram, so you could always get in touch with him that way."

Ella turns her gaze to the window and looks out across the vast expanse of the retreat, consumed in her thoughts I watch her chew on the side of her mouth.

I know I'm correct about her and Fraser. I actually even got the impression Fraser still maybe loves her a smidge too, even though he's married. I feel terrible thinking this because I bet his wife is lovely, and he has a lovely son with her, but they say your first love is always the one you remember. He's never forgotten Ella. I watch Ella gazing out the window; she's never forgotten him either.

"Ah, how is Hunter?" My mum's face lights up.

I let go of Ella's hand and slide it back onto my lap, then drag out, "I... have... no... idea." And shrug my shoulders.

"Why, what happened, Eden? He's such a lovely boy. He's the first boy you've looked at since Jamie. Hunter is a catch and a half," she says, her eyes full of mischief. "You

two looked like you were having fun the other morning."
She giggles now.

Oh heck.

"Mum, he's not a boy, he's a man. You should know; you
got a good look at his Three Wood the other morning, and I
ain't talking about his golf club." Ella titters.

"That's enough, Ella." Mum points her finger at her.

"Well, he decided that I've to find someone local.
Because his job is complicated and I live in a fairy tale and I
deserve someone who can give me stability and a family,
and he can't give me that because he lives on the other side
of the world," I drawl out. "And... Yadda yadda yadda." I
finish my sentence, lean my head forward, and knock my
forehead against the table, tapping it lightly up and down.
"I. Give. Up," I say in time to my taps.

"Stop doing that, Eden." Mum scolds me and Ella
laughs.

"Christ, what are we like. At least Eva has her shit sorted
out. One out of three ain't bad."

"Ella, language, please."

"Oops. Sorry."

"I really like him, like *really* like him. He's just so,
everything. Although did you see what just checked in." I
roll my eyes, leaning against my seat. "His ex-girlfriend is
here. Her name is Jess. She is nothing like me. We're like
green grapes and rainbow chard."

"Green grapes and rainbow chard? What the hell are
you talking about?" Ella giggles.

"Well, I'm the green grape—tiny, boring, easy choice,
and plain. And she's the rainbow chard—long, lean,
extravagant, and multicolored. I saw you checking her in,
Mum. What did you think? And why is she even here?"

A dozen thoughts hit me. Is he back with her? This

sucks big-time, if it's true. My stomach knots. Was everything he said a lie? Was he expecting her, and that's why he ended us before her arrival? But then he was arguing with her in the driveway. He wouldn't do that if he was with her.

I hope it wasn't just about the sex. It didn't feel like that at all.

Not one bit. He made me feel like I was his.

Like I belonged, and he shared his inner feelings with me too. It felt incredible being together, but maybe I was wrong. I'm not great at this relationship stuff. But his words meant something to me; I absorbed every word deep. I believed him.

At least the benefits of working with a therapist have stood me in good stead. Over the past few days, I've been able to get on with my life using some of the Dr. Anderson's coping tools she has me do daily. I feel as fragile as a spider's web, but I'll be okay, again, eventually.

"She's all fur coat and nae knickers if you ask me." Mum interrupts my thoughts, and she waves her hand in front of her face. "I really shouldn't talk about our guests like that. And you, young lady, need to stop talking about yourself like that. You'll be glad you're nothing like her. You're more like a pitaya fruit—unique, beautiful, and intriguing."

Ella and I both laugh. Mum is so ridiculous.

"She's here with that Jax fellow. He informed me he's Hunter's agent." She continues. "They both checked in together and are sharing a cabin. They're together, together." Mum loves this gossip; her whole face beams with glee as she continues spilling. "They were chatting in reception. Hunter is *not* happy at all with Jess being here. And not that I listened that closely." Yeah right. Mum's words speed up now with the excitement of it all. "But apparently Hunter didn't even know that Jax and Jess were dating. Jess was whining to Jax about how upset she was because Hunter didn't want her here and that she's not allowed to speak to him." She puts on a fake squeaky American voice toward the end. Ella and I giggle again.

Well, now I feel like a complete bitch for thinking badly of Hunter. Maybe what he said is true. It felt true. All of it.

"They look like that detective and cartoon woman from that silly film I made you girls watch when you were little. It had a cartoon rabbit in it, but it was like an actual movie. It was always on at Christmas, anything to fill in a gap. What was it called again?" She furrows her brow.

"Eh, *Who Framed Roger Rabbit?*" Ella replies.

Christ, they really do. But Jax is slimier with his gelled back hair and Jess is not as classy as that cartoon woman, like not at all.

"How long are they here for?"

"Only four days." Mum shakes her head. "By the sounds of it, Hunter didn't even know they were coming or staying here."

"They were arguing outside, but I wasn't close enough to hear what they were saying. Hunter looked like he was having a proper hissy fit. I'm guessing if he didn't know they were coming, then that's why," I say.

Mum pours herself another cup of tea from the teapot and then stands at the end of the table, hugging her cup.

"You know girls, love is never something that comes easy. If it did, everyone would be happy and singing and dancing like loony bins, and everything would be joyous and there would be no relationship experts." Mum pauses and sits down beside us. "But love, true and real love, can be complicated. Look at your dad and me. No one wanted us to be together. Your gran and grandad tried to keep us apart.

The age gap between us was a big one, especially when I was only nineteen and he was ten years older than me. But I loved him from the day I laid my eyes on him. It really was love at first sight. We fought hard for one another and it was heartbreaking, awful, and then it was wonderful. And look at us now. The ten years between us doesn't even matter. We knew, both of us wanted to be together. And we have you girls and all this." She motions her hands in the air to all of her surroundings. "We love each other more now than we did back then. But we fought for what we wanted and for what we believed in."

I stare at my mum in awe. I'm not sure if I have the guts to go after what I want, but my mum did. She's so brave and inspiring. I think this is where I get my hopeless romantic ideals from; it's been staring at me in the face the whole time.

"And you know what, girls? We didn't see the entire road map, not at the time, but we took junction after junction; we figured our journey out *together* till we reached our final destination. I'm not sure we're even there yet; we still have so much we want to discover together. But love, girls, love, is everything. But you've got to fight for what you want; that's *if* you want it badly enough."

Mum smiles at Ella and me.

"Okay, I'll let you girls sit there and let that sink in. I need to sort out the beds in cabin three." Mum shuffles out the kitchen door. "Love you, girls. C'mon, Treacle, you come with me." She pats her leg quickly, beckoning Treacle. "Let's go find Dave the dog."

Ella and I watch as Treacle's little roly-poly ebony body wobbles following Mum reluctantly. We then look at each other.

"Mum's right, Eden. You need to fight. Fight for Hunter. I

never did with Fraser and I'm sitting here after all this time still living with deep regret. Do you want him? Truly think he's the one?"

I pick at the knots in the wooden tabletop with my nails. "Yeah, really, I think he is. Is that weird to say, even though we've only known each other this short time? Christ, I thought Jamie was the one, and he *wasn't*."

"Hunter and you, boy, it's nothing like what it was like with Jamie. After you told me yesterday what Hunter said on Monday, the sexual chemistry and the connection you have." She clutches her hands to her heart. "Your conversations are deep, like really deep. When you told me his reasons *not* to be together and how he feels, you know what I thought?"

"What?"

I was not expecting what she says next.

"I think Hunter's falling in love with you and he doesn't know how to react or how to work it all out. I think you're falling or have already fallen for him. And I don't think it's odd, not even in the slightest." She stares me down. "Fight, Eden. If you want this, then go after what you want."

I rub my temples at the thought of him falling in love with me and my heart stutters in my chest. Imagining this incredibly godlike guy falling in love with me, it feels surreal.

"Okay, but what do I do? How can I explain to him we can be together for more than just a few weeks? I don't have any of that figured out."

"Did you not just listen to Mum? You only have to get to the first junction, then the next, then the next, you don't *have* to have it all figured out. If it's meant to be, it will all work out. Figure everything out as you go. You're both overthinking everything."

It's so obvious now. Mum and Dad are living proof of doing the whole figuring it out as we go malarkey. I feel a little buzz of energy burst through my veins, and light glimmers from my inner shadows.

"So what do I do? I saw him today, and he barely looked at me."

Ella cunningly side-eyes me. "I think we need to make an impact. Something he can't deny or walk away from. We have to show him what he's missing." Rubbing her hands together, she gets excited. "I think I have a plan," she says with glee. "If he really is falling in love with you, then this is going to tip him over the edge. He won't be able to stay away, ever."

I have no idea what Ella has planned. Whatever it is, I'm all in.

"But I don't think you're brave enough." Ella wiggles her eyebrows.

"Are you challenging me?"

"Yup."

"Try me."

CHAPTER TWENTY

Pure barry: *Saying,* completely brilliant, wonderful, anything that's really good, fantastic.

Hunter

Half asleep, I'm roused by the ding from my phone. Eyes closed, I reach over and fumble to find my phone on the bed. Instant warmth spreads to my heart as I read Eden's name across the screen. Not reading the notification fully, I place my phone in front of my face and tap my messages app.

Eden: Hey, Hunter, I hate to ask, but could you come over to the studio later please? I need your help with something.

What does she need my help for?

Me: Is that a good idea? Can you not ask your dad?
Eden: I think you're the best man for the job. If you could, you'd really be helping me out.
Me: OK.
Eden: Great. Tonight? About 7:40 p.m. I have a class at 8 p.m. It won't take long.
Me: OK.
Eden: See you then, thanks.

Surely Eden has lots of guys around the estate to help her if it's something she needs help with in her studio? Baffled, I jump out the bed anyway and head to the shower, with a spark of excitement at the prospect of seeing her again today. I hope she doesn't ask me to fix anything; I am shit with a screwdriver and hammer.

Checking the time, I'll grab something to eat, then I head across at 7:40 p.m. How very precise.

Right on time I walk through the door welcomed by a dimly lit studio. As I walked through the trees, I noticed the studio blinds were closed, making me question if the place was even open.

"Hello?" I call out.

I hear the clicking of heels from the far end of the giant room.

A vision in white and black, Eden appears in the studio's office doorway. Her petite figure is draped in an oversized man's white shirt that falls to the top of her knees, black pantyhose, and black leather above the knee-high heeled boots. Is this her usual dance class attire for her late-night classes? She is a sexy treasure chest I want to open.

"Hey, Hunter. Thanks for coming," she purrs, setting all my senses on fire. "I really need your help with something. Could you pop yourself on that chair there?" She points to the middle of the floor, where I see a solo gray velvet chair facing toward the poles now fitted at the far end of the studio.

"Eh, yeah." I pull my brows together. "Are you sure your dad couldn't help you? I'm not good at fixing stuff, if that's what you need help with."

"Oh, I'm sure. You're the perfect man for the job. Sit," she instructs.

Okkaaaaay. I step slowly toward the chair with no idea what she needs me to *sit* and help her with.

"So." She looks me dead in the eyes. "I just need some general advice. I need to show you something, then I'll need a little feedback. Is that okay?"

Frowning, I say, "Sure, I think." I sit on the velvet chair, more confused than ever.

"Great." She smiles seductively. "Now, I need you to pay attention. Pay *very* close attention. Because your advice and feedback are really important."

As I'm about to reply, she sashays across the studio floor toward me, with the sound of her clicking boots against the floor echoing through the room.

"Ready?" she asks.

"Eh, yeah, I thi—" I don't get time to respond as the sound system loudly fires up, making me jump as the first beat of "Naughty Girl" by Beyoncé booms through the room.

I'm about to ask Eden what's going on, but she starts dancing in time to the music. Swaying back and forth, she seductively rolls her hips and rolls her body in time to the Middle Eastern style song.

I can barely breathe as I watch her delectable body move in immoral ways.

Shifting her weight from side to side with intention, she shimmies to every beat of the music, moving closer toward me before standing before my feet, swishing her incredible hips back and forth. Frozen solid to the chair, I can't take my eyes off her.

What's happening?

Rolling her body from head to toe directly in front of me, she crouches down, with hands on her knees, feet on the floor, she splays her legs wide with her hands. My eyes zone in between her legs and all I can see is the outline of her lower lips, clothed in a slither of black wet look fabric.

Fuck.

Me.

I then get a perfect view of her toned thighs covered by lace thigh-high holdup stockings. I groan.

Gliding her hands up her thighs, she snakes her hips side to side to a standing position as she moves in time to the breathless vocals.

Brain fog hits me hard, my head now stuffed full of cotton wool.

When the song hits the chorus, she runs her hands up my thighs, then suddenly hops onto my lap and straddles me with her curvaceous body. I feel my cock leap with joy as I let out a breath I didn't realize I was holding and gulp for fresh air.

Christ, it's gotten really hot in here suddenly.

Grinding her pelvis into me, she rolls her head back in a circle, grabs the chest of her shirt, and rips it open, like she's fucking Superwoman, catapulting buttons everywhere.

My eyes bug out as she exposes her splendid breasts, covered in a matching strappy black bra top that does nothing to hide her deep cleavage and full breasts.

Rolling her shoulders, torso, and hips simultaneously, she skims her hands from her hips up her waist, over her breasts and neck, then interlaces her fingers into her hair, wildly whipping her head, all the while moving back and forth across my now rock-hard cock.

Instinctively, I raise my hand to touch her as electricity runs through me like a bullet train.

"Ah, ah, ah, no touching," she purrs, rolling her obscene hips into my aching hard crotch.

She slides backward off my lap and dances off toward the poles. I watch her ass and hips swish back and forth in her barely there black hot pants. Her firm toned butt cheeks spill out everywhere as she bounces and moves across the dance floor, twisting and turning as she goes.

As if by magic, she jumps onto one of the poles and starts wrapping her legs and body around it, spinning as she moves from one move to the next.

My eyes bore into her as she slithers and curls around the pole, legs curling one way and then the other.

Without warning, she lowers her feet to the floor, walks around the pole, jumps into it, hugs it tight, turns herself upside down, then draws an air arch with her legs, executing the perfect pair of splits while suspended in the air.

Dear Universe, please forgive me for all the truly dirty thoughts I'm having.

Eden slowly glides down the pool, turns on her front, and begins crawling back toward me on her hands and knees.

Midway, she pumps her shoulders and ass in a pounding motion in rhythm to the music.

Magnetic eyes locked on me, she prowls, lithe as a lioness, forward, like she's hunting her prey.

Her tits jiggle and spill out of her top with honey hair swishing over her shoulders to the floor in waves.

My heartbeat shoots through the roof as she arrives at my feet. I'm not sure how I'm still alive at this point. I think a mild heart attack is on the horizon.

Running her hands up my shins, she grabs my knees, then slowly leans back on her heels and weaves her way upward, slinking her hips in a figure eight motion till she's at full height.

A strangled moan leaves my throat as I stare transfixed by her seemingly effortless movements.

I don't think I can take anymore. But she continues torturing me as she starts to belly dance, swooshing and twisting her hips in slow fluid waves. Her aqua belly ring glints in the light as she hypnotizes me with her lascivious hips, tilting her shoulders one way, her hips another.

Arms stretched out in front, she hooks her hands on to my shoulders and thrusts herself back onto my lap, straddling me again.

My heart hammers in my ears as she slides her hands up my neck, leans in, licks my neck with her delectable mouth, all the way up to my ear, and lightly bites my lobe. I'm a goner.

Goosebumps of desire cover my entire body as she triggers all my sinful thoughts of what I want to do to her. "I'm so glad you could help me tonight, Hunter," she whispers in my ear in her gentle Scottish accent that lights my soul.

I try to clench my eyes shut and shake my head to clear

this fog that's taken over my brain, but my body has a mind of its own and they shoot back open.

Without warning, she takes one leg, arches it high in the air off my lap, pivots her foot that's planted firmly on the ground, and pushes herself away, just as the music fades out, and she starts walking, wiggling her hips back in the office's direction.

She disappears into the office and the door closes. I'm then left sitting by myself in the middle of the studio with a furrowed brow, completely puzzled.

Eh, mmmmm. What. The. Hell?

The studio door behind me opens with a whoosh and I spin around in my chair in a panic, wondering if something else is about to happen, only to find Ella drifting through the doorway.

"Hey, Hunter. You alright? What are *you* doing here?" She frowns.

"Gee, well, I'm not sure," I say, flustered, and try to cover my hands over my crotch.

Ella ambles toward me with a tilted head. "Are you feeling okay?" She palms her hand to my forehead as soon as she's beside me. "Yikes. I think you have a temperature. You feel really hot. You should go home and lie down or have a cold shower. That might help," she says with a poker face.

I lean forward, figuring it will be the only way to cover up my throbbing erection. "Yeah, I think I should do that. Can you just give me a second? I'll just sit for a couple of minutes. You know I feel light-headed." I rub my temples.

"Sure, yeah, but we have a class in ten minutes. The students will be here soon; you may not want to hang around."

I scratch my head, trying to think of my job, golf swings, the weather, anything to help my cock go down.

A click from the office door turns both our heads toward the sound. Eden, the she-devil that she is, smiles a full-on provocative smile, now dressed in purple leggings and an off-the-shoulder white tee shirt. "Hunter, you don't look so good; are you okay?" Teetering behind her is Eva. Christ, was Eva in the office the whole time?

"I'm fine," I say through gritted teeth.

"You sure? You look a little flushed," Eden says coyly.

"He's boiling, feel his forehead. I think he's got a temperature. I suggested a cold shower; that always helps. Don't you agree, Eva?" Ella says.

Is this some sort of a test?

"Good idea. You should rest too. You don't want anything raising your temperature more now, do we Hunter? Stress can do that to you. Have you been training hard this week, Hunter? Adrenaline can also cause your temperature to rise too." Eva says, and I detect a sarcastic tone in her voice. They are all loving this.

"Did you know, if your heartbeat rises, it stimulates your temperature too? You should be careful, Hunter. You don't want anything raising your heartbeat or blood pressure either," Eden retorts, unblinking.

What is going on here?

Ella turns to Eden. "You look nice today. But I thought you were wearing all black and a white shirt earlier?"

"Nope, I've been wearing this all day." Eden firmly locks eyes with me and winks.

Fucking vixen.

New voices enter the studio.

"Here comes our students. You had better go. You okay

to stand?" Eden asks me, like she would ask a child as she tilts her head.

"Yes," I grit out.

"Great, I have a few things I need to ask you, you know feedback-wise? I'll text you later. Have a great night, although your night may have peaked already." The corners of her mouth curl upward, flashing a smile of innocence.

Finally able to stand, I lean down toward Eden, but she doesn't give me the chance to say anything.

"You can go now. Thanks."

And just like that, I'm dismissed.

You are in so much trouble, Cupcake.

She bats her lashes back at me. "I'll text you later." She turns her back on me and starts addressing the room with a loud clap, as if I'm not here. "Evening all. Okay, let's get started early tonight 'cause Eden has stuff to do after class."

With a deep frown, I glance back over my shoulder. Did I imagine what just happened? I look around, searching for answers. Shake my head in bewilderment. Nope, it really happened.

As I push the heavy door open to leave, I come face-to-face with Luke, who's leaning against Ella's black Fiat 500 with a grin wider than the Grand Canyon. "Oh, man, you are so fucked."

"What the hell, man, did you know about this?"

"Nope. I still don't really know what those girls are up to. All I know is you were getting your own private pole show this evening."

I pull the back of my neck.

She well and truly got me.

Luke's right, I'm fucked.

Sitting outside, enjoying the fresh Scottish evening air, I lean back against the bench outside my log cabin and take a long drink of my cold beer. I need it to refresh my brain. It was fizzing when I returned from the studio.

I'm so ill-equipped to deal with Eden's transformation from Virgin Mary to enchanting urban sex goddess, and it's taken almost an hour to reorganize my thoughts and for my cock to settle down.

All I wanted to do was reach out and touch her. Make her mine and never let her go. But I don't think she wants that. I think she's punishing me for all the things I said the other night. It's payback I reckon.

A soft ding brings me out of my fumbled thoughts, indicating a new text message. I'm hoping it's Eden. Although this could be yet another ruse.

A quick look at my phone screen confirms it's her.

Here we go.

Eden: Thank you so much for taking part in my research tonight. I just have a few questions to ask. Are you free now to answer via text?

Me: What are you up to, Cupcake?

Eden: I am not *up to* anything; this is for research purposes only.

Me: OK, what do you want to know?

Eden: On a scale of 1 to 10, with 1 being strongly dissatisfied and 10 being highly satisfied, how would you rate the quality of my performance this evening?

Me: 10.

Eden: That is high, thank you. Next question.

Eden: Thinking about the routine itself, do you think it needs more or less pole routine?

Me: Less pole.

Eden: And can I ask what you suggest putting in its place?

Me: More lap dancing.

Eden: This is great feedback; you have no idea how grateful I am for your time, Mr. King.

Me: What are you doing, Eden?

Eden: Patience, Hunter, patience.

Eden: On a scale of 1 to 10, with 1 being very low and 10 being very high, how likely would you come back for a second showing?

Me: 10.

Eden: Brilliant, you must have really enjoyed the routine then. Next question.

Eden: How fast did your heart beat in your chest when I was dancing? Again, with 1 being very low and 10 being very high.

Me: 100.

Eden: Yikes, that is high, next question.

Eden: How much did I turn you on? With 1 being not at all and 10 being super high.

Me: 10 multiplied by 20.

Eden: That's a lot, next question.

Eden: How hard were you as I thrust myself against you? With 1 being soft and 10 being rock hard.

Me: 10 multiplied by 100.

Eden: Gosh, these stats are going up and up, next question.

Me: It was really up.

Eden: Shush now, stop distracting me.

Eden: Do you think I should test my routine on other guys to gather more research?

Me: HELL TO THE NO.

Eden: That's quite a strong, firm no, noted, next question.

Eden: So not appropriate to have asked my dad like you suggested?

Me: Definitely not!

Eden: I agree. Next question.

Eden: Do we have an undeniable connection? Answer Yes or No.

Me: Yes.

Eden: Is the attraction toward me so strong you find it difficult to stay away? Answer Yes or No.

Me: Yes.

Eden: Has sex with me ever felt like it does with anyone else? Answer Yes or No.

Me: Yes.

Eden: What?

Me: I'm only joking, the sex with you is mind-blowing.

Eden: Phew, you had me worried there, next question.

Eden: Reservations aside, do you want to be with me? Answer Yes or No.

Me: Yes.

Eden: My heart just did a funny flippy thing, that's pure barry.

Me: Mine too, what the hell is pure barry?

Eden: Ah, it means that's utterly wonderful and fantastic.

Eden: Next question.

Eden: Do you think you are feeling things for me in a way that scares you? Answer Yes or No.

Me: Yes.

Eden: I thought so - well Ella and Eva did.

Me: Are they both in on this too?

Eden: Maybe, next question.

Eden: If I tell you, even though I have only known you for a brief time, that I'm *falling* for you, would you say that you are *falling* for me too? Answer Yes or No.

Me: Yes.

Eden: The girls were correct, and that scares you?

Me: Yes.

Eden: Me too.

Eden: But...

Eden: I have a proposal on the *us* thing, would you be willing to hear it? Answer Yes or No.

Me: Yes.

Eden: A wise woman (my mum) once told me (just today) that you don't have to see the entire road map; you just need to get to one junction, then the next and then the next. Meaning we don't have to have it all figured out, but if we don't try to take this beautiful journey together, we may live to regret it for the rest of our lives. Just like Ella does with Fraser. Imagine, if we do drive through all the curves and ups and downs together, we could be each other's ultimate destination. Would you be willing to take one junction at a time with me? Answer Yes or No.

Eden: You're making me nervous by keeping me waiting.

Eden: Maybe you need a little time to think it over.

Eden: Did I lose you?

Eden: Bum.

Eden: OK, it was worth a shot.

CHAPTER TWENTY-ONE

Smourich: *noun,* a kiss! **Pronounced:** Smoor-ikh (yet again, the kh is more of a throaty, back of throat sound. Fish bone stuck in your throat sound, say it fast, yup, nailed it, again).

Hunter

"Yes." I bound toward her through her security gate, not caring I haven't closed it behind me.

Startled, she lifts her head from her phone.

Eden lays her phone on the step, stands with urgency, jumps down the studio steps with a loud crunch, and starts walking across the gravel.

"Yes? Really?" she says, wearing an astonished enormous smile.

Beaming, I quickly close the distance between us; we mellow our strides as we get closer.

"You want to give it a try with me?" Eden points to her chest. She steps closer.

"Yeah, I really do. It was wrong of me to tell you to find

someone else. You're *it* for me. All I want is you." I move next.

"Yeah?" She swoons, swaying back and forth with her hands clasped together.

"Yeah. Your mother's a wise woman."

I move closer again.

"She really is."

Another small step.

"So we're doing this. We're going on a journey together, you and me? And you don't hate me?" I take a deep breath and one large oversized step. We're now inches apart.

She slows her normally rapid accent to a gentle, breathless wave. "Yes, we are. For the first time in my life, I'm going after what I really want. We can suss everything out as we go. It may not be perfect, and may be a little bumpy at times, but we are doing this. And I don't hate you, Hunter."

"You want me even after all those utterly stupid things I said the other night? I hate myself for saying them."

"Yeah, I do." She slowly blinks.

"Then take me; I'm all yours."

Eden bounces up on her tiptoes, rising as far as she can. I bow down to meet her before landing a tender kiss to her soft pillowy lips.

We kiss and kiss, worshiping each other's mouths, over and over again, with fervent care, knowing this is the first of millions to come. Circling my protective arms around her, I pull her flush against me, deepening our kiss. Without hesitation, our tongues collide and we groan softly. Simply lost in one another. I bathe in this overwhelming feeling of belonging and oneness with this irresistible girl I now never want to be without.

Unhurried, our kisses slowly lessen before I entwine my hands into her hair, plant a soft kiss to her cheek, and embrace her with everything, trying to show her she's my main squeeze. The girl I know is my ultimate other half, the girl who gives my butterflies butterflies and the girl that is going to change my life for the better and forever.

We stand and hug together as the birds sing around us, basking in the evening's dusk.

I whisper, "You are a naughty girl, Miss Wallace; you knew I was a sucker for your dancing."

"It was really all Ella's idea. You can be angry with her." She chuckles into my chest. "And my mum said some very smart things today, so I made a plan for us. A long-term one. I want to show you."

"You know for someone so small and delicate, you keep surprising me with your sassy tenacious side. I think you've been spending too much time with Ella," I goad.

"Stop it." She pokes my ribs as I lean out slightly.

Turning her face upward, she says, "I listened to Ella talk about Fraser today and I don't want to have any regrets with you. She talked some sense into me; you should thank her."

"What's up with her and Fraser?"

"Well, she denied it, but I think Ella is still in love with Fraser. It's complicated, but she's now regretting not moving away to be with him. She's never had a boyfriend since Fraser, like ever, lots of dating and interest from guys, but no boyfriend. I think she's realizing now she could have been with him. He wanted her to move, but she stayed here with us, her sisters. Anyway, I don't want to talk about Ella now. I have a plan I want to show you. A plan for us."

"Okay, but you have got to fill me in on the Ella stuff later. Give me a *wee smourich* first, then show me your plan. I'm intrigued."

"A smourich?" She smiles widely. "Have you been reading your Scots dialect book I bought you?"

"Aye, a huv," I say in the worst Scottish accent imaginable that sets Eden into a confetti of giggles.

It's my favorite sound.

"Well done, Mr. King, nice try, but please don't do the accent again." She wipes away her tears from laughing.

"I promise I won't do it again. I pinky swear," I say, sticking my pinky out for her to take it. As she locks hers with mine, I pull my fist into my chest and draw her to me, stealing my kiss.

"Thank you for my smourich," I breathe.

"Thank you for saying yes to starting a new road trip with me."

I will be this girl's happily ever after.

I lace our hands together and start walking toward the studio.

"I think you need to perform for me again first, you know, so I can give you more accurate feedback this time, I may have some more suggestions." I raise my eyebrows in hope.

"Not tonight, Mr. King, another night. We have a plan of action to go over. Come on." She tugs my hand, leading me away from the studio to her house.

"Okay, I suppose so, show me your plan. I want to know everything." We walk around the corner to the front of her house.

"Wait, am I seeing this right? Does your new car have eyelashes?" I ask, dumbfounded, staring at a new shiny mint-green Fiat 500.

"Yes, now she really looks like Bambi," she jokes.

"You are so strange, Miss. Wallace."

"I know, that's why you're *falling* for me."

"It really is, and what's the reason for *you* falling for me?"

"Because you have great abs, and there's something about your bronzed forearms that makes my lady bits light up."

"Reeaallly?" I start waving my forearms about.

"Stop it, you'll make me all hot and flustered, we won't make it to read my epic master plan."

"Ah, but that's *my* plan." I laugh.

"Later, I promise, but for now come see."

I grab her hand as we enter her house. Let's see what my girl has in store for us.

Currently sitting in the first class section of the train, Eden and I are Edinburgh bound for the weekend. I reflect on a week of our emotional roller coaster.

True to her word, Eden thought of everything. I watched her give an almost office-like proposal, outlining all the things we should do once The Cup is over and I leave Scotland for the next tournament back in the States.

Speaking to each other every morning and every night and being honest with one another, were her two absolute nonnegotiables. Watching films online together over video call, watching similar television shows so we have lots to talk about, set up new music playlists together, she'd thought of everything. Even phone sex and sexting. She'd researched the best apps to allow us to do this safely, blowing my mind in the process.

She plans on visiting or touring with me once every couple of months, and I have agreed that I can schedule in Scotland visits every other month.

She'd already spoken with Pippa, asking for access to my

schedule, so she would know the places I was traveling to and from, and when.

Eventually, she said that we need to set our life goals together, not now, see how it all goes first, then look at our Forever Goal, is what she called it.

She's so damn smart; she astonished me with the level of detail she went into. I don't know why I didn't think of it myself.

Once she'd finished her proposal, I was so turned on by her intensity to make us work, I fucked her right there on the kitchen table, not giving a damn who saw or could see in.

She came all over my cock lightning fast as she clawed at me to go deeper and harder with every thrust. Her insatiable appetite for sex turns me on so bad and we can't get enough of each other.

Eden proposed we go away for the weekend as soon as my meeting with the Golf Association was over. This pleased me no end, not wanting to be around Jax and Jess for yet another day. Although I would have taken great delight in waving them off.

Got to give it Jax, he pulled a brilliant deal my way moneywise on my latest sponsorship deal.

Although I have something else, I'm dealing with Beth separately without Jax. I want to share the plans with Eden, but not yet. Not until I sign the contract. I'm hoping to do that soon. I've also asked Beth to keep quiet. It's something divinely inspired following Eden's proposal.

Relaxing back in my seat across from Eden, I watch her admiring the scenery whooshing by. She's beautiful.

"Keep your eye out for seals; they sometimes bathe in the rare sunshine along the coastline. Just further along here." She points, smiling out the train window.

We've already had lots of laughs together today, which seems to have set the tone for the weekend.

Eden almost broke a rib laughing at the hilarity of me trying to get my six-foot-four frame into her tiny car.

With my head touching the ceiling, I had to crouch slightly. I pushed the seat as far back as it would go, and still my legs were struggling for space.

If I'm going to be visiting more, she has got to get a bigger car.

Also, she scared the shit out of me. She enjoys going fast. She informed me her Fiat is an Abarth. It's a fucking pocket-rocket, like her. At one point I thought we were going to end up in another field again as she Tokyo drifted around the Scottish countryside roads. That reminds me, I must buy travel sickness tablets for the ride home.

"Fancy playing a game?" I ask.

I've got something I want to ask her, and I figure this will be the best way.

She blinks her blue eyes my way and smiles. "Yeah, what do you have in mind, Mr. King?" She leans forward across the table between us.

"Weeellll, I was thinking, like a get to know you kinda game."

"Okay, you go first, Hunter."

"First question, when did your obsession with Minnie Mouse start?"

"Seriously? That's your first question." She rolls her eyes. "Okay, honestly, I'm not sure, but it's gotten worse as I've gotten older. Probably because I don't give a crap about what anyone thinks. Eh, maybe about age five or six."

I smile back at her. "Your turn. What do you want to ask me?"

"What's your house like back in Florida?"

"We have really similar taste, actually. It's quite like yours, but needs a woman's touch. It's a bit of a bachelor pad. Five bedrooms, when I only really need one. Big kitchen. I love cooking. Glass and wood like yours, but bare. You need to restyle it for me; you have great taste."

"I would love to do that. I am rubbish at cooking though, so you can do all the cooking for us." Her face lights up. "Can I ask, is this the same house where you lived with Jess?"

"How do you know she lived with me?"

"It came up when I Googled you."

Bloody internet.

"Ah. Yeah, I kicked her out faster than I moved her in though, you'll be pleased to know," I reassure her. "What else did you learn about me online?"

"Pah." She giggles. "They said you had a massive putter."

I scoff. "Jesus Christ. Is it true?"

"Nope, they exaggerated; it's tiny." She smiles innocently with the eyes of a doe.

"Minx," I whisper.

"Did you see how much I was worth?"

"Nope." She shakes her head. "I didn't."

"You're such a rare find, Miss Wallace."

"When you win a tournament, do you get a lot of money then? I honestly have no idea how much you guys earn."

I sit back in my chair and clear my throat. Sometimes money does strange things to people, and I know Eden isn't like Jess at all, but it worries me she will see me differently. Eden is unique; she's even paying for this weekend. I love that she's fiercely independent and self-supporting.

"It's okay. You don't have to share with me; I was just curious," she says.

"It's fine. Sooooo, my last win, I won… one point nine million dollars."

"You're shitting me?" She stares openmouthed at me. "Holy crap, and that's just one competition?"

"Plus, there are lots of sponsorship deals and I've modeled a few times for some of the fashion brands, and fragrance ones too. Have you never seen me in an ad?" I ask.

"No, never. You forget I've wrapped myself away for a few years. You are such a surprise, Hunter. You're like the secret millionaire next door." She laughs. "I'm guessing you don't see it all. With staff and expenses, and I bet the tax man loves you." She smiles.

The thing about Eden is, she gets it. She runs a business; she knows the ins and out and how it all works. She's grounded and real. I really love that about her.

"I'm nothing like Jess, if that's what you're thinking, Hunter."

"Believe me, I know that. You're a lifetime away from that bitch."

"She really hurt you, huh?"

"Mmm, I don't know if she hurt me, not love-wise, 'cause I was never in love with her. For her, our relationship seemed like it was all about the money, parties, and who she could befriend to climb up the social ladder. After our breakup, she sold her story to the press about us. Well, she sold made-up stories about me and made me look like a dick. I was the innocent party, not her. All along she was cheating on me with Jax Parks apparently, my douchebag of an agent." I rub my head.

"I have to admit. Her and I are nothing alike." Eden smiles with a twinkle in her eye. "That fur coat, I am so jealous of that though. I might need to get me one of those." She winks.

"Stop it. What was I thinking?"

"I have no idea," she says with a mischievous look in her eyes.

"So I've made some mistakes in my life; what about you?"

"Well, I dyed my hair pink when I was fourteen, trying to be all artsy-fartsy like, and it fried my hair. I went skinny-dipping at a beach party once and someone stole my clothes. Not my best idea, and I think my biggest one has to be Jamie."

Part of her regretting Jamie makes my heart sing, but part of it also makes me jealous. Jealous because she held on to him for so long, wishing he'd come back. Jealous he got so much time with her.

"Do you think if he came back you would speak to him?"

"That's a tough question. I was angry at him for leaving, but we had a child together. I think if he wanted to talk to me about Chloe, then probably yeah."

I'm not sure that answered my question.

My girl has been through so much, but she probably needs closure.

"I bet she would have been beautiful, like you. Chloe that is," I whisper.

Her face lights up. "Thanks, Hunter. She would be three now, almost four."

"I think you'd be a wonderful mum. I've seen you with students; you're kind and patient. I know you've said you may not be able to carry a baby again. Is there no solution?"

"I have something called an incompetent cervix. That sounds so awful when I say it. Which means my body opened too early for Chloe. It can be silent. You have no idea it's going to happen, or even if you have it. But I hadn't been feeling well for a few days before I lost her. I had some pelvic pressure, backache, and pulling sensations in my belly. I thought it was all normal for pregnancy. But every case is unique. There are a few things I can do to help prevent it happening again," she says wistfully. "Do you think you want a family?"

I reach out and take her hand. "Yeah, I want the whole nine yards."

I could see myself having it all with her.

"Trust you to use a golf pun for that." She chuckles softly.

We sit in calm silence.

"Do you think you would want to try again and have a family, Eden?"

"I do, yeah. I really would love a family."

We want the same things.

I change the subject. "Your turn. Ask me something."

She ponders. "What would you say if I told you I had three things booked for this weekend from my bucket list and you're doing them all with me?"

Suddenly I'm trying to recall what's on her list.

"You do? What are *we* doing? More castles no doubt, they seem to be everywhere in this country."

"We do love our castles. Well, tomorrow morning we are going to visit Edinburgh Castle, then afterward I'm booked to have a tattoo with an incredible tattoo artist. I booked him weeks ago when my list first came through. Don't worry. It's just me having a tattoo done."

"Really, what are you having done?" I ask, smiling with surprise.

"I'm having an unalome style symbol with a sunflower integrated into the design."

"What's an unalome?"

"I'll show you." She pulls her phone out of her purse.

"The symbol signifies a path to enlightenment. It's a Buddhist symbol, and I love its meaning." She turns the phone around to me. "This is what he's drawn for me." She points to the screen. "You see these spirals? They symbolize the turns and twists throughout our life, and the straight lines at the top signify the moment we reach enlightenment, harmony, or contentment if you like. The sunflower is for me, well, Chloe and the boys we lost, to represent hope. Hope for better things to come."

I gulp. "It's beautiful, Eden."

"It really is. And now that we're together, these twists and turns represent us too. Our path to harmony together is coming," she states confidently.

I love this girl. Do I really love her? Not just falling for her? Holy shit.

Interrupting my thoughts, she asks, "What does your tattoo represent? It's massive, by the way. How long did that take? Mine is tiny by comparison. I'm only booked for an hour."

"About three sittings. It is only six months old. I decided to get it when I was making progress with my strength and my back felt better and stronger. But it took me ages to pluck up the courage to get it. And as cliché as it sounds, it represents my career rebirth. Despite having gone through my surgery, it's about my journey through the fire and adversity."

"Sounds like us too, representing something new, our strength and our eternity."

My throat suddenly goes dry. I want to tell her I love her. I love all her curves and curiosities. I love her soul and body, and most of all I love that fucking giggle I can't get enough of. I want to make her mine forever 'cause I don't want anyone else to have her.

Unaware of my thoughts, she says, "Oh, then on Sunday morning..." She takes her phone out of my hand. "We're going to feed the penguins at Edinburgh Zoo." She almost shrieks.

"We are what?" I ask slightly flummoxed.

"Going to feed the penguins at the zoo. It's on my list. But I've booked you too."

"Damn, have you got any idea how badly they smell? Like, reek of shit and fish." I gag at the very thought.

"But they're so cute with their little waddles and stocky bodies."

I break out in a cold sweat just thinking about how close to the smelly fuckers we'll get if we're feeding them. Oh well, I might as well lean into her bucket list.

"Annnnd the third thing you have planned?"

She claps her hands with excitement. "Well, it's actually four. But we can do two together at the same time. Tonight —" She closes her eyes and takes a deep breath to pull herself together. Christ, it must be something big if she's this excited. "Tonight, we are going to see Lewis Capaldi outdoors at Princes Street Gardens." Her eyes are as big as saucers now while I sit there deadpan. "How can you not be excited? Do you know who Lewis Capaldi is?"

"Sorry, Louie Capaddy who?"

"Are you kidding me? He's Scotland's answer to Beyoncé, the most wonderful love song writer slash singer. He's huge in America; how could you not know who he is?" She shakes her head at my ignorance. I laugh at her broad Scots accent she shifts into now and again. Sometimes it's really strong, and she uses lots of slang, and other times it's more subtle and delicate.

"I do, Eden, I'm pulling your leg," I tease. I love how Eden gets so excited by the little things in life.

"You'd better appreciate these tickets. You've no idea what I had to do to get them off Eva. These tickets are like rocking horse poop, Hunter. Be more excited."

I throw my hands in the air mockingly. "Woo-hoo."

"Much better, thank you." She laughs.

I could listen to her giggle all day.

"So you like Lewis Capaldi then?"

"Yes, I love him. But not as much as Minnie Mouse though." She lays her hand out flat and tilts it back and forth. "But maybe same level love, but differently. I think that's more like it."

Eden is so refreshing and youthful in her thoughts. Today she's wearing a cropped pink sweatshirt with a 'This is my day off sweatshirt' slogan. I love all her foolish ways and sense of vitality.

"So, that's three, what's the fourth?"

"That's easy. Kiss under the stars. We're doing that tonight at the concert." She wiggles her eyebrows. "That's number eleven on my list."

All I can do is smile.

"Let me see your bucket list again." I know she keeps a printout of it and takes it with her everywhere for reference. I'm gearing up to ask her my question.

Digging around in her purse, she eventually pulls out her tatty list.

"Number one you've done... me. Number two? Did your vibrator arrive?"

"Keep your voice down," she hisses.

"Well, did it?"

"Yes."

"Great, we can have fun with that and all this proposed phone sex we're going to have that you've scheduled in."

"I didn't *schedule* it in, Hunter. It'll be spur of the

moment and romantic. Oh, and also, you're going to love this." She lowers her voice and leans in further. "I bought one of these remote Bluetooth vibrator things for us. So no matter where you are in the world, you can control it with your phone, Hunter, and I just pop it in."

I let out a hearty laugh.

"We're gonna have some fun, you and I, over Wi-Fi." She wiggles her eyebrows.

"Wow."

"It will be wow." She giggles.

Unexpected is the only word I can think of to describe my girl. I have no words as she blows me away each and every day, and I feel her relaxing more and more around me. She wants this, me and her.

Clearing my throat, I shake my head and turn my attention back to her list. "So, are you still going to see your therapist?"

"Yes, but I only have one more booked and I think my mind has been changed forever. I am good to check out, baby."

"You got a pen there?"

"Yeah." She digs into her Mary Poppins style backpack and pulls out a pen.

Taking it from her, I score through list number twenty-four.

"You're not doing that one."

"Ella said I have to do them all; you can't change the rules, Hunter. Bad. Very bad. Which one is it?"

"One-night stand. Or two. Nope. Not. Fucking. Happening."

"I agree, not happening."

Smiling, I run my eyes down the list to find the one I'm

really after, number twelve, and I read it out loud. "Book a vacation to Disney World?" I lift my head.

"Yeah, I still haven't spoken to Toni and Beth about that. I really should, you know getting the girls to take time off is more difficult that you would imag—"

"Come with me."

Unblinking, she stares back. "What?"

"Come with me. To Florida. Next weekend for a week. Probably not as long as you would want, but come home with me. I have a photoshoot I need to be physically there for. It's just me going; the rest of my team are staying here in Scotland. The photoshoot and press conference I have booked won't take up much time. I want to show you my home." I'm rambling now.

"You want me to come with you? To Florida? Actual Florida?" she quizzes in shock.

"Yes, actual Florida. I've asked Eva and Ella to cover your classes; it's all done. They checked your passport for me, and it's up to date. I only organized it yesterday, so it's all really last minute. I live a couple of hours away from Orlando, but I've booked us a hotel inside Disney World for three nights, and we get to have breakfast with Minnie and Mickey. I've booked fast track passes for all the rides, and I thought we might do one or two of the other parks, like Universal Studios maybe? I know it's not as long as you would want to go, but I want to take you to see the fireworks at Magic Kingdom. That's number..." I run my hand down her list. "Twenty-two." Then I lift my head.

Aw, shit. Too much too soon? She sits as if frozen in time. I'm not even sure if she's breathing.

I wave my hand in front of her eyes. "Hel-looo?"

Her lips tremble.

Shit, what did I do?

"Hey, what's up, baby?" I move from my seat, circle around the table, and shuffle myself in beside her. She turns her head, her eyes glazed.

"You organized all that for me?"

"Yeah, did I do something wrong?"

"No." She bows her head, shaking it from side to side. "No one's ever done anything like that for me before. You're so thoughtful."

"So you're not upset?"

"No," she gasps. "Upset? Hell no, Hunter, I'm so happy and excited." She launches herself at me and rams her lips into mine with such force I think she made me bleed. It's a messy, wet kiss I can only grin through.

"I'm really going to Florida with you next week?" She's giddy now with excitement.

I bob my head in confirmation.

"Holy shit, you're getting it tonight big-time. Ocht, this is pants though. Here was me thinking I would take you to see a concert in the gardens, kiss under the stars, stay in a hotel overlooking the castle, make love with the curtains wide open, and you top me by booking bloody Disney World." She sits back in her seat in wonder.

She said make *love*.

"It's not a competition, and I did not know you had these next few days booked for us. To me, yours is way more romantic than mine. Bloody Minnie Mouse? Romantic? Hardly."

"Ooooooh, to me it is, Hunter. Seriously..." She turns back to me again. "You are something kinda wonderful."

"And so are you," I say back.

Leaning in, I kiss her and she takes that as an invitation to almost hop on my lap. She would if there wasn't a table there. We kiss like the sun will never come up again.

"Fuck's sake, man, get a room," someone shouts from a few seats down in a really broad Scots accent.

But we don't stop as our mouths dance together with delight. When my girl is soft, she's so gentle, but she lets me know when she needs it hard, and this kiss is exactly that. I bite her bottom lip, stretching it out a little. Kissing her will never be enough. I want her all the time, every second of the day. I love her.

I thrust long, deep strokes into Eden with everything I have. We are back at the hotel, on the top floor, overlooking the castle that's flooded by the moonlight. We had a brilliant, fun evening at the concert, but I couldn't wait any longer to get her back here to the hotel room.

I need her. I need to bury myself in her so deep. I'm not sure where we begin and end together.

"Come again for me, baby."

"My God, I don't think I can take it. I feel so dizzy," she breathes.

"I've got you." I reluctantly slide out of her and move my long, lean body beside Eden on the bed. "Turn your back to me."

Shuffling in, I pull her close, her back to my front, and hook her supple leg up over my thigh.

This feels fucking incredible.

With ease I slide my thick, throbbing, hard cock back into her now soaking wet core and dive into her neck, devouring that sweet spot behind her ear that makes her feral.

With better access to her tits, I tease her nipples, changing it up between slow and fast. We rock together, like we've been doing this forever. Her body lights up like a star on a clear night at my touch.

"Lick my fingers," I command.

I guide my fingers to her mouth, and she licks them gently, but as I go to remove them, she sucks them hard, lapping her tongue around them, then bites down slightly.

"Holy shit. I'm gonna come if you keep doing that," I gasp.

She releases my fingers and watches as I coat her swollen clit with my wet fingers. Small, gentle rubs. Between my cock buried deep inside her and me biting at her neck and circling her clit, her pants and moans become louder, making me instantly harder. I urgently need to fuck her senseless.

"I might pass out from all the sensations," she whimpers.

White-hot ecstasy builds within me, and I never want this to end. I'm so addicted to this feeling with her. To make her feel like this. Knowing no one but me has ever made her feel so good.

"I'm gonna come, baby; come with me."

"Yes. Now, Hunter. Now."

I really let her have it, pounding deeper and harder.

"Tighten that pussy for me and come," I growl through clenched jaws, pounding into her hard and fast.

Like the devil himself leaves my body, I growl out in a fury of pants and deep moans as an almighty orgasm hits me and pleasure pools in my balls as passion radiates through my spine.

Her body squeezes around my cock, milking me with everything she's got as I jerk into her.

Arching her spine, she grabs the back of my neck and pulls my mouth to hers in a wet, urgent kiss, desperate for the connection. Her mouth forms the shape of an *O* as we moan into each other's mouths with wild abandonment. Coming together, hard, losing control, we breathe deep, openmouthed, lips still touching.

This is nothing like I've ever felt before. It's beautiful. She's beautiful.

Together we are an astronomical explosion of emotions and sensations.

As our breathing subsides, still connected, I brush delicate kisses over the back of her neck and shoulders.

I want her forever.

Eden

My heart pounds with newfound emotions at this bewitching man, holding me tenderly, looking after me, caring for me.

It sprinkles tingles all over my neck and shoulders, driving shivers down my spine.

Hunter slides himself out of me slowly, leaving me feeling empty. He's the other half of me and I want him to be inside of me always.

I turn around and lie half over him and smile with contentment. He sweeps his thumb up and down my arm that's wrapped around his athletic body.

He sweeps my never-ending hair to the side, bows his head and kisses my neck. Like always he's tender and loving.

Hunter squeezes me and kisses the top of my head. "Go to sleep, Cupcake. We've got a busy two days ahead."

As I drift off, all I can think is, I love this man.

CHAPTER TWENTY-TWO

Scran: *noun,* food. **Pronounced:** Sc-ran.

Eden

"It was wonderful from start to finish. He took us on his private jet. I've never been on one before. You should see, it's so plush and luxurious. There was champagne as we boarded and he even organized some Disney movies for me to watch too. Annnndddd, I joined the mile high club, girls." I laugh from a little nervousness.

This all so new to me, sharing my newfound sex life with the girls.

Believe me, it's not just sex; it's a supercharged connection on steroids.

"I think sex in the air heightens all your senses or something. It was extraordinary."

"Is that jet his, then?" Eva asks me.

"Yes and no. He is part owner, along with another four or

five golfer friends. Apparently, they all travel together if it's a team tournament and stuff. I felt like a princess."

"I've never met anyone who owns their own jet," says Eva with a deep sigh.

"Hey, are you okay? You've been really quiet recently, and dancing classes aside, I've hardly seen you," I ask.

Eva lowers her chin to her chest. Sensing Eva's weariness, I walk over and give her a hug. "Is something wrong, Eva?" I give her a good squeeze.

"Ignore me. I'm just having a bad few weeks. Things aren't right between Ewan and me. I don't want to talk about it. You've had such a great time away. I want to hear everything."

"We'll chat later. Okay?" I whisper into her ear.

Pulling out of our hug, she weakly smiles at me. I don't like Eva being sad. It's not like her at all. She and Ewan are like couple goals to me.

Toni pipes up. "How was Disney, Eden? Was it just how you imagined?"

"Disney World was magical," I say in awe. "I met Minnie at the breakfast table in the morning. She's so cute. When I met Cinderella at the meet and greet with the princesses, she asked me if I traveled by pumpkin to get there. It was so funny and better than anything I could have imagined. I got new ears, and I made Hunter wear them too. I don't think he was too impressed by that. There was the parade, and aww, it was a-ma-zing. The fireworks at night in Magic Kingdom were spectacular. I have never seen a fireworks show like it. Tink flies across the sky," I squeal. "Hunter even took me swimming with dolphins too. We squeezed so much in. It was all so fantastical." I bounce across the kitchen toward the kettle and flip the switch on.

"Sounds like hell; thank fuck you didn't take me there. You have the mind of a five-year-old," Beth drawls.

"Oh, be quiet. Stop being a stuffy CEO boss bitch. Eden's excited. Let her tell you about her ultimate dream coming true. You're never too old for Disney," Toni says warmly.

The girls have come over for a quick cuppa because I haven't seen them since I got back over a week ago. The week after Edinburgh, Hunter and I spent so much time together. We have so much in common and haven't stopped chatting, laughing, and discovering everything about one other.

Going on vacation with Hunter—well, back to his home —it felt like we've been together forever. We are perfectly synchronized.

I also watched his photoshoot with his new sports sponsor too. Having never attended a professional brand photoshoot before, I was fascinated by everything, including Hunter's delectable brawny abs. The way the stylist greased him up. Holy hell bags. I couldn't take my eyes off him for one second. It was difficult keeping my hands off him. Well, that was until we went into his dressing room.

The man is a dream.

It's only a couple of days now till The Cup starts and the town is getting really busy, but so have Toni and Beth's jobs too. The town demands their attention during these four intense days.

"You don't need to listen to me for long; Hunter and I are going out for some scran, anyway. He's due here in about ten minutes," I say, looking at the clock. "I need to go get ready. He's taking me to Wee Oscars tonight." I beam.

"I think I preferred you when you were depressed all the time. Now you're too sparkly and shiny and bouncy and shit. You make me think my entire life is boring now compared to yours." Beth leans back against her chair in my kitchen and folds her arms.

"Have you seen his Instagram? All the girls are asking who the girl is in the photos at Disney World and at the penguins. They're all commenting on how cute you are." Toni bounces her shoulder in excitement. "You're practically famous."

"I thought Hunter was gonna barf at the penguins. The smell was horrendous. Did you see the comments on that photo? Some of them are mean. One of them called me a poison dwarf. Pffft," I moan. That one hurt, I have to admit.

"Ignore them, they're just jealous. The sunflower field date Hunter took you on was insanely romantic, Eden. He's so thoughtful," swoons Eva.

I can't help but smile. "I know. He's everything, girls. I feel so lucky. That was a tremendous surprise. He had a little table set up with champagne and a cheese board, surrounded by sunflowers as we sat and watched the sunset. It was beautiful. He pays attention to everything I say, and he knows how important sunflowers are to me."

Toni beams. "He posts pics of you guys all the time. He really likes you."

"I don't think I can take any more of this," Beth grumbles.

"And you should see his house. It's huge, like five times the size of mine, and he has a pool. We made love in his pool too." I smile at that memory. "I'm ticking that off my skinny-dipping and sex in the sea items from my bucket list. I'm not doing it here in Castleview Cove—uh-uh, no way. It's too bloody cold." I continue. "You know, he even had a new bed arrive for his bedroom so I didn't have to sleep in the same bed that his ex, Jess, did. He's so thoughtful. He really looks after me," I say dreamily.

"God, I think I'm going to throw up," Beth mutters.

Toni swings around to Beth and whacks her on the shoulder. "Will you just bloody stop? For Christ's sake, since you and Billy called it quits, you've been a cranky old trout. Now stop it and let Eden have her moment. Our girl is happy, Beth, happy." She urges her to get on board.

I can't help but smile. "I don't care what you think, Beth. I am happy and so in lo…"

I stop myself.

"Love? Were you about to say love?" Eva quizzes me, wide-eyed, and the girls all stop what they're doing.

I move my eyes sideways, deep in thought. Shit. I don't want to tell them. I want to tell him.

"You so are, you're in love with Hunter!" Toni yells and it echoes loudly throughout my open-plan house.

Simultaneously, Hunter walks into the kitchen. Aw, hell.

I forgot I opened the sliding glass doors earlier as it's been a super-hot day. With all the glass it was like a furnace in here. He must have come through them and not my squeaky front door, or I would have heard him.

Hunter stands there, hands in his pockets, staring at me in his white dress button-up shirt tucked into his charcoal-gray dress trousers. He looks so handsome with his endless deep tan.

"Annnnddddd… I think that's our cue to leave, girls," says Beth as she stands, gathers the mugs, and places them carefully in my Belfast sink.

"Lost for words, Hunter?" Toni teases as she walks out of the kitchen.

Hunter hasn't taken his eyes off me.

Briefly Beth pats Hunter's back twice. "See you in a few days, King."

Eva waves and behind Hunter's back, she silently mouths, "Oh my God."

Then it's just Hunter and me standing in the kitchen.

Bloody hell.

"Did you hear that?"

"You love me?" He frowns.

"Okay, so you heard that." I crinkle my nose and clench my eyes shut.

"I'll ask again, do you love me, Eden Wallace?"

"Eh, would it be alright if I did, or does it complicate your feelings or anything? You know, it's okay if you don't feel the same way, and hell, I never wanted you to find out like this. This is not how this is supposed to go. So. Not. Romantic," I say abashedly, rubbing my elephant necklace as I look away.

"Say it," he commands. "Look at me." He's so sexy when he's bossy.

I slide my eyes to him.

"Say it, Eden."

"I love you, Hunter," I say almost inaudibly.

"Louder, baby," he says with an I-dare-you grin.

Screw it, nothing we ever do together is conventional. I raise my hands in the air and give it my all. "I love you, Hunter." My voice bounces around the open space.

Hunter dashes toward me, cups my face, and squeezes his face to mine as we lock in a hard kiss against one another. I think he's trying to pull my neck out of its socket.

"I love you, Eden. More than anything in this world, I love you. I've wanted to tell you for weeks now."

Oh my, I think my heart may burst, or I might faint, or both. He loves me.

Melting together as we share a long passionate kiss, we claw, scramble, and breathe against each other.

"I want to do this all night, but we have dinner reservations," he mumbles against my mouth.

"We can continue this after."

"I can't stop, but you need to get dressed. You are not going out in a bright-pink bra top and cycling shorts to Wee Oscars." He laughs into my mouth. "They'll not let us in."

"I think I look great."

"You look better naked."

I love the way he says naked and baby. It comes out like nay-kid and bay-bee and makes my tummy spin.

"We need to stop kissing, or I'll never be ready in time."

"Fuck it." He picks me up and places me on the edge of the kitchen table.

"Someone might see; it's not dark enough yet," I squeal.

"Don't care," he says, undoing his dress pants quickly. "I need to be inside of you now. Shorts off."

So this is happening fast. I whip my stretchy pink shorts off and just as I drop them to the floor, he glides his cock along my already wet, swollen folds. I moan and arch my back, begging him to do it again.

"This is gonna be quick, hard, and fucking wonderful. You ready?" he says with a broad grin, teasing his long, hard length at the entrance of my sex.

"Yeah, Hunter, I want you." I pull him to me.

I can never get enough of this man.

I'm already throbbing.

In one swift move, he rams his dripping cock hard inside me.

Ouch.

But oh, so good.

I arch my back off the table.

"Give it to me, Hunter."

Looking up, I take in this man who loves me. I feel so

lucky to have him in my life. Nothing comes close to how he makes me feel. I feel stellar. I watch him as his eyes roll back in sheer pleasure, lost in us.

"Ah," I gasp as Hunter pounds into me and shapes his hands on my tiny waist.

"My hands are carved for your curves."

I love when he tells me how he's feeling. He short-circuits my brain.

Like always, there's that electricity thrumming between us, but I need closeness, so I reach up. "I want more."

In one fluid movement, Hunter lifts me up, moves me so I'm now at the other end of the table on my back, then crawls on top and glides his thick cock back inside of me.

"Take your top off, Hunter. I want to feel you against me."

"Take yours off too."

Unrelentingly, he keeps thrusting into me as he leans back and pulls his shirt over his head, exposing his glorious body, then grabs my hips. I feel my orgasm weave its way up my spine, warming my thighs and sex.

"Kiss me, Hunter," I beg.

He bows his head and licks my new tattoo between my cleavage, dragging his wet tongue up my body before landing on my lips. Urgently, we kiss as his naked chest melts into mine.

"Roll your dance hips for me, baby," he mutters breathlessly.

I move in time, meeting his intense rhythmic thrusts. He moans out, "I can feel everything inside you. It's like your magic spot is rubbing the head of my cock. Wrap your fucking legs around me, now," he demands, rolling his eyes back.

I want him to go deeper. Tilting more, I loop my legs

around his waist and hook my feet together, begging Hunter to drive into me deeper. He grabs the edge of the tabletop to get the anchor he needs.

I can't think straight as our slapping skin and moans echo through my house. "Oh my God, that's so good, Hunter." I moan frantically, digging my nails into his muscular back.

I feel my orgasm coiling down my spine and into my hot, deep core. A tidal wave of sensations flow through my body as my orgasm surges.

Like a rocket discharging, a shower of golden stars flash behind my eyes.

Clenching hard around him, we both pant wildly as we photo finish climax together loudly, and he spills himself inside me. It's beautiful and out of this world. Sinful and fuck hot. He's my light in my darkness. I don't care that this man now owns my heart. I want him to. I want him to own me and make me his. Forever.

"I love you, Eden. So, so much," he pants uncontrollably.

Wrapped in glowing ecstasy, descending together, I lock eyes with him. My heart beats a thousand times faster as I'm consumed with emotions that feel alien to me.

"I love you too, Hunter. I've never loved anyone before until you. My heart's been waiting for you," I whisper.

Leaning up on his elbows, Hunter's eyes darken, lost in our moment, then he kisses me with his delectable full lips.

He murmurs against my skin, "Mine's been waiting for you too."

"I don't want you to go in a few days." My heart saddens at this thought.

"I promise you, baby, we're going to make this work. I know we will."

I know we will. I know we can. But it hurts at the thought of him not being here all the time. I think this is going to be harder than I thought.

I pull in a breath.

"Now no more sad thoughts, Cupcake," he says faintly, smoothing his thumb over my temple. "It's a new beginning for us. A new part of our journey. We're gonna be just fine. I promise." We kiss our most delicate kiss, creating a wild butterfly flutter between my heart and throat. "Now, I hate to do this, because this kitchen table is becoming one of my favorite places to be with you, baby, but you have half an hour to get ready." He points to the stairs as he slides out of me.

"Easy-peasy," I say, jumping off the table before stealing a quick kiss. As I run to get ready, he swats a firm slap to my behind. I yelp and laugh at the unexpectedness of it.

I laid my navy and white spotty wrap jumpsuit out earlier and I'm putting my hair up tonight in this sexy bun thing I watched how to do on YouTube last night.

As I dash into the shower, I bathe in the feeling of being loved. He loves me.

Hunter King loves me. Little Eden Wallace of Castleview Cove.

I don't think things could get any better.

But sometimes we can't predict what's going to happen next, and it's probably just as well I didn't.

"Only two more days till The Cup then. Do you think you're ready?" I ask Hunter as I finish the rest of my glass of prosecco.

We've had the most incredible meal. Wee Oscars is a traditional Scottish dish restaurant, owned by my dad's friend, Oscar. It creates every dish with a twist. Selecting as many plates as you want, everything is dinky but bursting with flavor. I even managed to persuade Hunter to try haggis. I don't think he'll try it again. His nose flares gave him away as he proceeded to tell me it was nice, but he looked like he was chewing wasps.

"I hope so. My swing is great. Luke and Evan are happy with my form. I feel good. I got the girl; I'm in love." He dreamily leans forward, puts his elbows on the table, and cups his face, gazing at me.

"You're such a flirt, Mr. King."

"I know, but it always gets me what I want."

"Yeah, and what's that?" I push my finger into my mouth, then lick and bite the tip openmouthed, teasing him.

"Stop doing that, naughty girl. Or I won't be able to stand," he moans. "I want you. Only you."

I bat my eyelashes and grin.

"In all seriousness, are you going to be okay when I leave after the winner's ball? I hate having to leave so soon and I will hate not seeing you every day. But we have video calls. I'm looking forward to the phone sex you've promised me." He winks.

My heart drops a little at this thought. I haven't been able to think of anything other than him leaving in a few days. But it will be okay. We have a plan and I'll see him again in eight weeks. Eight long weeks. He has back-to-back tournaments and I have the dance showcase coming up so eight weeks is when we can see each other next. It's all booked and I'm flying out to Florida.

"I know I'm going to miss you too. You make me happy. So happy." I lay my hand out for him to take it, which he does.

"Well, let's not think about that now. Let's focus on the

fact we still have six days together. I know four are Cup days, but I'll see you every night. I've arranged VIP escorts for you and the girls for the last day of the tournament. Come for a couple of hours here and there too throughout the other days if you want to. But on the last day, there's always a huge buzz. I have also arranged access to the player tent. It's free booze; I'm sure Ella and Beth will be all over that. My mum and stepdad will be here too."

"They really will devour that drinks tent. I'm looking forward to meeting your parents."

We've met over FaceTime and they seemed lovely.

"I want to be at every hole you play for the final," I say confidently.

"Really, the final? Are you that confident I'm going to be in the final?"

"Yes, I'm sure of it. I want to be there with you when you win."

"Do you?" he asks in awe. "You don't want to be at every hole on the last day. You'll be bored."

"I know diddly squat about golf, but I'll always support you, Hunter."

He lifts my hand to his lips, and plants a soft kiss to my inner wrist. Each and every time he does that I get a little shiver down my spine.

"Thank you for letting me find you, Eden."

"Thank you for finding me, Hunter."

"I actually hunted you down. I've been hunting for someone like you all my life. I think I subconsciously willed you to crash that night," he joshes.

"You sure did. I didn't stand a chance."

"Pah, you're one to talk. Bloody pole-dancing tease. I want another one of those." He raises his brows high.

"I can do that."

"Yeah?"

"Absolutely. Can we go home now?"

"Now that's an offer I can't refuse."

Hunter raises his hand to the server to get the check. "Shall we go get an ice cream? I only have eleven more to check off my list."

"You've done better than me. Although I have a year to complete my bucket list," I say. "C'mon, let's get ice cream. 'Cause there's always room for ice cream."

As soon as we're outside, the queue to get into the restaurant snakes down the narrow cobbled lane. I hate to tell the hopeful diners that they stand no chance of getting in. Luckily, my dad wangled tonight for us.

A few of the hopeful diners recognize Hunter and start chanting his name and wishing him well.

The town is packed tonight. I forgot how busy it gets during the tournament.

Hunter signs a few autographs and then wishes them well. He pulls me in close as we take a leisurely walk along the street to Castle Cones.

"We'll be lucky to get a taxi tonight, you know," I say lazily.

"We'll be fine. There is no way I am letting you walk very far in those sky-high red heels. Although, I think you should keep them on when we get home. You look super sexy in them, and I quite like the idea of them wrapped around my ears tonight. How the hell do you walk in those, anyway?"

I giggle and I'm about to answer when someone calls to Hunter from behind. Turning around, Fraser is jogging toward us.

"Hey, guys. I'm so sorry I haven't been able to see you. It's been a crazy few weeks. You all set for the tournament?"

"As ready as I'll ever be."

"I actually wanted to catch you too, Eden, and thank you for speaking to Ella for me. It meant a lot. Thank you."

Ella got in touch with Fraser? Interesting. I'm going to put salt instead of sugar in her cup of tea when she visits next time; she never told me. She's such an introvert sometimes.

"You're welcome, Fraser. I hope you guys worked things out. It's been a very long ti—"

"Sorry I'm late, Fraser. I couldn't get the car parked, and it's so busy."

My blood drains from my body at the sound of that voice. I'd recognize it anywhere.

As if in slow motion, the town around me spins like I'm in a blender. With everything becoming a blur, my body shivers and shakes as I slowly turn toward the voice.

"Eden?"

"Jamie!"

"Fuck," I hear Hunter mutter under his breath.

CHAPTER TWENTY-THREE

Baw bag: *noun,* an insult, an ignorant, vulgar, obnoxious or otherwise debatable person. A scrotum. **Pronounced:** Baw bag.

Coorie: *Verb,* to snuggle, nestle, cuddle. **Pronounced:** Coo-ree.

Eden

Fate, karma, the universe, whatever you want to call it is a funny old thing. Life is so unpredictable. Often unexpected. It never pans out how you think it will, and sometimes you just have to go with the flow.

Like now, for instance.

I'm sitting at my kitchen table, the very table Hunter and I fucked each other senseless on the other night, across from the man I never thought, maybe recently secretly wished, I'd never see again. He's never changed. Still dirty-blond, blue eyes, average height, unkempt, pale, all-around average.

He's sitting here, cocky as ever. As if the last few years never happened. He looks well. Not broken like he was when he left. I wondered to myself if he may have sought the help he needed for his post-traumatic stress disorder. I hope he did. He needed it, although I thought I smelled a faint whiff of alcohol as he walked past me at the front door.

Following the surprise encounter with Jamie the other evening, I stumbled away in shock, not wanting to talk to him. Hunter wrapped his huge protective arms around me and bundled me into a taxi.

He didn't ask me anything or press me to talk about Jamie afterward. He made me a cup of tea and snuggled up with me on the couch. He always knows exactly what I need.

Jamie turned up on my doorstep the next morning, wanting to talk. I wasn't ready. So I asked him to come back in a few days. And here he is.

I've psyched myself up to speak to him. Having him in my house unnerves me, though.

"What do you want, Jamie?"

"Please don't be like that, Eddy."

"Don't call me that. You lost that right when you left me," I say deadpan.

My shield of armor is firmly up.

"You look great."

Bawbag.

"Where have you been all this time?"

"Glasgow."

"Glasgow? What? As in an hour and a half away from here Glasgow?" I ask in confusion. "You've been there all this time, doing what?"

"Working for a building contractor. A friend of mine got me the job not long after I left."

So he's been in Glasgow, close to Castleview Cove and holding down a job. Doesn't sound like he's been going crazy out of his mind worrying about me, and I'll be damned if I let him know it's only within the last three months I've got my life back on track. I feel so pathetic for holding on so long. What a waste of my years.

"What are you back for? Why now?"

"Fraser's back for The Cup. I thought it would be a good time to return. See Mum and Dad, and I haven't met my nephew before either. It's been a family reunion of sorts."

Great.

"Since when did you become the family man, Jamie?"

"Please don't be angry with me, Eddy. I can't go on another year with you hating me."

"You think I hate you? I don't care enough about you anymore to hate you."

"Ouch. Fucking hell, since when did you become so feisty?"

"Since you left me. Since you never attended your own daughter's funeral. Since you didn't get in touch to let me know you were fine and well. Since I discovered you were cheating on me, for years, I might add, with Fiona *fucking* Evans. Nothing like choosing the town slut. Classy choice, Jamie. Real classy. So take your pick," I spit out.

"Shit," he whispers with his head bowed.

What a prick.

"You know the best bit. I now know we were never in love with each other. Our relationship was deeply flawed, but I wasn't the problem. You were. The boat and losing the boys aside, we had issues way before then. Our relationship was based on lies. I was a pushover. You used me. I was a simple choice."

"You really think that? Seriously. I love you, Eddy. I never stopped. I thought about you all the time."

What the actual hell is he on about? Is he for real?

"You love me?" I try to keep my cool. "I'm sorry, but you clearly do not know what love is. It's trust and honesty. It's being looked after. Being made to feel special, and it's a joint partnership. Ours..." I motion to the gap between us. "Was very one-sided, in every single way. It all leaned in your favor. Trust me, I know that now."

I feel my face getting hot and flushed as my heart beats in my ears with rage.

"And tell me, how many girls did you screw when you were with me? And since you left me? Did you ever think to get in touch? Love me? You're an asshole." I shake my head in disbelief.

"I love it when you're feisty."

What a cocky twat.

"After all this time, you come back here and throw this shit at me with the word love and you sit there like the last few years never happened. You've got a helluva nerve. You are the last person on earth I want to spend any time with anymore," I spit out.

"So you're spending all your time with Hunter King now?"

"He's five times the man you are."

I get the distinct feeling Jamie isn't back because he cares about me; it's because he's jealous.

"Oh really, is that why they pictured him with his ex a few weeks ago in Florida. Weren't you with him there too?"

What the hell is he talking about? Hunter and Jess? Couldn't be. I was there with him the whole time. Apart from the morning we were due to leave, he nipped out as he had some 'loose ends' to tie up, he said before heading back here to Scotland.

"How the hell do you know I was in Florida? Stalking me now, Jamie? You're pathetic."

Why is he doing this? And what picture? I need to Google when he leaves.

"I can't believe you're here, and you expect me to just act like everything is normal. You haven't even asked about Chloe, our baby." I clutch my chest. "Why didn't you come to the funeral?"

"I didn't know. My family didn't know my whereabouts, so they couldn't get in touch. And I was a mess, Eddy; I couldn't come back. I wasn't ready."

"But you're ready now?"

Ready now, because I have Hunter. He's been checking out Hunter's Instagram. I think this is who Fraser texted that day on the beach. He was texting Jamie all along.

"Yes, I am. How do I make things right with you?"

A loud bang from the front door startles us, and Hunter starts talking before he enters the kitchen. Oh boy, how do I explain this?

"Hey, Cupcake, I'm home," he bellows. "Day two, baby, and Hunter King is back in business. My game was on point today. I'm winning this championship. Your predictions were correct, baby." Dropping his keys, I hear them clatter on the top of the wooden console at the front door. "I want to celebrate. First, though." I hear him getting closer and his voice hits the kitchen before he does. "I want to devour your lips and then... I've thought of nothing else all day but your pretty little lips wrapped around my co—"

Hunter stops as he turns the corner into the kitchen and spots Jamie and me at the table.

"Shit," he says under his breath.

Jamie sneers. "You were always pretty good with your mouth, Eddy," he mumbles.

I think I'm going to pass out.

"What the fuck did you just say?" Hunter booms.

"Stating facts, Hunter," Jamie calmly replies.

Christ, Jamie's braver than I thought. Maybe he is drunk.

"Stop it, both of you."

Jamie sneers at me. "So you're screwing the retreat residents now. If that's how this works, maybe I should check myself in," Jamie says, his voice thick with venom.

A sudden declaration of war between them, I watch as Hunter readies to launch himself at Jamie. I fly from the table, running, and place my tiny frame in front of him with my hands up, pushing his chest back.

"Don't let him get to you. He's baiting you, Hunter. You have your game to think about. Your hands are your winning chance. Ignore him."

"And you." I whip around, coming face-to-face with Jamie's sinister smile. "Get out of my house, now. You can speak to me about Chloe and Chloe only. You know, your baby? That you haven't even asked about. Do you even know what happened? You're a self-absorbed prick. Thank Christ Chloe isn't here to witness how much of a fucknugget you are. You would have made a shitty dad. Now get the hell out of my home. Now." I point in the door's direction.

I continue to stand in front of Hunter as I watch Jamie slide his chair across the floor, making an almighty shriek from the legs across the floor. How fitting it sounds like my inner voice, shrieking to remove me from this situation.

Raising himself to his feet, he catches my eye. "I do want to speak to you about Chloe, Eddy. I really do. I'll be in touch." He then sniggers at Hunter.

"Don't bother," Hunter growls though clenched jaw.

"That's not for you to decide."

"Like hell it isn't," Hunter roars at Jamie.

"C'mon now, Hunt—" I lower my voice.

"Hunt suits you, rhymes with cun—"

"That's enough, Jamie. Get out now," I yell.

Hunter and I both watch as Jamie skulks through my house. We hear the front door close with an almighty bang.

I slowly turn to face Hunter.

"Eddy?" Hunter scrunches his face up in disgust. "You're not fucking seeing him again."

I've only ever seen Hunter mad once, and that was when Jess was here. Which reminds me, I must look that picture up of her and Hunter Jamie mentioned, if it even exists.

"Ocht, it's what he used to call me. I told him to stop. You're right; I don't want to see him again, but if he asks about Chloe and wants to go see her memorial and where we laid her ashes by the tree, then I will take him. But only for that. You can't tell me who I can and can't see."

Hunter stands, breathing heavy in and out, hands on hips, as he tries to calm himself. "You shouldn't even see him for that. I won't allow him to speak to you like that. He's your ex and I don't trust him. I would never ask you to stop seeing anyone but him. I can't allow it."

"I don't want to fight. Please? It's his daughter too, Hunter. Believe me, I agree with you; however, I do not do tit for tat. That's not how I behave."

"Okay, but if you see him again, someone should be with you. I don't think I'm that person. I may do something I regret." He stops in deep thought. "How can he be Fraser's brother? They are nothing alike." He frowns.

"I don't know."

"What made you decide to see him?" Hunter quizzes me with a frown.

"I just thought it would be better to get it out the way. Like ripping off a plaster, or Band-Aid is what you call it. Get it done. Trust me, I'm not exactly part of the Jamie fan club either. All I want to do is show him Chloe's tree, and then I'll never have to bother with him again. He's just said he lives in Glasgow. He has a job and stuff, so he's no intention of staying. You have nothing to worry about."

Hunter folds his arms, deep in thought.

I steer the conversation in a different direction. "He ruined your big news. Let's forget about him. Tell me everything about today; we can watch the highlights together on the television tonight. I want you to tell me all about the pars and under pars, birdies and eagles annnnd... those are the only golfy type words I know; I don't even think they're correct." Hunter laughs at me. "Mmm, and shaft and hole, they sound naughty." I laugh, trying to lighten the mood.

"I don't care if you don't know, Cupcake, as long as you're there for the final, because it looks like I'm on target for that." He bounces up and down on his feet with excitement. "Then you can call all the golf words after types of fruit for all I care."

"Come here," I beckon him with my pointer finger to me with flirty eyes.

Hunter strides over and wraps his muscular arms around me, nuzzling into my neck. "Fancy a shower, Cupcake?"

"I thought you'd never ask."

"Unfortunately, I can't stay tonight as Luke and Evan have strategy to discuss and I need to study the golf course again. Plus, I have a couple of appointments I need to attend; I really need to go to those. But we can have a shower. I'll make us something quick to eat, but then I need to go."

I groan. We only have a few more days left and I want to spend all my nights with Hunter. What appointments does he have so late on in the evening?

"Well, if we only have a little time together tonight, let's make the most of it," I say as I slap his ass and start running for the shower. "Race ya."

"Hey, you cheated."

I make it into the shower before him.

Hunter appears behind me, encasing me with his solid, naked body, placing feather kisses to my shoulder and neck. We shower in silence and Hunter bathes me with the utmost of care and intimacy, kissing and cuddling me under the trickling water. Never have I felt so cared for.

"Shall we just order food in? Save you cooking, you've had a long day," I say as I get out the shower.

"So have you. That's a great idea. I have that local food app on my phone; my passcode is my birthday. Just pick anything, I'm ravenous."

I nip out of the shower before Hunter to order ahead.

"Haggis it is," I tease as I walk out of my bathroom.

'Don't order haggis, uh-uh," he bellows from the shower.

"I thought you loved it."

"Yeah, sorry, it was delicious. Order me five portions." I hear him gag.

Laughing, I grab Hunter's phone off the bed, tap in his code, and there in front of my eyes is Hunter's text message app he hasn't closed.

.   .   .

Jess: I'm so happy we saw each other today. It was great and Florida was pretty special too. Can't wait for this week to be over so we can get back to the States.

It's from today. *See each other, great, Florida, special, we?*

Bile rises in my throat.

He didn't reply. It was delivered just as he arrived at my house. Jess is here. So he saw her in Florida. What did he see her for? Is that who he's seeing tonight for his alleged late-night appointment? It can't be. He's said many times he doesn't speak to her, and I saw how he was with her when Jax and she arrived together. Was, is, *this* all an act?

"What are we having for dinner then?" Hunter saunters into the bedroom, rubbing his hair with a towel.

I swipe his messages away quickly, my heart beating fast, and start scrolling to find the app.

Flustered, I say, "Eh, I don't know what to have Chinese, Indian, or Italian. You decide."

"Let's have Chinese tonight."

I place our order and then get dressed, a million different thoughts and scenarios whirling through my mind. I pass Hunter his laundered clothes I did for him today, and he casually chats away as I mumble a yes and no here and there. Once he's dressed, we head downstairs.

A little niggle enters my head. Hunter never tried to have sex with me tonight. That's not like him. He normally can't get enough.

Breaking my thoughts, he says, "I love your house, Eden, it's incredible. I can't believe you designed this yourself." He bounces down the stairs, looking around at the space.

I get our plates and cutlery ready. "Well, along with the architect I did, yeah."

"You have an amazing eye for detail. Your shower is like a luxury five-star hotel."

"I know, and I have a Kim Kardashian worthy walk-in wardrobe too." I'm trying to keep a level voice that doesn't give away my upset.

"With curves and booty to match."

I give a weak laugh.

"Would you ever consider building another house?"

"Yes, definitely. I love it here, but it's attached to the studio and can sometimes be noisy with the cars and drop-offs and music and stuff. We do appear to be outgrowing it though. I have a feeling we could do with a new dance teacher to join our team to cover me when I come to visit you too. I think it's too much for Ella and Eva."

"I wouldn't worry about that for now."

Does he mean because I won't be visiting him, anyway? I feel sick.

"Hey, you okay?"

"Mmmmm... I'm so tired tonight. I taught four classes today with Eva off. I felt a little light-headed earlier too. I'm fine, really." I fan my face with my hand.

"Well, as soon as we've finished dinner, I'm going, and you can have an early night," he says. "Then we only have tomorrow night together." He protrudes his bottom lip out like a sulky child.

"The winner's ball is on the night of the final. Which means we have to come back here, fast turnaround, change, then straight back out. My flight is so early the next morning." He wraps his arms around me.

He can't be cheating on me; I don't believe that. It simply can't be true. I know how he feels about cheating. It has to be something else.

"What do you want to do tomorrow night?" I ask, feeling

saddened by his departure and the discovery of Jess' text messages.

"I would love to sit on the sofa with you, cuddle, or what do you guys call it, coorie. I love that word. I want to coorie in with you, watch a film, kiss you all over, and sleep here tomorrow night. Then the big day the next day." His eyes twinkle.

"Sounds perfect."

After our meal, I clean up and walk Hunter to the door.

"Tomorrow I have back-to-back classes. I'll see you tomorrow night then?"

"Yeah, I'll text you as soon as I'm off the course." He leans in and places his plump lips to mine. "I'm going to miss eight weeks of these lips and this cracking arse of yours," he rasps with an almost Scottish twang as he smooths his hand down my back and gives my butt a good squeeze. I've noticed he's been using more Scottish British slang, like arse. It doesn't suit his accent at all, the way he tries to roll his letter *r*'s.

"I love you, Hunter. I really do. Be careful with my heart, please."

"Hey, hey, baby, look at me. I will always look after your heart. I promise."

I smile softly.

"What appointments are you going to tonight?" I ask curiously.

"Eh, it's just a Golf Association thing."

"Okay, well, have fun and good luck tomorrow."

"See you tomorrow night, Cupcake. Love you."

"I love you too."

I stand and wave him off till he's around the corner.

Heading back into the house, I quickly grab my phone and text Beth.

Me: Do you have something on this evening at the Golf Association with Hunter?

Beth: Not at this time of the night, no, why?

Me: I must have got mixed up, sorry.

Beth: He's doing really well in The Cup. Everyone's rooting for him to win. His agent is an asshole, though, and his ex. She goes everywhere with him.

Me: Was she there today? I was there for an hour early this morning but didn't see him or her.

Beth: Yeah, in the VIP area all day, winding everyone up and making out she and Hunter were so close. She has no class.

Me: Great. Can't wait to meet her. I'll see you on final day.

Beth: Forget her. See you then. Love you, babes :)

I pull up Google next and search for Hunter's name. Sure enough, there, in all its glory, is a photo of Hunter embracing Jess outside what looks like an office. He's wearing the clothes he wore on his flight back to Scotland with the headline, *King of Golf Dumps Highland Fling for Old Flame.*

What?

Jamie was telling the truth. I'm not sure how I missed this.

A cold sweat washes over me, and I make a dash toward my downstairs bathroom as I'm hit by a sudden wave of sickness.

I don't like this feeling.

Please don't let this be true.

CHAPTER TWENTY-FOUR

Stooshie: *noun,* a row or fracas, commotion. **Pronounced:** Stoo-she.

Hunter

"Hell, man, what a day. You're in the final tomorrow. You smashed it today." Luke beams in disbelief as we get out of the car and I tip the driver. The privileges of being a player in the tournament, you're assigned a driver for the week. We're now back at the retreat and I am buzzing.

What an adrenaline rush today. Luke, Evan, and I have been nonstop talking about my technique since we got in the car.

"I can't wait for tomorrow now. First. Shower and then I'm off to see my girl." I grin wide as I walk toward my cabin. "Have a great night, guys; thanks for today. Bring on tomorrow." We all start whooping.

Just as I'm about to push my key in the door, I notice two

people standing off in the distance at Chloe's tree. I slide my bag off my shoulder and place it on the doorstep.

I slowly walk across the path and onto the grass for a better view.

Eden and Jamie.

My excitement bubbles burst all around me.

I watch as the pair of them chat and Eden smiles briefly, shaking her head. They have so much history together; I wonder what they're talking about.

Eden brings her hands to her face suddenly as her shoulders shake.

Oh, baby.

Snaking his arms around Eden, Jamie pulls her into him, and she dips her head into his shoulder. I can only watch as he kisses the top of her head.

I close my eyes in pain; I can't watch this.

I shouldn't be watching this.

It's their child.

Not mine.

His and hers.

That connection will be there forever.

He's here in Scotland and I'm about to leave.

Reluctantly I turn and walk back to my accommodation; my body now feels as heavy as an 850-ton engine.

Since Jamie appeared the other night after our meal, Eden has become really quiet and I've had this overwhelming feeling that she's pulling away from me. Her texts have been one-word answers since last night too; it's very unlike her.

The combination of me leaving and Jamie's return hasn't been the best timing.

Following my bit of a stooshie with Jamie. That's what Eden called it. Apparently, it means strong words were exchanged. Their language makes me laugh. It made me feel wretched for her. It was wrong of me to react. It's what he wanted and his vile words, the way he spoke about Eden, were so disrespectful.

We never spoke about it, not really. I'm unaware of how she feels about the whole thing. She also never told me much about what he wants or what they spoke about.

She held her ground though, and I admire how strong she was with him. I'm hoping it's because I was there and she doesn't back down when others aren't around to defend her.

She's much stronger now. Not the fragile woman I met in that field, she's growing in confidence every day.

Not wanting to push her after Jamie's abrupt exit, we simply spent the night having a soothing shower and takeout dinner together. Wanting to show her it's not about the sex for me all the time, which we do a lot of, and it's phenomenal, but connection and conversation in other ways, with Eden, is incomparable. We always have so much to say. However, last night, she was a little quiet and reserved.

An odd sensation coils in my stomach.

I need to pull myself together. She told me she wanted to show Jamie Chloe's tree. Closure is what she's seeking, I think. I hope it's exactly that because she and Jamie look very close.

Jealousy is not usually an ugly trait of mine, but with Eden, it runs deep and I truly don't trust Jamie with her. I can't help but wonder if Jamie wants her back or plans on staying around. All I know is that I don't want him around my girl.

Remembering that broken girl back on the pier all those weeks ago, I saw how hurt she was as she recounted her not so splendid memories of him, Chloe, and fresh evidence of Jamie's infidelity.

It wasn't pleasant to watch. And I never want her to feel like that again.

As I push and twist my key to open my door, trepidation swamps me and I can't help feeling that I'm about to find out what the universe really has in store for me, none of it planned by me.

Entering Eden's dark entryway to her home, I wonder if she's even in. I took my time showering and getting ready to come over, giving Eden the space to freshen herself up after visiting Chloe's tree. I cannot imagine what losing a child must feel like, and she's always very reticent after her tree visits.

"Hello?" I call out.

Walking cautiously into the living room area, I spot a single lit candle on the coffee table with a little note under it.

I'm up the stairs.

No kisses, embellishments, or smiley faces, like she would usually add.

I pad up the creaky wooden stairs, not knowing what to expect. Mixed emotions flood my heart knowing that we have a bittersweet couple of days left together combined with the vision of her and Jamie together earlier too. My head feels tight and heavy.

Upon entering her bedroom, as I slide the heavy-duty barn-style door along the industrial wheel railings, I'm welcomed by a gust of warm heat with dozens and dozens of white candles lit throughout the room. Their light dances across the surfaces of the walls and ceiling, and I'm hit by a cocktail of exotic fragrance in the air.

"Hi." A soft whisper makes me shift my focus toward the bathroom door and I gasp.

Surrounded by the glowing light from the bathroom behind her and the light of the candles, Eden leans against the doorway in nothing but a soft pink and black feather lace bra, the smallest matching lace micro thong, garter belt, and black lace top stockings.

My throat dries up. She's so seductive and sexy, but tonight I wanted to spend it cuddling on the couch and relaxing with her. Just simply *being* with her is more than I needed tonight. I was not expecting this at all.

"Hey, baby," I whisper back.

"I wanted to surprise you."

"You certainly have managed that." I hold out my hand, motioning her to take it. "I only got to see you briefly this morning down on the course. I've missed you today."

She glides across the room toward me and takes my hand but doesn't confirm she missed me too.

"You okay?" I ask with worry.

"Yeah, I'm good, Hunter. I don't want to talk. I want you to make love to me. Slowly." She purrs as she rises on her tiptoes. I lean down to meet her soft lips and like always, the urge to devour her inches around my body.

This is most unlike Eden; she's becoming more and more comfortable and confident with me; however, something feels a little off.

She slides her hands downward to the hem of my shirt, then pulls it over my head. Not missing any of the divots as she moves south, she plants wispy kisses across my washboard abs.

Dipping her hands into the waistband of my jeans, she

locates the top button. Painfully slow, she unbuttons them, popping one at a time. With ease, she drops my jeans and black fitted boxers to the floor, and I step out of them.

Palming my cock with her hand, I let out a long moan. The blood rushes to my cock, becoming harder as she strokes me up and down with her delicate hand.

"You like that, Hunter?" She holds my gaze.

"I love it, Eden. I love you."

I cup her face with my hands and we kiss tenderly, softly. Nothing in this lifetime comes close to how I feel about Eden. With every thud of my beating heart, I love her. With all my soul. I want to move my life to be with her.

"Make love to me, Hunter."

Dipping slightly, I grab the back of her thighs, lift her up and walk over to the bed, and lay her down gently. Against the bed she looks divine in her contrasting light and dark underwear. So sexy and so angelic all at the same time.

I ply her with kisses across her body, building the anticipation of what's coming, she pants and whimpers with lust.

I pull her miniscule thong to the side and run my finger down her wet folds where I find the sweet spot between her legs. Instantly she starts oooooohing and writhing at my touch. Dipping my finger into her wet pussy, I pump slowly in and out, then add another finger.

Her pants become loud and shallow, with every plunging finger fuck.

"Yes. I want more, I need you, Hunter."

Pulling her panties further to the side, I slide my hands up her body, over her sheer stocking tops, then pull and snap the straps of her suspenders against her skin. She gasps as I cover her lips with mine, slowly kissing her over and over as my now dripping pre-come cock slides in. She wraps her slender legs around my waist, tight.

This is where I belong. With her like this. We are explosive together. It's like coming home and she's the best welcome home party.

We rock slowly, taking our time, kissing, exploring one another.

Rolling us carefully, Eden now on top, I push her back slightly and rise to meet her. Sitting upright like this, this closeness I feel with her, it's sublime. Looping my hands around, I unclip her bra, expose her full breasts, and suck her pebbled rosy nipple into my mouth.

Eden grabs the back of my head, begging me to suck harder. She has such sensitive nipples of late; me doing this makes her crazy.

Lazily, she slides up and down my cock as I move across to her other nipple, giving it the same attention as the other.

"Ooooooh," she whimpers.

Cupping her peachy ass, I spear her harder up and down.

She pulls my face upward hard into hers and our tongues dance and sing together in harmony. We breathe rough and fast with each pump as she pounds herself onto me again and again.

We lose ourselves in one another.

Spur of the moment, I throw my arms around her back, lie down on the bed, taking Eden with me, and spin us around with Eden now under me.

"Ah, Hunter, yes, there, that feels so good."

I spread my knees wide, thrusting rough and deep.

Smoothing my fingertips across her body, I bow down and pin her arms slowly above her head.

I entwine our fingers together, hands palm to palm.

Inches away from each other, I ride her like there's no tomorrow. Without warning, I get an overwhelming sensation that we aren't getting tomorrow. We have no more days for at least another two months.

This feels like goodbye as she looks deep into my eyes. Why does it feel like this? I stop moving.

"Why did you stop?" she blinks and asks breathlessly.

"I just wanted to look at you. You're so beautiful, Eden. I want to remember everything about this face. I'm going to miss you so much."

Her eyes glaze with emotion and I move in to kiss her with the lightest of touches. Our kiss is soft and sweet as our tongues tap each other briefly, teasing one another.

With slow movements I undulate my pelvis in waves, thrusting in and out again, not slow, not fast, but with meaningful momentum. Our moans flood the warm candlelit room. Our shadows flicker across the walls and ceiling.

Eden is glowing; she's my twin flame.

"Hunter."

"I know, baby, I know."

In perfect sync with one other, her heart beats with mine, our impending orgasms build and build. Warmth and rapid-fire spasms at the base of my spine spark. I'm at the point of no return, as the sensation at the tip of my cock builds fast, becoming super sensitive. Feeling my muscles pull from my stomach and thighs into my balls. I can no longer hold it and we come together, hard, screaming each other's names. Eden clenches around me over and over as I come inside her hot, wet core, emptying myself deep.

Leaning back slightly, I rivet my eyes to her exquisite face as she loses herself in us. It's blissful and euphoric all at once.

We slowly come down together. Eden peeps at me with her ocean-blue eyes and gives me a half smile.

"What's up, baby? You feeling sad?" I pant.

Instantaneously, tears pool in her eyes and slide down her temples.

She sniffles. "I love you so much, Hunter."

This isn't goodbye. Why does it feel like she's saying goodbye?

Planting a soft kiss to her forehead and then her temple, I rotate us onto our sides, still connected.

"Everything's going to be just fine," I say, although I'm not convinced myself. Eden's quietness and distance the last few days have kind of thrown me off. Jamie turning up and then the tree encounter has done nothing to eliminate my dreaded thoughts either.

Eden snuggles into me. I pull her in tight as if trying to mold her body, heart and soul with mine so she can be with me everywhere all the time.

"I have something that might cheer you up. I made the final," I whisper.

"Why didn't you say?" She lifts her head up to catch my eyes.

"Eh, because you seduced me as soon as I arrived. Annnddd you told me no talking." I chuckle.

"Fair point. So tomorrow, huh?"

"Yeah, tomorrow. Final."

"I'm so happy for you. Does this mean more sponsorship opportunities and stuff?"

"That, plus it moves me up the World Golf Ranking too." I bug my eyes.

"You're so talented, Hunter. For the few hours I've come down this week, you're so driven and focused. You're a joy to watch."

"Did you just give golf a compliment?"

"Yeah, it's still boring though. I just like watching you."

"It's the forearms again, isn't it?"

"Yup, it really is. When you bend down to pick up your ball and flex your arms, oshhh. It gives me fanny flutters."

"I had never heard that term until now. To us a fanny is a butt."

"I know. I've taught you lots of Scottish and British words since moving here. You can take it all with you when you leave and educate the masses for me."

Still inside Eden, not wanting to be anywhere else, we lie together, holding one other.

"When did Jess and Jax get here? I didn't see them, but Beth said she did."

"Please don't spoil the night mentioning those two. I don't want to talk about them. Tell me, after you left the course today, did you do much later?" I ask, fishing to see if she'll tell me Jamie visited Chloe with her.

"Nope. I ran five classes today plus a lunchtime tap class. Then I went to buy this underwear from the little lingerie shop in town. I'm sure Isla will have texted the entire town, knowing we're together. And then I came back home. I bought us food too. Are you hungry?"

Eden's reply has suddenly left me with no appetite.

I can't help thinking she's not telling me something. A sense of unease washes over me, and I wonder why didn't tell me she was with Jamie today. "I'm not very hungry."

"Me either. I've been feeling sick for a few days."

"Have you?"

"Yeah, I'm fine, really. I think it's the heat in the studio these past few days," she reasons. "Wanna have a shower?"

"I've just had one, but you made me dirty again." I slide

out of her. "C'mon, baby. You look fucking hot. But we need a shower."

She giggles. But not her usual full-hearted one. We make our way into the shower and the rest of the evening goes by too quickly.

Knowing I have a big game tomorrow, I don't care as I have a sensational last night with my girl. Kissing her, caressing her, loving her.

We are complete opposites, where countries and careers divide us.

We are happy and sad.

American and Scottish.

Golfer and dancer.

Tall and short.

America and Scotland.

We are one, but are we though?

I'm holding on to some of Eden's hope she speaks of.

Hope that we can make this work.

I have to make this work.

CHAPTER TWENTY-FIVE

Reekin: *adjective,* a state of inebriation. **Pronounced:** Ree-kin

Eden

Waking up to an empty bed this morning set my mood for the entire day. Hunter had to be up and away at the crack of dawn.

I feel sadness as it weaves into my bones.

Wearily, I walk through the busy and noisy VIP tent on my way to the restrooms. Beth's been checking where Hunter is so we can watch him coming in toward the final last four holes. He's doing extremely well, and he's eighteen under, which apparently means he's winning the Championship.

I've been chatting with Hunter's mum, Elizabeth and stepfather, Frank. Both of them are wonderful people, but I've been holding back knowing that I may never see them again. They truly love Hunter and are the perfect doting parents.

Last night was wonderful with Hunter, but thoughts of us being apart from early tomorrow do things to my heart I don't like.

I wanted to ask Hunter about his photo with Jess and why he didn't mention it after meeting her in Florida.

I wanted to ask him about the Golf Association meeting too, that apparently never happened, but I couldn't bring myself to ask either.

The reality of my impending heartbreak is setting in.

All I wanted was one last night with Hunter. Probably selfish of me. But to love him is what I am meant to do.

My heart is his. His is not mine. Especially if he's been seeing Jess. I feel like such a fool; however, the last thing I want to do is throw him off his game. I may be a lot of things, but being a bitch or stealing someone's dream, nope, that's not my style. I'm letting him have his moment before I fade into the background and become a distant memory for him while he lives his life in Florida. With Jess. If he is lying to me, then he's a great actor, I'll give him that.

So, today for me, is all about the show again, back to that old chestnut. I'm here to support, and then he'll be gone tomorrow, taking my heart with him.

My heart feels heavy as I enter the bathroom. Having done my business, I stand and wiggle side to side, pulling up my super skinny black jeans. I feel it all happening at once. My phone slides up my back pocket as my butt cheek stretches out the fabric. It jumps out of my pocket and slides into the toilet with a loud plop. "Oh, fudge nuggets," I gasp and whip around. Instinctively I throw my hand out, knowing good and well I would not put my hand in there. But like karma herself has turned up to lay everything on me today, a slight wave of my hand triggers the auto sensor flush and before my very eyes, my phone is gone in the whirling water. *Poof*.

"Well, that's just great. Thanks." I raise my head to the heavens and roll my eyes.

I quickly wash my hands and stomp back to the tent.

I call out to the girls, "I just dropped my phone down the toilet." I raise my hands in the air, slapping them back down on my outer thighs.

"Shit." Beth laughs. "It would only happen to you. You can now tell everyone you have shitty reception."

"Oh, very funny. What a day."

"Hey, hey, this is a great day." Beth loops her arms around me. "Forget your phone; you'll get a new one. You're in love, and your boyfriend is in The Cup final, which I might add we need to make a move to watch his last four holes. Plus, we're drinking champagne; the sun is shining; the place is buzzing. What have you got to be sad about?"

If only she knew about the text messages, the photo, and his lie.

"Nothing." I paint a smile on my face.

"Girls, let's make a move, shall we? We can't stay here getting reeking."

"I have no phone, so please don't lose me, ladies."

"We won't. First things first, Hunter said to grab his bodyguards from the staffing station, Liam and Noah. Then we can get to the front for Hunter's last shots. C'mon, let's go." Beth rounds us up, downing the last of her champagne and plonking her glass onto the table.

Once Liam and Noah are with us, Eva, Ella, Toni, Beth, and I huddle between them, protecting us from the crazy busy crowds.

"I feel so important," says Toni.

"We are." Ella points to her VIP pass.

We all giggle.

As we head toward our destination with Liam and Noah as our protectors, I teeter in my black wedge strappy sandals, trying to keep up with my herd of gazelles.

We arrive just in time to see Hunter and his caddy, Jim, who I only met the other day, walking up the fairway toward the hole Hunter's playing. Waving to the fans as he passes, they cheer and clap him on, calling his name and wishing him well. The crowds love him.

He's shining out there and loving every minute, chatting to his caddy and reveling in the moment.

Standing near the front, I hope he spots me with my white tee shirt featuring a sequined gold crown on the front, but he spots Jax and Jess first and gives them a thumbs-up. *Fucking Jess.* Then he spots me and waves in my direction with a cheesy smile and winks. Giving a small wave back, my heart melts at his smile. He's such a good-looking man. He's the only man I know who could pull off wearing a pair of skintight white pants. He is hot and his ass should be illegal. But he's not mine.

Pushing my gloomy thoughts aside, I focus on Hunter for the next few holes as we walk toward the last hole.

The tension throughout the crowds is palpable. The fans respectfully clap Hunter and his opponent on, but when asked to stay quiet while they take their shots, they're all as quiet as church mice. The buzz and thrum of people around is contagious.

I never knew golf could be so exciting.

"Okay, Eden," Beth leans in and whispers in my ear. "This is the final hole. Hunter's opponent has made his shot. If Hunter makes this putt and the ball goes in the hole. He's won." Thank Christ for Beth. All I know is that he was winning, but no idea by how many shots on this hole or how many he needs to win.

I grab Beth's hand and squeeze it tight.

The steward holds up his baton, instructing the crowd to be quiet.

Then there is complete silence.

In the distance, all that can be heard is the crashing ocean waves and the odd shriek of a seagull here and there.

A thrum of excitement rolls through the 40,000 strong crowd.

This is it.

This is Hunter's shot.

Crouching.

Assessing.

Aligning.

Silence.

Hunter gets himself into position, does a little side-to-side patter of his feet. Swings his putter back and forth before committing to the shot.

I do not know how Hunter must be feeling, but I feel my own heart beating like a loud set of bongos in my chest.

With one gentle, expert stroke, the golf ball rolls across the green, taking its time to fall with a dip into the hole and makes a clatter sound indicating he's won.

And that's it.

The crowd cheers and claps with excitement. People sitting up high in the spectator stands rise to their feet in honor of Hunter, whooping and chanting his name.

He's a legend. Pulling himself back from the brink to this moment of glory.

Hugs, back pats, and handshakes are dished out to his caddy and his opponent. Walking over to his parents, sister,

Evan, and Luke, they all embrace with well wishes and excitement for Hunter.

The king is most definitely back.

Hunter is so calm and composed. I don't know how he does it. He moves away from his family, claps his hands, then walks in a circle, in delight, thanking the crowd for their support and basking in his win.

A mixed grin of elation and relief dons his striking face.

As he circles around, he spots me in the crowd and strides toward me with intention.

Ella nudges my back, prompting me to walk toward him. I start tentatively moving. But then he puts his arms out and I run to him. The crowd goes wild as I leap into his arms.

I hear clicking cameras all around us as the paparazzi go nuts at our sudden display of affection.

"I did it, baby."

"You really did, Hunter. I'm so proud of you."

Dropping me onto my feet, he leans down, cups my face, and kisses me full on the mouth in front of thousands of people. I wonder how many people are watching this on television from all over the world. I cry with happiness for him.

The cheering takes a new turn, getting louder and louder as we stay in our own little bubble for a few seconds, longer than we should.

Hunter leans back, grabs my hand, and punches his hand in the air. The whooping and cheering that follows is deafening.

A girl could *definitely* get used to this.

"I love your tee shirt." He turns to me, pointing at my sequined crown tee.

The crowd spots what he's doing and laughs along with us.

"I wore it for you. You're my king."

"And you're my queen, baby."

Am I?

Leaning down once more, he taps a quick kiss to my lips, then informs me he's got to get ready for the official ceremony and interviews.

"You can watch the presentation if you want, Cupcake, then I know you'll be keen to get away quickly so we can change for the ball tonight. I'll come pick you up. I have some news I need to share with you, plus something else I really need to tell you," he says.

He looks worried.

"Okay."

I wonder if he's telling me it's over tonight, and this is all show for the press. He did say a few weeks ago to me that the press is good for his brand.

As he dashes off, Liam stalks toward me, ushering me back to the safety of the girls and Noah.

We watch Hunter being presented with his trophy and give his quick speech, thanking all his family and his support team. He mentions the fact that Castleview Cove will always have a special place in his heart. He will in mine too.

Afterward, we all disperse, going our separate ways. Ella is attending the ball this evening as Luke's partner, and Toni is going with Evan. For Beth it's a work event so she'll be there, anyway. No, Eva today or tonight. She's currently having a sabbatical from the studio. She won't tell us why, but we agreed to respect her wishes and give her the space and time she said she needs.

"Ladies, see when you're all better dressed." Beth laughs.

As Toni, Ella, and I jump in the car Hunter organized for us, we wave Beth goodbye.

We're all getting ready at my place. I have bought new everything for this evening.

This last week has gone too quickly for my liking.

Last night together. What a horrible thought.

Dread washes over me in waves at our impending farewell.

One last night before he becomes someone else's.

❋

Sipping glasses of sparkling prosecco in my kitchen, Toni, Ella, and I wobble about on our heels. Fixing, preening, and altering hair, lipstick, and pulling at our dresses here and there.

A loud knock at the front door indicates the arrival of the boys.

Clicking across my wooden floor, I head to answer the door as Hunter walks through it.

I'm greeted by Hunter in his tuxedo. Good heavens.

What a sight.

He's so handsome and I can feel the energy bouncing off of him. He's as high as a kite from the adrenaline of winning today.

He rushes in, but then stops. "Aw, man, you'll hate me if I ruin your lipstick."

"I really will," I say, agreeing with him.

"You look fabulous." He steps back to get a better view.

The dress I picked out for tonight is a strapless navy satin number with a higher front and dramatic dipped hemline at the back. My Bardot neckline bodice features an oversized print of blush pink, royal blue, and red peonies design, and the inside of the dress is lined with the same material of my bodice. It's royal and luxurious, and it makes me feel like a queen.

"Your boobs look sensational," he says lustfully.

"I bolstered them into this dress; I'm sure they're getting bigger," I say, shifting my upper body from side to side and pulling my top up slightly. I had to go up a size in my dress. Hunter and I have done nothing but eat. Florida food was epic. "I'm one sneeze away from popping out."

"That, I would like to see." He laughs. "Are you ready?"

"Yes," I say, bending slightly to adjust the thin strap on my blush-pink strappy heels. "Let me just grab my bag and the girls."

Grabbing my keys, I head out the door. I slide my red satin clutch under my arm as I watch the girls leave the house before me. Ella is wearing a tight and super stunning to-the-floor black-and-gold silk dress, and Toni is wrapped in a deep-berry mermaid fit figure-hugging tulle gown. Inspecting my hair in the hall mirror, I adjust my caramel beachy wave style that took great effort to do but now looks effortless. How I pulled it off, I'll never know. I take a deep breath in. "Here we go. Last night together," I mutter.

With a loud clunk, I pull my front door closed, lock up my house, and drop my keys into my bag. With no phone, I realize I have so much more space for everything in my tiny bag.

Taking my first step, I raise my head and stop moving in shock. Hunter's standing beside a shiny black limo, in all his tuxedo glory, hands in his pant pockets, relaxed and dashing, just waiting for me.

"My goodness."

He raises two fingers up in a peace sign. "Two more off your bucket list. Number nine, attend a ball and number thirteen, ride in a limo."

He wouldn't be doing this if he was seeing Jess behind my back. Although I never knew Jamie was cheating on me. Detective Wallace, I am not.

"You did this for me?"

"Yeah, baby, I did."

I can't help but smile.

Hunter opens the door for me, and instantly the girls scream.

"Are you girls going to be like this all night? You are loud girls. Very loud." Luke covers his ears as I dive in.

There doesn't appear to be anything further going on between Luke and Ella, although I think Luke would like that. Ella has said nothing, but as always, she's holding back.

On the other hand, Toni and Evan have become really close. Toni's been really sad these past few days. I think she feels the same as I do as the inevitable departure.

Happy endings are not for everyone.

Taking it all in, the smell of the leather, the popping of the champagne, giggling from the girls, my handsome man. I want this night to last forever. In a time loop, I don't want to move on to the next twenty-four hours. I'd like to stay here.

CHAPTER TWENTY-SIX

Giein it laldy: *saying,* to give one's all, to be vigorous or energetic. **Pronounced:** Geen it lall-day.

Eden

Hunter hasn't left my side since we arrived. He's been attentive and introduced me to everyone.

From the corner of my eye, I spot Fraser and his family across the room. Sitting next to him is Jamie. Why is he here? I didn't see him come in.

I notice Fraser boring his gaze through Ella, who's standing over at the bar.

There's something going on there. I must ask Ella about that later. God, this is exhausting. Between me and Hunter, Ella and Fraser, Eva and Ewan, I don't know if the three of us are coming or going.

An announcement is made from the stage to indicate the first dance.

"C'mon, winner first." Hunter places his hand to my lower back, ushering me to the dance floor.

Hunter takes my hand and circles my waist with the other in a ballroom-style hold.

"Can you dance?" I ask, looking up.

"Nope, but I can sway and sidestep."

"Maybe I should lead."

"You probably should," He jokes.

Orchestral strings float through the air as we're hit with the sultry tones of Beyoncé's version of "At Last."

"You may have a Scottish Beyoncé in Lewis Capaldi, but in the States we actually have Beyoncé." He crinkles his nose. "Since that first time you danced for me in the studio, how passionate you were about song's words and the emotion behind them, I started listening to the words of every song that plays on the radio. This song. These words. This is for you. For us. We're together at last."

A lump balls in my throat.

We glide and sway together, moving over the floor as other couples join us. And Hunter's a really wonderful dancer.

Jamie and the gossip mags are wrong. Hunter is mine and only mine. He's not seeing Jess. I feel it. I think.

I listen to the mesmerizing words.

He is my at last, not for long enough though.

The night goes by filled with lots of laughing, joking, and dancing with my girls. Ella's been giein it laldy all night, ignoring Fraser's glares.

Heading to the bar to get myself a drink, I glance around the room. Jamie is across the room chatting with Jax. I've only met Jax once, but I do not get a good vibe from him. Two slimeballs together, deep in conversation.

Shifting my eyes around the room, I spot Hunter way

over in the far corner chatting to a woman in a bright-red dress and skyscraper heels. Jess.

She reaches up and rubs her hand down his arm. He doesn't even flinch. He flashes his statement smile at her and he looks very at ease, unlike before around her.

Turning back around, I bow my head to the bar as my stomach sloshes around like a washing machine.

"They're closer than you think."

Jax Parks.

Great. Just what I need.

"Really. Do you know that for sure?" I ask, not really wanting to know the answer.

"Jess informed me they met up in Florida a few weeks ago and she slept with him so, yeah, I know."

I feel sick to my stomach. "Why would she tell you that? And why would you stay with her?"

"Easy pickings. Easy lay," he sneers.

Yuck.

"I knew you two would never last. You're not good enough for him. He likes party girls, fake blondes, and fake tits. Factor in a long-distance relationship. They never work. You're just a toy to him. He has a girl in every city and town around the tournament trail. You know little to nothing about him and you're so not his type." He looks me up and down with distaste as he sips his whisky. "Jess, now she fits right into this scene. Party girl. Knows all the golfers and their families. Free to travel. American. Lives in Florida. Likes to share, if you know what I mean."

A mix of shock and anger flood my head. I can't listen to another minute of this.

"I wouldn't trust him if I were you. Being away all the time with temptation everywhere. Pfttt. Good luck." Before I can move, he decides for me as he turns on his stout feet and walks away.

Relief washes over me.

What a head fuck.

My puzzle of conflicting emotions is all over the place. I'm getting mixed messages from Hunter's words and actions, but the text, photo, and sneaking off to nonexistent meetings don't match.

I turn again to see if Hunter is still talking to Jess, but he's nowhere to be seen and neither is she.

Walking back over to the table, needing to freshen up, I grab my clutch and make my way to the bathrooms.

Twisting through the maze of corridors in the five-star luxury hotel, lost in my thoughts at Jax's words, I come face-to-face with a swaying Jamie. He's so drunk. He's clearly been drinking for a few hours.

"Hey, you alright, Jamie?"

"You." He points at me viciously. "You should be with me, not him."

Panicking, I look around to see if anyone is around to help in case this goes south.

"You are mine. Not his. You always have been."

"I'm not yours, Jamie."

"Yeah? Well, you're not his either. I saw him with Jess earlier and she's filled me in on all of her and Hunter's recent hookups. Sneaking around and fucking behind your back."

Why is this happening to me again?

"What did she say?" I whisper as I watch him swagger back and forth.

"She said that they have arranged to be together once Hunter leaves here. He's never coming back for you. They have plans. Together," he slurs.

Jax was right. Jess and Hunter.

A vicious pang of jealousy pierces my heart.

Mum was wrong. Going after what you want was a stupid idea.

The man I love doesn't love me.

I stumble backward away from Jamie.

"I have to go."

"Don't go," Jamie shouts. "Eddy, come back." I hear him howl.

Running through the corridors toward the back of the hotel, I burst open the giant fire exit door that leads to the back parking lot, for fear of running into paparazzi hanging about at the front.

I can't breathe as I bend over with my hands on my knees. Gasping for air outside, my chest feels tight and heavy.

"Eden?"

I turn around to face Hunter.

Spotting my tears, he says, "Hey, baby. What's up? I saw you racing along the corridor."

"Don't call me baby," I spit.

"Hey, hey, what did I do?" He laughs.

"Everything. You've lied to me for weeks now."

"Lied to you?" he asks, puzzled, as I stomp toward the parking lot.

"About everything. About us, Jess, your intentions with me. Everything. I saw you back there. She was touching you; you never stopped her. I've seen the text messages from her. You met her in Florida, Hunter, and you never said."

Hunter clenches his jaw.

With anger, I pour out everything I've discovered these last few days. "It was all over the gossip mags. I saw it with my own eyes, but I didn't want to believe it. You were with her. Hugging her. And Jax said—"

"Oh, great, continue. What did Jax say? This I have gotta hear." He stops walking and folds his arms.

"He said you and Jess met when we were in Florida and you fucked her. Did you? I feel sick."

"You didn't just ask me that, did you?" He drops his head. "I would never, ever cheat on you. I have always been faithful to you, with all my girlfriends. Unlike your ex."

Jamie clumsily walks out of the heavy door with a clatter, then stumbles and weaves toward us.

"Speaking of the devil." Hunter glowers.

"Don't listen to him, Eddy. He's lying to you," Jamie slurs.

"Am I now, and how would you know? You fucking drunk. Fraser's filled me in on all your latest antics. Your life's a mess. No home. No job. Alcohol dependent. You need help."

"Shut it, Hunter. You don't know what you're talking about," Jamie mumbles.

"Shut up, both of you," I yell. "Jess told Jamie all about your secret rendezvous, Hunter, and how you've been planning a life together when you leave here. Jax even confirmed it. He said our relationship is a lie and we would never last. You have women everywhere you go.

"You're only using me while you're here. But Jess, well, she supposedly fits right in, no commitments, no ties, easy girl, and knows the golf scene." I hold back the tears I feel forming. "You lied to me the other night when you said you were going to a meeting late at night. You weren't there. I checked."

Someone must have alerted Toni, Beth, and Ella as I watch them tentatively join our *Jerry Springer Show* moment in the hotel parking lot.

"Great. An audience. Well, why don't I fill everyone in where we're up to, shall I?" Hunter says a little too calmly.

"Eden here thinks I'm cheating on her with Jess. I'm a lying, cheating asshole and our relationship is a lie. Isn't that what you said?" he turns to ask me through narrowed eyes.

The girls all stand in complete shock.

I don't like this at all.

"Oh, and the best part, that information came from Jax and this jerkoff here..." He points to Jamie. "...and Jess apparently too. Three fine human specimens with no backbone, no loyalty, and not a scrap of honesty between them. You actually believe them over me?" He points to his chest.

"I don't know," I answer, because I really don't know anymore.

"Are you fucking kidding me? I've had the best day of my life today. I win The Cup and the girl, and you pull this shit on me." He shoots me a furious glance.

Resting his hands on his hips, he raises his head to the sky, trying to calm himself down. "I wished you hadn't done this tonight. Do you want to know the truth, Eden? Because you could have asked me. Or is it because you're so wrapped up in Jamie since he came back that I've been swept aside so you can make way for him."

"I don't know what you mean." I sniffle.

"Pah, really, who's lying now? You've been quiet, reserved, holding back. Not sharing every thought with me, which is most unlike you. The icing on the cake, I asked you last night what you'd been up to yesterday, and you never told me this asshole visited Chloe's tree with you. I saw you."

"I didn't want to upset you," I whisper.

"But, here, now, this is a better time to upset me?" He paces. "You know what. I can't do this. You'll never believe me. He may have cheated on you, Eden, but I never would. I am nothing like him."

"Fuck off, Hunter," Jamie mumbles.

"No, you fuck off, Jamie. I've learned more about this girl in a few weeks than you ever took the time to in seven years. I know what's going on here. You saw Eden in the papers, getting her life back, with me, and you're fucking jealous. But you left; you walked away from this incredible girl and your baby. You don't want her, but no one else is allowed to have her, is that right? Fuck, I bet you're loving this. Tell me, did you concoct all this crap about me alongside Jax to cause what's happening here? To place doubt in Eden's mind? From what I hear, manipulation is one of your strengths. Did Jax pay you to tell these lies?"

Jamie's sheepish face says it all as he looks away from us. He lied to me about Hunter and Jess. It's written all over his face.

I cover my mouth with my hand and let out a muffled shriek.

"I put money on the fact he told you he's still in love with you. Did he tell you that too, Eden? The other day in the kitchen? Is that what he told you, because you told me jack shit about what you spoke about. Did he?"

"Yes," I whisper.

He shakes his head in disappointment. "You'll always be searching for reasons not to be with me. Let's face it, you've been looking for an excuse since we started dating to get rid of me or waiting for me to fuck up. Because of course you don't deserve happiness and love in your life, isn't that right, Eden? You deserve scum like him." He points at Jamie again. "This time it's cheating on you. The other week it was because I live too far away. Then it was because of things Jamie made you believe. Even though I've done everything to show you otherwise. You drew up a master plan for us to be together. I'm one hundred per cent all in with you. Or was that a lie from your end? Was all that a ruse to make me believe this would work?"

"No, it was never like that, Hunter," I'm not lying, I love him. A cold sweat breaks out across my skin as I start to panic.

"Well, it feels like it." He pulls his hair. "Do you really want to know what I've been doing sneaking around and who I've been meeting at night?"

I don't get a chance to answer.

"Realtors, or estate agents, whatever. I've been buying land so I can build a fucking house to move here, so I can be with you. Man, I feel like such a fool." He rubs his hands into his eyes. "I've had meetings with my realtor via video calls this week, staying up late so we can list my house in Florida, getting all the paperwork in order."

What have I done? My world plummets around me.

Hunter can't stop his river of defense. "Jax Parks. I fired him this afternoon, straight after my win. He's been screwing me over for months now. It's his revenge, Eden. Do you not see this? Getting a drunk involved worked out brilliantly for him. He told you lies about me. It's fucking fake news, and you bought it. He wants this to happen. I'm surprised he's not out here ringside." His voice is suddenly as hard as steel. "I can't believe I'm having to justify myself when I've done nothing wrong."

"Jess?" He paces with fury. "I bumped into her when I had an appointment with my lawyer. To start my visa application to move here to Scotland to be with you." He points at me.

My bag drops to the ground as I place my head in my

hands and sob into them as tears of reality fall. I don't think I want to hear anymore.

"Jess was at the gym. I decided I didn't want to hold any bitter grudges toward her anymore. We made our apologies to each other. I let go of the past so I could move on with my future. With you. Tonight she was just saying congratulations. That was all." He rubs his eyes.

"When we chatted in Florida, she invited me to go to her spinning class with her. I was polite and said I would, knowing damn fine I will not be there, because I'm moving here. My lawyer's office is located next to her gym. It was a chance meeting, Eden."

Hunter lets out a strangled groan.

"I don't even think I can stop it now, but my visa application is underway. It takes eight months to process, and I wanted to start as soon as possible. Having spent all that time with you in Florida, I realized I couldn't be without you. I'm no liar. I'm the opposite of that. I'm the most honest guy you'll ever meet. Everything I said was true. I love you with everything. But tonight I don't recognize you."

I feel bile rising in my throat. He continues his onslaught of honesty.

"I know you've been hurt. I know what you've been through. But you've been trying to convince yourself you're not worthy of love again. My love. You've fucking crushed me with all this high school bullshit tonight. This is such childish behavior. I can't win with you. You want me, but you won't allow me to have you. Not really. You're still wrapped up in him and believe his lies." He stares at Jamie. "I never stood a fucking chance once he came back. You certainly won't let me love you fully with my whole heart. I wanted to share my life with you. Last night, when I made love to you, you were saying goodbye to me already. I knew it. I could feel it with every touch. You'd already made your decision we would not work." With glassy eyes, he rubs his nose with the back of his sleeve.

"You want me to back off and be the bastard you so desperately want to believe I am, then have at it. You're getting what you want, Eden." He tugs furiously at his bow tie to loosen it.

"I was moving heaven and earth to be with you. I even signed a deal the other day, in private, behind Jax's back, with Beth and the Golf Association to set up a new golfing scholarship, identical to the one I have back home. I was going to help run it here, with Luke and Evan running the facility in Florida. I wanted to cherry pick my tournaments, me winning Majors allows me to do that. Then coach, here in Scotland, in between that. Looks like that's going to change now."

He looks over to Beth. "I need you to get me out of that contract, Beth. Pronto."

I yell, "No, Hunter, please don't do that." My charming American boy is so hurt. I did this. I've never seen him like this before. Pain funnels fast into my heart; I think I may pass out.

He shakes his head at me. "You messed up, Cupcake. The issues you have with trust were never about me. If we don't have trust, we have nothing."

We stand in silence. I'm utterly lost for words.

"Long distance will never work without trust, Eden. We are doomed from the start. And please don't waste your tears. Not for me. Save them for him. 'Cause he seems to get everything. He wins every time with his lies and deceit."

His eyes full of pain connect deep with mine. "You'll never trust me being away all the time. It will eat you alive and I can't allow that to happen. You've hurt us both enough tonight. Just so you know, I've never loved anyone the way I love you. I've tried to show you how much. It's been a whirlwind; you've had me in a spin since I met you. Fuck." He squeezes his eyes tight. "I gave you my heart. You had me." He glances over at Jamie. "But I can't live in the shadows of another man. For the record, unlike him, I'm not leaving you, Eden. You pushed me."

He turns, marching toward the hotel, muttering, and disappears through the glass sliding doors. All I can do is stand and watch as my future melts away like snow in a thaw.

I don't know what to do.

"What have I done?" I bawl.

"We can be together now, Eden," Jamie leers.

"Do the right thing for once in your life and fuck off, properly this time." Toni shoots him a vicious glare.

Detecting the mood, Jamie wobbles away toward the town center.

"How do I fix this?" I look at the girls.

One by one they walk my way. Ella pipes up, "I don't think you can, babes. He's hurt. You've done some pretty stupid shit in your time, but this takes the biscuit. I would normally stand by you through hell or high water, but you fucked up tonight, Eden. What the hell were you thinking listening to Jax and Jamie?"

Shivers of panic wave like a violent storm.

"I'm going to be sick." I bend over fast, emptying my pain, sadness, and stupidity all over the tarmac.

When there's nothing left, I turn back to the girls.

"I'll call you a taxi." Beth taps on her phone as they all start walking away.

"Are you not coming home with me?" I ask.

"We're staying here, Eden. You need to go home, clear your head, get perspective on what happened here tonight. You need to buckle up because the next few days are going to hurt like a bitch. He leaves tomorrow, baby girl. You blew it." Ella's stoic voice has thrown me.

My girls always have my back. But not tonight. This is awful.

"I see," I say, wiping my face, trying to pull myself together.

I turn my back on them. "You can all go now."

Picking up my bag up from the ground, I walk slowly toward the curbside to wait for my taxi.

Shoulders back, I take a deep breath in, knowing that I've just changed my direction forever.

I hold back my tears, the large ever-growing lump in my throat threatens to strangle me.

Behind me, I hear the girls clicking heels go back inside the hotel, and then it's just me.

Alone again.

Just how it should be.

Destined to be by myself forever.

I blew up my own world tonight.

Tears pool in my eyes again as that familiar friend called pain weaves itself through my veins.

Hello, old friend. Oh, how I've missed you.

CHAPTER TWENTY-SEVEN

Ella Wallace

Arriving early at Eden's house with the girls, we decided we should attack this head-on. We will not let Eden wallow around for the next few months.

I understand her grief will never subside for Chloe. But the sadness, or worry for Jamie's whereabouts, went on for too long.

This time, we're not letting that happen.

This is going to be worse. Because she actually loves Hunter.

None of us can wrap our heads around what Eden did last night. It makes no sense.

Expecting a shocking day ahead with tears and sadness, we've come equipped with cupcakes and coffee at nine in the morning.

I could do without this today after Fraser's confession last night, and we've been waiting for Eden to answer her door for ages now.

"Should we get the key from reception?" Eva asks.

"I don't think she's in."

I knock again.

"Her car is here." Toni points.

"She's not in the studio, is she?" Beth frowns.

We make our way around to the studio. The door is open wide, and all the blinds are up.

We shuffle through the door and head in the office's direction at the back.

Sure enough, here she is, dressed all in black. Hair up. No makeup. Sitting behind the laptop with the office phone under her chin.

She looks tired but there are no signs of any red eyes or tears.

Dozens of newspaper article printouts are scattered across the desk of Hunter and her embracing at the final yesterday. They made the front and back page of all the mainstream newspapers.

"Yeah, that's great, thank you, and my new phone, that will be here tomorrow by courier, will it?" she questions whoever is on the other end. "Great. Thanks for your help."

She puts the phone back into its cradle and looks up.

"What are you lot doing here at this time of the day, on a Sunday?" she asks as if last night never happened.

"We brought cupcakes and coffee, because you know, we thought you might need cheering up today," says Toni.

"I'm not hungry," Eden replies flatly.

This is not what we were expecting at all.

"You lot can all go. I'm busy."

"Eden, come on now. You had a brutal night last night. We know that you'll be feeling like shit today. We're here for you," I say.

"What, like last night, Ella? When you all walked away

from me? Whatever," she says deadpan. "Did you have an enjoyable night in the end?"

"We left not long after you. The boys all left before us too. Hunter was really upset."

She chews the inside of her mouth and turns her attention back to the laptop.

"What are you doing, Eden?" Eva asks.

"Working, Eva. We have new student enrollments starting tomorrow. The accounts need doing and all those boxes behind you are sponsorship opportunities to make bank. I've worked out that there's about ten grand in those. I'm making a start on that today on Instagram and looking at ways to be more profitable." She sits back in her chair.

"She doesn't mean with work, she means now, with Hunter?" Beth barks.

"That, well, I blew it last night with Hunter. Isn't that what you said, Ella? I watched Hunter pack up and leave real early this morning. He's gone. Without a goodbye. This is all I know how to do. Work and dance. So this is it for me. That okay with you all?"

Oh, Eden.

"C'mon, Eden. This is not like you," Toni whispers.

"But moping around, losing myself in a man, being sad. That's me, is it? Or is it the stupid childish playful side that's me? Because Hunter made it pretty clear last night that I was, now wait, how did he put it again? High school and childish. Yeah, I think that was it. He's right. It's time to grow up. So this is me. Working and dancing. It's what I do best. Keep myself to myself. Look after number one and I don't need or want any of you. You made that very clear last night that I fucked up when you left me."

A red, angry rash starts creeping across her neck.

"I may have been fooled last night and completely

played by two spiteful twats. Fed lies to like a hungry lion, but I would always, always stand by you all no matter what. Even if you messed up. But then none of you share anything with me. So I don't really know that much about what goes on. And why is that? Because I'm the baby of our messed-up little group. Short and stupid. Just a silly, naïve, dress like a five-year-old little girl who saw the fun in everything again, or is it because I'm not very experienced in relationships? What the fuck is that all about, eh? Because I pay my taxes, run a home, run the business, built a house. I look after myself, like a big girl, but you all treat me like I'm an idiot."

She stops for a moment.

"And you, Eva. I bet you've told everyone apart from me what's going on with you and Ewan, but aw no, our little girl can't take it, so we won't share with her. What the fuck ever. Now would you all just fuck off? I don't need you; I am not a charity case," she yells now, raging.

"That's enough, Eden," Eva lowers her voice at Eden.

"And what about you?" She points at me. "What exactly is going on with you and Fraser?"

"I don't know what you're talking about."

"Really. You could have fooled me," Eden spits.

"And you, Beth, huh? What the fuck is wrong with Billy exactly? Doesn't meet your CEO standards? You're too pigheaded to admit you're in love with him and just be with someone for being normal and grounded. But no, he doesn't tick Mummy and Daddy's boxes. Doesn't earn a million a year and doesn't have six million pounds' worth of investments."

"You've gone too far, Eden. Shut the fuck up," I yell.

"No, I will not. You all like getting up in my shit. None of you ever share anything with me. Toni, what about you? Too scared to tell us that your mum and dad would prefer you to marry an Italian guy? Is that why you hide every single boyfriend? What will happen exactly if you don't marry one? Will they take ownership of the parlor away from you?"

Toni cries.

"Thought as much," Eden mutters.

Eden shoves her chair back, pushing herself up from it. She picks up her car keys off the desk, along with a little white box with a big red bow and a white envelope that was underneath it, and circles around from the desk.

"Well, if you lot won't leave, I will," she says.

"Where are you going, Eden? Please just stay; let's talk about this," I plead.

"Nope, not talking. Don't want to. I've no phone, so don't bother trying to find me. And you can delete me from your stupid WhatsApp group too." She dashes through the studio.

"Please, Eden. We need to talk about you and Hunter, about last night." We all run after her.

Spinning around, she furiously spits out, "What, so we can talk about how I messed up my life again? How I was lied to last night? How stupid I feel? How I self-sabotage? How I don't trust? How I'm an idiot? How fucking painful it all feels? How I lost the one and only man I've ever loved? How I lost the man who was going to move his entire life to be with me, but now he isn't? So we can all talk about me again? Fuck that. No, thanks. My life might be a disaster. But you all have problems of your own. You all think I don't see it, but I see everything. This isn't *Sex in the City*. We're all twenty-seven years old and still fucking about like we're eighteen. Except for Eva, I think, but then again, what do I know." She storms out the doorway.

We run after her, watching Eden stomp across the gravel toward her car.

"And no more crying. You heard Hunter," she calls out over her shoulder. "I'm not to shed any tears for him. So I'm following his command. I'm doing as I'm told, like a good girl."

Face-to-face with the car, she rips the eyelashes off her headlamps and throws them to the ground.

"Better grow up now, huh? And you can both sell your cars. I'm trading this in tomorrow, for something less childlike. Also, take your pissing bucket list and shove it too."

We watch as she furiously skids away down the drive through the stones, making them fly everywhere.

Shit.

"This is bad. Really bad," Beth says as she loops an arm around Toni's shoulder.

"What do we do?" Toni asks, wiping her tears.

"Should we text Hunter?" Eva suggests.

None of us speak.

I don't know what to do.

"Text him," Beth whispers.

I pull out my phone.

Me: Have you really left?
Hunter: We're about to take off in ten minutes. Yes.
Me: It's not good, Hunter. Eden's bad, really bad, like crazy.
Hunter: I texted her this morning to say goodbye, but she didn't reply.
Me: She dropped her phone down the toilet yesterday at the final. She's not got a phone.

Hunter: Shit. Will you tell her I love her, and I will never forget her for me, please?

Me: She's not talking to any of us. She's just taken off in her car at high speed. She's angry. Furious. You should have heard what she's said.

Hunter: Why did you let her drive like that? Was she crying?

Me: Nope, no crying. No tears. Just pure rage. She said it's time for her to grow up. We didn't get a chance; she was too quick.

Hunter: I can't come back. I won't. Eden and I are over. I can't be with someone who thinks I'm a liar, Ella. She doesn't trust me. If trust doesn't exist with us, then I can't do this.

Me: I think you're wrong. I think your impending departure left her feeling vulnerable and susceptible. Jamie and Jax saw that. This is not like Eden at all, Hunter, you know her.

Hunter: I have to turn my phone off now, but will you please try to find her for me and text me as soon as you can to let me know she's safe?

Me: Gosh, this can't be it, Hunter. Surely not? You love her, don't you?

Hunter: With everything I am, but I have to go. I have three back-to-back tournaments and all this visa and house sales shit to sort out now. I'm sorry, Ella. Eden and I were not meant to be. Not in this lifetime.

Ella: You don't mean that, Hunter.

Hunter: I don't know anymore. I left her a gift on her doorstep late last night; I planned on giving it to her last night but didn't get the chance.

Me: She had it in her hand when she left, I think. A white box and red bow?

Hunter: Yeah, that's it.

Me: Until next time, Hunter. Good luck.

Hunter: Thanks, Ella.

"He's gone, girls." I look up from my phone.

"We have to find her," Toni mumbles.

"Beach?" Eva suggests.

"Let's go," I summon them all.

CHAPTER TWENTY-EIGHT

Eden

Numbness. That's what I feel, or don't feel.

Complete numbness.

He's gone.

He left me.

I pushed him.

I believed an ex-boyfriend who's a natural-born liar.

I believed his ex-agent seeking revenge.

I believed them over him.

I feel like such a naïve little girl. A failure.

Barefoot, I walk along the beach, hands clasped around a little white box with a red bow and envelope in my hands. I can't bring myself to open them.

As I left for the studio at four a.m., these two little things were perched on my front door mat with the simple word Cupcake across the front in Hunter's handwriting.

Wondering if Hunter had just left it, out of curiosity, I snuck through the security gate toward the mansion house.

Hunter and his team were loading all their gear into two of their rented Range Rovers, indicating his departure.

Piercing anguish screamed in my heart.

Seconds later, I walked back through my gate toward the studio. I couldn't watch.

Hunter's hit the nail on the head. I need to grow up.

From now on, I'm going to focus on myself and stop listening to others.

I let out a tremendous hollow breath and sit cross-legged on the sand.

Looking down, I thumb the pretty red silk bow. Against the stark white box, it looks like my heart. Bleeding. I'm angry and hateful toward myself.

A soft, "Hey," breaks into my thoughts.

Looking up, I see it's the girls.

God, I was so mean. I'm a bitch.

"Hi." I drop my chin to my chest.

"Can we sit with you?" Eva inquires.

I don't reply.

One by one they sit down to form a circle.

"Do you want us to stay here while you open that?" Eva points to the pretty box.

I can't speak.

Picking up the box, I pull the bow at one end. It delicately slips off the box.

Slowly, I lift the lid.

Inside sits a shiny solid gold Yolo.

I suck in my breath.

Beside it is a small card with Hunter's handwriting.

I read it out loud.

I love you more than anything to change my entire life for you. I would give you my last chocolate too. Hunter xo

Lost for words. We all sit in silence.

I reach for the envelope. Tearing it open, I pull out a piece of paper with a printed email.

On further inspection, I realize it's Hunter's visa application submission. Across the top he's written, *Getting to the first junction is always the hardest. Here's to our new journey together. xo*

"I've really messed everything up. I'm so sorry," I talk aimlessly to both the girls and Hunter, hoping he hears me.

"He's gone? For good?" I ask them all.

They nod their heads, confirming what I already feel. I know he's gone.

I pull my lips into my mouth and fiddle with the red silk ribbon.

Swallowing the giant lump in my throat to make it go away, I rapidly blink my eyes and roll my head back, holding in the tears I know I won't be able to stop.

"I'm going to go. Thank you for coming to find me. I'll be fine," I say, standing to leave. "Can you put that in the safe for me, please?" I point to the box and paper.

Eva scrambles to her feet. "We can help, Eden; please don't push us away."

"I would like to be alone." I look each of the girls in the eye.

I walk back up the sand toward the dunes, through the cars, as loneliness strikes me like a blow.

Here's to my new journey.

Alone.

Because everyone leaves eventually.

CHAPTER TWENTY-NINE

Stravaig: *verb,* wander aimlessly. **Pronounced:** Stra-vague.

Hunter - three weeks later

Three long weeks since I saw her last. It feels like a lifetime.

Three weeks of grueling touring, meetings, and interviews. It's been crazy since my Cup win.

My game is fucked at the moment. Good, but not great. Not the way it should be. My head's not in the game.

I can't even remember what town I'm in. I don't care.

I pick my phone up from the bar and do what I've been doing every day since I left her. Tap the Instagram app open to see if she's posted anything today, hoping to see her beautiful face.

There she is. It's a different photo than normal. I read the post first.

Ten-year school reunion. What a blast. Good times.
#highschoolfriends

I zoom in. Standing next to her is Jamie with his arm around her slim shoulders.

My heart clenches in pain.

She's not smiling.

She looks somber and serene.

Her sparkle duller than normal.

She looks how I feel.

Nothing has ever felt like this.

"Want to talk about it?"

Pippa.

"Don't want to."

"Call her, Hunter."

"Can't."

"Can't or won't."

I don't answer.

"Talk to me. It's been weeks now and you haven't spoken to anyone about what happened," Pippa urges me to talk.

"Don't want to."

"You have got to stop saying that. You are driving us all crazy." She groans.

I bow my head and rest my arms on the bar.

"Look. The last person you need advice from is the Olympic winner of shitty relationships, but I think you should call her, Hunter. Sort it out. Get it out of your system. Thrash it out with her. Let her explain. Eden is a kindhearted girl, inside and out, and you know it. There's not a nasty bone in her body. Okay, so she messed up, but she's not a bad person, Hunter. Two snakes misled her, and you sneaking about behind her back. That was a stupid idea. You should have told her your plans."

"I wanted it to be a surprise," I say through clenched teeth.

"I am fully aware. But when you've been hurt in the

past, it does strange things to you and makes you act completely out of character. Trust me, I know. It's like your common sense gets thrown out the window and someone else steps in, possessing all your rational thoughts."

Pippa was hurt really badly four years ago, and she's been single ever since. A cheating fiancé will do that to you. She doesn't let people into her life easily, and I can see she has a point with Eden.

"Remember, she hasn't known you that long either. What I know though is she loves you; everyone could see that. Her past, although her past, it's part of who she is. When you've been hurt, it stays with you. And it takes a very long time to trust again. To leave without saying goodbye, you messed up, Hunter. Regardless of what she accused you of. You know, none of it was true. But you walked away from her probably when she needed more reassurance from you."

I should have stayed.

"You are better than that. Better than any man I know. But you messed up too."

Fuck, that hurts when Pippa puts it like that.

I want Eden.

I need her.

I can't see him with her.

Feeling discomfort everywhere, my body groans.

"Eden's fears of abandonment, trust, and being alone are feelings that were caused by her past, other people, circumstance, whatever it was, but you were her future. She needed you."

I don't respond to Pippa.

Still holding my phone, I close Instagram. I open up my photos and scroll. I've done this every day for hours, gazing at pictures of us together. The penguins, her laughter, the concert, Disney, us kissing, her smile.

"Well, I'll go back to my room then. Great chatting to you as always." Pippa huffs and pats my shoulder.

My steps feel heavy around every course I've walked around.

My soul feels dark. She's the light I need in my life.

I fell off the precipice and into paradise, but it didn't last long enough.

Without her, I don't feel whole.

There's nothing for me but her.

But she's not mine to have anymore.

She pushed. I ran.

I should have stayed.

Watching the television above the bar, it all passes in a blur. I don't have a clue what's going on. There's a sea of people around me, but I can't hear any of them as I'm lost in my world of torture and loathing at myself for leaving. For being stubborn. For not hearing her out. For not reasoning.

I need her lips on mine to ease this suffering. She drowns everything out when we're together. The passion and fire I feel for her still burns deep.

I don't know how long this agony will last, but I hope it ends soon as I can't take it anymore.

※

Eden - one week later

"Hey, Eddy. I didn't know you were coming around to see me today."

"I thought I would surprise you, Jamie." I drag my pointer finger down his chest as I push him through the doorway of his mum's house.

"Yeah?" Jamie's face lights up.

"Ooooooh, yes, babes. I saw your mum and dad leaving. Fancy doing something fun and outrageous?" I ask, teasing him.

"Yes, honey, I so want to. You haven't even let me kiss you yet these past few weeks."

"I know. I'm making sure you're ready for me," I say, licking my lips.

I watch as Jamie locks his eyes on them.

"Let's go up the stairs, shall we?" I raise my eyebrows in question.

"Hell yeah," he marvels and starts running up the stairs.

As I enter his bedroom, I realize not a single thing has changed in all these years. Football posters, awards, and high school photos still line his walls.

"So," I say. "Here are the rules. You lie back on your bed. No touching until I say so. This is all for you, Jamie. Your pleasure only. Forget about me. But no touching. Alright?" I purr.

"Sounds good to me."

"Clothes off. Then I'll show you what I have on underneath this long coat."

He scrambles, trying to pull off his clothes lightning fast.

I widen my eyes and smirk. "Great, now on the bed, Jamie."

He flings himself on the bed.

"Your turn, Eddy. Take that coat off."

"Uh, uh, uh." I wave my pointer finger back and forth. "First of all. I hear you've been a naughty boy. Have you?"

"Yes, bad, bad, very bad."

"I thought so." I wink.

"That's what these are for." I pull out two sets of handcuffs from my pockets.

"Crap. Are they for me?" He frowns.

"Yeah, they are. I'm going to handcuff this bad boy right here." I point to him. "Then I'm going to ride that hard cock of yours so good."

"Holy shit, Eddy. What the fuck happened to you over the years? You are fucking hot, girl. Handcuff me, honey." He willingly puts his hands out.

Grabbing one wrist, I lock it in place, then pull his hand up over his head and secure the other side of the cuff around the metal frame of the bed.

"That's too tight," he complains.

"It's fine. You won't be in these long, Jamie," I say reassuringly.

I grab his other wrist and do the same.

"This is not very comfortable, Eddy."

"You're going to love it, Jamie. Now imagine your hands on my body. Can you remember what it was like before?"

"Yeah, you've always had a fucking hot body and your lips are fucking amazing. Wrap them around my cock now."

"Not yet. Just hang on. Remember, you've been a naughty boy." I pout. "Are you hard for me?"

"Fuck yeah. I need you, Eddy."

"How bad do you want me?" I lick my finger and drag it down over my red-coated lips.

"So bad, so, so, fucking bad." He writhes about on the bed.

"Well, isn't that a fucking shame, 'cause you're never going to get it," I snap with venom.

His face drops.

"You, Jamie Farmer, are a fucking asshole. One I should have dumped in high school."

Not being able to look longer than a few seconds at his

puny body and less than impressive cock, I slide my eyes away from him.

"You have lied to me repeatedly. These last few weeks I've been leading you on, you dumbass. You were never getting so much as a kiss from me, never," I spit.

"You fucking bitch," he sneers.

I burst out laughing as he lies there helpless.

"You lied to me about Hunter. You teamed up with Jax to make me believe you. You lied throughout our entire relationship. You cheated on me. You left me to grieve by myself for our child. You, Jamie, are a disgrace to men. I never want to see you again. Take your fucking pathetic drunk ass, get out of this town, get the help you need for your drinking and never come back." I walk out the door.

"Where are you going?" he cries with panic.

"I'm leaving," I calmly state.

"What the hell? You can't leave me here like this!"

"Oh, hang on. I forgot," I say, digging about in my pocket.

I pull out my new phone. "Smile." I take a picture.

"What the fuck are you doing?"

"Taking it as a memento. You know, just in case I want to be reminded of what a truly dreadful person looks like. And yes, I can leave. I just have to walk through this door." I tap the frame. "It's dead easy. Watch." I place my foot outside the doorway. "I don't know why I'm showing you because you're the expert. You would know. You walked through one of these real easily when you left us, remember?"

I pop my finger in the air as if having a lightbulb moment. "Ah, there are no keys for those. I threw them away," I say, swishing through the door.

"You'll pay for this. You bitch."

"No, I won't, Jamie. No, I won't. Pack your bags and go." I

laugh and walk down the stairs. I hum to myself as I close the front door behind me.

"Argh," I hear him screaming loudly.

I giggle to myself as I jump in my car. This is the lightest I've felt in weeks. I've been stravaiging about the beach for weeks by myself. Spending time alone. Getting my life in order. Changing everything. Working out my own life plan.

I pull my phone out of my pocket again to get my daily fix.

I tap open the app and type in the search bar, *Hunter King*.

A new post on his Instagram grid today. A screenshot of his playlist.

Lewis Capaldi's "Someone You Loved."

"Hunter. I'm so sorry."

I scroll down to the photos of us on his grid. The only photos I have of us are the ones on his Instagram account I screenshot. He never removed them.

Not backing up my old phone for months left with me nothing of Hunter on it. It was as if our time together didn't happen.

It's a distant memory.

It's where it will stay.

In the past.

Self-hatred threatens to choke me as the tender knot twists around my still beating heart.

I'm beyond pain. I'm simply hanging on to survival.

CHAPTER THIRTY

Baffies: *Plural noun,* slippers. **Pronounced:** Baff-aiz.

Bahookie: *noun,* a person's buttocks. **Pronounced:** Baa-hook-ee.

Eden - Two months later

"I'm not staying," I say as I clatter my car keys on top of the parlor booth table in front of me.

"Stay for one ice cream," Eva begs.

"No, I'm parked on double yellow lines outside. I'll get a ticket if the traffic wardens are around. I only stopped by to say a quick hello and because I need a pee. Another one." I roll my eyes.

"Go then. Come back quick. I have something to speak to you about. Plus, we haven't seen you in over two months. Now you're not in our WhatsApp group anymore I have no idea what you're up to these days. I miss you. We miss you.

And also, I have a lot of questions about the fire department being called to Jamie's house. Go." Beth points to the bathroom doors.

I groan and grin simultaneously. "Okay, but if I get a ticket, you're paying for it."

Coming out of the bathroom stall, I realize how big I'm getting.

Having washed my hands, I dry them on the hand towel.

From the side, my bump looks huge.

I walk over to the mirror and gently stroke my black fitted tee over my ever-growing tummy.

My babies.

Hunter's babies.

Our babies.

I turn to the side again and my heart does a flutter.

I'm so in love with my bump. I spend hours talking away to it. If I could sing, I would do that too.

To say it came as a shock when I found out why I was sick all the time is a colossal understatement, and it took me a few days to get used to the news.

Without question, these babies are meant to be. It's part of my story. My journey.

It's not a junction; it's a pathway to something new and wonderful.

I look down. How can I be this big at only four months pregnant? I'm going to be the size of a house full-term, and my boobs? Well, don't get me started on those. Balloons is the only word for them.

I've been taking every precaution to prevent the same thing from happening before. Vitamins, eating well, rest, and I'm being closely monitored too by my OB. So far so good.

I smile at myself in the mirror, but with a heavy heart

that Hunter isn't here to share this magical experience with me.

My accusations and my lack of trust drove him away. I never wanted that to happen. I also don't want him to think I am after his money. I don't need it.

I royally messed up, and now I'm living with the consequences. I'll be a single mum at twenty-eight. *Deep joy.*

"I hope you're not sad, babies. Well, happy sad. 'Cause that's how I feel, munchkins." I rub my tummy and head back into the parlor.

I'm now sitting around the table with the girls. "So what do you want to know?" I ask them.

"We just want you to confirm or deny, that's all." Toni swipes her hand through the air in front of her.

I smile. I miss my girls.

"And I have something important to tell you too, Eden. We need this information first," Beth says.

I've distanced myself from everyone. Even Mum and Dad. I've been running the office and not doing any classes to ensure my babies are safe and well. I've left Ella and Eva to run the classes.

I'm enjoying being pregnant and focusing on rest and being strong for when the little ones come along. I had my twelve-week scan. I went alone; they said everything was fine so I am focusing on that.

Everything is fine.

I miss joking around and laughing though. I have done little of that since Hunter left.

A prickling sensation of aching twinges my soul. It's a sensation I know so well. It dips in and out in waves every now and again.

I focus back on Toni.

"Ted heard from Lewis, who heard from Richard, who

heard from Colin, who heard from Christ knows, I've lost track now. That a certain little blond bombshell showed up at Jamie's house and handcuffed him to the bed in a sordid tale of *Eden's Revenge*," Toni rasps in a demonic voice toward the end. "Then his parents returned and had to call the fire brigade, where they cut him out of his metal bed frame."

She taps a fake mic in her hand as if testing it. Then she places it under her mouth. "Can you confirm or deny, Ms. Wallace?"

She holds the invisible mic under my mouth.

I belly laugh and lean in. "Confirm. It was me."

Toni splays her fingers and lets the invisible mic drop.

"You are a badass." Beth whoops and the girls all start clapping.

"I knew nothing about the fire brigade, though. That's news to me."

"Well. It's all over the town. Jamie deserved that. He's told everyone. How embarrassing for him. Apparently, the firefighters had a good laugh at his expense." Ella chuckles.

"I took a photo, but I'm not showing you."

"You're no fun," Eva dramatically huffs.

"He had it coming. Did he leave town; does anyone know?" I ask.

"Apparently, he left a few weeks ago. No idea where, but he's gone, Eden," Ella confirms.

Goodbye to old news.

I get out of the tight booth. With my head facing toward the table, I ask if anyone wants a drink or ice cream.

"I'm never going to get out of here in a few months. Look how big I am already." I stand to the side and show the girls.

But they aren't looking at me. They're looking past me. All wide-eyed and openmouthed.

"What are you all look—" I twist my head around.

Standing in the middle of the parlor.

Hunter.

My legs almost go out from under me, and I grip the table for support.

He's still so dazzling, instantly setting my body on fire and making my heart race.

"Ah, that's what I needed to speak to you about," whispers Beth.

Hunter mumbles something under his breath that I can't make out. He swipes his eyes down my body. His eyes bug out as they zoom in on my bump. Promptly, he turns on his heel, walking away from me.

Frozen solid, I watch as he places his hand on the back of a tall brunette. Ushering her out the door, they're gone in a flash.

I clench my eyes shut and breathe deep.

Turning around quickly, I grab my car keys to my new boring mum car off the table in haste.

"I have to go. I just remembered I have to go do something," I stutter.

"Eden, stay. Please don't go," Beth pleads. "I was going to tell you. I promise. He's only here for a week. He's launching a new initiative for us. Shit. I'm sorry I should have texted to warn you."

"It's fine. I'm fine. Do you think he saw?" I look down.

"He saw."

"Oh, yeah."

"Mm-hmm."

"Couldn't take his eyes off it."

They all speak at the same time.

Aw, poop.

What if he wants joint custody and takes my babies

away to America? I sweat at the very thought of it. This can't be happening. I've already lost Chloe.

In a fluster I dash away from the girls and mutter over my shoulder that I'll see them soon.

※

Hunter

She looked beautiful today.

She's cut her hair to half its length.

And it's darker than before.

My angel dressed in black.

But she's not mine anymore, and she's pregnant with *his* baby.

I feel sick at the thought.

Throwing the sheets back, I get into bed. There are no words for how I feel.

I lost her to *him*.

Sleep is the only thing to take the torturing ache away. I roll over, hoping for sleep to come soon. I'm somewhere between mourning and heartbreak.

Between worlds.

Between the land of having what was and now can never be.

As I drift off, all I see is her behind my eyes. My Eden. My place of paradise.

※

Not knowing how long I've been asleep for, I'm abruptly awakened to the loud persistent ringtone from my phone.

"Who the hell is calling at this time?" I say groggily, trying to locate my phone on the bedside table in the dark.

I open my eyes. Squinting from the brightness of the glaring screen.

Ella?

I swipe open the call.

"Ella?"

"Hunter, you have to come to the hospital."

"Why?"

"It's Eden. She fell down the stairs. She's been bleeding. They're not sure if the baby is okay yet."

My heart skips a beat.

Confused as to why Ella is calling me, I rub my eyes with my hand. I feel sympathy pain in my chest as I feel Eden's pain. "Okay, but why are you calling me exactly?"

"Eden's going to kill me for calling you."

She pauses.

"It's your baby, Hunter."

I catapult upright.

"What?" I exclaim, now instantly awake.

"The baby is yours."

"Not Jamie's?" I ask to confirm.

"Jesus Christ, Hunter, for someone smart, you sure are dumb. She's four months pregnant. The baby is yours. And she never went with Jamie."

Holy shit. She's having my baby. I swipe back the bedcovers at high speed. My stomach somersaults with giddiness and anxiety.

"I'm on my way. Where are you? In fact, text me all the details and zip code or postcode or whatever the hell you call it."

"See you so—"

I cut her off.

Dashing around the room, I pull my clothes on at supersonic speed.

I call Lisa, my new agent, to let her know what I'm doing. I check the time. We're supposed to be launching this new scholarship with the Golf Association in a few hours' time. My lawyers couldn't get me out of the contract I signed months back, so now I'm committed, traveling back and forth. That sounds exhausting.

But maybe not.

"Forget it, we can always push to the next day if we have to. Get your girl." Lisa yawns through the phone.

"Thanks, Lisa."

"Oh, and Hunter?"

"Yeah?"

"Congratulations."

I smile.

But she's fallen.

She didn't tell me.

Our baby.

Holy shit.

I run out of the hotel room to go see my girl.

Eden

I don't remember falling asleep, but I'm still lying on my side when I wake up. It's the only comfortable position I can lie in now.

As I flutter my eyes open, I come face-to-face with the most incredible set of dark-chocolate eyes I know so well.

I miss these eyes.

Chin balanced on top of his tent of strong fingers, he stares straight at me and blinks twice.

"Hi," he whispers.

I reach out to touch his face. Then I realize what I'm doing and pull back.

Familiar goosebumps appear, making all the hairs on my arms stand on end. He's like static electricity.

"Hi," I whisper back.

We stare at each other as I place my hand back on the bed. I don't know why he's here, but I feel so much relief that he is.

He's my person and my calm, but he's no longer mine, remembering the girl from the parlor.

"How are you feeling?" he asks eventually.

"Sore. I think my bruises have bruises. Wooden floors are not ideal when you fall down the stairs." I groan, now noticing the pain in my backside and thigh.

It all happened so quickly. My front of my flip-flop style baffies caught on the edge of the stair and before I knew it was on my ass, bumping down each one. I hit my thigh and bahookie, hard, and the right side of my stomach.

Those stairs will not work with tiny feet running about.

"How did you know I was here?"

"Don't be mad. Ella called me." He keeps staring at me.

"So you know?" I close my eyes.

"What, the baby is mine? Yeah, I know. That's why I'm here."

He's only here for the baby.

I clench my eyes as I feel tears forming. I haven't cried since he left. I can't because I don't think they'll stop if I start.

"Why didn't you tell me? I'm crazy mad at you for not telling me. I'm the dad."

I can't hold them back and my tears flow like a river. "Because of what I did to you. The things I said. The things I believed about you. I'm so sorry, Hunter. I've hurt you enough, and I didn't think you'd want to be involved. I'm not after your money. You have a busy life and what I did is unforgivable. I understand if you don't want to speak to me." I sob. "I don't want you to take the baby away to America without me. I lost Chloe; I don't want to lose another baby." I cry out my worst fear.

"Hey, hey. No crying. You've had enough upset for one night. Sh, sh, sh," he coos, thumbing my tears off my cheeks. "The doctor says you're to have complete rest and no upsets. C'mon, Cupcake. Look at me."

I open my eyes to his reassuring and honest face.

I've missed my nickname.

"I would *never* take your baby away from you. Never. Ever. Just because we live on different sides of the country, I will try to be here when you need me. Our baby will stay with you." He strokes my temple with his long fingers, which I love so much. I love everything about him.

I wish I could take the evening of the ball back.

"You're in control here. I will respect all your wishes. We will sort this out between you and me, Eden. No matter what, we will make it work. Everything that's been, has been, we have to forget the past. We have to move on from that. For the baby's sake, we can't hold on to any of that now. We have lots to talk about. We'll do that before I leave again, but you need to rest and relax."

My body sags slightly with relief. But he's leaving again. "I am really sorry, Hunter. I truly mean that; please believe me."

Anguish washes across his face, and I feel all hope finally leaving my body.

"I forgive you, Eden. I can't hold on to grudges. It's been eating away at me, every minute of every day. I can't stay mad at you. Look at this face." He delicately thumbs my cheek. "I've missed you." His mouth trembles.

I've missed him so much too.

"Can we please be friends again, Eden?"

Friends.

That's more than I was expecting because I didn't think he would want to speak to me ever again.

Hunter is such a lovely guy; how he's able to forgive me, I'll never know. I let serious trust and vulnerability issues cloud my judgment all those months ago.

"I'd like that. We are going to be parents together so I am guessing we have to speak to each other once in a while, huh?" I say.

He takes my hand and squeezes it before letting go, then rests back in his chair, deep in thought.

I want to know what he's thinking. We sit in comfortable silence.

Once I've calmed down, I turn around to check the time.

"Where is everyone else?" I ask.

"I sent them all home. I said I would stay and keep them up to date."

"But what about your girlfriend? Do you not want to go be with her? She'll not like you being here with me. God, why do I always make everything so complicated?" I clench my teeth. "I'm so sorry about the baby. I didn't get pregnant on purpose. My bloody implant was due for renewal; we never took extra precautions, and I missed my reminder letter before we went to Florida. You can have a new life with your girlfriend, Hunter. I won't stop you. I'm not like that. I won't hold you prisoner. I promise," I say adamantly but with a painful chest. I don't want him to ever find someone else.

"Girlfriend? What the hell are you going on about?" he asks, standing up now.

I push myself up the bed. Hunter helps me rearrange my pillows.

I look up. "Yeah, the beautiful brunette you were with yesterday, in the parlor."

"Lisa? Hell no. She's my new agent. Jesus Christ, Eden. You don't half jump to conclusions. And she has a *girlfriend,* Eden." He rolls his eyes.

Relief washes over me as I suddenly can't make eye contact with him, feeling dumb at yet another accusation.

"Sorry, I just assumed."

"You need to stop assuming and ask me. Communicate with me. Text me. Call me. Just come out and ask. Anything. Everything. I wished you'd done that before. It also would have been nice if you'd told me we were having a baby. You don't have to do all this yourself. This is a big deal. Huge deal. I think I need a stiff drink from this news, but *we* are having a baby, Eden." He points to us both. "You need to speak to me."

Here goes. "Babies. Plural."

He stops what he's doing.

"I beg your pardon." He dips his head to his chin, raising his eyes toward me, like he's peering over the top of a pair of glasses and frowns.

"*Babies.* Three. Triplets." I hold up three fingers.

I count down from five... Five... Four... Three... Two... One.

"I think I need water and a seat. Or a fan. Has it gotten really hot in here suddenly?" He pulls the neckline of his tee shirt back and forth quickly. "Three babies. Three. Not one. Three," he mumbles. "Are they sure?" He looks at me.

"Yes, they confirmed it again last night on the scan. I

have told no one yet. And that's why I'm so big. I've known for a few weeks." I stroke my stomach.

"But where are they going to fit? You're so tiny." He paces. "That cannot be good for someone your size. Will it be cesarean delivery then? Or how does that work? Will you be okay? Are you okay?" I laugh and cover my mouth to hide my amusement. "Oh, I feel faint. I think I need to lie down." He walks over to my bed. I shuffle across carefully so he can get in next to me.

"You okay? Should I get a nurse?" I ask, confused and amused.

"Maybe I think I'm having a seizure. Or a heart attack or a panic attack—maybe all three." He puts his hand to his head. "Feel me. I'm burning up."

Someone clearing their throat startles us. "Mr. King. You're not supposed to be on the bed."

The doctor.

"I think I'm dying."

I've missed this incredibly funny man in my life.

I look at the doctor.

"I just told him it's triplets."

"Yeah, that's going to tip you over the edge a little." He laughs. "Do you think, Mr. King, you could get off the bed and die elsewhere, please? Eden's had a fall, and she requires space and rest."

"You have no heart, Doctor," Hunter says, sliding his feet back to the floor.

"Are you good for me to continue, Mr. King?"

"Yes. Are you okay, Eden?" Hunter looks at me.

"I'm perfectly fine. You've cheered me up. Let's listen to what the good doctor has to say, Hunter. Okay?" I say reassuringly.

I think it's four babies I'm having.

"You're good, Eden. You are fine. Everything looks perfectly normal on the scans. You're doing all the right things. Your bruising will feel worse these next few days. You really took quite a tumble. But otherwise, you are good. You have no other symptoms other than the spotting you had last night. The disruption from you falling has caused the bleeding, but the babies are healthy. Their heartbeats are strong. We want to keep you in for the next few days for observation, just in case. And I think..." The doctor cranes his neck out the door. "Here it comes now. We're just going to do another scan."

"Ready to meet your babies, Hunter?" I ask.

He's nervous, but his eyes are sparkling with excitement. I can tell.

With everything set to go, the radiographer slides the handheld probe across my skin and in full black-and-white picture, our babies appear on the screen.

Hunter leans in to get a good look. Instinctively, he takes my hand.

"Look at them, Eden. They're ours. We made people," he says in awe. "What size are they now?" he asks.

"About the size of an apple or avocado. Roughly," the radiographer replies. "Would you like to hear their heartbeats?" she asks, staring at Hunter.

Yup, he's very difficult not to look at.

"Would I ever."

With that, a multitude of fast-racing *thunks* sound throughout the room.

"You hear that, Cupcake?" He squeezes my hand.

"I do."

"Would you like to record it on your phone, Mr. King?"

"Can I? Thank you, ma'am."

He's so polite.

I watch as he digs about in his pocket for his phone. Before it opens, I see his locked screen photo is a selfie he took of us at Magic Kingdom. I'm kissing his cheek and his face is all scrunched up. We look so happy.

He hasn't changed it. My heart does a hopeful swoop.

Once he's finished recording, the radiographer then prints out a couple of copies of the scan for us, and then it's just us again.

"So tiny." He swoons over his mini munchkins photo.

"They don't feel it," I say, rubbing my tummy.

He tilts his head. He's thinking. "Hmmmm, can I feel? Your tummy?" He motions with his head to my stomach.

"Yeah. I'd like that. Excuse the hospital paper pants, Hunter. So sexy," I say, pulling up my hospital gown and revealing my swollen stomach again.

"You could wear a tent and still look beautiful and sexy," he says.

I think he's just saying that to make me feel better.

Tentatively, he gets closer to the side of the bed, reaches his hand out flat, and places it gently on top.

"It's firmer than I thought it would be."

I smile.

"And really hot."

"I'm like a furnace now. I have triple insulation."

"No belly ring?"

"Nope, I had to take it out."

"That's a shame." He winks. "Although it's probably the reason you're in this dilemma now with these three monkeys. I could never resist that crystal blue belly bar of yours."

I laugh and blush.

"Oooh, that goes tight when you laugh. That feels so

odd." He explores my skin and tummy with his long, lean fingers.

He bends down and whispers to my belly, "Hey, you three. This is Daddy. We haven't met before. Now you're not to give Mummy a hard time. She's been through a lot already and you've got to behave. Okay? Are we on the same page?" He bends down and kisses my belly.

My heart clenches at his action and I burst out crying.

Covering my face, I sob. I can't do this.

I can't keep pretending I don't love him.

I can't be around him and not want him.

The tears I've been holding in pour out.

I love this man. Now more than ever.

He's so tender, loving, caring.

And I pushed him away.

I want him back.

There is no way he would ever want me, not after what I did. I hurt him deeply.

Hunter sweeps in and cuddles me tight, pulling my head onto his shoulder, and I'm encased by his citrus smells that trigger all the memories of our past.

"I'm really so sorry," I say on a hiccup. "I always dreamed of a family. Not like this. With a mum on one side of the world and a dad on the other. I'm so sorry for everything. I know you said you forgive me. But I ruined everything. I can't forgive myself, so I don't know how you can forgive me."

Sniffling and mumbling into his chest, I keep repeating how sorry I am. He continues to cradle me but says nothing.

"Heavens, please tell me the baby is fine," I hear Ella gasp as she enters the room.

I can't work out why anyone still cares about me anymore; I've been horrible to everyone.

"It's fine. The babies are fine. Eden is fine. We're fine, Ella. Eden's just a little upset," Hunter reassures Ella.

"Phew. Thank God for that." She puts her hand to her chest. "Wait a minute, did you say *babies*? As in more than one?" She gasps.

"We're having triplets," I say, slowly removing myself from Hunter's hug, and I wipe my face, which now feels red and hot.

"This is a risky business, this whole triplet thing, huh? I'm so not getting into that game. Holy crap, Eden. Three? Shit, how the hell are you going to do this yourself, Eden? It's just as well Mum and Dad live beside you."

I throw my hands in the air in defeat. Honestly, I do not know how I am going to do it either.

I watch Hunter's face drop. I would love to know what he's thinking.

Ella moves over and gives me a kiss on the cheek. It's the closest we've been for months.

I miss my family and my friends.

I miss my sisters.

I miss Hunter.

"You okay, Cupcake?" Hunter asks me.

"I'm fine. I'm sorry. Ignore me. I'll be just fine," I reply.

"I hate to do this, but since you're here now, Ella, I have a launch thing on today with the Golf Association. It's been scheduled for weeks. I'll be back as soon as I can, though. I promise."

"Yeah, Hunter. Go do your thing. That's what you came back for, after all. Go do it," I say, blowing my nose.

Hunter leans in to give me a kiss, then realizes what he's doing and steps back.

"Okay." He puts his hands in his jeans pockets. Text me

if anything changes. That's a warning. Com-mu-ni-cate. Yes?" He smiles.

I salute. "Got it."

This is so odd.

"See you later."

I give a small wave as I watch him leave and Ella chases after him. "Eh, Hunter. Can I have a quick word with you?"

I lean back against the bed; I hope Ella can help me shower, and I pray she's brought me clean panties.

She and I, we're not as close as we used to be, but I need her help today. I should apologize to her. I've treated her terribly too.

I feel blue.

I've pushed everyone away.

It's me, the babies, and now Hunter, again. He wants to be part of their lives.

How will we do any of this together? I'm unsure. I'm not sure how I will manage when Hunter has a new girlfriend and maybe a wife. My heart won't take it.

God, that feels painful. What if the babies love her more than me?

The poor guy just had a whole lot of information thrown at him. I wouldn't blame him if he actually ran away this time for good.

I'm so tired. I close my eyes. And drift off and dream about the perfect little family I could have had.

✻

Hunter

I sit down next to Ella on the chairs near the exit of the hospital.

It took all my strength not to kiss Eden back there. To hold her for eternity and never let go.

She's the missing part of my jigsaw puzzle; I'm not complete without her.

We're having triplets. My mum is going to be beside herself. So will Pippa.

I'm going to be a dad. To three.

But it's a mess. Me in America and Eden in Scotland.

The physical pain I'm in feels worse than ever.

Leaving her again and my children.

I never wanted to be a part-time dad. This was *definitely* not the plan, uh-uh, no way.

"Thank you for coming last night," Ella starts, breaking me from my thoughts. "I know you're just back and I have no idea what you and Eden were talking about. Or if you're sticking around for the babies and stuff, but I wanted to speak to you, Hunter. Away from Eden. Just to fill you in a little about her since you were here the last time."

I don't like the sound of this.

"Before you start, I'm sticking around, Ella. I'm their dad. I'll have to travel back and forth, but I'll be here for the babies."

"You're such a lovely guy, Hunter." She smiles. "You should know, Eden's sad. Like, really sad. Next level sadness. It's so hard to explain, but it's palpable. She doesn't speak to any of us anymore. She walks by herself on the beach. She's changed her car. She's thrown out half her clothes. The childish ones she said. Because you said she was high school and childish that night of the ball. She wears black all the time. She's so unhappy. Did you see yesterday, she's cut all her hair? It's never been this short. It's not a statement. It's a sign of complete torment in my eyes. Trying to be someone she's not. She hasn't cried once since you left."

"Never?"

"No. Never. Just now is the first tear I've seen. She's angry. Silent angry. She spends no time with any of us. Yesterday was the first time I've seen her outside the studio in two months. Toni and Beth don't see her at all anymore. She's removed herself from our WhatsApp group. She doesn't text any of us. All of her sparkle has gone. You'll see for yourself. She's not the same girl you left behind. She's so hard on herself. She can't forgive herself. She can't move on, and Mum and Dad are so worried about her. This is not the same as when Jamie left. This is *so* different because she loves you; you're the only man she's ever loved, Hunter."

My heart shatters as her words punch deep. She loves me. Still.

Ella starts crying.

"She works in the back office now at the studio. She hasn't danced since you left. She may look fine, but she's dying inside. I feel it. I feel all her pain. Eva does too. It's so fucking painful, Hunter." She clasps her hands to her chest.

"What do you need me to do, Ella?"

"I don't know. I don't think there is anything you can do. But I just wanted you to know." She looks around. "She doesn't speak to me anymore. We aren't even friends. She hates me. I left her that night standing outside the ball. She's angry at me. Angry with Jax and Jamie. Angry at herself for believing their lies. Angry with the world. It runs deep. She's punishing herself and everyone around her. She feels alone and unloved, but we're all here. It's just so painful to watch. And she's blooming. Have you seen her? She's beautiful pregnant. But she's somber. She's going to have sad babies. They must feel her despair." Ella mutters tearfully.

This whole situation is a beautiful disaster.

"She's sad, heartbroken, and lonely. She loves you,

Hunter. You're embossed in her heart forever. I know in my own heart she will never go with another man. Never. She gave her heart to you. It doesn't belong to anyone else but you. One of the things I do know about my sister is that she is loyal to the core. I wasn't that night of the ball. I should have stayed with her. And now you're having triplets together." She runs the back of her hand under her nose. "Now that is a surprise. She's fiercely independent and will want to do it all herself. I think we get that from Mum."

She gives a half-hearted laugh and suddenly stands. "Anyway, welcome to fucked-up Wallace-land. I'll see you later, Hunter, and I'll text if anything changes." She walks back to the ward.

"Bye. And hey, Ella." She turns. "Thank you for telling me."

I need to fix this.

For Ella.

For Eva.

For her parents.

For her friends.

For our babies.

For us.

CHAPTER THIRTY-ONE

Kirk: *noun,* church, specifically Church of Scotland. **Pronounced:** Kirk.

Eden

I'm not sure what I expected, but it's been three days since I was discharged from the hospital, and Hunter has only dropped in a few times to see me. Well, the babies. To see how they are.

He seems a little off since the hospital. Distracted, erratic, and on edge.

Making cups of tea and preparing food for me. He's certainly kept himself busy when he's been here.

But he's kept his distance. Not getting too close and we've had some awkward small talk, and that's about it.

Not what I was expecting at all. In fact, I'm not really sure what I was expecting.

I'm guessing with the full-on Golf Association launch

this week, my surprise that 'you're going to be an instant daddy to three' hasn't helped.

His impending departure is in the cards. Two days and then he's gone again. I'm not good at goodbyes. I am certainly not good at people leaving period. It triggers all my abandonment issues.

He has mentioned how he wants to be here when the babies are born. Having a scheduled caesarean will work out perfectly for him because Pippa can plan it into his busy calendar. It all feels really clinical. He was very matter-of-fact about it all.

Remembering how close we were as a couple bears no reflection of us now. We're not the same anymore, and that destroys any hope I had left.

What a truly sad situation.

Hunter has mentioned how he wants to sort out visitation, and how it would be best to do it all kosher through a lawyer. I agreed with him; it's best we do everything correctly from the start, then we both know where we stand. I want my children to know their daddy, and I would never prevent him from seeing his children.

Just because I destroyed what Hunter and I had, doesn't mean I need to mess up our children too.

I look around my lovely home. I'm sitting on my gray sofa; it's become my best friend these past few months. I'd most definitely win the award for 'best efforts for working on your groove' category.

I've been flicking through Netflix for twenty minutes now, trying to decide what to binge on next. Decisions.

This last week, the only excitement I feel is when Hunter visits. As fast as he arrives, he's gone, and poof, the light goes out in my heart again.

A knock against my front door indicates I have to get up.

This could be difficult. Rolling off the couch, I hoist myself to my feet. I can't imagine myself at full-term; at only four months, you can roll me like an Easter egg.

Opening the front door, there's no one there. Hmm.

However, sitting on my doorstep is a black dress bag; resting on top is a shiny gold envelope.

Puffing as I bend, I pick both up, close the door gently, and make my way back to the couch.

I curiously open the gilded letter first.

It's an invitation.

Your presence is required at seven p.m. this evening. Wear the dress. I'll pick you up. Please RSVP. Dad x

Opening the dress bag next, I pull out a soft and delicate chiffon rainbow striped, to the floor maxi dress in pastel lilac, pink, and mint green. Each color merges into each other like striped watercolors. I stare in wonder. It's stunning. The top part of the dress cinches in with a solid band just under the bust before flaring out.

At the bottom of the bag lies a pair of pale-lilac lace low-profile sparkly trainers with a little label Dad has tied around the laces. *'I don't trust you walking in heels. Don't worry, your dress is petite; it's the perfect length.'* This makes me smile. There is no way Dad picked this out; this is all Mum.

Picking up my phone, I text him.

Me: I'm so confused. What is this? x

Dad isn't the best with text messages; I should have called. He takes forever to reply.

Dad: I have something to show you. Be ready for seven p.m. x
Me: But it says RSVP. Do I have to come?
Dad: For goodness sake, Eden just wear the dress. I shouldn't have asked you to RSVP. It's not optional :)
Me: Well, I guess I'll see you around seven then
Dad: Be ready, little one, love you x
Me: Love you too, Dad x

This is most unlike my dad. He's not known for his spontaneity. Dad's a planner like me.

I text Ella and Eva next on our group studio chat.

Me: Have you had an invitation from Dad?
Eva: Yeah, what's it for? Do you know?
Me: Nope. No clue.
Ella: I have one too. It's maybe for Mum and Dad's wedding anniversary this week. Meal maybe? Also it's our birthday next week too.
Me: Ah, of course. See you all later then?
Ella: I would like that. I miss you, Eden.
Eva: So do I :(

I swallow my pride.

Me: I miss you too.
Ella: We'll chat later, okay?
Eva: I need a hug from both of you. We're stronger together, all three of us.
Me: Omne trium perfectum - everything that comes in threes is perfect.

Ella: We are. I need you both in my life.

Eva: I need you both more now than ever.

Me: I'm here, I'm so sorry for being the rotten egg in our trio.

Ella: You are not, Eden. We all have things going on, but we need each other to get through it all.

Eva: We really do. I love you both, no matter what.

Me: I love you both too.

Ella: Tonight's outlook just got better. I can't wait to spend time with you all this evening. I've no gift for Mum and Dad's anniversary. Did you get anything, girls?

Eva: No, I actually forgot all about it.

Eden: I think if they know we're all friends again, that may be the best gift.

Ella: I agree.

Eva: Me too.

Eden: See you all soon then. I need to go get ready.

I took my time getting ready for tonight, enjoying preening, beautifying, and plucking.

Although shaving my legs and lady bits has already become a problem. I'm going to have to book myself in for a monthly wax unless I choose to let myself go wild. Nope, not doing that. There are certain things I am not willing to do, and that is one of them. Note to self, book in waxing for three weeks' time.

The last time I went out was the Winner's Ball, and that didn't go so well. I'm so angry at myself for being so foolish.

Since we had our little text conversation with my sisters, I feel a little lighter. It's amazing how a few lines of words can make all the difference to your mood, I'm actually looking forward to tonight.

Hearing the door now, I pull my shoes on, tie the laces

quickly, and grab my little pink clutch as I hear Dad walking into the house. "Eden?" he calls out to me from the bottom of the stairs.

"I'll be right there, two mins."

Carefully walking down the stairs, I meet Dad at the bottom. My dad is such a handsome man. My mum calls him her silver fox. Silver hair and beard and tanned all year round, with all the work he does around the estate. He's dressed in a tartan dark-green, navy, and red, Barbour button-up shirt with navy dress trousers and brogues. He's more handsome now than ever and still cool.

"You look beautiful, Eden." He holds out his hand for me.

"I'm a pudding."

"A beautiful pudding." He smiles.

"You're not supposed to agree with me, Dad," I say, fluffing out my hair. I've kept it down tonight and it's super shiny from not straightening it for months. Now half its length, it takes half the time to style.

"Why do I never learn? There is no winning with you four."

We laugh as we head out the door.

"Where are we going? I spoke to the girls earlier; they said they're coming too."

"It's a surprise." Grinning, he makes air fireworks with his hands.

"How romantic. Mum is a lucky woman."

"She wasn't saying that when I let Dave the dog out earlier and he rolled himself in fox poo. I disrupted her *getting ready time*," he says, making air quotes.

"Oh, dear." I giggle.

"Nope, not a deer, a fox."

"Your jokes never get any better, do they?"

"They really don't. Now let's get this show on the road," he says, rubbing his hands together as we walk toward the mansion house, then summons me to loop my arm through his.

"Are we leaving from your place?"

"Yes, we are."

Arriving at the reception area, Dad then hops into one of the retreat's pristine white golf carts adorned with yellow bows.

"Where are we going in this?" I point to the cart, confused. "And where are the girls?"

"They're already there. Hop in." He pats the seat next to him.

I wrap my arms around myself and tilt my head.

"Get in, Eden." He holds his hand out for me.

Okay.

"I'm so confused."

Dad stays silent as we make our way past the cabins, up over the grass, and past Chloe's tree.

As we reach the top of the grass hill, I spot my dream church nestled down the other side of the hill, glowing in the distance. Outside, a small crowd of people are gathered.

"My goodness. Did you do up the kirk?" I gasp.

"Yup."

"When did you do this? Mum is going to love this."

"Mmmmm-hmmmm."

As we get closer, everyone stops chatting and turns around to us, waving.

The entire area outside the old stone church is dusted with fairy lights.

Dad has chopped many of the trees down, allowing the church to breathe again. But the trunks of the two larger trees on either side of the church are wrapped in delicate lights around their branches. It's magical.

The tiny building stands there in all its historical glory. It's breathtaking.

"Am I the last to arrive?"

"No. Mum is."

Noticing now that we're closer, there's a table with lots of food and nibbles on and a gentle wave of music flows through the air.

"This is lush, Dad."

Leaving my bag in the golf cart, I step out and I'm greeted by Eva who pulls me into a deep embrace. My nephews are running about, pretending to be airplanes. "They are driving me daft tonight. So hyperactive. You have all this to look forward to," Eva says, exasperated.

I groan. "Don't remind me. No Ewan tonight?"

"No. I'll call you tomorrow. We'll chat then. Okay? Not tonight though," she says with her head still on my shoulder.

"I understand." I rub her back. "This all looks so fabulous. Dad's done an outstanding job."

"He has," I hear Ella behind me. "I've gotta get in on this." She joins us. "We miss you, Eden."

"I know. I miss you both too. I really am so sorry, girls. I really need you now."

We hold each other tight, confirming to me I have them. Eventually we all pull away.

"I love your dress." Ella smiles.

"There is no way Dad picked this." I spin around. "Look how pretty it is. I feel like a mermaid."

"Better than your usual black these days," Eva says.

"Let's not spoil the evening," I say and look around.

Dad has created seating made from the felled trees.

I do, but what the hell has this got to do with tonight?

"Tonight, this is another one of those little turns in *your* journey. A beautiful curve, we will call it. You've had a detour, but it's time for you to get back on track." She smiles.

"Me?"

"Yes, Eden, you."

"But I though—"

"Sh." She lets go of my hands. "That door there..." She points to the little door that takes you through to the main church. "Is the start of your new journey. I want you to hold on tight and never let go, no matter how bumpy things get."

She walks away through the main door.

"What are you talking about, Mum?"

But then she's gone, leaving me alone in the foyer. All I can hear is the soft thrum of guitar playing inside the church and a slight scream or two from my nephews outside.

Curiosity gets the better of me. I reach for the tarnished brass doorknob to take me inside the main church.

Here goes nothing.

I do not know what is on the other side of this door. Mum made it sound monumental.

The door creaks open. I'm bathed in a dazzling yellow glow illuminating the tiny church.

Dozens upon dozens of elegant tall glass vases bursting with sunflowers are scattered down the aisles and between the straightened-up wooden seating pews. The soft thrum of "Perfect" by Ed Sheeran wafts around the glorious space.

Delicate fairy lights spiral around the sandstone columns and the light splinters off the sparkling stained glass windows. This must have taken ages to do.

Walking down the center aisle, I let out an audible gasp as I gaze all around.

"This is beautiful."

"Just like you." I jump, startled by a familiar husky voice that echoes throughout the space.

The voice that makes my heart somersault with joy.

Stepping out of the shadows of the altar, Hunter comes into focus.

I think I'm hallucinating. But the vision keeps walking closer toward me. I'm glued to the higgledy piggledy cobbled floor as my heart races.

I palm my hand to my forehead. "Are you real? Tell me I'm not having a moment. If I'm not hallucinating, then what the hell are you doing in here? I'm having a strange evening so far."

"You're not hallucinating, Eden. I'm here." I watch Hunter slowly move closer to me. He looks so handsome in his mint-green polo shirt—not his usual color choice—his hands in the pockets of his black dress pants.

"Huh, we match." I look down at my pretty dress. What a stupid thing to say. Gosh, I'm so nervous. He always has the ability to make me lose my senses.

"We do. We *are* the perfect match, Eden."

I think he means we *were* the perfect match. Until I ruined everything.

"What are you doing here? This is supposed to be Mum and Dad's anniversary night."

"Who told you that?"

I scratch my head. "Eva, I think, and Ella." Now I'm not so sure. I double-check my memory and come up short. His scent, which I love so much, encroaches the space, messing with my brain. I can't think straight.

"You're not here for your mum and dad tonight, Eden."

I make a face.

"You're here for us," Hunter says softly.

What?

"Okay, you're going to have to explain. For us?"

My heartbeat kicks up a notch, mingling excitement and confusion.

"Yes, *us*."

Okay.

He's so close now. Hunter pulls his hands out of his pockets and wraps his warm hands around mine.

I look upward and meet his emotion-filled eyes.

"Eden Wallace, since the day I found you in that field all those months ago, there hasn't been a second of any day that I haven't thought about you. You've taken up permanent residency in my head and heart; there's no space for anyone else."

Blood pumps faster around my veins. Oh boy.

"I love all your kooky ways. Your kind and gentle heart. You're funny, smart-ass mouth, and most of all, I love your awful cooking."

"That's a low blow, Hunter." I laugh, wide-eyed.

But he's not wrong, my cooking is awful.

"It is, but true." He grins back. "These last few months have been awful without you. I've missed you so much. I can't live without you." He rubs his thumb across the back of my hand. "I refuse to live another moment without you. I can't do it. I won't do it. I want everything you want, the house, the family. I want it all, with you."

He takes a deep breath in and closes his eyes before continuing.

"I love you, Eden."

I was not expecting this tonight. Butterflies flutter in my throat.

"Still?" I ask, confused.

"I never stopped. I won't ever stop loving you."

"Sweet baby Jesus," is all I can say as my chest rises and falls fast. I may hyperventilate.

"You are loved more than you can ever imagine. By me, your family, and your friends. All those people out there, they are here for *you*. I'm here for you. For our babies. For us. Forever. I love you more than anything to give up everything to be with you."

I feel him slip a heavy weight of metal into my hand.

I turn it over. It's my gold Yolo.

"Forever?"

Hunter lets go of my hands and takes a step back, dropping to the floor. On bended knee, he looks up.

"What are you doing?" I cup my mouth.

"What I should have done the moment I met you."

Hunter pulls out a Tiffany blue leather box from his pocket, revealing an extraordinary yellow diamond engagement ring.

"Oh my goodness." I fan myself.

"Little Eden Wallace from Castleview Cove. Will you marry me?"

My face breaks out in the most enormous smile as I'm overcome with a feeling of warmth and happiness all over my body.

Inaudibly I breathe out, "Yes."

"Was that a yes?"

I say vigorously, "Yes, yes, yes."

"Really? Christ, I'm gonna love you so hard." He slides the ring on my finger, then he quickly stands as his face explodes into a megawatt smile.

"I hope so," I say through glazed eyes.

Looking down, I inspect the dazzling jewel Hunter slipped on my finger.

"That's what the sunshine yellow diamond is for Eden.

To signify your sunflowers. For your hope. Our hope. We have hope."

"We have everything, Hunter. I love you so much." I reach up and cup his face. "Kiss me."

"I've wanted to kiss you so bad since the hospital. It's been torture these last few days." He bows his head. "Oh, two seconds."

Hunter bends down and pulls out a wooden box between the pews.

"Stand on that," he says, holding my hand.

"You brought me a step." I giggle.

"Yes, I did, so you don't have to stretch too much."

"You are so ridiculous," I say, stepping on top of the box. We meet eye to eye.

"See, perfect height now."

"This works," I say, leaning in again. "Now kiss me like I'm yours."

"You are mine. You always have been."

Hunter gazes into my eyes and smooths his thumb across my cheekbone. "I've missed this face," he says before planting a gentle kiss on me. His lips envelop my lips as we tentatively kiss each other, and like always our kiss turns desperate. Hunter pulls me in close. "This bump is going to be a problem," he mumbles against my mouth.

I smile. "Tell me about it."

Hunter runs his fingers up through my locks and pulls my face hard to his. We breathe deep and heavy as our tongues dance with glee together once again. We both groan loudly. We can't stop. I don't want to. As Hunter shifts his hands down my back, he cups my bum and gives it a little squeeze.

"I've missed you, baby," he breathes.

"I've missed you more."

Nothing has ever made more sense than this. We fit perfectly together. Goosebumps scatter across my body as a familiar warmth builds between my legs.

No one makes me feel the way Hunter does. Like home, like I belong, like I'm safe, like I'm loved, like I'm sexy, like I'm beautiful.

A loud pounding on the door makes us jump and we both laugh.

"I think that's our sign to meet our guests." Hunter rests his forehead to mine.

"Gosh, did you do all of this?" I ask.

"Yes. For three solid days. That's why I've hardly been around. Plus, I think if I'd been around you too much, I would have let the cat out of the bag. It was so difficult not to tell you. I was so excited. I had to throw you off the scent. That's why I mentioned all that child visitation crap and lawyers."

He had me fooled.

"Was the church your idea?"

"This is your dream, Eden. I want to make all your dreams come true. Your dad and most of the staff have helped me clear the trees and clean up inside here. They wired electricity too. But your mum, Ella, and Eva organized the flowers, your dress, and the food."

"They knew?" I gasp.

"Everyone knows. They were sworn to secrecy."

"Well, they are excellent actors. I'll give them that."

"In between that, I also had an online consultation with Tiffany in London, and they couriered up your ring. It only arrived late this afternoon. I was panicking. You almost had a gummy sweetie ring. I've been sweating a lot these past few days."

"Sounds super intense."

"It was. Thankfully, this time, to my surprise, all went well. Phew."

"I won't ever doubt you again, Hunter. I promise."

"Hey, we've moved on from that. You won't ever have to have any doubts again because we are spending our time together forever."

"Is that so?" I beam.

"Yes, that is so."

"What about your visa and touring and everything?"

"That's easy. I never canceled my visa application. I couldn't because my contract with the Golf Association was locked in tight. So everything I had organized previously is still in place. It was meant to be. This fate thing has a funny way of working where you and I are concerned."

Hunter places a soft kiss to my lips and the air sizzles between us.

"And..." he says.

Gosh, there's more. I don't think my heart can take it.

"We are flying back to Florida together. I have a doctor lined up to travel with us. You are coming with me so I can sort out my house, lawyers, paperwork, and belongings, and then we are finally moving back here together."

"But what about the studio?"

"Ah, well, from what I've heard, you don't teach anymore, so it doesn't matter, plus the girls have been advertising for a new teacher this week to cover you while on maternity leave."

"Gosh, you really have thought of everything."

"I'm going to look after you, baby."

Bay-bee. I love how he says that.

"We can only marry, if you agree to a couple of things though."

My heart flips.

"You have to get rid of that horrible bloody car you've bought. That is not a fun-sized pocket-rocket Eden car."

Phew. Thank you, Universe.

"I can do that." I laugh.

"And you have to grow your hair back and recolor it to the way you had it before. Come out of the dark. You are light and luminous, baby."

He has a point. I don't feel like me at all with it this short and darker. "Okay."

"There is one small thing I have arranged, but I'm not sure you'll be happy with me." He leans back slightly.

"Yeah? What's that?" I ask with wonder.

"I've set a date for the wedding." He scrunches his nose up. "It's in eight weeks' time. I want to get married before the babies come along because we're going to be so busy with three kids. Christ, that sounds weird when I say it." He shakes his head. "Is that okay? It's in here." He looks around. "I'm hoping that softens the blow."

"It's perfect." I smile. "I'm going to be bigger again in eight weeks."

"I know, but still beautiful."

I lower my eyes. "This is the best night of my life, ever. You're an incredible man. With a kind heart and incredible soul, Hunter."

"Well, with you being my twin flame and all, Cupcake, we *are* the perfect match."

"Oh yeah, I'm sure you're just saying that so you can get your visa quicker. Marrying me is your ticket out of the States."

"Aw, man, you figured out my plan. Dammit."

A louder thump on the door echoes throughout the church. "C'mon, you two, we're dying out here. And it's bloody freezing; we want to come in," Ella bangs on the door again.

"I think we had better open the door."

"I think we should. Also, I flew in Luke, Evan, Pippa, and my parents for tonight. They've been hiding in the cabins."

"You really thought of everything."

"You're my everything, Eden."

"I love you, Hunter."

"I love you too, Cupcake."

CHAPTER THIRTY-TWO

Eden

As I roll onto my back, I raise my hand in the air, gazing at my sunshine diamond and tilt it slowly back and forth. Mesmerized, I watch it glint and sparkle as the early morning light cuts through the gap of my balcony curtains.

I'm getting married. To Hunter King.

To say I'm still in shock would be a massive understatement.

Three days on and I still can't stop smiling.

Ella knew all along; all I had to do was open my heart to possibility. I ticked number thirty-one off my bucket list. Fall in love. That's the only item I care about.

Hunter and I celebrated our engagement surrounded by our family and friends. It's an evening I will never forget. It really was magical, and the fog that's surrounded me for months disappeared in a flash. All I needed was Hunter to make it dissipate.

"What are you doing, Cupcake?" a groggy, half-asleep Hunter asks.

"Making sure it's still real."

"It's real alright and so is this." He thrusts his morning glory into the side of my hip.

This man is always ready to go.

The day after our engagement, I called the doctor to make sure it was fine for me to have sex.

I hadn't even considered asking before. It's not like I planned on having sex while I was pregnant or anything. According to the doctor, I'm to have total pelvic rest, which totally sucks as my horny hormone levels are through the roof, but it's a big fat no.

It's been complete torture for me these last few days.

Turning on my side to face him, he reaches out and starts pinching my nipples.

"Would you like me to help you with that?" I palm his cock over his boxers.

"Nope," he groans. "If you can't, I can't. It's not fair. Although fuck knows how I will last the next few months. You're way too sexy and your tits turn me on so bad." He bows his head and sucks one over the fabric of my vest top.

"Ah, you really have to stop, Hunter." I roll my eyes into my head. "The risks are too high. One orgasm can trigger a contraction." I breathe. "I want you so bad, but we can't risk it."

My medical history is just too big a risk, so we have to abstain altogether. Well, I have to.

"I'm sorry, but these are just so big. You have actual melons. So crude, but it's the only word for them." He laughs as he lifts his head and gives my boobs a good squeeze.

"I don't like melons."

"Nope? Okay then, juggernauts?"

I flick his ear. "No, not that either."

"Milk monsters?"

"Ew, that's worse, but they will be soon. Or rather we'll have three milk monsters."

"Don't keep reminding me. Every time you say the word triplets, babies, plural and kids, again plural, and having them all at the same time, I think I age another year. We need nannies. A squad of nannies." He groans.

"They will have aunties and grannies, not nannies. Ah, and I did wonder why I spotted some gray hairs coming through yesterday. It's the worry."

"I do not have gray hairs coming through." He leaps out of bed.

I stifle a giggle as I watch Hunter inspecting his hair in my dressing-table mirror.

Skimming his beautifully sculpted bronzed body with my eyes, I appreciate his mighty fine backside encased in snug black boxer shorts.

Hot damn, he's all mine now.

"There is no fucking gray here, you little minx. You will pay for that after these babies are born." He leans back over me on my bed. "We have to get up. Lots to do today before we head to Florida. But first I have something I want to show you."

"What is it?"

"It's a surprise." He bows his head and kisses my swollen belly. "Good morning, monkeys. Be good for Mummy again today. Stay in there; we only have a few months to go. Hang tight."

It's not just my belly that's swollen; it's my heart too. The love I feel for this man bowls me over.

He's been the biggest surprise of my life.

"Another surprise?" I ask.

"Yes, now come on, beautiful girl. Up." He holds his hands out to help me.

"You shower. I'll go make your favorite, boiled eggs on toast."

"That would be lovely. I keep craving eggs. Who knew I would go off cupcakes?"

"I know, shocker. I'll be surprised if Cupcakes & Castles sustains a business without you. C'mon, beautiful. Time to get in the shower." He points.

Once we're fed, watered, and ready to go, we jump into Hunter's new shiny black Range Rover Autobiography. I have no idea how I'm going to drive this thing once we have the babies, but apparently he's getting me one too. It's so bloody high. Mine is going to have rose gold trimmings though; I am so bloody excited about that.

Luckily, Hunter has his fitted with automatic electric side steps for me so I can hop in and out easily. I'm getting those too; that's a must.

"Where are we going?" I ask, smoothing out my figure-hugging pink maternity midi dress. Since the other night, I've ordered so many dresses. They are so comfy, complete lifesavers while preggers. They also go great with my giant trainer collection. Thank the heavens above for next day delivery.

"Patience, Cupcake, patience." Hunter drives us, twisting through the countryside roads.

"Here we are." Hunter pulls into an opening and drives into a development site.

It's only a few miles from the retreat. Someone's been building a house here for the last few months. I've driven past this almost every day, admiring the fast progress they've been making.

I gaze in wonder out the window. It's dazzling. It looks like an enormous glass box overlooking the entire landscape of Castleview Cove.

The views they have must be breathtaking.

"Whoever is building this house has really gone all out. It's so striking. You'd better not hang about here; they won't let you turn in the construction site."

"Eden. This is our new home."

"Sorry, what?" I gape.

Hunter motions his eyes to the car door. "C'mon, they're expecting us."

He jumps out and runs around the front of the car to my side to help me.

I grab on to his shoulder as he helps me down the step.

As Hunter and I walk hand in hand toward the captivating home, my jaw drops at its size.

"Holy shit, Hunter."

He laughs. "This is our new beginning, baby."

"But how, why, when?" I scratch my head.

"I never stopped the sale going through or the build. I was always going to need a place to live when I was toing and froing between here, golf tours, and Florida. So I just kept building. The difference now is, this is going to be my permanent place to live, and we have three kids' bedrooms to consider. That's where you come in. You get to decide what you want to do with the layout. As well as loads of other stuff. You have way better taste than me."

"But what about my house?" I ask, walking through the giant charcoal and glass front door.

Hunter grabs a couple of hard hats from the floor. "We need to put these on. Your house, well, that's up to you. You look cute in this." He pats my work hat. "You can sell it. Keep it. Rent it out. Or you can convert it into a bigger dance studio. That, my beautiful girl, is up to you. But with only three bedrooms, it's not big enough for us, especially when my family comes to visit."

"How many do we have in here then?" I ask, looking around at the crisp white walls.

"Seven. But we can change the upper level."

Holy shamoly. Seven bedrooms.

"Everything is up to you. This will be your project until our three monkeys arrive, Cupcake. All you have to do is pick what you want, colors, finishings, soft furnishings, kitchen, bathrooms, everything. Um, and a wedding. No pressure," he says sheepishly.

I hold on to Hunter's hand tight as he shows me around the incredibly bright space, squeezing it to make sure this is all real. "Can I have a walk-in wardrobe again, please?"

"Already done. So is that a deal breaker for you moving in?"

"Yeah, I think it is." I smile as I take it all in wide-eyed.

Hunter moves us through the giant open-plan living space.

With wall-to-wall windows, the Cove comes into view as we move closer.

My heart skips a beat.

Sunlight beams through the seamless windows, making the dust in the air glitter.

"Wow. Hunter, this is stunning. Is this really yours?"

"Ours, Eden, this is ours."

I stare out the window, watching the waves crash along the shoreline.

"Hey, look, you can see the old McGregor's fruit field from here too." I move over to the side window. "That's where I crashed." I point. "Where you found me."

I turn around. Hunter is standing directly behind me.

"Correction, it's where I hunted you down, remember?" He pulls me into his arms.

"I remember now." I bounce on to my tiptoes and press my lips to his. "So that's where we started. And here is where it all ends, huh?" I ask.

"No, baby, this is where it starts. This is where we take a new junction and begin our new journey together."

No matter where I am, I know Hunter will be with me, right by my side, holding on tight, navigating the way with me, and I am never letting go, no matter how rough the ride may get.

I will never be lost again.

He never hunted me.

I willed to be found.

The End

Stick around - Bonus extended epilogue plus sneak peek of Chapter One of Book 2 - Inevitable Ella - Fraser & Ella's story.

EPILOGUE

Hunter - Four years later

"Hi, Edith. I didn't think you were coming by today." I say to my mother-in-law.

She's enjoying the afternoon sunshine out on the deck off the living area.

I drop my car keys on the outdoor table.

It's a very rare warm day, and the views across Castleview Cove spread into the horizon as the sun spills across the town. It's the perfect bluebird day, minus the snowfall from the evening before. Although, snow falls here more than I expected. I don't think my Floridian bones were made for snow.

"I stayed for a cuppa. Eden called me earlier as she needed a hand."

"Hey, boys," I call for their attention. "What are you doing?" I watch as Lewis, Lachlan, and Lennox lift their dark-haired heads up from the sandpit.

"They are up to no good; that's what they are doing." Edith laughs, standing up.

"Hi, Daddy." They all say in unison, waving their chubby, dusty paws.

I love my boys.

"Have you been good for Mummy today?"

"Lenny been bad today," Lachlan tweets in his little voice.

"Tattle taywl," Lennox responds.

"Um, not."

"Wes woo are Lacky." Lewis joins in.

My boys. They don't half make me smile. Unprompted they all have nicknames for each other—Louie, Lacky, Lenny. They are too cute and make my heart melt.

Eden ended up having a minor procedure to keep those boys in. They were determined to come out. Such a massive worry. Now we have them, and we live and breathe for them.

They keep us on our toes; that's for sure. Strong-willed is an understatement. No idea where they get that from. We travel as a family when I tour, and they join me whenever they can. There is no better feeling than having them all there perched on the greenside watching me. The press devours my boys and love their little souls bounding over to me when I scoop the wins. We are the dream team.

The fun we have as a family is incredible. Eden is an exceptional mum. Her never-ending free and youthful spirit is infectious, and it's normally Eden who starts the water balloon fights and sandcastle building competitions.

She gets us all involved in those stupid social media challenges too. I'm positive she uses those as an excuse to climb my body like a koala. However, she informed me that our three mini-me's and my shirtless abs get more views than the dance routines for the studio. Anything for my girl.

The thing I most regret buying is those stupid foam dart blaster guns for us all. Eden takes great pride in gathering her triplet army, and the four of them get me every time I'm in the bloody shower.

It's become my coming home ceremony. If they get close enough, they don't half smart and leave a mark. The boys think it's hilarious. Of course it is.

When you're told you're going to be a dad to three, all at once, and how hectic it can get, you're not actually listening. I certainly wasn't.

Our life is noisy, messy, chaotic, fun, and crazy, but I wouldn't have it any other way.

Between me touring and coaching, Eden teaching dance, and our three three-and-a-half-year-old boys, I barely remember if I put on underwear most days. Although for Eden, that's a given.

"Where's Eden?" I ask.

"In the bathroom. She's been there a good twenty minutes so far."

"Oh boy. One of those days?" I ask.

"Yup. Do you want me to take these three away for a few hours and you can come and get them later or they can even stay the night? They have loads of clothes at our place," she says as she walks to go fetch them from down by the garden. "As you know, Charlie loves having them over for the night. I think he wished he'd had boys, not girls. Any excuse to get the mini digger out tonight."

"Is that okay? You don't mind?" I ask.

"Nope, enjoy your Saturday night together. Go get Eden. I'll sort these three terrors out. Forget about them. Come get them tomorrow."

"Boys. Be good for your nana and papa."

No reply. Typical.

I turn into the house and bound up the stairs two at a time.

"Eden.".

I try the bathroom door, but it's locked.

"Eden, baby, open the door."

"Are you with anyone?" she mumbles from behind the door.

"No, it's just me."

"You sure?"

"Yes, Cupcake, now open the door."

The door unlocks with a clunk. She opens it at high speed, then yanks me in by the wrist, giving me whiplash, before she shuts the door, quickly locking it again.

"Christ, what are you doing?"

Eden slides her back down the gray tiled wall and sits on the floor. I notice a tray of six cupcakes, with three already eaten.

"I'm hiding."

"From?"

"The boys. I think they're trying to kill me." She stuffs another cupcake into her mouth.

My heart melts. I try to keep a straight face as I crouch down.

"Lewis stuck a stone up his nose today and Mum had to help me tweezer it out. Lennox put my phone down the toilet and then flushed it. That's my third phone this year," she says, spraying crumbs everywhere. "And Lachlan reprogrammed my Kindle and now it's all in Spanish. Can you have a look at that for me, please?

"And to top it all off, I reversed the car into the garage and dented the bumper. The boys demanded I turn the volume up to "Baby Shark" and it overwrote the reversing sensor beeps. Now I have that to sort out."

I have to wrap my lips around my teeth to stop myself from laughing.

"It's *not* funny, Hunter. I'm a mess. Mum says it's karma. She's no help at all." She huffs.

"I beg to differ. That unhelpful mum of yours has just taken the boys away for the night."

Eden stops chewing her cupcake. "You're kidding me? But I never got kisses and cuddles from my babies."

"You'll see them tomorrow and you can video call them later from my phone."

"True. We're free?"

"We're free."

Eden relaxes and puts the rest of her cupcake back in the tray. "Can we have an early night and lazy morning tomorrow and everything?" Her eyes smolder.

"Yes. What's everything?"

"You know?" She raises her eyebrows, eyes glinting.

"Yeah?"

"Oh, yeah," she says as I pull her to her feet, and she plants a kiss on my mouth.

"What, now?"

"Yes, Hunter, now."

"But you've got cake between your teeth."

"Then lick it out." She laughs against my mouth.

"You're disgusting."

"I know, you love it. Clothes off. Let's shower." She grabs her toothbrush from the vanity unit. I watch as she quickly brushes her teeth and whisks off her leggings and bra top.

I don't have to be asked twice with Eden. We can never, ever get enough of each other.

"I've thought about this all day. You're so fucking wet, baby." She bounces up and down my rock-hard cock. "And beautiful."

"Hunter, that's the spot." Straddling me, she gasps as she gyrates her hips.

We had a tiled seat fitted at the far end of our shower for this very reason. Sex in the shower with Eden is fucking epic.

"Baby, you're gonna have to come fast." I clench my jaw and dig my hands into her hips.

"Now, Hunter, now."

Eden plunges her hands into my hair and pulls it hard, and that's it, I'm a goner. I piston her up and down fast as her wet, hot pussy pulses around my cock.

We cry out as we climax together; our cries echo in the steamy shower.

With Eden and I, it gets better and better each and every time. We always make time for each other because when we're together, there is no better feeling.

We're entwined around each other's hearts forever. Discovering each other still and figuring everything else out as we go.

As we descend, our hearts calm down to their gentle contentment, and I nuzzle into her neck.

"How did I get so lucky?" I breathe into her neck.

"You've got that the wrong way around. I'm the lucky one." She kisses my temple.

Placing my hands on either side of her face, "I love you, Eden."

She blinks and smiles. "I love you too, Hunter," she replies, as sweet as music, then she kisses my lips. "Can we have takeaway pizza tonight?"

"How the hell can you go from telling me you love me to then asking for pizza?"

"Easy, two things I love." She gazes at me and plays with my hair. "Well, three, cupcakes too."

"I love golf, but I don't ask you if we can go for a round of golf straight after I tell you I love you, especially when I'm still inside of you." I thrust my hips.

"Don't do that, or we will never get out of here tonight." She gasps.

"That's the plan."

"I like your plan," she says, leaning in and kissing me desperately.

Here we go again.

And just like that, we are one.

We found each other.

Meant for one another.

We crashed into each other.

We are each other's happily ever after.

✳

Want more Hunter & Eden? Grab the *BONUS extended epilogue*>>>

WANT MORE HUNTER & EDEN?

If you're not quite done with these two beautiful souls just yet, then why don't you leap into Hunter and Eden's future with this funny and beautiful extended epilogue.

https://bit.ly/extendedHE

Read on for a sneak peek of VH Nicolson's next book, Inevitable Ella, Book 2 in the Triple Trouble Series. Ella & Fraser's Story...
Coming soon.
Sign up to my newsletter to keep up to date.
www.vhnicolsonauthor.com

SNEAK PEEK: INEVITABLE ELLA
CHAPTER 1 - UNEDITED

Ella

The wind's thumped out of me at high speed.

"Sorry, say that again Fraser. You *love* me? Tell me I heard that right?" My Scottish lilt vibrates through the musty hotel stairwell.

Either my ears are playing tricks on my brain or I've had one too many tequilas tonight.

"Will you keep your bloody voice down Ella. For Christ sakes." Fraser says through a clenched jaw as he cranes his neck upwards to make sure no one is listening on the floors above.

I watch him wipe his dirty blond locks from his tanned brow. Pacing now across the concrete floor in his black patent leather dress shoes.

I wish he wasn't so flipping handsome.

He's tuxedoed up to the max and wearing it like it's his second skin.

We're at the Winners Ball.

The flagship golf tournament, The Championship Cup,

takes place every four years in our historical little town of Castleview Cove. Today was the final and this evening we're celebrating the winner. Fraser came in fourth place this year.

His desperate and frenzied words I've longed to hear again, for years, poured from his delicious lips with ease a mere few moments ago. Straight after he manhandled me through the heavy fire exit door.

Three powerful words I never thought I'd *ever* hear again.

"Keep my voice down? You don't get to play with my feelings like this, Fraser."

Determined to deflect the tears I feel forming behind my eyes. I dig my nails into the delicate fabric of my black silk, to-the-floor, evening dress.

"We spoke on Instagram for the first time in seven years. To help us move forward. To be civil to one another. Because you asked me to." I say through clenched teeth.

It was not to confess our undying love for each other. I'm so confused with his words. What the hell is actually going on?

My sister Eden, bumped into Fraser on the beach. He begged her to speak to me, for me to get in touch with him again.

Hesitation held me back until I finally gave in and messaged him. I've tried so hard to release him and let go. But try as I might the feelings I feel for him still surround my heart.

Not knowing what to say, it took me a full morning to form a few simple, keep-it-breezy-how-are-you sentences. Swithering to send it or not, I hovered over that button before eventually pressing send.

Our brief conversation was exactly that, brief. We both

agreed that we harbored no hard feelings towards each other. He apologized. I was all water under the bridge, and it's fine.

I thought it would help me move on. Bury the hatchet, but nope, it didn't make me feel any better. Not even one little bit.

But this? Well, I never expected *this*.

What the hell is he thinking?

"You left Castleview Cove to pursue your dream of becoming a pro golfer, Fraser. I never stopped you. You achieved what you set out to do. We split up. You finished with me. It's done." My voice cracks as I remember the weeks that followed his departure.

When Fraser left I was only sixteen, Fraser was two years older than me, but I knew then no one would ever replace him.

He was, and still is, my one and only true love.

After five years of dating from afar, I became accustomed to the distance.

Then he broke up with me. Breaking my heart in the process.

Fraser swings round to face me. "I never for one minute, ever, stopped loving you Ella. I never wanted to split up with you. I *had* to."

What does he mean he *had to*?

I stumble backward in my sky-high black strappy heels.

"I'm pretty sure that's a fucking lie, given the fact your *wife* is sitting in the ballroom of this very hotel we're in. I shouldn't be here with you, alone. This is wrong."

So wrong.

Fraser slides his hands into the pockets of his black dress pants and drops his head to his chest. "Everything's a fucking mess. My life's a mess."

This is news to me. His social feeds and posts certainly don't reflect his words. Fraser's life looks like one big happy holiday in California. Perfectly preened influencer wife and a handsome son. Carefully curated home. Posts from dozens of cities and tournament golf courses from around the world. He has a picture-perfect life.

And his wife's not just beautiful, she's striking. Gorgeous in fact. Long brunette locks, sparkling straight white teeth, endless tan, and envious legs, with boobs I would trade my mother in for. Nothing like me at all. She's from great stock. Wealthy and highly influential. Her family owns half of California I believe. Well, I know, because I stalk, way too much, I stalk. Her father is a sports agent, he only represents the most successful athletes, including Fraser.

Being married to that family suits Fraser.

He's living the dream life we always dreamed of together. Stepford wife style.

"You're lying," I say.

In all the years I dated Fraser, he was never a liar. However, this man standing in front of me now, I no longer know. It's been so long.

"I am *not* lying. I promise." His weary crystal blue eyes meet mine. "Ella you know me."

"I don't know you anymore."

I really don't.

When he left our quaint little Scottish seaside town years ago, I believed, in the beginning, we could make it work. I was young and naive then.

Fraser won a golf scholarship in America. He was so excited. I was too and for what it would do for our future together.

As time passed though, *I* slid out of his heart.

"I don't know why you're doing this. This isn't a game." I whisper.

"I'm not *doing* anything, I'm telling you how I feel Ella."

"This isn't fair."

"What's not fair is watching you tonight from afar. With someone, I know very well. Knowing that *I* should be with you. Are you with Luke?"

"No, I'm not *with* Luke. Not that it's any of your goddamn business. You're fucking married." My voice echoes through the concrete and metal space. "You think it's fair for me to watch you with a wife. And child, Christ, you have a kid. I've watched your new life play out from afar for years. So don't stand there and tell me what's fair and what isn't. *You* ended *us*. You split up with me. I never had a choice."

"*I* never had a choice either."

"What do you mean *you* didn't have a choice? You got married then had a son in quick succession. Tell me, were you with her before you broke up with me?" Clenching my fists by my sides, I grip my dress tighter.

"Did you cheat on me with her?"

"No. Never." He bellows.

"Then what happened?

Silence.

I wait. "Speak to me."

Nothing.

This is pointless. As I turn to leave, Fraser reaches out and grabs my wrist. "Please stay." An instant zap of static electricity sparks between us, reigniting our dying flame. It takes my breath away as I feel his touch sparkle everywhere.

I whip around. "Please stop. You have to stop." He has to before I do something really stupid.

"I don't want to." He dusts his calloused fingers,

reminding me of his profession, upward across the smooth skin of my pale arm, over the spaghetti straps of my silky dress.

"We can't do this Fraser."

"I know we can't. But I *want* to."

I feel his other hand grip my waist. He pulls me in close and grinds himself into me.

Someone send help.

Welcoming his six-foot-two stature as I tilt my head upward, we face off eye to eye.

Our weighted breaths reflect each other.

He faintly taps his fingertips into the nape of my neck before weaving them into my long platinum locks.

Dipping his head to mine, he fuses our foreheads and lets out a heavy sigh. My pulse picks up speed faster than an Eminem rap.

"I miss you so much, Ella."

He roughly pulls me in closer still, his solid athletic frame against mine. Sliding his hand downward from my waist, he cups my backside, pressing himself against me. I feel his hot hard cock through his dress pants.

Instinctively my body wakes up. It's been waiting all this time for him and my sex begins throbbing at his touch.

It takes everything within me not to reach out. I keep my hands firmly glued to my sides. I fear touching him and never wanting to stop.

I want him. His body, his mind, and his soul I love so much.

But he isn't mine and I've never forgotten how he discarded me like I meant nothing. Like *we* meant nothing.

My heart swells with both misery and desire, striking hard in my chest.

Shallow puffs of air wisp against each other's skin as he pulls his cheek to mine.

Desperate to connect once again. He moves his hands and cups my cheeks with his expert hands. His tender touch flips my pulse into a frenzy.

"I meant what I said." He says, bowing his head closer to the curve of my neck.

I close my eyes, inhaling. Delightful warmth trickles across my skin as his sandalwood and musk scent awakens all my senses.

"Tell me you feel the same." He presses.

I do feel the same.

I've longed for this moment.

I want him and only him.

I want him to kiss me, to take me.

I've never stopped wanting him.

No man has ever lived up to him.

Fraser feathers his generous lips against my neck and I can't stop the moan escaping my chest.

Particles glimmer between us and it's everything I remember feeling. His touch is everything my body desires but we shouldn't be doing this.

Realization suddenly hits hard. "What I know Fraser..." I whisper. "...is you're not a cheater and *I* am most definitely not a home-wrecker."

I step backward forcing myself out of his arms, and whip around to grab the emergency door handle, instantly missing his warmth and touch.

"You're right Ella, I'm not a cheater."

I ping pong back to meet his icy eyes.

Oh god, poor Fraser.

"Is your wife cheating on you?"

He doesn't reply.

My perplexed heart free falls as outrage takes flight.

"Is that what this is about? Your wife is cheating on you, so you decide to cheat on her too? Fucking hell Fraser, I thought you were better than that."

"No." He exclaims. "It's nothing like that. It's complicated."

"Then enlighten me."

"I can't." He expels a long groan.

Furrowing his brows, he digs his palms into his closed eyes.

I have to draw a line in the sand right now. "Since high school, I have been so in love with you."

His hopeful eyes pop open.

"It's only recently my mum informed me I could have trained to be a dancer anywhere, she would have let me move with you. I regret not moving." I tuck my lips into my mouth before continuing. "The girl in high school would have swooped into your arms with your flippant three words of I love you. Those are words I don't take lightly and the old Fraser, the one I do know, would have been careful and handled my heart with care. You and I? We are done. We were over a long time ago. You made sure of that."

"But you just said..."

"I know." My eyes glaze over. "But you finished us and married someone else. You replaced me instantly."

Ouch, that hurts. It's really is time for me to move on. It's been seven long years since we split and I really feel I have to move on for my own sanity. I'm so pathetic.

He's married.

"I never stopped wanting or loving you, Ella. Never. I've thought about you every.single.day." His husky voice now thick with torment.

A lone tear rolls down my cheek as sadness engulfs me. Why is he doing this now?

"You have to stop saying that." I bow my head.

He tentatively scuffs towards me again and lifts my chin with his pointer finger.

I love his eyes. I've dreamed of his kind cool crystal blue jewels I could butterfly stroke in, for thousands of nights.

"Please don't be upset Pixie."

When Fraser discovered my name means goddess fairy maiden, he started calling me Pixie, which I loved because he's the only one who used to call me that. I haven't heard it in a long time.

"Don't call me that." I plead.

"I can't explain to you what's happening or what's going on. I want to, but I can't. I have always loved you. I have never cheated on Anna. But I don't love her." His forehead creases.

"And I *never* cheated on you. It's you, it's always been you. Christ, it's so fucking complicated."

But he married her. None of this makes sense.

Gently strumming his rough thumb across my jaw, my stomach backflips.

"I've lost count of how many times I picked up the phone to speak to you but I couldn't dial your number. I'm so fucking sorry. I wanted to reach out when I saw you at Chloe's funeral but I fucked everything up. I don't blame you for not wanting to speak to me."

I still love his throaty husk. "You sound so American. Where did your lovely Scots accent go, Fraser?"

He scoffs. "I know, my mum says I think I'm bloody Gerrard Butler. Flipping in and out of Scots and American. I don't even know I'm doing it."

I pull a half-smile.

This is so confusing. Us. Him.

"What's changed Fraser, why are you telling me this now?"

His defeated shoulders sag.

Our eyes magnetized to one another.

Fraser leans in and kisses my forehead. *Oh boy.*

This feels so familiar as erratic flutters batter around my heart.

"There are things I can't tell you. My life... it's not... Anna... she's not..." He doesn't finish.

I don't know what he's trying to tell me.

We stay like this. Firmly planted against one another. Neither of us willing to spoil our precious trip down memory lane closeness.

"Tell me please Fraser, you can trust me," I whisper.

Without warning, he releases my face, "I can't. I so want to be with you. But you're right, this is wrong." He steps back quickly with a look of utter anguish across his face. "Fuck," he mumbles. "Please know that I'm not lying and that I'm still in love with you, Ella. I was forced to stay away from you." He then spins on his heels and sprints up the concrete stairs, leaping two steps at a time, around the corner, up the next set of stairs out of sight.

"Fraser," I call.

I battle the urge to run after him but I know I have to let him go, again. Even although I have so many questions.

With that, I hear him abruptly leave through the fire exit door above with a deafening bang it bangs closed.

I jolt and the bottomless pit feeling resurfaces in my heart.

Forced to stay away from me? But why?

I'm dumbfounded by his words, what a surreal twist of events. Forced? By who?

What couldn't he tell me? Is his wife really cheating?

I breathe a sigh of relief knowing he'll be gone tomorrow heading off to the next golf tournament hopefully it's as far away from Castleview as possible.

Who the heck would *force* him to stay away from me? No one cares about me like that to keep Fraser away from me. What happened all those years ago? I try to recall and come up short.

My head starts thumping in time with my aching heart.

I do really have to get over Fraser. It's been too long. What has been, has been between us, it's time for me to set sail on a new voyage, so no more Fraser fog clouding my vision. Nope.

Although that crushes me, I have to do this.

I'm a silly bitch for harboring the feelings I've had for him for so long.

Relaxing my hands, I try to smooth out the clusters of my dress I've been desperately holding on to with valor, but my efforts fail to dust out the crushes. Fuck it. It will have to stay like that.

Everyone will be wondering where I am and this dreary staircase is making me claustrophobic.

With luck Fraser and his wife leave the ball early. I don't think I'll be able to look her in the eyes. Fraser and I didn't do anything but what we discussed and the way Fraser held me feels deceitful.

Right Ella, pull yourself together. I dab under my eye in the hope I haven't ruined my makeup and mascara.

Shaking my head to straighten myself up, I comb my fingers through my icy strands. As I glance upward a small grey fluffy feather floats across my face and lands perfectly at my feet. Since Fraser left all those years ago. I find feathers everywhere I go, some days I find two or three.

I started finding so many that I had to Google it. Apparently feathers are a positive omen for better things to come. But here I am, still waiting for the Universe to jump on board and deliver whatever those things are.

Although, thinking about it, there's probably doves nesting in this grotty space. Nothing good could ever happen here that's for sure.

Head held high I stride back through the staircase door where I throw myself straight into the path of Toni and Beth, my two friends.

"What have you been doing in there?" Toni quizzes.

"Eh, I was just getting some fresh air."

Toni and Beth both frown.

"In there?" Beth grabs my hands. "Whatever, Eden needs us out in the car park."

"What's wrong?" I ask.

"No idea, but shit's going down apparently." Beth strides toward the back entrance of the hotel, pulling me with her.

"Christ she won the guy. The very guy who won The Championship Cup today, what the bloody hell is wrong with my sister now?" I huff.

Just like that my moment with Fraser in the staircase set the tone for the rest of the evening.

Sorry, who re-tuned the night to Poop Parade FM?

Not me.

I never asked for any of this.

And what made Fraser say all those things to me tonight?

I need more tequila to get me through the rest of the night.

Forced? By who?

ACKNOWLEDGMENTS

It takes a party of people to write and co-ordinate a book and these are the gorgeous souls I want to give a mahoosive shout out to.

Firstly, a huge thank you to my incredible husband and son for their never-ending support and belief in me. They cheered me on page after page and also put up with all the midnight tapping against my keyboard like a crazy woman as each chapter unfolded - they deserve a medal, and sleep.

Thank you to Kimberly, my editor, who put up with all my strange Scottish slang words and has the patience of a saint. I'm grateful to have you on my team.

To my mum, dad, and sister... thanks for all the little messages of encouragement. As well as the vitamins my mum provided when she thought I was writing too late into the night. Love you, mum.

A huge thank you to the most incredible mentor and Queen of all Swans, TL Swan, who without, I would never have written this book. She formed a special group of girls over lockdown and we all had a dream—to become authors. She went above and beyond to help and support us. There is not a chance in hell I would have come this far without her stream of knowledge or without that group of beautiful Cygnets. Thank you to each and every one of you. I will forever be grateful for your guidance, cheerleading, and virtual hugs.

To Laura and Sadîe thank you for always having my back on messenger. You girls rock!

Rosie, Carolann, Sarah, Sorrel, and Alison... my beautiful beta readers... thank you for reading for me. Your constant messages of encouragement gave me the zest to keep on writing every single day. Thank you for being a huge part of this journey. You girls will always have a special place in my heart.

Naomi, thank you for just being a super-duper awesome human being. You encouraged me to initially put pen to paper and write the goddamn book. Your words, *"you've got the idea, just do it, get it out there,"* have been in my head since day one and you've given me the nudges and kicks up the bum when I've needed them. You are a special woman Naomi, and you mean so much to me. Thank you for being in my world.

And to you, the reader, thank you for sticking around to the end to read my debut book. Thank you for taking a leap of faith on a new author, you have no idea how much that means to me, I am eternally grateful. THANK YOU! Mwah x

ABOUT THE AUTHOR

VH Nicolson is an emerging author of contemporary romance. This is her first book and is now completely smitten with writing love stories with happily ever afters. VH Nicolson was born and raised along the breathtaking coastline in North East Scotland. For more than two decades she's worked throughout the UK and abroad within the creative marketing and design industry, as a branding strategist and stylist, editor of a magazine and sub-editor of a newspaper. Married to her high school crush, they have one son. She has a weakness for buying too many sparkly jumpers, eating Belgium buns, and walking the endless beaches that surround her beautiful Scottish hometown she's now moved back to.

Printed in Great Britain
by Amazon

62976088R00274